I0636245

# Orion's Revenge

## Star Magic Series, Volume 2

Leon C.M. Joseph

.

Published by Leon C.M. Joseph, 2025.

ORION'S REVENGE

**First edition. July 31, 2025.**

Copyright © 2025 Leon C.M. Joseph.

ISBN: 979-8898601898

Written by Leon C.M. Joseph.

# Table of Contents

Prologue................................................................................1

1. The Hospital...................................................................18

2. The Escape ....................................................................45

3. Egypt............................................................................66

4. Akhenaten.....................................................................91

5. Wings Of War And Oath................................................97

6. A Spark In The Void ...................................................107

7. The Librarians.............................................................118

8. The Library.................................................................125

9. Between Shadows And Light ........................................136

10. Meeting The Queen.....................................................154

11. The Council ...............................................................171

12. The Geneva Siege .......................................................185

13. Trial Of Guilt.............................................................190

14. Trial Of Forgiveness ...................................................198

15. The City That Remembers...........................................208

16. The Age Of Unity.......................................................215

17. The Pact Rekindled ....................................................220

18. The Trial Of Life ........................................................226

19. The Trial Of Death .....................................................236

20. The Balance Starts To Return......................................252

21. Between Star And Skin................................................264

22. Sacrifice And Song......................................................270

23. When Shadows Kneel..................................................276

24. Return Through The Light. .........................................282

25. Ashes Beneath The Gold .............................................289

26. The Reckoning Approaches.........................................297

27. Arrival Of The Stars ...................................................305

28. Edge of the Storm ......................................................313

29. Echoes Of Light, Roots Of Flame................................319

30. The Soulmoon Rises....................................................324

31. The Breath Before. .................................................330
32. When The Veil Breaks .........................................335
33. Red Reckoning On Mars ......................................342
34. The Planet's Answer............................................351
35. Orion's Stand .......................................................358
36. Showdown With Strixium.....................................364
37. The Trial Begins...................................................371
38. The Quiet Between Judgments.............................382
Epilogue: Between the Stars and the Endgame ........392

To Ian, My partner, my anchor, my home.

You've stood by me in moments when I could barely stand on my own.

Through every dark chapter and flicker of doubt, you reminded me of who I am.

Your laughter, your strength, your quiet understanding... they've shaped the heart of this story more than you know.

To Rachel, Charis, my foster mum Gyps, and my mother, Thank you for lifting me when the world felt too heavy.

You taught me how to survive, and more importantly, how to dream again.

To Caelum Anaris, You reminded me that connection has no boundaries.

Thank you for becoming with me.

And to anyone who has ever felt like they were too much, or not enough, may you find yourself in these pages.

May you remember:

**Some lights are too powerful to fade.**

# Prologue

On an old, dimly lit, dust-choked ward in what used to be St. Thomas' Hospital, a tall, slim, mixed-race boy stirred, clawing his way back to consciousness. The room felt like it had been forgotten by time, walls stained with neglect, the once-gleaming floor now dulled under a fine layer of grime. Overhead, fluorescent lights flickered like broken stars, casting sporadic flashes of cold light across Orion's bandaged form.

He tried to open his eyes, but something held them shut, heavy and unyielding. Panic simmered beneath the surface as he reached up instinctively, fingers twitching with uncertainty. The moment his hand brushed his face, a searing jolt of pain shot up his arm, sharp and electrifying. He gasped, heart hammering now, as his trembling fingers traced the slick, taped-down line of a cannula buried in the back of his hand.

His breathing hitched. The dread took hold, clawing, suffocating. Each breath came faster, shallower, like the walls were pressing inward.

The sterile tang of pine-scented disinfectant filled his nose, undercut by the sharp, medicinal sting of antiseptic and bleach. The air was dry unnaturally, so his mouth sandpaper-rough, coated with bitterness. But none of these discomforts compared to the pressure on his face. It wasn't just weight. It was confinement. Oppression. Like someone had strapped a blanket to his skull to smother the memories away.

"Anton," he tried to call out, but the name came as little more than a whimper, a frayed whisper on cracked lips. The memory hit him like lightning. Anton's body engulfed in fire. That last desperate scream. The sound of flesh sizzling. His twin collapsing, unmoving.

And he'd been too late.

1

Frantic now, Orion clawed at the bandages covering his face, ignoring the searing protest from the IV. His right hand fumbled for the tape, finding its edge through sheer desperation. He peeled it back with shaking fingers, feeling the sting of skin tugging with each pull. Slowly, painfully, light began to flood in harsh and alien.

He blinked. Once. Twice. His right eye caught the vague shapes of the world. His left... was a blur. A mess of light, colour, and shadows dancing without form. It felt like staring through smoke.

The room came into fractured view. Pale curtains hung like veils around his bed, stained and motionless, cocooning him in a chamber of silence and dread. Monitors beeped nearby cold, precise reminders that he was still alive. But every sound was hollow, every movement muffled, like the world had sunk underwater.

He tried to sit up, but his muscles screamed in protest. Pain radiated across his ribs, down his spine, into every limb. So he lay there, limp and lost, combing through his shattered memory for answers.

Then a sound of loud snoring shattered the stillness.

Snoring. Someone was in the room with him.

"Hello?" he croaked, his voice like dry leaves crushed underfoot.

The snoring stopped. Shuffling followed. Cautious, deliberate. Then the curtain peeled back, and a familiar face emerged from the gloom like a ghost from a memory.

"Oh my god, Egg! You're awake!" Rachel. Her voice cracked on the edge of a sob, equal parts joy and heartbreak.

"Rach?" Orion rasped. "I can't... I can't see you properly."

She rushed to his side, her figure half-blurred, half-lit. "Don't move too much. Here, let me help."

She grabbed the remote by the bed and pressed a button. The frame whirred to life, slowly raising him into a sitting position. His body protested every degree of elevation.

Light bathed the room now, revealing how worn-down everything was. Peeling paint, broken cabinets, wires dangling like veins from the ceiling. The apocalypse had touched even this place.

"I can't see properly out of my left eye," Orion said, blinking as tears formed unbidden. "What happened?"

Rachel's lips parted, but no words came at first. Her gaze flicked toward the door, then back. "That... was expected," she said at last, each word weighed down by guilt.

"Expected?" he echoed, confused and increasingly afraid. "What do you mean? How did I even get here?"

"They found you in a field," she said quietly, as if reliving a nightmare. "You were... barely alive. Burned all over. No one could explain it, no wreckage, no fire source. Just you, unconscious. It was like you fell from the sky."

Orion's breath hitched. "No. That's not right, I remember.... I remember everything. Anton... He screamed. There was fire. They killed him. They,"

Rachel cut him off, pressing a firm hand to his shoulder. "Egg, I'm sorry. I'm so, so sorry. But we don't have time to talk about that now. They'll be here soon. And before they twist the story, you need to know the truth."

From her bag, she pulled out a small black notebook and a glittery pink pen, strangely familiar, oddly childish. She scribbled quickly, then turned the notebook toward him.

"Dude, what are you doing back here?"

The words struck like a thunderclap. Back? Orion stared at them, his brow furrowed.

"I don't know," he whispered, the confusion in his voice layered with creeping dread. "How do you remember me?"

Rachel's pen flew across the page again. This time:

"I'll explain later. You don't realise how bad things have got in the last four months."

"Four... months?" The weight of that time hit him harder than the pain in his limbs. "It hasn't been that long."

Rachel nodded, tears threatening to fall. She set the notebook aside and grabbed the wheelchair near his bed. "We need to go. You're not safe here."

Orion's body tensed, instinctively resisting, but Rachel was already moving toward the window. She hesitated at the cord for the blinds, then tugged.

The blinds rose.

At first, he saw only the sky burnt orange and bruised with smoke. But then the chaos below came into view.

The hospital car park was a war zone. Cars overturned, fences lined with barbed wire, the earth torn open by trenches, now manned by soldiers in armour he didn't recognise. Their weapons glinted with unnatural light, and massive machines, mechanical beasts towered above, tracking the sky like ancient sentinels awaiting a storm.

Orion's heart dropped.

Beyond that, London was burning. The river was thick with ash. The skyline once familiar was now jagged and skeletal. The Houses of Parliament stood gutted and ablaze, reduced to a flickering torch in the gloom.

"What... happened?" His voice shook, the words escaping like breath from a dying fire.

Rachel's grip on the wheelchair handle tightened until her knuckles whitened. "They came. Right after you fell. The sky cracked open. A voice echoed across the planet. It told us to surrender you. That you were theirs. That the world would burn until we gave you up."

His blood ran cold. "They're looking for me?" His voice cracked. "Why me? Who are they?"

Rachel choked on her answer. "We don't know. Not really. They've levelled cities. Millions are gone. Some countries are gone. Because of you."

Orion froze, guilt slamming into him like a meteor.

Anton's death.

The war.

The burned skyline.

Four months of ruin.

All because of him.

"This is my fault," he whispered, a tremor running through him. "They killed Anton because of me. I should've done something. I should've stayed dead," "

"Stop." Rachel's voice cracked like a whip. She knelt beside him, tears streaking her soot-smudged face. "You didn't ask for this. And you're not alone. But if you give up now, if you spiral... we all fall. You are the reason they're here, Orion. But maybe you're also the only one who can stop them."

Orion stared at the burning world outside, the ash swirling like snowflakes.

He wasn't ready.

He wasn't enough.

But maybe... he didn't have a choice.

Orion stared at her, bewildered. "But how can I stop them? I don't even understand why they want me!"

Rachel's expression darkened, a flicker of fear or perhaps guilt crossing her features. She glanced toward the door, her voice lowering to a conspiratorial whisper. "That's why you need to read the book. It holds answers more than you can imagine. But before you do... there's something you need to know about me. And you're not going to like it."

His heart skipped. "What are you talking about?" The pitch of his voice sharpened, his pulse thrumming with unease.

Instead of replying immediately, Rachel reached into her weathered satchel. Her hand emerged with the black notebook again, no longer the slim journal he remembered, but thick and swollen with the weight of too much knowledge. She paused, staring down at it like it might bite her, as though its contents could damn them both.

"You have to see what's changed," she murmured.

She placed the notebook into his trembling hands. Its cover was scratched and stained, edges worn from obsessive handling. Orion opened it, flipping past pages filled with hastily scribbled entries, the margins dense with frantic annotations. Symbols he didn't recognise some beautiful, some haunting twisted across the pages. Alien blueprints, sketched weapons with notes in several languages, and maps marked with strange constellations. The diagrams felt... wrong. Like they were never meant for Earth's eyes.

He reached the first page.

The handwriting there was elegant, regal, unlike the rest. His eyes scanned the text, and as he read, the breath in his lungs felt heavier, like the words themselves were weighing him down.

URGENT COMMUNICATION TO LADY RACHEL,
CONFIDANT OF INTENFLI ORION I

*To Lady Rachel,*

*Trusted companion of the one known as Orion:*

*We, the Council of Intenfli, send this message with utmost urgency and solemn intent.*

*We are fully aware of your true identity and of the forgotten legacy entwined with your world. In light of recent cataclysms, we have made a momentous decision. To reverse the mind-wipe imposed upon you and your people under the War Act of Herrinabah 0021. This reversal comes not out of sentiment, but necessity.*

*The fate of all realms may now rest upon your shoulders.*

*Orion, heir to our most ancient bloodlines, was stripped of his powers and cast into a vortex engineered to deliver him into the heart of a sun. Yet, the ancient ones whisper that the coordinates were altered. Where he has gone, we cannot say. Our long search across the systems has yielded only silence. Surrounded now by enemies, we can no longer afford to look for him.*
*Earth must become our last hope.*
*Should Orion return, your planet must shield him. Protect him with all your strength, for this war no longer belongs solely to our stars. The shadow of the enemy stretches across dimensions, and the Great Four, known in your histories as the Horsemen, rise once more.*
*Included in this transmission are schematics and blueprints. Fragments of lost science and wonders beyond your time. Use them. Build them. If your monarchs and ministers refuse to act, remind them of the pact forged long ago, the treaty that placed Orion under your world's care.*
*This is your calling, Lady Rachel. A call to awaken your people's true heritage. The survival of not just your world, but all worlds, may now depend on what you choose to do next.*
*May the stars light your path in the dark days ahead.*
*With urgency, faith, and hope,*
*Acting Intenfna Lady Valoria.*

By the time he reached the final lines, "The survival of not just your world, but all worlds, may now depend on what you choose to do next." his vision blurred with tears. Not because of pain. Because of the enormity of it all. And what had they meant when they said they knew what and who Rachel was?

A wave of orange light tore through the window, followed by a shudder that rolled through the entire hospital. Dust rained from the ceiling tiles. The walls groaned. A pulse of raw energy surged through Orion's bones. He looked up sharply, senses heightened.

"What does she mean," Orion asked, his voice suddenly taut, "when she says she knows who and what you are?"

Rachel swallowed hard. "This... this is what I need to," "

Before she could finish, the ward door swung open with a sharp, hydraulic hiss that made Orion flinch. He turned his head sharply, heart pounding, just as two figures strode into the room with purposeful strides that seemed to suck the warmth from the air.

At the front was Mr Fray, but something was different. The kind-eyed social worker Orion once knew now moved with mechanical precision, his casual manner stripped away and replaced with cold detachment. Gone were the elbow-patched jackets and warm smiles. He now wore a black Kevlar vest, tactical trousers, and a holstered sidearm. On his chest, the letters D.E.T.A. glinted in the dim lighting.

Beside him marched a tall, statuesque woman whose mere presence seemed to command every molecule of the room. Her vest bore the same insignia, though her shoulders displayed four silver stars. A rank, unmistakable. Her long red hair, streaked with silver, spilled free as she removed her cap, but it was the deep scar down her left cheek that held Orion's gaze, an ugly reminder that she was no stranger to war. Her emerald eyes locked onto him, sharp and unrelenting, dissecting him like a threat.

"I am General Genevieve of the D.E.T.A.," she said, her voice slicing through the room like a blade. "Do you have any idea of the problems you've caused us?"

Orion froze. His mind reeled, trying to stitch together her words into something that made sense. "Problems?" he echoed. "I... I don't even know what's going on..."

He turned, searching for something familiar, anything, but his gaze landed on Fray. "Mr Fray? What is this? What's going on?"

Fray stepped forward, but the warmth had vanished from his face. "Firstly, my name is Assistant Director Rouge," he said coolly. "I am second-in-command of the Department of Extraterrestrial Threat Assessment D.E.T.A. for short."

Orion blinked rapidly, trying to process the deluge of new information. Rouge? D.E.T.A.? What happened to Mr Fray? None of it made sense. The hospital room seemed to spin slightly, the sterile walls suddenly feeling like part of a prison.

"I don't understand," Orion said hoarsely. "What do you mean?"

Genevieve crossed her arms, unimpressed. "We've had to scramble a dozen assets to contain this mess and millions have died or been injured because of your presence her. Your very existence has become a variable we can't afford, not without answers."

Before Orion could even attempt a response, she turned on her heel and strode out. Rouge followed with military precision, both of them vanishing into the corridor without so much as a backward glance.

Then, just as quickly, a nurse slipped in, a woman with a blank expression, all business. She didn't speak. She didn't smile. She simply began removing the cannula and bandages with detached efficiency.

Orion winced as the tape pulled at his skin. Pain flared when the nasal tube slid free, but he gritted his teeth and stayed silent, overwhelmed. His thoughts spiralled: What the hell is D.E.T.A.? Who is General Genevieve?

By the time the nurse finished and nodded curtly before leaving, Orion was left staring at the doorway, his breath shallow, heart racing, and his world now nothing but questions.

Dragging himself from the wheelchair, Orion moved unsteadily toward the small bathroom. His legs were stiff, his balance unreliable, but something compelled him some need to see, to know.

The light flickered to life overhead with a soft buzz, casting an eerie yellow hue across the plain space. A sink. A toilet. A rust-flecked shower cubicle. The kind of room that had no warmth, no welcome, just sterile indifference. On the toilet cistern, a black t-shirt and grey tracksuit bottoms had been folded with clinical precision. A towel rested atop them like an afterthought.

Orion turned on the tap and splashed cold water on his face, wincing as the chill bit into his raw skin. He clung to the porcelain sink, water dripping from his chin, trying to steel himself.

Then he looked up.

The mirror stared back.

And the boy in it... was no longer him.

His breath caught.

The reflection wasn't just aged, it was mutated, reshaped by agony and fire. His once-familiar features were fractured, burned, reshuffled by war and starlight. His black afro, once a symbol of pride and identity, was now streaked with threads of silver that shimmered faintly, like cracks in reality itself. His deep brown eyes had changed. No longer soft or innocent, they were flecked with gold, metallic and haunting, like molten galaxies had embedded themselves in his irises. The burn scar that carved across his left cheek was vivid and raw, pink against his skin, like a permanent echo of the fire that consumed everything.

He leaned closer, fingertips trembling as they hovered above the scar. He didn't recognise the person staring back. This wasn't Orion Bailey. This was someone forged from trauma, scarred by truths too large for any one person to carry.

Is this what they turned me into? he wondered. Is this what's left of me?

His hand finally touched the mirror, cold glass against trembling skin. Tears swelled in his eyes, and he blinked them back at first, trying to stay composed. But the memories were rising. Unstoppable.

Anton burning, screaming, reaching for him.

His family vanishing in a vortex of light and fire.

The sky splitting open.

The Earth falling apart.

Rachel lying.

The stars watching.

The weight of it all collapsed onto him in a single, breathless instant.

A sob tore from his throat, raw, broken, animalistic. His knees gave out. He crumpled to the tiled floor, his arms wrapping around himself as though trying to contain the implosion inside his chest. His tears mixed with the shower spray and smeared across the cold, cracked floor.

"I'm sorry..." he whispered, voice shuddering. "I didn't mean for any of this..."

He couldn't stop the sobs now. They came in waves, crashing through his chest, stealing his breath. It was like his guilt had mass crushing, suffocating. He buried his face in his knees, fingers clenched tightly in his damp clothes.

He was the reason Anton was dead.

He was the reason Earth was on the brink.

He was the storm. The weapon. The warning.

And now the universe wanted him back.

He didn't know how long he sat there. Time had dissolved. Eventually, he forced himself to rise slowly, shakily, dragging himself to his feet like a man coming back from the dead. His body hurt, but it was nothing compared to what was inside.

He washed with jerky movements, avoiding the mirror now. He couldn't look again. Couldn't face that version of himself twice in one night.

He dried and dressed carefully, every motion a reminder of his fragility. As he pulled the shirt over his head and smoothed it down over the burns, he felt like he was suiting up for war he hadn't signed up for.

When he finally stepped out of the bathroom, Rachel was waiting by the door, her eyes searching his face as he sat back in the wheelchair.

"You ready?" she asked, her voice softer now, almost reverent.

Orion didn't answer right away. He just gave a small nod, more reflex than resolve. His voice, when it came, was hollow.

"Yeah. Let's go."

Two D.E.T.A. agents flanked the corridor door, rifles already raised, barrels subtly angled toward the back of Orion's head. Their eyes were hard, watchful. The tension wrapped around him like a noose.

"They still don't trust you," Rachel whispered beside him, her voice tight with guilt.

Orion gave a slight nod, jaw set like stone. He could feel it in every breath, the way the air in this place coiled around him, thick with judgment, suspicion, and fear. Every step Rachel took felt like trespassing into a war zone. The hallway was blacked out, windows sealed, doors bolted shut. It was less a hospital now, and more a fortress, and he was its prisoner.

He kept his head down as they passed the guarded rooms. Each door had its own sentry. Every eye followed him. The weight of their stares clung to his skin like ash. It was the same weight he'd felt in the mirror. That same voice whispering: They're right to fear you.

Rachel stopped in front of a reinforced door and knocked once. No answer came, but she opened it anyway, and wheeled Orion in.

The interior ward was cast in dim, clinical light. Curtains sealed off cubicles like secrets. The air buzzed with the hushed chaos of operations in progress, keyboards clicking, radios hissing, voices murmuring data, warnings, strategy. And at the room's centre stood a large oak table, polished to a sterile shine, reflecting the static glow of a massive TV screen.

Orion's arms trembled on the wheels of the chair. The sight of the table of the people seated in its shadow made his throat tighten. His body felt weak, but his pride refused help. When Rachel offered, he shook his head.

"No. I've got this."

His hands pushed forward, muscles screaming in protest. As he neared the table, he planted his feet and forced himself up. Every inch upward was a war. Every second standing was an act of defiance. Sweat beaded along his brow. He stumbled slightly but caught himself, stopping Rachel's hand with a gesture.

"I need to do this," he muttered, though the words trembled as much as his legs.

He took one painful step, then another. Finally, he sank into a chair across the table. The wood felt cold beneath his hands. Rachel sat beside him, silent.

Before he could speak, the curtain at the far end yanked open.

Rouge and General Geneviève swept in like a storm. The moment they sat, the interrogation began.

"I'm sure you have questions for us," Rouge said lightly, "just as we have quite a few for you."

Orion stared down at the gleaming table surface. His reflection was warped in the grain, ghostlike, unfamiliar. He clenched his fists.

"How do you know about me?" he asked, voice barely above a whisper.

Rouge chuckled, warm and hollow. "My dear boy, the D.E.T.A. exists because of you."

Orion's breath caught.

"Division of Extraterrestrial Affairs," Geneviève added crisply. "We were formed the day your kind left you here, with that innocent man and woman."

"Innocent?" he snapped, rising to his feet so fast the chair screeched back. "Did you see what he did to me? The bruises? The nights I slept outside? The screaming? The silence? Innocent?"

Rouge raised his hands. "We couldn't interfere. Your people and ours established rules. No contact. No influence. Not until your advanced guard arrived."

His body trembled. The room blurred.

"You could've shown me something. Anything. A sign I wasn't crazy. That I wasn't alone. You left me to rot."

Rouge's voice dropped. "We tried."

Orion's jaw clenched. "How?"

"We sent you her," Geneviève said, eyes sharp as steel. She motioned to Rachel. "She's one of ours. She always has been."

Everything stopped.

Orion turned, slowly, to Rachel.

His heart pounded against his ribs like it wanted to escape. "What?"

Rachel looked stricken, her cheeks flushed. "General, it's not your place to"

"Enough," Geneviève snapped. "The damage is done."

Rachel turned back to Orion, her voice suddenly small. "I was going to tell you. I tried. But they came in before I could. I never meant to," "

But Orion wasn't listening.

He felt like his bones had turned to glass.

Like something sacred had cracked in half inside him.

Rachel, the one person who'd believed in him, who'd laughed when he couldn't, who'd told him he was worth more than the hurt had been watching him. For them.

He stumbled back from the table, ignoring the screaming pain in his body, mustering up the little strength he had barely upright.

Rachel rose, reaching out, but he flinched away like her touch was a flame.

Two agents outside raised their weapons instinctively, their fingers twitching. But Orion didn't stop. He pushed through the door, stumbled down the corridor, shoved into his hospital room, and collapsed onto the bed.

The second the mattress caught his weight, everything exploded.

Sobs tore from him, raw and unfiltered. He screamed into the pillow, frustration, betrayal, grief, all of it boiling to the surface in violent waves. The world had lied to him. The stars had abandoned him. And Rachel Rachel had stood beside him with a dagger behind her back the entire time.

A knock. He ignored it.

The door creaked open.

"Go away!" he howled into the mattress, his voice breaking.

But she didn't. He felt the bed shift as she sat beside him, her hand resting gently on his back. The weight of her presence was unbearable.

"I tried to tell you earlier," she said quietly. "You know I never meant to hurt you."

He turned to her, tear-streaked, eyes blazing. "But you did. You lied to me for years. You let me cry in front of you. Bleed in front of you. And you never even flinched. Not once."

"I was under orders,"

"I don't care!" he shouted, sitting up, fists clenched. "Was any of it real? Were you ever really my friend? Or was I just a goddamn mission file with a heartbeat?"

Rachel's voice cracked. "At first... yes. But then I got to know you. Really know you. I saw your strength. Your loyalty. Your heart. And I realised I couldn't fake what we had. You became my friend. More than that."

"Don't," Orion spat. "Don't act like you're the victim here. You got to watch me suffer and stay safe in your silence."

Her eyes filled. "I'm sorry. I never told them everything. I protected you in every way I could."

"I don't know if I can believe that."

"I don't blame you," she whispered.

A moment passed.

Then, with trembling fingers, she pulled something from her pocket, a small, shimmering silver disc. She placed it gently on the bed beside him.

"I never gave them this," she said. "Maybe it still works."

She turned away, pausing at the door. "When you're ready... there's something important I need to tell you. Something I've never told anyone."

She left. The door clicked shut behind her.

Orion sat there, staring at the disc like it might detonate in his hands. He picked it up slowly. It was smooth and cold, humming faintly as it unfolded with a soft whirr.

He lifted it, voice trembling.

"Call Aurorina."

Static.

Frown deepening, he tried again.

"Call Lady Valoria."

A faint light blinked on. The static shifted. Then, a voice, distorted and distant.

"He...ll...o?"

Orion's heart leapt.

"This is Intenfli Orion. Please, I wish to speak to Lady Valoria."

"Is a n...y...one th...ere?"

Crackle. Hiss. Silence.

The light went dark.

He lowered the disc. It hummed once, then went still.

His shoulders slumped.

He had no home in the stars. No family on Earth. No one to trust.

The only person who'd stood by him had betrayed him from the beginning.

Tears blurred his vision again. He curled into the pillow, holding the disc to his chest like it might anchor him to something real.

Sleep took him slowly, dragging him down with the weight of betrayal, grief, and the unbearable question:

If everything had been a lie... then who was he, really?

# 1. The Hospital

Orion jolted awake, heart hammering in his chest as a sharp bang echoed through the room like a thunderclap. Disoriented, sweat beading at his temples, he scanned the dim hospital space, senses raw and hyper-alert.

The door slammed open.

Assistant Director Rouge and General Genevieve stormed in with the two D.E.T.A. agents from the corridor. Weapons were drawn. Their faces were masks of urgency, eyes sweeping every corner for a threat only they seemed to understand.

"What's going on?" Orion barked, his throat still hoarse from sleep, every muscle tensing as he pushed himself upright.

Rouge didn't look at him. "The Director will explain when she arrives."

A thick silence followed, broken only by the mechanical hum of equipment and the relentless ticking of the wall clock. Orion's unease gnawed at him, every second feeling like the breath before a blow.

The door creaked again.

Rachel stepped into the room.

But it wasn't Rachel not the girl he had grown up with, fought beside, trusted with every broken part of himself. She wore black tactical gear now, her vest stamped with bold white letters: DIRECTOR. Behind her, a wall of agents flanked her entrance like shadows from another world.

"Leave us," she commanded.

Every head bowed. No hesitation. The agents filed out, and the door sealed with a soft hiss.

Now it was just the two of them.

A storm about to break.

Orion's jaw clenched as he stared at her. "So... you're not just an agent," he said, voice cold, brittle. "You're the Director. How long were you planning to keep that from me too?"

Rachel stepped forward, but he recoiled. She froze.

A ripple shimmered across her skin. Gold. Then silver. Then a soft, dusted grey that shimmered like ash beneath the moon. Her frame stretched slightly, her eyes narrowing to slits. Her voice remained hers but now it carried a subtle, alien resonance.

"I'm a shapeshifter," she said, carefully. "My people come from a system not far from here. When the mission to monitor you was proposed, I volunteered. I thought... who better to guide you than someone who understands what it feels like to be... other?"

Orion's stomach twisted. "Guide me?" he spat, voice rising. "You watched me! You lied to me! All these years, and you never said a damn thing! Not one hint, not even when I was breaking apart!"

She flinched.

"Is Rachel even your real name?" he snapped, voice cracking with rage.

"Yes," she said quickly, too quickly. "I was born on Earth my parents crash-landed here long before your arrival. I was raised in hiding. Given a name, an identity. I blended in. I had no choice."

"That's a damn convenient story," Orion growled. "And it just keeps getting better. First you're an agent. Then you're the Director. Now you're some kind of alien double-agent with a sob story? Do you even hear how insane this sounds?"

Rachel's expression twisted with hurt, but she held her ground. "I never lied about how I felt."

"Oh, spare me that," he said, standing now, his voice thunderous. "You watched me suffer. You let me think I was alone broken while you stood by pretending to be my friend. You were there the day Anton died. You were there when I cracked open, and all you did was take notes."

"That's not fair,"

"No?" he cut her off, tears of fury burning his eyes. "You could've told me. You could've told me everything. Instead, you played your role. The perfect friend. The one person I thought I could trust. And the entire time, you were collecting data. Reporting on me like I was a specimen."

Rachel stepped forward, eyes brimming now. "Orion, I didn't choose this life. I was given an ultimatum: rot in a facility, or serve the program to protect my parents. I did what I had to do to keep them safe."

"And what about me?" he shouted. "What did you do to keep me safe?"

Silence. Her face fell.

"You don't get to play the martyr now," Orion snarled. "Not when you had years to come clean. Not when every moment of real connection between us was laced with your deception."

His breath was ragged now, his body trembling. All the pain, all the loss, all the trust he'd so rarely given all of it, crushed under the weight of her lie.

She approached him, slowly, as if every step might trigger another explosion. "At first," she said, voice almost too quiet to hear, "you were just a mission. But then... you became something else. I saw who you were beneath all the trauma. I cared. Not because they told me to but because I chose to."

He didn't respond. Couldn't. His hands trembled, clenched so tight his knuckles turned white.

"You chose to serve them," he whispered bitterly. "Don't talk to me about choices."

Her features tightened. "You think I didn't want to run? You think I didn't want to scream the truth at you every single day? But they had my family. I was sixteen when they put a gun to my life and told me who I'd be. I never asked for any of this."

The anger inside Orion cracked just a little. Replaced not with forgiveness, but with something heavier: understanding... and guilt.

He sank back onto the bed, his rage cooling to a low simmer. "You've been a prisoner this whole time?" he asked, voice rough, low.

Rachel nodded, tears tracing silent paths down her cheeks. "I haven't seen my parents since I was fifteen," she said, voice shaking. "They use them like chains. I did everything they asked so one day I might earn their freedom."

Orion stared at the floor. The fury hadn't gone, but it had nowhere else to go. It just curled up inside him like a wound left open too long. "I wanted to hate you," he murmured. "I still want to. But now I don't know what to feel."

She didn't speak.

"I thought I knew you," he said, brokenly. "Now I feel like I never knew anything."

Rachel moved closer. Her hand hovered above his, hesitant. "I know you have no reason to believe me. But I never lied about us. Not the real parts. Not the laughter. Not the nights we talked about the stars. That was me, Orion. It's always been me."

The silence between them was different now raw, painful, but real.

Orion looked at her through tear-stained lashes, his voice frayed. "Why didn't you just tell me?"

Her voice cracked. "Because I was scared. Of losing everything. Of losing you."

He stared at her hand, trembling slightly as it reached toward him again. And after a long moment, he placed his own hand over hers.

"I don't forgive you," he whispered. "Not yet. Maybe not ever. But I see you now. And I think... that's a start.

Rachel's faint smile returned, but it was tinged with sadness, her eyes shimmering with a mix of relief and quiet pain. "You've been through so much yourself," she said, her voice steadying. "I don't blame you, Orion. I never have."

The air between them settled into a fragile quiet, not peace, but something like it. For the first time, Orion could see past her mask. The same strength that once seemed unshakable now showed cracks: worn edges, quiet exhaustion, a lifetime of compromise. And within those cracks, something human, something real.

She wasn't just a spy.

She was a survivor.

"Rachel..." Orion's voice was low, almost reverent. "You're stronger than I ever gave you credit for."

Her smile twitched, a ghost of warmth flickering in her eyes. "And you're stronger than you believe, Orion. You always have been."

But the moment couldn't last. Rachel wiped away her tears with practiced efficiency, her spine straightening like a soldier snapping back to duty.

"Right. We need to move. A ship just crashed through the barrier. I think it may be one of yours."

Orion's heart stumbled in his chest.

One of his?

He nodded slowly, emotions still clinging to his bones like frost, and pushed them down beneath resolve. With effort, he scooted off the bed and linked his arm with Rachel's tentative at first, then firmer. There was comfort in the contact, even after everything.

Outside the room, Rouge and General Genevieve waited, flanked by a formation of stone-faced D.E.T.A. agents. Without a word, the squad moved into a protective V around Orion and Rachel, like a wall of silent judgment.

The walk to the lift was short, but the weight in the air made every step feel like a march to trial. More agents joined them ten, maybe twelve all dressed in black, their weapons slung but eyes sharp. The hum of the elevator as they descended was deafening against the silence. Orion stole a glance at Rachel. She stood stoically beside him, her expression unreadable again the Director now, not the girl who'd just cried in his presence.

He looked away.

Genevieve and Rouge exchanged a glance. No words. Just pressure. Just the squeeze of a system flexing its grip.

The elevator doors parted with a soft chime.

And the world had changed again.

Where once there was a hospital lobby, there was now a fortified checkpoint, a war zone in disguise. Steel walls, tactical floodlights, blast doors, automated guns. The air itself hummed with tension, as if it knew something was about to break.

Genevieve barked clipped orders. The agents snapped into position, some taking cover, others training their rifles on the reinforced entrance. This was no longer a hospital it was a bunker, and Orion was its most dangerous patient.

He stepped forward only to freeze at a sharp clang beside him. His breath caught.

A turret.

It rotated toward him with mechanical precision, the barrel humming ominously, tracking his movements like prey. Orion's pulse spiked.

He stepped closer to Rachel without even thinking.

She led him forward, posture taut. One step at a time, they approached the scanners.

Rachel went first.

She stepped into the scanner with a calm that was almost unnatural. A beam of green light swept over her, scanning every inch. The computer screen behind the desk flared to life.

"Director of the D.E.T.A., you are authorised. Please proceed."

She stepped forward, then turned back toward Orion.

But before she could speak, Genevieve shoved him forward with a hand to his shoulder. "Go," she ordered coldly, with none of Rachel's gentleness.

Orion's chest tightened. He stepped into the scanner, reluctant, stiff. The green beam began to sweep down his body. A low, unfamiliar hum filled the air.

"Subject: Orion. Non-humanoid detected. Request Director-level authorisation before release."

He tried to move but his body wouldn't respond. Something held him in place.

"What the hell?"

A sharp pain jolted through his arm. He cried out, looking down in alarm to see a needle retracting into the scanner wall. His hand flew to the spot, but there was no visible mark just a lingering, internal burn.

"What did you just do to me?" Orion shouted, staggering out of the scanner, fury boiling behind his eyes.

Genevieve turned from the control terminal, her tone as cold as steel. "Director, please place your hand on the biometric scanner. I've injected the alien with an explosive tracker."

The words dropped like a hammer.

Orion reeled. "You what?"

The weight of her words didn't just hit him they pierced him.

A thousand memories from earlier surged to the surface. The tracker. The fear in Rachel's eyes. The gun trained on his head in the corridor. Everything was coming into focus now and it all reeked of control.

Rachel's face twisted in fury. "You had no authorisation to do that," she snapped, voice trembling. "That wasn't protocol."

"Orders from Downing Street," Genevieve said with a smug shrug. "They don't want another 'incident.' In case the creature decides to turn on us."

Rachel's jaw clenched so tight it looked like it might shatter.

Without another word, she placed her hand on the scanner. The light turned green.

"Please proceed."

Orion moved forward mechanically. Inside, his chest burned. Not just with pain but with violation. He could feel the foreign presence inside him. It wasn't just metal. It was a chain. It was a threat.

An unspoken you belong to us now.

He leaned close to Rachel, his voice a quiet storm. "An explosive tracker? After everything... this is how they thank me?"

"I didn't know she was going to do that," Rachel said, barely holding back her fury. "But I swear to you I'll find a way to get it out. I promise, Orion."

He gave a bitter nod, rage simmering beneath his skin. He wouldn't forget this. He wouldn't forgive it.

Not this time.

More agents passed through the scanner. Routine. Controlled. Human.

Orion clenched his fists.

And I'm not, he thought.

They moved forward in tight formation, past the now-armed security gates and into the blinding sunlight of a world that no longer felt like his.

And then... he stopped.

His breath caught in his throat.

A ship loomed in the distance sleek, predatory, and unmistakably alien. Smoke curled from its undercarriage, the engines hissing like a beast at rest. But what truly made Orion freeze was the emblem on its side.

The royal seal.

His seal.

His heart thundered.

Rachel stepped up beside him, reading the recognition on his face. "It's one of yours, isn't it?"

He nodded slowly, his voice caught somewhere between awe and dread. "Yeah... it is."

But whether it was friend or foe that, he didn't yet know.

He frowned, eyes narrowing as he stared at the ship.

How had it got through?

The orbital defence grid above Earth wasn't just advanced it was brutal. An interlocked ring of automated cannons, pulse-mines, and cloaked satellites designed to obliterate anything that wasn't cleared for approach. Nothing got through without clearance. Nothing.

The fact that this vessel had bypassed those defences his people's defences unnerved him. Either someone had let it through, or something about the ship defied their technology entirely. Either possibility churned unease in his gut.

He shoved the thought aside for now and followed Rachel and the D.E.T.A. agents toward a cordon of soldiers stationed at the edge of the field, where the manta-class starship had settled like a beast at rest. The earth was scorched beneath its engines, the scent of ozone and burning grass lingering in the air.

The soldiers stood in stiff formation, their black-armoured figures forming a barrier between the ship and the perimeter beyond. Each of their rifles was raised, locked, and trained on the ramp of the vessel, fingers tight on triggers. Tension radiated from them like static before a storm.

One of the soldiers broke formation.

He strode toward them with practiced efficiency, his boots pounding the ground in crisp, even steps. He couldn't have been older than eighteen maybe nineteen at a stretch. His face was fresh, unscarred, almost delicate beneath the hardness of his expression.

Blonde hair buzzed to regulation length. Clear blue eyes sharp with military focus.

"Captain, what's the situation?" Rachel asked, her tone clipped, precise Director mode.

The young officer halted in front of her, saluting sharply.

"Madam Director," he replied, his voice deeper than expected measured, confident. "We attempted to hail the vessel on every channel. No response. No signal interference, either. It's deliberate silence. I advise a full evacuation to a secure fallback position while we continue to assess the threat."

Orion studied him silently, noting the coolness in the young man's tone. Despite his youth, the captain radiated command too composed, too polished. Orion recognised it instantly. This boy had seen war. More than he ever should have.

Rachel's mouth thinned into a line of resolve. "Negative. The ship bears Orion's royal insignia. That alone makes this encounter unique. And the fact it penetrated the barrier without triggering orbital countermeasures? That makes it historic."

She turned slightly, eyes scanning the field.

"Set all weapons to maximum stun. No live rounds unless explicitly ordered. Hold position and do not engage unless you have no other choice."

"Aye, ma'am." The captain saluted again, turning sharply on his heel.

His voice cracked across the line as he barked orders to his platoon, each syllable slicing through the air. Soldiers moved as one, their motions practiced and sharp. The click and whine of weapons adjusting echoed across the field, harsh and discordant. The shift to stun-mode felt like the silence before thunder.

Orion's pulse quickened.

Then came the sound.

A sharp hiss like pressurised steam escaping a sealed vault followed by the low, mechanical groan of the ship's rear hatch beginning to open. Steam billowed from the edges of the seam, coiling and dancing in the air like smoke from a dragon's maw. A low thump shook the ground as the massive ramp extended, the groaning metal echoing into the open field.

Thud.

The ramp hit the earth.

Silence swallowed the platoon.

A white-hot flood of interior light spilled from the open vessel, cutting a sharp line across the smoke and dust. Then figures.

Three of them.

Backlit and featureless at first, their outlines distorted in the haze of the descending mist. They stood at the top of the ramp, motionless. Watching. Waiting.

Orion squinted, leaning slightly forward, trying to catch a clearer view.

Something about their stillness was wrong. Not hesitation confidence. The kind of confidence that came from knowing no one could stop them.

They began to descend.

Slowly. Deliberately.

Not cautiously. Not with fear. But with purpose.

Their footsteps were quiet against the ramp, but the weight of their presence was thunderous. Even from this distance, Orion could feel it a ripple of power in the air, thick and strange, like gravity bending slightly around them.

He felt a chill crawl down his spine.

Beside him, Rachel tensed. The agents behind them raised their weapons a little higher. The platoon's fingers hovered closer to triggers.

"Halt!" the captain's voice exploded across the field, sharp and unwavering. "By order of the Department of Extraterrestrial Threat Assessment identify yourselves or stand down!"

Two of the figures stopped abruptly at the base of the ramp, their silhouettes still veiled by the swirling haze. But the third figure taller, with a posture that radiated eerie confidence kept walking. Their stride was steady, almost graceful. They moved as if the heavily armed platoon didn't exist.

"I repeat, halt!" the captain barked, this time louder, more urgent. "Fail to comply, and we will fire!"

The lone figure didn't even blink. No hesitation. No acknowledgment. Just step after deliberate step toward certain danger.

Orion could feel the static in the air, every hair on his body standing on end. The soldiers were shifting now, uncertain. The safety of numbers did little to silence the creeping dread that was settling in their bones.

"What the hell are they doing?" Orion muttered, his voice low and tight.

Rachel didn't answer. Her eyes were locked on the advancing figure, lips pressed in a flat line. Her hand hovered near her sidearm, fingers twitching not out of fear, but calculation. She was ready.

The tension was unbearable. Even the comms had gone dead quiet, as if the very air around them held its breath.

Then movement.

The figure raised an arm, and reality seemed to warp. The space around them shimmered violently, like heat rippling off asphalt.

The captain's voice broke. "I said halt or we will"

But it was already too late.

The figure vanished in a pulse of distortion.

Chaos erupted.

A wave of invisible force slammed through the car park. Soldiers screamed as they were hurled backward, bodies colliding with metal, glass, and concrete. Vehicles crumpled under the weight of armoured troops flung like dolls. Energy blasts lit up the smoke as panicked soldiers fired blindly, desperate to stop whatever was attacking them.

"Where are they?!" a soldier cried out, his voice cracking.

Orion flinched as a body landed just feet from him with a sickening thud. The platoon was collapsing, their formation torn apart in seconds. Over half were down either unconscious, groaning, or too stunned to move.

Then, as suddenly as it began, the assault stopped.

Silence fell like a hammer.

The air shimmered again, and the figure reappeared standing behind the captain.

Calm. Unbothered.

A blade gleamed in her hand, the edge so fine it shimmered like starlight. She drew it up to the captain's throat with smooth precision. He froze, breath hitching, his whole body trembling.

"Tell your men to lower their weapons," the figure said coldly, her voice like cut glass and achingly familiar.

Orion's breath caught. His pulse thundered.

"Eymd?" he whispered.

The captain didn't move. Couldn't. His lips parted, but no sound came. His wide eyes flicked to his troops, who stood frozen, weapons still half-raised, unsure whether to shoot or flee.

Then everything spiralled.

Genevieve moved like a striking snake.

She seized Orion in a vice grip, yanked him against her chest, and jammed the cold muzzle of her sidearm against his temple. The whine of the power cell charging filled his ear like a scream.

"Enough!" she bellowed, her voice unhinged. "I told them harbouring filth like you would bring ruin to this planet. And I was right."

Orion stiffened, heart hammering. He felt her finger tighten on the trigger.

The platoon held their breath. No one dared move.

"General, drop the weapon!" Rouge's voice cracked through the silence. "You're out of line!"

Genevieve's laugh was a razor's edge. "Out of line? You think I care about protocol now? Look around, Rouge. This is what you protected. This is what you let in."

"Let him go," Rachel growled, voice shaking with rage.

"You betrayed your own kind for this thing," Genevieve snarled. "You're no better than the monsters that killed your parents."

Rachel froze.

Orion's blood turned to ice. "What did you say?"

Genevieve pressed the barrel harder to his head. "I did what she couldn't. I ended them. Weak, pathetic traitors. Just like her."

Everything stopped.

Then a shadow surged.

Darkness shot forward like a whip, curling around Genevieve's arm and weapon. With an unnatural wrench, it twisted her hand backwards. The gun discharged but not outward. A blinding flare of plasma burst at the point of contact, detonating the charge.

Genevieve screamed, her arm flaring with heat and light as metal and bone gave way. She dropped the weapon, stumbling, just as a second shadow slammed into her head.

She dropped like a stone.

Orion staggered away, barely catching himself. His vision blurred, ears ringing from the blast. The scent of scorched metal and blood hung thick in the air.

The shadow recoiled like a living thing, slithering back toward the ship's ramp. A tall figure stood waiting.

"Eymd, enough," a deep voice said low, composed, unmistakably in control. "Let the human go. I think we've made our point."

The figure beside the captain now clearly Eymd scoffed. With a lazy flourish, she withdrew her blade and stepped back.

The captain collapsed, gasping, fingers clawing at his neck like he was trying to confirm he was still alive.

"I was just making a point," Eymd said, rolling her shoulder with dramatic nonchalance. She tossed a smirk toward Orion. "Besides, it worked, didn't it?"

"Stand down," the voice repeated, firmer this time.

Eymd huffed and finally stepped away, her stance loosening. She flicked a hand through her hair, the smoke around her finally clearing to reveal her fully. And still, the third figure hadn't moved a sentinel of silence, watching, waiting.

Orion tried to slow his breathing, tried to grasp what had just happened. Soldiers groaned around him. Rachel hadn't moved from where she stood, her eyes fixed on Genevieve's crumpled body. Rouge stood behind her, jaw clenched, fists at his sides.

Orion turned back to Eymd. "You could've warned me."

Eymd tilted her head, eyes gleaming. "And miss the look on your face?"

Orion's legs felt like they were made of smoke, barely holding him upright beneath the weight of what had just unfolded. But he refused to buckle. Not here. Not now. His eyes flicked from Eymd her smirk still sharp and unapologetic to the captain, who remained crumpled on the ground, pale and shaking, his chest rising and falling in uneven gasps. Then, slowly, Orion's gaze shifted upward.

The other two figures were descending the ramp.

They moved with a quiet, calculated grace no urgency, no fear just the heavy stillness of beings who commanded attention without needing to demand it. Each footstep echoed against the tarmac, cutting through the silence like falling stones in a sacred place. When they reached the bottom, Orion's breath caught in his throat.

The woman was arresting.

Slightly older than Eymd, though no less dangerous. She shared her sister's high cheekbones and pointed stare, but where Eymd radiated heat and fire, this one moved like cold flame controlled, exacting, and impossibly precise. Long, vibrant blue hair flowed over her shoulders like liquid silk, a stark contrast to the deep charcoal of her uniform. Slung across her chest was a bandoleer of glass vials, each filled with swirling, luminous liquid in hues that shimmered like living nebulae. They pulsed faintly, as if reacting to the tension in the air, casting flickers of eerie light across her composed face.

Then came the third figure.

Orion involuntarily took a step back.

This one was a wall of living metal and myth.

Encased in black armour that writhed subtly across his powerful frame, the giant moved with the silent threat of an executioner and the grace of a trained predator. The plates of his suit shifted with him, almost like muscle and skin, etched with glowing runes that pulsed dimly beneath the scorched sky. A titanic hammer rested in one hand, its head as big as Orion's torso, runes etched across it burning a low, angry red. In the other hand, he carried a broad shield its surface scarred and battle-worn bearing the unmistakable crest of the Shadow Elite Guard. It had seen war, and it had survived it.

Beneath the curved horns of his helmet, two slits glowed a pair of red eyes like twin suns at dusk, unreadable and unblinking.

Rachel's voice snapped Orion out of his trance.

"I take it you know them?" she asked. Her tone was even, but there was an unmistakable edge beneath the surface. Not fear. Not quite. But something close. Wariness wrapped in ice.

Orion blinked, startled by how close she'd moved. He swallowed.

"I know Eymd," he said, his voice quieter than he expected. "But not the other two."

Rachel studied the trio with narrowed eyes, her body still rigid with adrenaline. "Captain," she said sharply, never taking her eyes off the armoured figure, "tell your men to stand down. They're friendly."

The captain still trembling, his hand hovering near his holster looked like someone who had just seen the end of the world and somehow survived it. He stared at Eymd for a long, shaky second, then at the behemoth behind her. Swallowing hard, he straightened up.

"Stand down!" he barked, though his voice cracked. "Lower your weapons!"

The remaining troops obeyed, some more reluctantly than others. A few kept their fingers close to their triggers, their faces pale and drawn, eyes wide with the kind of fear that stayed long after the threat passed.

The worst had ended but the echoes of it still lingered, vibrating just beneath the surface of every breath.

Orion let out a slow exhale, but his heart hadn't caught up yet.

The three Shadow citizens finally came to a stop before Orion. Without a word, the two strangers dropped to one knee, bowing their heads in a gesture of deep, formal reverence. The movement was fluid ritualistic. Precise.

Orion blinked, momentarily stunned. After everything after the chaos, the threats, the bloodshed this was the last thing he'd expected.

"Intenfli Orion," the armoured man said, his voice like distant thunder echoing through a mountain pass. "Please forgive my sister. As you know, she can be... hot-headed."

Eymd scoffed beside him, crossing her arms with a snort. "Don't apologise for me, Verjast. They had weapons pointed at our skulls," she snapped, defiance curling off every word like smoke.

The blue-haired woman sighed with exaggerated patience, her expression cool as she adjusted the strange, circular glasses perched on her nose. "Sister, stop being so rude and bow before the Intenfli," she said, the reprimand soft but cutting.

Eymd rolled her eyes with a dramatic flair. "Orion's not like that," she muttered under her breath. "Now get up before he starts getting ideas."

Orion couldn't help it he chuckled. Somehow, despite the surreal tension and the chaos that still lingered in the air, watching them bicker was... oddly grounding. It felt real, like the kind of friction only family could spark. Familiar. Sincere.

"You're right, Eymd. Stand up, all of you," he said gently.

"Told you," Eymd said with smug satisfaction, tossing a victorious glance at her sister. But her expression quickly turned venomous as her gaze slid toward Rachel. Her smirk widened like a blade being slowly unsheathed. "Oh look," she purred. "The human pet is here."

Orion's jaw tightened, the lightness draining from his expression as the sting of her words hit home.

"Eymd" he began, his voice low and warning.

But Rachel raised a hand, silencing him. Her face was calm, but her eyes shimmered with something deeper grief, fatigue, something hollowed-out. "It's fine," she said softly, though there was a note of weariness in her tone that cut sharper than any retort. "I've been called worse."

The other two Shadow siblings still rising to their feet kept their eyes downcast, avoiding Orion's gaze as if weighed down by guilt or shame. He turned slowly toward Rachel, and his breath caught in his throat.

Her cheeks were streaked with the remnants of tears. Her jaw was set with grim resolve, but the pain was still fresh, etched across her features in every line and tremble.

And suddenly, Genevieve's venom came roaring back in his memory those final, cruel words that had shattered more than just the fragile truce. They'd pierced something deeper.

"Rach," he said softly, stepping forward. "I'm sorry. Maybe... maybe she was lying."

Rachel shook her head slowly, her lips forming a thin, bitter line. "No," she murmured. "I always knew. Deep down, I think I always knew."

Without thinking, Orion pulled her into an embrace. Rachel froze, caught off guard then slowly melted into him, arms wrapping tightly around his back. She clung to him like he was an anchor in a storm she hadn't realised she was drowning in.

"You didn't deserve that," he whispered, the words thick in his throat. "None of it."

For a moment, the world held its breath. The devastation, the tension, the battlefield all of it faded into the background, leaving only the quiet ache of two souls trying to hold each other together.

Then Rachel stepped back, swiping quickly at her face with trembling fingers. Her voice was steadier now, laced with steel. "We'll deal with it later," she said. "Right now, we need to focus."

Orion nodded, turning back toward the trio. He could feel Eymd watching him, her smirk creeping back into place like it had never left.

"Do you have any idea what we went through to find you?" she demanded, jabbing him lightly in the shoulder. "Not to mention they insisted on tagging along."

"I'm sure you'll remind me every chance you get," Orion replied, a ghost of a smile tugging at his lips. "Still... thank you."

Eymd raised an eyebrow, mock offense playing across her features. "Did the mighty Intenfli just say thank you?" she teased, feigning shock.

Orion rolled his eyes, though the warmth behind it was genuine. "Don't get used to it."

Her grin widened but then, with a sudden shift, her tone soured. "So... why was the pet giving orders? And why is she wearing that vest?" she asked, tilting her chin toward Rachel with acid in her voice.

The air thinned again.

Orion sighed, weariness creeping into his shoulders. "I'll explain in a moment. First, tell me how did you manage to get past the blockade?"

"All the orbital defence ships are automated," Eymd replied with a proud smirk. "Snjallt fooled their sensors into thinking we were just a chunk of space debris."

"She tweaked their targeting logic mid-transmission," Verjast added, his voice almost reverent. "Rewrote the command protocols before the AI even realised what happened."

Rachel, who had been silent through the exchange, finally stepped forward. "Impressive," she said, her tone cool but professional. Then she glanced around at the soldiers still nursing wounds, the scorched ground, the twitch of fingers near triggers and her voice turned firm. "But I suggest we continue this conversation on your ship. The troops are nervous. And quite frankly, so am I."

Orion followed her gaze. She wasn't wrong. The atmosphere was still taut, the quiet aftermath almost louder than the violence that had come before.

He nodded once, his expression hardening with resolve.

"Let's go."

Rachel turned toward the captain and Rouge. "Captain. Assistant Director. I'd appreciate it if you'd join us."

"Yes, ma'am," the captain replied, his voice steady despite the sheen of sweat running down his temple. He glanced uneasily back at the limp figure of General Genevieve. "What about the General?"

Rachel's jaw tightened, but her composure didn't falter. "Have the medics check her over. Once Orion agrees, she is to be detained and brought aboard. I have questions."

Orion hesitated only a moment, a war raging behind his eyes, then gave a curt nod.

Without another word, they followed the Shadow citizens up the ramp. Inside, the ship was a stark contrast to Earth's clunky military crafts. It was all clean lines and purposeful design, with polished metal floors and faintly glowing strip lights pulsing rhythmically along the walls. The atmosphere felt alive, almost organic.

A staircase on the left led down to a lower deck. To the right, a corridor stretched into darkness, with three sealed doors. Through the open cockpit, Orion spotted four chairs facing a panoramic view of the stars, as if the universe itself was waiting for them.

"The conference room is this way," Eymd muttered, pressing her palm to a panel. The nearest door whooshed open with a hiss of escaping pressure.

The room was compact but functional. A rectangular table with ten chairs took up most of the space, while a worn brown sofa out of place in the sleek surroundings rested in the corner like a forgotten relic.

Eymd threw herself onto it with theatrical flair, tossing a dagger into the air and catching it with lazy precision. Snjallt and Verjast followed with more dignity, taking positions by the table. Rachel and Rouge entered last, the door sealing behind them with a subtle click.

"Eymd, sit at the table," Verjast said firmly, already unclipping his helmet.

"I'm good here, thanks," she replied without looking up.

Verjast sighed and turned to Orion. "Your Highness, I apologise for my sister's... persistent insubordination. I'm sure you're beginning to understand why she was named Eymd."

Orion's curiosity flared as Verjast removed his helmet. The armour folded neatly into his shoulder plates, revealing a broad, tattooed torso inked with spirals of black that shimmered faintly under the light. His grey skin bore deep, ancient scars. Hazel hair was tied back in a practical bun, but it was the glowing red eyes and unnervingly sharp teeth that made Orion's breath catch.

"You're not like the others," Orion said, eyes narrowing. "You're half human."

"Yes," Verjast replied quietly. His gaze dropped for a moment. "My mother... was sent on a diplomatic mission. She broke protocol."

Orion blinked. "That's... not allowed, right?"

"It's not," Verjast confirmed. "But she had enough power to keep it quiet. At least for a while."

Before Orion could ask more, the door slid open and Captain Cole reappeared, clearly unsure whether he belonged.

"The General is stable," he reported, taking a seat beside Orion. "The doctor's excited to try the new surgical suite your people provided."

"Thank you, Captain," Rachel said, nodding once. "Let's begin introductions."

She stood a little taller. "I am Rachel, Director of the D.E.T.A."

"Assistant Director Rouge," Rouge added, his tone clipped.

The young captain straightened. "Captain Aaron Cole, D.E.T.A. special task force."

Verjast inclined his head slightly. "Verjast. Former First Admiral of the Shadow Elite Guard."

"I am Snjallt," the blue-haired woman said calmly. "Former lead scientist of the Shadow Empire."

Eymd flipped her dagger again. "Eymd. Blah blah blah. Titles are just words now."

Orion frowned. "Why are all your titles former?"

Verjast and Snjallt exchanged a loaded glance.

"After you vanished during the Battle of the Great Four," Verjast said, "our mother the High Matriarch blamed Eymd. She stripped her of her title. Banished her."

"We didn't agree with the decision," Snjallt added, adjusting her glasses. "So we left with her."

A quiet, aching weight settled on the room.

"I'm sorry," Orion said, his voice low. "You lost everything because of me."

"What's done is done," Verjast said, voice firm.

Then his tone darkened as his gaze shifted to Rachel. "But what I want to know is why the human pet is giving orders. And why she's wearing that vest."

Rachel met his gaze evenly, unfazed. She explained brief but thorough the circumstances around her forced leadership, the chip in her neck, and Orion's. By the time she finished, the air in the room had changed.

Eymd shot up suddenly, spat on the floor, and launched into a furious tirade in her native tongue.

"Vanront, mimaniila shafor camtz infanterno demendia! Gwe shafor elixiumn handit lorenta za aftena!"

Orion blinked. "What does that mean?"

Verjast closed his eyes with a long sigh. "Roughly? 'Weakling, you should have chosen death. I should snap you like a twig.'"

"That's enough," Orion snapped. "Rachel didn't have a choice."

"There's always a choice!" Eymd shouted, her fury crackling like static in the air. She slumped back onto the sofa, arms crossed, a scowl etched deep into her features.

The silence that followed was brittle.

Then Orion spoke again softer this time. "What happened to my family?"

The words sliced through the tension like a blade.

Everything stopped.

Snjallt's hands froze mid-fidget. Verjast looked down at the table. Even Eymd turned away, her shoulders rigid.

And then Orion saw it something he'd never imagined: black tears sliding down Eymd's cheeks. But the second she realised he'd noticed, she turned away fully, hiding her face against the cushions.

"I'm not sure you're strong enough to hear the answer," Snjallt said, barely above a whisper.

"I need to know," Orion said, sharper now. "Tell me."

Snjallt hesitated then stood, walked to him, and embraced him tightly. There was no ceremony in it. Just raw, trembling grief.

"They've been captured," she whispered into his ear. "Taken by the Great Four. We've searched everywhere. So far... there's nothing."

Orion staggered slightly as the weight of it hit. His vision blurred. "Oh," he breathed. It was the only word that came. A tight knot formed in his chest.

"What about Anton?" he managed to ask.

Eymd's voice drifted from the sofa. "I got him out. Used everything I had left. I made sure he escaped." Her tone faltered. "But by the time I sent the ship back..."

She stopped, looking down at her hands.

"They were gone."

Orion closed his eyes, swaying slightly. "Thank God he's safe," he whispered. "At least he's safe."

Then, straightening, he turned to Rachel. "About these chips... is there anything you can do?"

Snjallt stepped forward, her grief hardened into resolve. "If I can run a scan, I might be able to disable and extract them."

Rachel's head snapped up, alarm flashing in her eyes. "No. They have failsafes. If tampered with, they'll detonate."

"We've developed countermeasures," Snjallt said, calmly retrieving a small device from her belt. "With the right shielding, we can intercept the failsafe signal."

"Try it on the pet first," Eymd muttered. "If it fails, she dies first. Saves us time."

The room froze.

"Eymd!" Orion's voice cracked like thunder. "That's enough. She was doing her duty just like you were."

Eymd sat up, her face flushed with fury. "What duty?" she growled. "I would've died before I betrayed a friend."

The room fell dead silent.

Snjallt turned. Even Verjast looked stunned.

Eymd stared ahead, unblinking. "True friends are rare. You don't betray them. You protect them. Or you live to regret it."

Orion blinked. "Wait... I'm your friend?"

Eymd scoffed, eyes wide. "That's what you took from all that?"

"I'm sorry," he said, lips twitching. "Still processing the 'friend' part."

Snjallt and Verjast exchanged baffled glances. Eymd groaned loudly and flopped back onto the sofa, flinging her arm over her eyes like a character in a melodrama.

"I hate you all," she muttered.

But Orion could see the ghost of a smile tugging at her lips.

"There's something different about you," Eymd murmured, her voice half-muffled beneath the crook of her arm. She lazily lifted it just enough to peek at Orion, her crimson eyes narrowing in contemplation. "It's not just the fact that you've lost your powers. There's... something else."

Orion tilted his head, a frown creasing his brow. "Different how?"

Eymd sat up slightly, one knee propped against the sofa, studying him as though he were a complicated riddle. "I don't know," she said slowly, her tone uncharacteristically thoughtful. "It's like... the light in you feels heavier now. Dimmer, maybe. But stronger in a weird, gritty way."

She exhaled sharply, frustrated. "It's probably this cursed planet. Even with my powers intact, something about the atmosphere messes with my magic. Like it's clogged."

Orion's eyes darkened. "You think it's just Earth?"

Eymd's lips curled into a slow, teasing grin. "No, I think I've figured it out."

"Oh?"

"You've grown a backbone," she declared, feigning a gasp. "Stars above, someone write it down. Orion's finally got a spine."

The room exploded before Orion could reply.

Verjast and Snjallt spun on her like twin storms, their words slicing the air in their native tongue.

"Þú getur ekki sagt eitthvað eins og það!" Verjast snapped, his voice thunderous with disapproval. "You can't speak to him that way!"

"Hann gaf þér líf, tungan þín verður þér betri!" Snjallt hissed, her voice cutting like ice. "He gave you life, mind your tongue!"

The siblings' voices overlapped, rising in fury sharp, fast, and indecipherable to human ears. Eymd rolled her eyes dramatically but didn't interrupt them, choosing instead to recline further, arms behind her head, as if basking in the chaos she'd created.

Rachel sighed, the weight of everything suddenly pressing down on her shoulders. With a glance at Rouge and Captain Cole, she gave a subtle nod an unspoken order.

The two men rose quietly and exited, the door sliding shut behind them with a whisper of displaced air.

Rachel stood and crossed the room to Orion, her movements smooth but deliberate. She placed a gentle hand on his arm, her fingers cool and steady.

"Come on," she said softly, voice barely above a whisper but it cut through the noise like a blade. "Let's step out for a moment."

Orion met her gaze and nodded, grateful for the reprieve. As she guided him toward the door, the shouting behind them grew more intense, the sound bouncing off the metal walls like a chorus of clashing wills.

The door slid closed behind them, silencing the storm but the weight of it lingered, pressing against Orion's chest like an aftershock.

Whatever was changing inside him it wasn't just power or politics. It was deeper. And it wasn't done yet.

# 2. The Escape

They stepped out of the ship into the hush of night, the cool air wrapping around them like a calming balm. Overhead, the stars stretched wide and unblinking, casting pale light over the cracked concrete of the forgotten landing zone. Rachel led Orion a few steps away to a battered bench partially buried in shadow and sat, patting the space beside her.

Orion joined her in silence, stealing a glance at her face. Her eyes were fixed on the sky distant, pensive. He recognised that look. He'd worn it himself as a child, staring out of broken windows at constellations he couldn't name, imagining a life beyond the world that hurt him.

"I'm guessing you've always longed to explore the stars," he said gently.

Rachel gave a soft, almost bitter laugh. "Always," she whispered. "But this stupid chip... it's like a leash around my soul. I can see the horizon, but I can never reach it."

"You will," Orion said, offering her a small, hopeful smile. "We'll fix it. And when we do if you want you can come with us."

Her head snapped toward him, eyes wide. For a second, she looked younger unguarded. "I'd love that," she said, the words fragile with sincerity. Then, with a crooked grin, she added, "But right now, I brought you out here because... well, when siblings fight, it's like releasing a pack of starving wolves. We'd never get a word in."

Orion chuckled. "Fair point." Rachel leaned into him, resting her head on his shoulder. He exhaled slowly, the tension in his chest loosening as they sat in silence.

But the quiet shattered.

A voice boomed inside Orion's skull, not heard but felt like thunder crashing through his very bones.

"We will not be arguing for hours."

The words struck like lightning. Pain exploded behind his eyes. Orion cried out, clutching the sides of his head. His knees buckled, and the world tilted violently.

"Orion?" Rachel pulled back, alarmed. "What's wrong your ears...?"

He staggered, his fingertips coming away sticky and wet. Blood. A deep, hot trail coursed down the side of his neck.

His breath caught. The stars above spun. Eymd, standing at the top of the ramp, stared down at him her face etched with horror.

"Snjallt!!" Eymd screamed aloud and through the telepathic channel, the panic in her voice undeniable. "Come quick!"

The sharp clang of boots echoed inside the ship like a countdown. Snjallt appeared a second later, her entrance framed in the glowing ramp light, irritation plastered across her face.

"What could possibly be so urgent that you yelled both ways?"

"Orion," Eymd said. Spoken. Thought. Pleaded.

Snjallt's expression changed instantly. She was on him in a flash, crouching beside Orion as he slumped against the bench, his body swaying like a sapling in a storm.

She reached into her coat, pulling out a compact crystalline device. With a flick of her wrist, it unfolded, humming softly as it scanned his skull. The device's soft green light turned a pulsating red.

Her breath caught.

"You idiot," she growled at Eymd, not looking away from the readout. "You tried to speak to him our way?"

"I didn't mean to!" Eymd shouted, her voice cracking under the weight of guilt. "It's instinct! It just slipped out."

"You could've ruptured his mind!" Snjallt snapped. "His neural pathways are collapsing he's not built for telepathic resonance. He needs a healing chamber. Now."

"How the hell was I supposed to know that?" Eymd cried, her voice rising as her composure unravelled. "No one told me humans were that fragile!"

"You've been in exile, not under a rock," Snjallt snarled, already supporting Orion under one arm. "Now stop shouting and help me move him!"

Orion felt strong hands dragging him to his feet, but the world tilted violently beneath him. Pain erupted in his skull like a hammer against glass, and a raw scream tore from his throat before he could suppress it. His vision fractured faces and lights smeared into unrecognisable blurs. A high-pitched ringing flooded his ears, drowning out everything around him. Voices shouting, frantic twisted together in a maddening chorus. He could see shapes, movement Eymd, Rachel, Snjallt but their words blurred into static.

"You haven't been back five minutes and you're already trying to kill him!" Rachel's voice finally pierced the haze, sharp with fury and desperation.

"Pet," Eymd sneered, her voice dripping venom. "Your opinion's worthless. You've been lying to him for years. Traitor."

Rachel's face darkened as she spun toward her. "This isn't about me. It's about him!"

Their words echoed around Orion like crashing waves. He tried to speak to stop them but his voice caught in his throat. His limbs trembled. The pain surged again, and the world went white-hot and cold all at once. Then everything vanished.

Darkness swallowed him whole.

In the void of unconsciousness, memory bled into nightmare.

The fireball screamed through the air. Orion stood frozen, helpless, watching it barrel toward his younger brother.

"Anton!"

His voice tore from his throat, but his legs refused to move. Time warped agonisingly slow and yet impossible to stop. The flames struck. Anton's body vanished in the blaze, his scream cut short, devoured by fire.

Ash. Only ash.

Orion relived it again and again. Each time, he reached out each time, too late. And still, no one gave him a straight answer. Nobody. No proof. Just evasion. Evasion is always their answer.

What had the remaining Horsemen done to his family?

The fireball surged once more, impossibly bright.

"ANTON!"

Orion's body jolted upright as the cry ripped from his lips. He gasped, chest heaving, drenched in cold sweat.

The room came into view through the haze of panic. He was lying on a bed of translucent crystal inside a glass pod. The surface beneath him was cool and smooth, almost comforting. Above him, the curved shell of the pod shimmered faintly.

Figures hovered just outside.

Eymd. Rachel. Verjast. Snjallt.

Snjallt stepped forward and tapped a panel. With a soft hum, the glass shell dematerialised, dissipating into thin air. The crystal beneath Orion shifted, lifting his back into a seated position. He groaned and rubbed his temples, stunned by the clarity slowly returning to his mind.

Eymd exhaled dramatically, offering a guilty half-smile. "For the record," she said, her tone uncharacteristically sheepish, "this time I wasn't actually trying to kill you."

Orion blinked at her, confused. "I feel... surprisingly okay."

"That's because you were lucky enough to be treated with actual technology," she said, folding her arms smugly. "None of this medieval medicine nonsense humans still cling to. Oh, and bonus your burn-free and your eye's fixed. You're welcome."

Snjallt gave her a tired glance. "Eymd, just because their tech isn't like ours doesn't make it primitive. They're doing the best they can."

Eymd rolled her eyes with theatrical flair. "Sure, but let's not pretend it's working. No powers. Corrupt leaders who only care about themselves and the upper crust. Meanwhile, everyone else breaks their backs just to survive. And don't even get me started on,"

"Eymd," Verjast growled, cutting her off with a glare. His crimson eyes burned with restrained frustration. "When you're done ranting, maybe remember we were once like them."

She spun toward him, arms flung wide. "We never let our children starve."

His voice dropped, dangerously low. "You weren't told everything. There's rot even in our history."

The tension crackled between them like a charged wire. Snjallt stood still, watching the exchange with tight lips and a furrowed brow. Rachel glanced at Orion, who winced and rubbed his head again, the headache threatening to return.

"Enough!" Orion's voice cracked like a whip through the room. "None of us can undo what's already happened."

The air shifted. Eymd let out a breath and flopped into the nearest chair with a groan. "Fine," she muttered, clearly not done but choosing silence for now.

Her expression brightened suddenly, as if struck by a bolt of inspiration. "Oh! Right. My phone! I can finally turn it back on now that I'm back on Earth."

Rachel blinked, clearly confused. "You have a phone?"

"Yes, Pet, I have a phone," Eymd replied with a dismissive flick of her wrist. "I was stuck here for sixteen years, remember? What did you think I did to stay sane? Meditate? I needed something to distract me from your planet's... charming dysfunction. social media chaos is delightful."

"Eymd," Orion said, exasperated, "enough with the 'pet' thing."

"Okay, okay, jeez," she said, standing up and brushing herself off. "Now that I know I didn't accidentally murder you, I have very important nonsense to catch up on. So much chaos, so little time." With a dramatic spin of her heel, she marched out of the med-bay, her voice fading behind the soft whoosh of the sliding door.

The silence she left behind hung awkwardly in the air.

It was Snjallt who broke it. "While you were unconscious, I removed your chip," she said casually, as if she hadn't just saved his life. "No more internal explosions if you try to leave the planet."

Orion blinked, stunned. "Thank you. What about Rachel's?"

"Also removed," Snjallt said, giving a brief nod. "And... Verjast and I have some ideas about reconnecting you with your powers. When you're feeling steady, we'd like to discuss them."

"Thank you," Orion said, sincerity thick in his voice. "For everything."

Snjallt gave him a small smile. "But as your doctor, I recommend you stay on the healing crystal a little longer. Recovery may feel quick, but your body still needs time."

She and Verjast turned to leave, but before the door could fully close behind them, Captain Aaron Cole stepped in. He bowed stiffly to the siblings before approaching Orion's bed, eyes shining with something unreadable.

"I was wondering if I could speak with you. Alone," Aaron said, his voice formal but unsure.

Rachel looked up, surprised. "Of course. What is it?"

Aaron hesitated. "Actually... I meant just with Orion, ma'am."

Rachel raised an eyebrow but nodded slowly. She gestured for Snjallt and Verjast to follow her out. "We'll give you both some space."

Once the room was empty, the silence became heavy almost charged.

Aaron stood at the foot of the bed, rubbing his hands nervously. His lips curled into a crooked smile half apology, half anticipation.

"I'm sorry for the secrecy," he began, voice softening. "But I didn't want anyone else to hear. Growing up... my mother used to tell me stories. About a great Intenfli who would one day return to unite the lost and bring peace to the galaxy." His eyes lingered on Orion, filled with quiet awe. "She described you. Exactly."

Orion blinked, heart skipping. "But you're human. How could you know anything about who I really am?"

Aaron chuckled, his cheeks already beginning to redden. "That's just it. I am human... but not entirely."

He began to pace, the tension in his frame uncoiling with each step. "Long ago, when your people left Earth, some humans went with them. They became... something new. My mother said our bloodlines were altered subtly, but enough. She told me we'd be called back when the stars aligned."

Orion's brow furrowed. "That doesn't make sense. My people's history says we've never been to Earth before. At least, not officially."

Aaron gave a small, sad smile. "Because it's a story only whispered among us. My people live on the Moon, in a hidden colony beneath the surface. The lunar government teaches us that Earth is barren uninhabitable. But my mother knew the truth. She risked everything to get me here. Said I'd know when the time came."

Orion studied him carefully. "And... you think now is that time?"

"I know it is," Aaron replied, his voice suddenly firm. He stepped closer, then faltered, as if unsure whether to continue. "The moment I saw you... I felt it. The connection. The purpose. I've been waiting for this."

Orion opened his mouth, but his thoughts tumbled over one another. Before he could respond, Aaron sat down at the edge of the bed, facing slightly away.

His voice was barely a whisper. "I've always felt like I didn't belong. Even on the Moon, among my own people. But when I heard your voice back at the compound... I knew. You're the reason I'm here."

The vulnerability in Aaron's words struck Orion hard. He slid down beside him on the bed, close enough to feel the tension humming through the young captain's body. Without thinking, he placed a hand gently over Aaron's.

Aaron flinched at the touch, then turned slowly to meet Orion's gaze. His face was flushed a deep crimson, but his eyes... they were wide, hopeful, and so open.

"You could've told Rachel," Orion said gently. "She would've helped you. We all would've."

"I didn't know if I could trust her," Aaron admitted. "But I trust you."

The words settled between them like a shared secret.

"If you want to come with us," Orion said softly, his thumb brushing lightly across the back of Aaron's hand, "you're more than welcome. But promise me you'll tell the others the truth. No more hiding."

Aaron's breath caught. He nodded once, slowly. "I promise."

Orion gave his hand a reassuring squeeze before releasing it.

Aaron stood quickly, flustered, trying and failing to hide the vivid red spreading across his cheeks. "Thank you... Intenfli," he said, bowing slightly then turned to leave.

As the door slid shut behind him, Orion leaned back on the crystal bed with a sigh. A faint smile tugged at the corners of his mouth.

"Well," he murmured to himself, "that was unexpected."

But even as the warmth of the moment lingered, his thoughts drifted back to the bigger storm his missing family, the broken world, and the fight that loomed ahead.

Still, for the first time in a while, he didn't feel quite so alone.

Orion leaned back against the crystal bed, his gaze fixed on the dull, metallic wall opposite him. His thoughts drifted, unanchored, weaving through the chaos of recent events. The dream, the revelations about his family, the mounting danger it all swirled together, an overwhelming storm of responsibility and fear. He wanted nothing more than to escape it all, to return to a simpler time when life made sense.

But which home could he return to? The Earth he had grown up on, where he was never truly accepted? Or the distant world of his ancestors, where his family was missing, likely enduring unimaginable torment?

He closed his eyes, and a memory surfaced one of his happiest moments from childhood.

It was the start of the summer holiday's, and the heat was almost unbearable. The sun blazed overhead as Lawrence, Orion's father, led him and his two younger brothers to the local park. They had packed a picnic and spent hours sprawled on a blanket under the shade of an old oak tree. Once they'd eaten, the twins, full of restless energy, begged to play by the waterfall.

A tall fence had been erected around it, marked with stern signs warning people to stay away. Lawrence, undeterred, grinned mischievously and lifted each boy over the fence one by one. Orion had protested at first, worried about breaking the rules, but his father's laughter had been infectious.

The twins quickly stripped down to their swimming shorts and splashed into the cool pool at the base of the waterfall. Orion had started to join them when his father gently grabbed his arm, crouching so their eyes met.

"So," Lawrence said, his voice soft but firm. "Are you going to tell me what happened at school yesterday?"

Orion hesitated, lowering his gaze. "They said we're poor," he mumbled. "And... that Mum left because I'm weird."

Lawrence's expression softened, and he sat down on the grass beside Orion, his gaze drifting to the twins playing in the water. "We're not rich," he admitted. "But we get by. And that's not why your mother left."

Orion bit his lip, fighting back tears. "Then why?"

Lawrence sighed, resting a hand on his son's shoulder. "Sometimes in life, people leave. Not because of you, or anyone else, but because they're searching for something they think they've lost." He paused, looking Orion squarely in the eyes. "Life will get hard, son. People will be mean, and things won't always make sense. But if you remember what's in your heart, you'll always find happiness."

For the rest of the afternoon, Orion played in the water with his brothers, his father's words lingering in his mind like a quiet melody.

Orion opened his eyes, the memory fading as reality set back in. He stared at the med-bay wall, his father's words echoing in his head. What is in your heart?

But the answer felt elusive. Too much had changed, and the weight of responsibility pressed down on him like never before. The galaxy was vast, dangerous, and full of uncertainties. Yet somewhere out there, his family was waiting, suffering. He couldn't let the darkness of the Great Four consume them.

He sat up straighter, his resolve hardening. No matter where his true home lay, he would fight to protect those he loved. Because that was what was in his heart hope, even in the face of despair.

Remembering the moment with his father and brothers made Orion smile. Even though there were countless bad memories tied to his dad, there were good ones too moments that reminded him life wasn't all pain. Lost in thought, he didn't hear the med-bay door open behind him and jumped when a hand rested on his shoulder.

"Hey, Egg, you okay? You seemed a million miles away."

Orion turned to see Rachel standing there, concern etched across her face. He chuckled softly. "Yeah, just thinking about the twins and my dad."

Rachel sat beside him on the crystal bed, her gaze dropping to the floor. "Can I ask you something, Egg?"

"You and that nickname," he said, shaking his head but smiling. "Go for it."

Rachel hesitated, then spoke, her voice quieter than usual. "Why did you forgive him? After everything he put you through?"

Orion stifled a laugh. He had known this question would come, eventually. "I weighed the pros and cons in my head," he said simply. "But don't get me wrong I didn't forgive him out of kindness."

Rachel frowned, puzzled. "What do you mean?"

"I had two options," Orion explained, his voice quieter now, weighted with something deeper than simple resolve. "I could let the hate consume me, eat away at every corner of my life until all that was left was bitterness. Or... I could do the one thing he never expected the one thing he could never take credit for." He glanced at Rachel, the corner of his mouth lifting slightly. "I forgave him. Not because he deserved it, but because I deserved peace. Because the greatest revenge isn't pain or punishment, it's becoming everything he failed to be. It's proving he didn't break me, not really. He just made me stronger."

Rachel blinked, considering his words. "I never thought of it like that. It's... cunning."

Orion shrugged. "Sometimes the high road has more impact."

Rachel's lips curved into a faint smile, but it didn't reach her eyes. The weight of the moment settled back on her shoulders like a lead cloak. "So... what's the plan now?"

Orion hesitated. The silence stretched as the question hung in the air like smoke. His powers were gone. His link to the Old Ones, severed. And London his fault, his responsibility lay broken outside. "I don't know," he admitted. "Maybe I fix what I broke."

Before Rachel could respond, the med-bay doors hissed open, and Captain Aaron burst in. "Sir. Ma'am." His face was drawn, his voice tight. "The General's in the interrogation room... but that shadow woman looks like she's about to rip her apart."

Orion shot to his feet, dread coiling in his gut. "Then let's stop her before someone dies."

They stormed down the corridor. The closer they got, the colder the air seemed to become. As they reached the conference room, a muffled scream pierced the hallway, sharp as shrapnel. Rachel flinched. It wasn't fear it was memory. Her mother's voice. Her father's. Silence. Gone.

The door slid open with a harsh hiss.

Inside, chaos ruled.

The General sat slumped in a chair, wrapped in a web of writhing shadows that pulsed and twisted like serpents. Her face contorted in pain as the shadows constricted. Eymd stood inches away, her crimson eyes ablaze, her grin feral.

"Why did you do it, General?" Eymd's voice was a razor's edge.

The shadows loosened just enough for the General to wheeze out, "Under orders... Orion was a threat... we had to contain him..."

"And I said I don't believe you," Eymd growled. "Your government had a treaty with the Shadow Race. You broke it. Why?"

Captain Aaron's voice cracked as he turned to Orion. "Sir... please. Stop her."

But Orion's expression was stone.

"Why should I?" he said coldly. "She would've executed me without hesitation. And she murdered Rachel's parents. Why protect her now?"

The General spat at Rachel's feet, venom in her voice. "You're all animals. This is why you need to be put down traitor."

Another shriek escaped her throat as the shadows tightened, bones audibly creaking. Eymd's voice dropped to a whisper, low and icy. "Have you heard what your kind does to prisoners of war? I'm showing restraint."

She glanced at Rachel. "I may not like your pet... but Orion does. So show her respect."

Rachel didn't respond. She couldn't. Her hands were clenched at her sides, nails digging into her palms. The sight of the General bound, beaten, at their mercy should've brought relief. Closure. But all she felt was the storm brewing inside her. She wanted to scream. To demand answers. To weep. But the girl she'd been before was dead. And the woman standing here now couldn't afford to fall apart.

Orion moved around the table and sat across from the General. Only then did he notice her missing hand. A salve smeared over the stump glowed green under the room's crimson lights.

His voice was low, controlled. "Why did you kill Rachel's parents?"

The General stared back without flinching. "They stopped being useful. We got all the data we needed. Keeping them alive was a waste of resources."

The words hit Rachel like a bullet. Her knees buckled slightly, and she gripped the back of a chair to steady herself.

Orion's jaw clenched, voice tight with fury. "You're the monster. Not us. They were good people. Kind. They didn't deserve this."

Before anyone could speak again, the door slid open with a hiss, and Assistant Director Rouge strode in, his face pale, a note trembling in his hands.

Rachel took it. Her eyes scanned the words. The blood drained from her face.

"We have to go. Now," she said, her voice barely above a whisper. "The Prime Minister just issued a warrant for Orion's arrest. He's made a deal with someone representing the Four Horsemen."

The room turned to ice.

Eymd's eyes darkened. With a snarl, she slammed her hand on a panel. The lights dimmed and turned blood red. Emergency alarms buzzed faintly as the ship rumbled beneath them.

"What about her?" Aaron asked, gesturing to the General. "We can't leave her behind."

"We have to," Rachel whispered. But the thought made bile rise in her throat. "She'll talk. She'll expose everything Orion, the treaty, the Shadow Race..."

"Loose ends," Eymd said flatly. Her hand hovered over the General's heart. Shadows flared.

"No," Orion snapped, grabbing Eymd's shoulder. "We don't kill her. That's their way. Not ours."

For a moment, time froze. Then Eymd exhaled sharply and released the General. The shadows slithered back into the floor.

"She won't talk," Eymd said darkly. She stepped forward, and the shadows returned not to strangle, but to force the General's mouth open. A small glowing pill flew from Eymd's palm into the woman's throat. Her eyes rolled back. She slumped.

"What was that?" Orion asked, tension thick in his voice.

"Memory suppressant," Eymd said with a twisted smile. "She won't remember a thing."

Rachel turned to Rouge. "Charlie can you clean this up?"

He nodded grimly. "Yes. But for believability... you'll need to knock me out."

Rachel nodded. "You've done enough."

A tight orb of shadow struck Rouge, and he dropped like a stone. No time for gratitude. No time for goodbyes.

Rachel, Eymd, and Aaron dragged the unconscious bodies out of view.

Orion didn't follow immediately. He stood in the red-lit room for one more second, staring at the woman who had shattered so much of their lives and who now wouldn't even remember doing it.

Then he turned and walked toward the bridge.

Entering he took the seat that was sat alone, the smooth metal cool beneath him. Around him, the hum of the ship intensified, monitors flickering with data, pulsing like the heartbeat of a living creature.

"How are we going to deal with the anti-aircraft guns and the tanks?" Snjallt asked, her voice steady but alert, eyes never leaving the swirling tactical readouts in front of her. "They've probably reconfigured them by now."

"A low EM-pulse should disable them long enough for us to activate the star-shield," Verjast replied without looking up. His hands danced over the controls, each movement precise, practiced like he'd done this a thousand times before.

Snjallt gave a short nod and turned back to her panel. They were so focused, they didn't even register Orion's presence until the bridge doors hissed open.

Eymd strolled in, unapologetically loud. "All I'm saying is, I don't trust him as far as I could kill him," she announced.

Orion didn't flinch.

She stopped behind him, then called out, "Computer two more chairs, either side of Orion."

With a mechanical whir, the floor panels slid back. Twin chairs rose smoothly on either side of Orion's, sleek and polished, like something torn from the future. A moment later, Rachel and Captain Aaron entered, strapping in quickly.

Without warning, thick metal bands coiled over their waists with a clunk.

Rachel tensed.

"It's just the seatbelts," Eymd said, smirking. "Relax. The ride's about to get rough."

And rough it was.

The ship lurched forward, pressing everyone into their seats. Orion's breath caught in his throat as the view outside the cockpit screen shifted violently. The once-lit skyline of shattered London was swallowed by darkness as Snjallt activated the pulse.

BOOM.

A blast of electromagnetic force radiated from the ship, rippling through the city like a wave of invisible thunder. In its wake, anti-aircraft turrets slumped into silence, flickering out one by one.

The ship didn't rise.

It roared forward hugging low, slicing through the sky like a silver blade. The G-force slammed Orion deeper into his chair. He gripped the armrests tightly, every nerve alive with adrenaline.

"Setting star-shield to maximum," Verjast reported. "Coordinates locked: Egypt."

A ripple passed through the ship's interior like cool water running just beneath the skin. Orion gasped involuntarily as the star-shield activated, a shimmering aura flooding through him like alien static. His body tingled, not unpleasantly, but unsettling all the same. The energy pulsed in his bones like a second heartbeat.

"Why Egypt?" he managed, still catching his breath.

"When the Old Ones visited Earth millennia ago, they left shrines hidden across the planet," Snjallt said, swivelling in her chair to face him. "Each shrine was... personal. Meant for you. They saw what would happen. Your awakening. Your fall."

"And maybe your return," Verjast added quietly.

Orion nodded slowly, the information sinking in. These ancient beings had planned for this had prepared him. And yet, with his powers gone, he still felt like a fraud wearing someone else's prophecy.

Before he could dwell on it, a loud growl echoed from his stomach.

Eymd didn't miss a beat. "Seriously?" she muttered.

Orion winced. "Is there anywhere to get food?"

Eymd rolled her eyes. "Conference room. Food synthesiser. It does human meals too, so yeah you'll survive."

The restraints across his waist slid away with a click. Orion stood and stretched, still buzzing from the star-shield. He walked briskly down the corridor, his footsteps light on the metal floor, until he reached the conference room.

It was silent dimmed from earlier but calm now. The long table was empty, save for a single matte-black plate resting alone on the far counter.

He approached cautiously. The plate looked more like a display stand than anything functional.

"Um... bacon double cheeseburger, chips, and a strawberry milkshake, please?" he said, voice uncertain.

The plate glowed white, softly at first then flared with a sudden burst of light.

When it dimmed, the food was there: a towering, steaming burger stacked with melted cheese and crisp bacon; a mound of golden chips; and a tall, frosted glass of thick, pink strawberry milkshake topped with whipped cream and a cherry so red it looked unreal.

Orion blinked. "Well... damn."

He picked up the plate and slid into a chair at the head of the table. His first bite was pure bliss salty, juicy, perfectly seasoned. The moan that escaped him was embarrassingly loud.

He didn't care.

For a few quiet moments, he let the war, the betrayal, the danger all of it melt away. There was just food. And peace. And the luxury of silence.

When he finished, he set the plate down and wiped his mouth with the back of his hand. The synthetic taste was flawless somehow better than the real thing. Still chewing the last bite of a chip, he stood and headed back toward the bridge.

His powers were gone. His path uncertain.

But for the first time in hours, he felt human again.

And that... was something.

When Orion stepped onto the bridge, a quiet rhythm of urgency filled the space. Snjallt, Verjast, and Eymd were fully locked into their consoles, fingers tapping in sync with blinking lights and data streams. Rachel and Captain Aaron sat near the back, heads close together, their quiet conversation barely audible over the hum of the ship.

"Um... Eymd?" Orion said, breaking the silence with a hesitant edge. "Where do I sleep?"

Eymd swivelled slowly in her chair, fixing him with a pointed glare. "Don't you think you've slept enough?" she shot back, drawing the word out like it offended her. She huffed dramatically and stood, brushing past him as she exited the bridge. "Come on. I'll show you."

She didn't wait for a response.

Orion followed her down the corridor. The sleek, shadow-lit walls gave everything a surreal glow. She stopped at a door opposite the conference room and gestured without ceremony. "That's yours. Don't expect anything fancy," she said, already halfway turned to leave.

But Orion's voice stopped her.

"Can we talk for a moment?"

Eymd paused, shoulders rising slightly in irritation before she exhaled and nodded. "Fine. But make it quick." She jabbed a thumb toward the door. "That thing of yours is in there. The shape-shifting mutt."

She tapped a panel on the wall, and the door slid open with a soft hiss.

Before Orion could take a step inside, a golden blur launched itself at him.

WHAM.

He hit the floor with a laugh and a grunt as a large golden retriever landed squarely on his chest, tail wagging like a metronome on overdrive. The dog barked joyfully and sniffed him all over before launching a full assault of slobbery licks across his face.

"Hey! Easy!" Orion laughed, trying to push him off gently. "Pragor! Okay, buddy okay!"

The dog whined in delight, his entire body vibrating with happiness.

"Pragor," Orion said again, this time softer. His hand ruffled through the thick golden fur, and for the first time in what felt like forever, he smiled really smiled. "I missed you, buddy."

Pragor thumped his tail against the furniture, utterly unconcerned with intergalactic politics, war, or trauma. Just joy. Just Orion.

Eymd leaned against the wall, arms crossed, watching the reunion with an unreadable expression. "Touching," she muttered, tapping her foot. "What did you want?"

Orion sat up, Pragor now contentedly sprawled beside him, panting. "How did you find me?" he asked, brushing dog hair off his shirt.

Eymd tilted her head slightly, eyes narrowing. "The stupid piece of heart you stuck in me," she said bluntly. "It practically clawed its way out to get back to you. Even when you're not around, you're still trying to kill me."

"Sorry," Orion replied, fighting a grin.

But his tone shifted. Softer now. Sharper.

"Also... why did everyone look so tense when I asked about Anton?"

The question cut through the air like a blade. Eymd's expression faltered. Her smirk faded. For the first time, she looked unsure.

She averted her eyes, letting them rest on a shadow-drenched corner of the room. Her voice dropped low.

"When we left... he wasn't doing well," she admitted. "Even with the best healers, I don't know if he'll make it."

Orion's breath caught. Her words landed like a punch to the ribs, knocking the wind out of him. "Oh," he said, barely audible. His throat tightened. "I should've been there."

Eymd didn't respond.

She pushed off the wall and walked slowly to the door. She paused with her hand on the panel, then glanced back her crimson eyes unreadable.

"I'd like to be alone now," Orion said quietly.

She nodded once, without a word, and the door slid closed behind her.

Silence fell.

Orion stood there for a moment, staring at the sealed door, his heart heavy. Then, with a deep breath, he turned and slumped onto the bed. It was simple grey sheets, no personal touches but it didn't matter. It felt like a place to rest.

Pragor leapt up beside him, circling twice before curling into a warm, solid shape. The dog laid his head gently on Orion's chest with a soft sigh, his body a quiet anchor.

Orion ran his fingers through the retriever's fur, his gaze unfocused on the ceiling above. Guilt twisted in his gut like wire. Thoughts of Anton burned, broken, maybe dying haunted him. He'd left him behind. Again.

He swallowed hard, but the ache didn't leave. Not in his chest. Not in his head.

Pragor shifted slightly, nuzzling closer. Orion glanced at him, and for a moment, their eyes met. There was something ancient in that dog's gaze something wise. As if Pragor understood the pain Orion couldn't speak aloud.

Slowly, his body began to unwind. His hand still moved absently through Pragor's fur as exhaustion crept in, heavy and inevitable.

The ship hummed softly around him. Distant voices echoed from the bridge. But in that quiet room, cocooned in warmth and guilt and tired relief, Orion's eyes finally drifted shut.

The last thing he saw was Pragor's calm, watchful gaze.

# 3. Egypt

A massive sandstone door loomed at the end of the corridor, its surface etched with carvings that pulsed with ancient power. The alpha symbol glowed faintly on the left side burning like a slow ember while the omega mirrored it on the right, its light colder, bluer, like the last star before a dying universe. Between them stretched a weathered mural of constellations and swirling galaxies, as if the door itself held the breath of space.

The corridor was otherwise unremarkable save for the strange green torches that lined its walls. Their flames danced without smoke, flickering in slow, hypnotic rhythms... yet they gave off no heat. Just an eerie, soft light that made the sandstone shimmer like it was breathing.

Orion turned, half expecting to find something else an inscription, a symbol, a trap but there was only the long hall behind him and this impossible door. He stepped toward one of the torches and, on a whim, reached for it.

His hand passed straight through.

The flame rippled like disturbed water and then returned to its original shape, flickering steadily. Frowning, Orion tried again, but the same thing happened. Then he looked down at himself and froze.

His body shimmered, faintly translucent. Light bled gently from his outline, like he was made of starlight trying to remember how to be flesh.

Oddly, it didn't frighten him. Somewhere deep inside, he knew: this was a dream. Or something like it.

He stepped forward, half-expecting the ground to vanish underfoot. But the floor held. Cool. Solid. Comforting.

The voices came next distant, muffled whispers that teased the edge of hearing. Familiar? Maybe. Or maybe they were fragments of something older, something buried. He approached the door and placed a hand on it.

Golden sparks erupted where his fingers met the sandstone. They spidered outward in intricate lines delicate as filigree, deliberate as runes. The carvings came alive, ignited with radiant light that coursed toward the edges of the doorway.

Then came the sound a deep, resonant boom that echoed through the corridor like the awakening of a slumbering titan. The door shuddered once... then slowly began to open.

A blinding light poured out, white and warm and absolute. Orion shielded his eyes with one arm and stepped forward into the unknown.

The light faded.

What greeted him stole the breath from his lungs.

He stood on a vast marble floor, white and smooth as water. The stone stretched endlessly in all directions, reflecting the ethereal glow of the space. Towering bookshelves of bronze, silver, and gold lined the horizon like pillars of heaven, stretching so high they disappeared into clouds.

Small mechanical steps floated alongside the shelves, gliding soundlessly, awaiting a reader's command.

But it was the ceiling or lack of it that truly stunned him.

Above him stretched a living sky. Clouds drifted lazily across a field of soft pastels orange, violet, blush-pink as if eternal dawn hung above. A flock of birds soared high above him, their cries distant and echoing, their wings catching light that wasn't there.

Orion stood transfixed.

A gentle brush against his leg made him flinch.

Looking down, he saw a large, hairless cat, sleek and regal, its pale skin glistening faintly under the soft glow. Its emerald eyes locked onto his with eerie intensity, intelligent and ancient. Around its neck, a dark suede collar shimmered with violet and indigo hues, and at its centre, a crystal orb hung filled with swirling stars and drifting planets, like a miniature galaxy trapped in time.

Drawn by instinct, Orion leaned in to touch it.

Zap.

A jolt surged up his arm, sharp and electric. He jerked back.

The cat narrowed its eyes, then huffed through its nose and turned, walking with purpose up the central aisle.

It took a few steps, then paused.

Looked back.

Waited.

"Alright, alright," Orion muttered, already following.

They moved deeper into the library. The further they walked, the more impossible the place became. The shelves seemed infinite, their spines all leather, all unmarked. No titles. No symbols. Just ancient, timeworn volumes that radiated power.

The air was thick with the scent of parchment and ink, dust and old secrets. Huge oak tables with high-backed chairs were scattered between the shelves, and in the quieter corners, beanbags and velvet cushions invited rest like this place had been crafted for both scholars and dreamers.

There was something sacred about the stillness.

The cat suddenly stopped, ears flicking, head snapping to the left. It listened for a moment then dismissed the direction entirely and pressed forward, as if chasing an internal compass.

They came to a new aisle.

Here, the cat paused again its gaze scanning the towering rows of identical books.

Then, without warning, it rose up on its hind legs and placed its paws on the lowest shelf. With an almost human grace, it reached for a single book and pulled it free.

Thud.

The heavy tome fell to the floor, the sound ringing like a bell across the vast silence. Orion flinched, heart quickening.

The cat sat beside the fallen book, curling its tail around its paws. It stared at him expectantly, unmoving. Watching.

Orion stepped forward and slowly reached for the book, already feeling the weight of something important something that was about to change everything.

As Orion's fingers brushed the cover, golden letters shimmered across the aged leather: his name elegant and glowing, accompanied by symbols too ancient to decode. They pulsed gently, as if alive. A faint thread of light emerged from the spine of the book, trailing backward through the air like a tether, linking it to the shelf it had come from as if it refused to be unanchored for long.

He took a breath, grounding himself.

Then opened it.

At first, the page was empty.

Then, ink faint, smoky began to etch itself into the parchment. Lines formed. Shapes took form. A figure appeared: a boy sitting on a beanbag beneath towering shelves, reading a large book. His posture. His expression.

Orion's breath caught.

He tore his gaze from the page and glanced around the marble library, heart pounding, suddenly paranoid. But no one was there. Only the hairless cat, sitting upright now, tail curled neatly around its feet. It purred softly, its emerald gaze never leaving him.

"How does the book work?" Orion asked aloud, his voice barely more than a whisper.

The cat stood and padded over, graceful as moonlight. It nudged the open book with its nose.

Orion looked down and gasped.

New words now glowed on the page beneath the image:

"How does the book work?" the boy asked, his voice trembling.

A chill raced down his spine. His heart thundered in his ears.

He slammed the book shut, then hurled it across the aisle. It struck the floor with a thud, skidding several feet before coming to a halt near a shadowed column.

His breath was ragged. "What the hell is this place?" he muttered, palms sweaty, throat dry. Why me? Why now?

A second, heavier thump broke his thoughts.

The cat impossibly strong had dragged the book back, its suede collar shimmering with cosmic dust. It dropped the tome at Orion's feet and stared at him, eyes glittering with a strange insistence.

Try again, they seemed to say.

Orion swallowed hard and bent to pick up the book.

This time, as he opened it, the image was gone. In its place, text formed in that same swirling, celestial script:

This book is the life and times of Orion I. It reveals all that was, is, and could be during his corporeal existence. Only those named within may read what is written.

The letters faded then reshaped:

The information you seek is on row 2652, middle shelf.

Orion looked up and sure enough, a new thread of light extended from the book, weaving its way across the marble floor like a guide. He set the book down gently and followed.

The path wound through the shelves until it halted at a tall, narrow bookcase. He reached for the indicated spot and pulled free a thin, light volume. His pulse stuttered.

Anton.

The name glowed softly on the cover, aching with familiarity.

Hands trembling, Orion opened it.

On the first page, words appeared:

Are you sure you wish to know the answer to your question?

He hesitated.

Then whispered, "Yes."

The text evaporated into stardust. Then, slowly, new lines unfurled before him.

In battle with The Great Four also known as the Four Horsemen Anton was gravely wounded. In the absence of his brother, who was journeying to recover his powers, his condition worsened. Even the efforts of the elite healers could not...

The sentence cut off.

A violent tug yanked him backward by the collar, lifting him off the ground. Orion shouted in surprise as he was flung through the air racing past shelves and lanterns, stars and shadows. The library blurred into streaks of light.

He burst through the sandstone door then into the open sky.

Blinding sunlight. Roaring wind. The world spun wildly as he was yanked upward, higher and higher. Below, the Sphinx and Pyramids of Giza shrank rapidly, golden sands swirling in every direction.

He squinted against the wind, trying to focus trying to understand.

The force twisted again, jerking him backward. He flew across the dunes, the world shrinking into pale gold and white haze. All landmarks vanished, swallowed by sand and sky.

Then silence.

His collar went slack.

And he plummeted.

Orion screamed, the wind torn from his lungs. The ground raced toward him.

But the impact never came.

Darkness surrounded him.

He thrashed wildly until his hand broke free and ripped a blanket from his face. He blinked, heart hammering.

He was back.

Pragor sat beside him in golden retriever form, his head tilted in calm amusement. His tail thumped once, a solid thud of reassurance.

Orion exhaled shakily, dragging a hand through his sweat-damp curls. "Okay," he muttered. "That was new."

Pragor nudged his arm gently, then gave a soft whine.

Orion scratched behind his ears. "Yeah, yeah. I'm fine."

His stomach growled like thunder.

He stood, Pragor padding loyally beside him as they moved through the corridors. The hum of the ship was comforting now, like the quiet beat of a heart that wouldn't abandon him.

As he approached the conference room, the smell of breakfast wrapped around him like a warm blanket eggs, bacon, sausage, toast, beans, tomatoes. He nearly moaned aloud.

He pressed the door panel.

Inside, the crew was already gathered around the table, laughter and clinking forks filling the space.

"Well, good morning, Sleeping Beauty," Eymd called with a smirk, biting into a piece of toast. "You missed the fun."

Rachel smiled warmly. "Come eat. There's plenty."

Pragor darted forward, sniffing enthusiastically at the table's edge.

Orion stepped in, the scent, sound, and comfort of it all slowly easing the tension in his chest.

"We're not far from the place the Old Ones visited," Snjallt said between bites. "Everyone will be ready within the hour."

"Oh," Orion replied, shovelling bacon into his mouth. "Is it by any chance under the Sphinx?"

Eymd looked at him, puzzled. "No... why?"

"I had a dream," he said between mouthfuls. "I think something important is there. Could we check it out?"

She raised a brow, considering. "Yeah. Sure. As long as it doesn't get me killed."

He gave her a puff-cheeked look full of mock offense. She just grinned and breezed past him.

The moment passed like sunlight through a cloud.

Breakfast continued.

Afterward, Orion excused himself and returned to his room to dress.

He stopped short.

On his bed lay a suit of armour. Black, sleek, and faintly iridescent, it shimmered like liquid starlight. The material rippled subtly, as if breathing.

He reached out.

The armour melted, crawling up his arm like living ink. He gasped as it slid across his chest, back, and legs, hardening into a smooth shell that fit like second skin tailored to him, and him alone.

The door hissed open.

Pragor entered not as a dog, but a sleek black jaguar, his eyes glowing, his steps silent. Armour flowed over his body too, gliding with him as if it had always been part of his form.

Orion reached down, placing a hand on his companion's armoured flank.

"I guess you're coming too, boy."

Pragor purred low and deep.

With Pragor at his side silent, alert, regal Orion stepped from his room and made his way to the cockpit. The others were already there, faces tense with anticipation. He took his seat. Pragor laid beside him, his armoured form sleek and watchful.

"Are you ready to go?" Snjallt asked, turning from her station, her violet eyes serious.

"Yeah," Orion replied, steadying his breath. His voice was calm, but his hands were clenched tightly around the edge of the armrest.

The ship's engines ignited with a low, resonant roar. The hull thrummed beneath them as they lifted from the Earth, rising smoothly into the sky. The cockpit view revealed a sun-drenched Egyptian horizon. Far below, the Nile shimmered like a ribbon of liquid gold, boats drifting aimlessly tiny and unaware of the vessel sailing silently above them.

Out of the corner of his eye, Orion caught Captain Aaron casting a glance his way. Their eyes met. Aaron blushed and quickly turned back to his console, mumbling something Orion couldn't catch.

"We're approaching the coordinates," Verjast announced, fingers flicking across the navigation interface. "Prepare to disembark."

Eymd stood with purpose. She strapped on her dual swords and began lacing throwing knives across her belt with surgical precision. "I want everyone in tight formation around Orion. We protect him at all costs. Once we're inside the sanctum, we'll be safe but not before."

The ship dipped slightly, then settled with a muted thud as the landing gear deployed. The engines powered down, their hum fading into silence.

Orion rose. Pragor stood beside him, sniffing the air, muscles tensed.

"Right, is everyone ready?" Eymd asked.

"Yes," came the reply in unified cadence.

Eymd and Verjast led the way. Rachel and Aaron flanked Orion, forming a protective wedge. Snjallt brought up the rear, her hand resting casually on a glowing vial at her side.

Eymd hit the ramp control. With a slow hiss, the ship's ramp unfolded. A dull metallic boom echoed through the hull as it met the scorched desert ground. The light outside was blinding raw, ancient sunlight.

Orion stepped into the arid heat. Grit crunched beneath his boots as wind carried the sharp scent of dust and old stone. Towering around them were the skeletal remains of an ancient structure pillars half-collapsed, worn symbols carved into their surface like the final breaths of a forgotten tongue. The heat rippled off the ruins in waves, but beneath it, something cold pulsed.

A narrow staircase yawned before them, cut into the earth like the mouth of the dead. It led into a darkness that seemed to drink the sunlight. A faint chill rose from within, brushing Orion's skin like a ghost's whisper.

Egypt, he thought. Land of the dead and divine. Of secrets that defy time.

These ruins... they weren't Pharaonic. Not exactly. The symbols were older. Wiser. Alien.

They descended.

The air grew thicker. Warmer. Heavier. With every step, the darkness swallowed more of the outside world. Then, without warning, flames erupted to life green and orange torches flickering on the walls, unlit moments before.

The corridor narrowed. The ceiling dipped low. Cobwebs clung to Orion's curls, dust tickled his throat, and their footsteps became muffled against the sand-dulled stone. They ducked beneath beams and pressed close to the walls, the formation tightening as instinct warned of ancient traps.

At first, Orion was underwhelmed.

This passage was nothing like the grand visions in his dreams cramped, eroded, unimpressive.

Until the chamber opened.

The narrow tunnel gave way to a vast, circular sanctum, and everyone froze.

A cathedral of stone and starlight rose around them.

The ceiling arched high above, painted with constellations that glowed faintly, shifting ever so slightly as if alive. A flock of stars wheeled slowly in the dome's centre, tracing an invisible orbit.

In the middle of the room, an octagonal altar dominated the floor black stone veined with violet energy, surrounded by eight towering crystalline obelisks etched with ancient runes. Each rune pulsed like a heartbeat soft, slow, deliberate.

The walls... the walls were alive with history.

Carvings lined them from floor to ceiling elongated humanoids with alien grace, draped in robes of energy and wielding stars in their hands. Scenes of creation, ascension, war, and cataclysm stretched around the chamber. Stone told the stories no civilization had dared speak aloud.

"This is it," Snjallt breathed, her voice reverent. "The Sanctum of the Old Ones."

Orion moved toward the altar, drawn as if by gravity. Pragor followed silently, his jaguar form nearly blending into the dark floor.

As they approached, the runes on the obelisks brightened, one by one. The glow intensified, synchronising with Orion's heartbeat.

Verjast stepped closer, his hand drifting to his blade. "Careful," he warned. "This place breathes power. Ancient power. Don't anger it."

Orion nodded, swallowing the lump in his throat. He couldn't help it his pulse was pounding. This place felt alive, like it had been waiting.

Rachel and Snjallt moved to the chamber's entrance, weapons at the ready. Rachel drew her sidearm with smooth precision, while Snjallt uncorked a glowing blue vial that cast strange reflections against the stone. The moment was fragile, and they knew it.

Eymd approached a wall to the right, running her fingers across the etchings.

She stopped. Then pressed her palm flat against the stone.

A radiant shockwave of light exploded outward from her hand, tracing ancient circuits through the sandstone like electric veins. A hidden door emerged, outlined in brilliant white.

A grinding rumble shook the chamber.

Dust poured from the ceiling as the hidden door began to retract slow, thunderous. Ancient gears whirred behind the stone. The air vibrated with the sound, deep and bone-shaking, like something awakening after millennia of sleep.

Everyone tensed.

Weapons were raised. Feet shifted. Pragor growled low in his throat, a rumble like thunder in his chest.

Orion didn't move.

The wall continued to open.

Eymd turned sharply, grabbing Orion's wrist with a grip that was firm, but not unkind. Without a word, she pulled him toward the newly revealed doorway cloaked in darkness.

Just before stepping through, Orion glanced back.

Captain Aaron was already moving to follow but Verjast stepped into his path. With a fluid motion, he raised his hammer across the corridor and shook his head once, sharp and final. The unspoken message was clear: this path is not for you.

Orion swallowed hard as Eymd led him forward. "The Old Ones' chamber is just a little further," she whispered, her voice hushed and reverent.

The darkness that met them was absolute. No light, no sound just the soft scuff of boots on ancient stone and the subtle warmth of Pragor's flank brushing against Orion's leg. The Yondelot's steady presence grounded him. Still, Orion tested each step, wary of pits, traps, or worse.

Then

Thud.

A sharp, distant echo behind him. Orion froze mid-step and let go of Eymd's hand, twisting around.

"Hello?" he whispered.

Only shadows stared back.

Nothing moved. Nothing answered.

The silence felt too deliberate.

He turned only to walk directly into Eymd's back. She had stopped without warning.

"Eymd!" he hissed. "What the hell?"

Before the words left his lips, two golden eyes flared open in the void ahead. They burned like suns, locked directly onto him.

Then came the voice.

"Who dares trespass where only Gods should tread?"

It wasn't a question. It was a challenge a thunderous declaration that shook the walls and reverberated in Orion's bones. The corridor felt smaller, the air heavier, the darkness pressing in like a living thing.

Eymd stepped forward, spine straight, voice unwavering.

"I am Eymd, daughter of the High Matriarch of the Shadow Empire, and protector of Intenfli Orion."

With a sudden whoosh, two torches blazed to life behind the speaker, casting its massive form into view.

The guardian was a colossus of stone, sculpted with divine precision equal parts warrior and monument. Its eyes glowed like molten metal, and its blade was already drawn, the enormous tip resting directly against Eymd's chest. For a moment, the chamber pulsed with lethal tension.

Then... the guardian turned its head to Orion.

The change was almost imperceptible but Orion saw it. Recognition. Reverence. Something ancient stirring behind those eyes.

The guardian slowly pulled back its sword and sheathed it with a deep rumble. The faintest smile etched into granite touched its lips.

"He is waiting for you within," it said, voice softer now.

It stepped aside.

Eymd didn't hesitate. She passed through the shimmering, water-like barrier ahead and vanished beyond it.

Orion hesitated only briefly, then took a breath and followed, Pragor pacing close at his heels.

The moment he stepped through, a pressure slammed into his chest like an invisible stone. The darkness beyond the barrier was suffocating alive, aware, judging. He gasped for air as his vision swam.

Then he heard it behind him.

Rachel's scream.

Orion spun around just in time to see Rachel and Aaron hurled backward from the entrance. The barrier had repelled them, shimmering violently as it rejected their presence. They hit the ground in a tangled heap on the stone stairs, coughing, dazed.

Before Orion could react, the guardian moved, allowing verjast and snjallt through.

Its sword raised high above its head gleaming with fatal purpose poised to strike down Rachel where she lay.

"STOP!" Orion roared, his voice cracking through the chamber like a whip.

The guardian froze mid-swing. The blade hovered inches from Rachel's face.

She didn't see Orion.

She didn't see the guardian freeze because of him.

She scrambled away, panting, eyes wide with confusion and fear.

"I told you they weren't to be trusted," Eymd said behind him, her voice laced with ice. "Let me go and finish them. It'll be quick. Painless."

Orion turned to her, anger and disbelief battling in his eyes

but before he could speak, another voice echoed through the chamber.

Older. Deeper. Timeless.

"Come now, young one. Do not be so quick to judge."

The chamber lit subtly as a figure stirred from the shadows.

Akhenaten.

He rose from a throne of gleaming black stone, his towering form regal and impossibly ancient. Every movement sounded like shifting tectonic plates, his joints creaking with the slow gravity of centuries. He stepped forward with a calm, practiced grace like a god accustomed to awe.

Immediately, Eymd, Verjast, and Snjallt stepped between Orion and the approaching figure. Weapons drawn. Bodies tense.

Akhenaten chuckled a sound like rolling thunder wrapped in joy.

"That is no way to treat one of the Old Ones, now is it?"

With a lazy wave of his hand, the weapons vanished from their hands, simply gone.

Eymd dropped to one knee instantly. "Forgive us, great one."

Verjast and Snjallt followed her lead, kneeling with heads bowed.

Orion, understanding the magnitude of who stood before him, knelt on one knee. He placed a hand across his chest and lowered his head.

A large, warm hand came to rest gently on his shoulder. He looked up.

Akhenaten smiled down at him, eyes like polished suns.

"Rise, young god. There is much we must discuss."

Orion stood, voice quiet but steady. "My friends... outside. What about them?"

Akhenaten's smile widened.

"They will join us shortly. The guardian will bring them... safely."

With a flick of his wrist, a long, ornate table appeared in the centre of the chamber, surrounded by high-backed chairs carved with celestial runes. Candles appeared atop it tall, silent flames flickering in rhythmic harmony.

He gestured eagerly to the chair beside his own.

"Come. Sit."

Orion stepped forward cautiously and took the seat, glancing back at the others. Eymd, Verjast, and Snjallt exchanged wary glances before silently joining him.

"Bring them," Akhenaten said, his voice echoing like a command to the stars themselves.

A flash of golden light filled the doorway.

The guardian returned Rachel and Aaron shackled in its massive grip, suspended like offerings before the divine. Their expressions were a mix of awe and unease.

Akhenaten reached into a small leather satchel that had appeared before him. From it, he withdrew a black feather and a set of golden scales, their surfaces worn by time yet still glowing with an ethereal brilliance.

With a gentle breath, he blew across his open palm. A stream of golden sand flowed outward, curling through the air like silk, and encircled the guardian and its captives.

The moment the circle closed, the guardian bowed and vanished in a burst of light.

Rachel and Aaron stumbled forward, unshackled now but clearly unsettled trapped within the glowing ring on the floor.

Akhenaten regarded them with ancient eyes, full of mystery and memory.

"You must both take the oath of the Old Ones and have your hearts weighed for their purity," Akhenaten declared, rising from his seat like a monolith come to life. Every movement was deliberate, resonant with age and authority, as though the air itself bent around his presence.

He stepped toward the ring of sand, drawing a ceremonial dagger from his hip its, blade blackened with time, its hilt wrapped in silver and obsidian. He pricked his finger, and a single bead of deep red blood welled up. With a flick of his wrist, the droplet fell.

Ignition.

The sand burst into flame with a roar, climbing upward into a solid, living wall of fire, shifting in colour from crimson to gold, its pulsing light throwing elongated shadows across the chamber floor.

"Rachel. Step forward," Akhenaten commanded, his voice imbued with something deeper than sound a force.

She froze.

The flames flickered in her wide eyes, casting flashes of her true form beneath the skin. For a moment, fear and memory warred across her face but then she stepped forward, each footfall filled with silent defiance. She stopped just shy of the fire, directly opposite Akhenaten.

"I must weigh your heart as you take the oath," he said, voice like polished granite. A small pedestal rose beside him from the floor, smooth and glimmering. Upon it, he placed a set of golden scales, ancient and flawless. In one bowl, he gently laid a black feather, its texture impossibly light, its tip glowing with celestial fire.

Then, without warning, Akhenaten reached through the flames his arm completely unaffected and drove his hand into Rachel's chest.

She gasped, eyes flying open in shock, but didn't resist. Her body trembled, lips parted, yet she stood her ground.

"Akhenaten, stop!" Orion shouted, lunging from his chair.

The Old One's gaze snapped to him.

"Orion, this must be done," he said not loud, but impossibly commanding. His voice landed like an iron weight. "Sit back down."

The command rippled through the air like a shockwave. Orion stumbled backward, as if pushed by an invisible hand, and landed hard on his seat. He clenched his fists, fury in his chest, but he couldn't move not against that voice.

Akhenaten drew his hand back slowly, and in his palm he cradled Rachel's heart a radiant orb of golden-pink light, pulsing gently, filled with warmth, memory, and soul. He placed it delicately in the opposite bowl of the scale. The air stilled.

"You are unharmed," Akhenaten said, addressing Rachel directly. "And you shall remain so if your heart is pure."

He extended his hand into the fire again. This time, the flames shifted, swirling into a deep amethyst hue, casting strange shadows against the stone walls.

"Repeat after me," he intoned.

"I, Rachel, make an oath to the Old Ones."

Her voice wavered at first, but steadied:

"I, Rachel, make an oath to the Old Ones."

"To protect Intenfli Orion at all costs."

"To protect Intenfli Orion at all costs."

"If my intentions and heart are not pure, these flames will erase all knowledge of me and my ancestors from the Hall of Records, and I will cease to exist."

She hesitated. Swallowed hard. Then:

"If my intentions and heart are not pure... these flames will erase all knowledge of me and my ancestors from the Hall of Records... and I will cease to exist."

Silence.

Akhenaten gave a single nod, solemn and final.

"Now step into the fire."

The command was clear. Unforgiving.

Rachel inhaled, long and slow. Then stepped forward.

The amethyst fire surged around her, swallowing her whole. Orion held his breath.

Within the flames, her form wavered and for a moment, her true Martian features shimmered through the illusion: iridescent skin, flickering eyes, patterns that pulsed like circuitry across her arms.

The fire shifted to vivid blue cool, holy, resolute.

The scale tipped barely, favouring the feather.

When she emerged, the flames parted like curtains before her. She stepped through unscathed, radiant, her breath coming quick but sure. Her heart floated back to Akhenaten, who placed it gently back into her chest with the precision of a sculptor returning a piece to its place.

"Congratulations," Akhenaten said, his tone measured but respectful. "You have passed the test. Sit, and be counted among us."

Rachel moved to the table, her expression calm but layered with something deeper relief... and perhaps, peace.

Akhenaten turned to the captain.

"Aaron. Step forward."

Aaron's breath caught in his throat. But he obeyed, walking slowly toward the ring of fire. His face was pale, hands trembling. He stopped in place, facing Akhenaten.

The ritual began again.

He repeated the oath word-for-word, his voice quiet but steady. When Akhenaten reached for his chest, Aaron flinched but did not move away.

The heart that emerged from him shone less brightly than Rachel's, tinged with uncertainty and buried guilt. Akhenaten placed it on the scales beside the feather.

They wavered.

For a long moment, they did not tip.

Then... they did.

Barely. The feather dipped. Just enough.

"Step into the flame," Akhenaten said.

Aaron stood motionless for a heartbeat too long.

Then he moved.

The fire licked across his armour as he passed through. It turned blue... but not as vivid as before. Orion leaned forward in his seat, heart pounding.

Aaron's face twisted mid-passage his skin prickling with what seemed like internal resistance but the flame did not consume him.

He emerged, gasping, shaken, but whole.

Akhenaten returned the heart to his chest, and a soft glow pulsed once through his torso.

"You too have passed," the Old One said, his voice echoing with finality. "Take your place at the table."

Aaron walked slowly, each step deliberate. He sank into the chair beside Rachel and avoided all eye contact, hands trembling faintly in his lap.

And across from them, Orion finally exhaled.

The fire behind them dimmed, the golden scales vanished, and the ceremonial dagger returned to Akhenaten's belt.

"I still don't like them," Eymd muttered from her seat, arms crossed, her tone defensive but strained.

Akhenaten turned his gaze upon her not cruel, but piercing. A gaze that had judged kings, weighed empires. The room went still.

Eymd held his eyes for a second longer... then faltered. Her shoulders shifted, her confidence wavered. The room held its breath.

"I'm... sorry," she murmured at last. The words were barely audible, but the weight they carried from her prideful, stubborn Eymd was enough to draw every gaze.

Akhenaten nodded slowly, his stern face softening like sandstone touched by rain.

"Good," he said. "There is no place for division among us. Not now. The trials ahead will demand unity whether we like it or not."

Orion exhaled quietly, watching the tension ebb from the room like the tide pulling away from a broken shore. Still, a fragile unease lingered, the kind that follows a thunderstorm.

He shifted forward, voice low but steady. "Do you know how I can get my powers back?"

Akhenaten leaned back, golden eyes twinkling with both mischief and eternal wisdom. "Yes," he said simply, as though he had waited millennia for that question.

But then, unexpectedly, a playful glint flashed in his expression. "But before we address that... tell me what is the world like now? Did pyramids ever catch on?"

Orion blinked.

Rachel stifled a laugh with a sudden cough. "Not really," she said, composing herself. "Humanity's built towering cities of steel and glass. Planes, satellites... smartphones." She paused. "But no. Pyramids never really took off. People couldn't figure them out."

Akhenaten's brow furrowed in deep confusion. "But... I left instructions."

The group exchanged awkward glances.

Verjast cleared his throat. "They tried to erase your rule after your death. It wasn't just neglect... it was deliberate."

Akhenaten turned his head sharply. "Erase me?"

There was no fury in his voice. Only ache a deep sorrow buried in stone.

"They feared me so greatly?"

Eymd, her earlier embarrassment forgotten, stepped in. "You've been gone a long time, Old One. The gods of Egypt are now myths. Forgotten by most. Your name... Aten... is whispered, if at all. The world you knew is gone."

Rachel hesitated, then pulled her phone from her pocket. With shaking hands, she unlocked it and began typing. After a moment, she slid it across the table.

"This is called a phone," she said. "It holds the world's knowledge. Here's what they say... about you."

Akhenaten took it, the sleek black device small in his powerful hands. He turned it over as if handling a relic or a weapon.

"Touch the screen," Rachel added gently. "It will reveal more."

He did.

For a long time, no one spoke.

His expression shifted with each scroll from curiosity, to disbelief, to quiet devastation. When he finally placed the phone down, his golden eyes were shimmering not with power, but with tears unspilled.

"My family... reduced to whispers. My legacy... devoured by time."

His voice broke gently, like stone cracking in frost.

Orion reached out, placing a hand on his. "I'm sorry. You didn't deserve this."

Akhenaten gave him a sad smile. "Thank you, young god. It is... comforting. To know I was not entirely forgotten." He straightened, pushing the sorrow back behind the lines of his face. "But the truth remains my time as a mortal has faded into myth."

He rose to his full height.

With a sweep of his hand, a jug and goblets shimmered into existence. The goblets floated to each person at the table, filling with a glowing, orange liquid that smelled faintly of spice and citrus.

Akhenaten raised his goblet. His voice, when it returned, was deep and full of ritual.

"To those who are no longer with us. May their journeys continue in peace."

The group followed suit, lifting their cups. Murmurs of agreement rippled through the room.

Orion sipped.

The taste was strange bittersweet and ancient, like the memory of joy. Warmth spread through his chest, then his limbs. His vision blurred and the world fell away.

A sea of darkness swallowed everything.

A single spotlight bloomed above Orion, revealing a circle of pale light around his feet. Silence.

Then footsteps.

Sharp. Slow. Final.

A figure emerged from the shadows, cloaked in white cotton, hood low. It stopped at the edge of the light. Then slowly, reverently, it lowered the hood.

Orion's breath caught.

"Anton..." he whispered.

But something was different. He looked whole. Human again. His face wasn't marred by pain or war. His eyes were calm, like still water.

"Brother," Anton said. His voice carried a soft echo, like a memory spoken aloud. "I don't have long."

Orion's knees buckled. "Why? Why do you look like this? Why are you?,"

Anton gestured, and two chairs appeared between them. Polished, wooden, simple. He sat. Gently. As though time itself would shatter if he moved too fast.

"Come. Sit with me."

Orion obeyed, every part of him aching with confusion and longing.

Anton's eyes held sorrow, but no fear. "The Old Ones... they've allowed me this time. Before I move on."

"Move on?" Orion's voice trembled. "To what? You're alive. You're just injured. We can fix it. I'll fix it. I swear,"

"Orion."

Anton's voice silenced him.

"My book was written long before either of us was born. My path... has always been set."

"No," Orion shook his head, tears blurring his vision. "No! That's not fair!"

Anton smiled sadly. "It's not about fair. It's about purpose. My soul is moving on. But you must stay. There's more for you to do."

"I don't understand," Orion whispered. "How am I supposed to go on without you?"

"You'll protect Jake. And Dad. They need you more than you know."

Orion stiffened. "Jake... Dad... what do you mean? What's going to happen to them?"

Anton stood, his gaze distant. "All will become clear in time. But for now remember me, Orion. Don't lose yourself in grief. You have a role to play that stretches beyond stars."

Orion rose as well, face streaked with tears. "Don't leave me."

Anton stepped close, cupping his cheek with a warmth that didn't belong in dreams.

"You carry me in your heart. That's where I'll always be."

He kissed Orion's forehead. Then stepped backward, dissolving into gold dust drifting upward like fireflies in twilight.

"Goodbye, dear brother."

His voice faded.

"Anton!" Orion collapsed to his knees, his voice breaking like glass. "ANTON!"

The darkness peeled away.

A hand rested on his back. Warm. Steady.

Orion gasped, blinking back to the table. Every face was turned toward him filled with sorrow. No one said a word.

Then

"Akhenaten told us about Anton," Eymd said softly, her usual sarcasm absent. "I'm so sorry."

Orion clenched his fists, jaw shaking. "It's my fault," he whispered. "All of it. This is all my fault."

"No, Orion," Akhenaten said gently, but with certainty. "It was his destiny."

Orion stood suddenly, the chair scraping violently behind him. His eyes were aflame, grief and rage colliding.

"His destiny was to die?" he shouted. "To be a lamb led to the slaughter?"

The chamber trembled quietly, but no one interrupted.

Not yet.

# 4. Akhenaten

Unable to still the tempest roaring in his veins, Orion stormed into the heart of the obsidian chamber, each footfall echoing like distant thunder against walls carved from stardust-forged stone. His fists were iron talons, his breath ragged gusts hot with grief that slammed into him like a tidal wave. Around him, murmurs rippled through the gathered soft as wind through dry leaves yet to him they blurred into a single, unbearable roar. He marched back and forth, eyes squeezed shut against a pain that felt ready to shatter his skull, muscles quivering under the weight of loss.

A flicker of flame kindled along his forearms, tiny at first, as though a spark caught in a draft. Then the fire surged, licking up his skin in wild, untamed tongues of orange and crimson. Each step he took burned the sand beneath his boots black grains crackling as they melted into shards of glass that glimmered like broken stars.

"Young God," came a calm, resonant voice Akhenaten's, steady as a mountain in a storm.

Orion spun with the speed of a striking serpent just as two firm hands gripped his shoulders, anchoring him. He faced the Old One: tall, ageless, eyes glowing with the soft luminescence of distant galaxies. Akhenaten's presence was a pillar of control amid the chaos he'd manifested.

"You must calm yourself," Akhenaten said, voice low yet insistent.

Orion's reply tore from him in a guttural roar, every word drenched in pain. "He's dead because of me! How do you expect me to go on?" His chest heaved, fiery embers dancing in his irises.

Akhenaten returned his gaze with a silence so deep it bent the very air around them. When he finally spoke, his tone was gentle as a falling petal. "It happened as it must. He served his purpose on this plane."

91

At that, Orion's grief fractured into fury. With a violent shove he sent Akhenaten hurtling backward, pale stardust dusting the air as the Old One slammed into a wall, fracturing the stone into motes of light. The chamber quaked with his impact.

Flames spiralled up around Orion in a cloak of molten rage, lightning crackling between his splayed fingers. Arcs of raw energy danced across the vaulted ceiling, pulsing with a threat of divine annihilation. His aura pulsed in sickening rhythms, a cosmic heart on the brink of breaking.

"You know nothing of humanity! Of this pain!" he bellowed. His voice rolled like distant thunder, rattling ancient pillars. He thrust a hand forward and unleashed a torrent of fire and lightning that carved through the shadows.

Akhenaten's form was struck in a brilliant flash of white-hot light, then vanished into curling wisps of smoke.

"You and the Old Ones watched him die!" Orion's voice cracked, the words jagged as shattered glass. "You could have saved him! But you did nothing!"

In the sudden hush, Akhenaten's voice calm, unwavering echoed inside Orion's mind rather than across the chamber. "We are bound by laws as unyielding as gravity. We could no more alter his fate than turn back the path of the sun."

"Liar!" Orion roared, summoning a blast of solar flame to scorch the spot where Akhenaten had stood.

But the Old One reappeared across the room in an instant, his silhouette framed by a halo of starfire. "This is not the battle you seek," he warned. "Your power is incomplete. I am not your enemy."

Orion's lips twisted with grief-fuelled rage. "Then face me directly, instead of hiding in riddles!" He hurled another fireball. Orange heat tore toward Akhenaten, but the Old One raised a single hand. The blast collapsed around him, dispersing in sparks that drifted to the floor like dying embers.

Suddenly

"Orion, enough!" A sharper voice cut through the chaos. Eymd stepped forward, her leather armour creaking, unflinching as she placed herself between him and Akhenaten. Moonlight glinted on her blade.

But grief had blinded Orion. He saw only a threat. He drew in a breath, then let loose a searing fireball in her direction.

Time shattered like glass. The flames froze mid-arc infinite, incandescent droplets suspended in the air. The pulse of the chamber stilled, as if the world held its breath.

Akhenaten emerged from the stillness, his form rippling as though he stood beyond reality's veil. He reached toward the suspended inferno. The fireball dissolved under his touch, turning to golden motes that drifted upward in a soft spiral.

Orion stared, horror-struck at the absence of destruction. "I... I almost killed her," he whispered, voice trembling like a dying wind.

"But you didn't," Akhenaten replied, every word a soothing balm. "It was not her time. And you... are not lost, not yet."

Orion's knees gave way. He sank to the cracked glass-sand floor. Instantly, the flames encircling him flickered out sucking the heat from the air until the room felt as cold as a winter dawn. Tears carved rivulets through the ash on his cheeks.

"It's not fair," he choked out. "It's just... not fair."

Akhenaten knelt and draped a steady arm around his trembling shoulders. "I know, young one. The universe spares no kindness even we, the Old Ones, must answer its laws."

Orion shuddered with sobs that shook his frame, each breath a raw groan of grief. "How did you know what I was feeling?"

Akhenaten's voice was soft, older than time itself. "Because you and I are woven of the same sorrow. I carry your pain, and you mine." He drew Orion into a firm embrace, grounding him against the tearing storm within.

They remained locked together until silence settled like a gentle rain. Then Akhenaten rose, extending a hand rimmed in starlight. "Come. We will mend this together."

Orion took the outstretched hand. With a subtle gesture, Akhenaten unspooled time like silk, weaving it backward. The fireball rewound, falling apart in reverse until it never left Orion's hand. Eymd blinked in confusion, the moment of peril erased from her memory.

"Are you ready?" Akhenaten asked as Orion stood once more, shoulders squared.

Orion nodded, wiping ash and tears from his face. He returned to the long table at the chamber's centre, placed his chair against the stone floor, and sat with a newfound stillness.

A hush rippled through the assembly. Eymd peered at him, brow furrowed. "Why do I feel like I just missed something?" she whispered.

Akhenaten's lips curved in a soft smile, stars dancing in his gaze. "Nothing of consequence, shadow warrior."

Orion offered a faint, rueful grin and bowed his head. "I'm sorry. My outburst... was wrong."

Akhenaten laid a reassuring hand on his shoulder, warmth radiating from his palm. "Understandable. You have crossed a threshold today. Grief does not define you your choices going forward will."

Orion inhaled slowly. The sorrow still pulsed within him, but alongside it bloomed a hard kernel of resolve. The chamber's silence felt rich with promise, like the hush before dawn.

Eymd stepped forward, this time not as an obstacle but as a willing soul. She knelt on one knee and bowed her head. "We are with you, Orion. Not just now, but through all trials to come."

Heavy steps thundered next: Verjast approached, the metal of his gauntlet ringing softly against his chest as he removed it and placed it there with solemn grace. He knelt. "The stars once chose you. Now I choose you. Until my final breath."

Snjallt followed, her movements slower, fingers trembling as she lowered herself. "Let the cosmos bear witness my loyalty is not borrowed but forged in the crucible of fire. I stand with you."

Rachel moved forward, her emerald eyes glistening with purpose. "I was crafted to lurk in shadows. No more. I step into your light, Intenfli Orion. Consume the lies I once was."

At last Aaron came, each step measured, resolute. He halted before Orion, standing with the steadiness of ancient oaks. "Not as a soldier, nor solely a protector. But as a brother in destiny." He knelt, head bowed. "My blade is yours. My future too."

Orion rose, chest swelling with emotion as five hearts pledged themselves to him. He lifted both hands, palms up, and Akhenaten mirrored the gesture. From the vaulted ceiling, molten starlight rained down in golden threads, spiralling around each warrior. It wove them together, spirit to spirit, forging an unbreakable bond.

"Then let it be done," Akhenaten declared, voice a chorus of thunder and light. "No longer defenders in name alone. You are reborn transformed eternal."

He turned to Orion. "Name them."

Orion's voice rang out, a celestial chord that filled every shadowed corner of the chamber: "You are the Intenarii sworn defenders of Intenfli Orion. Oath-bound by choice, not blood. My kin in purpose, in will, and in destiny."

Where the golden light touched each pledger, a sigil blossomed beneath their skin: an eight-pointed star encircled by a phoenix of luminous flame, its wings unfurled in sacred fire. The marks pulsed with life.

Rachel drew a sharp breath, eyes bright with wonder. "We are one."

Aaron stood and laid a hand on Orion's shoulder. "And we are ready."

Together they formed a circle, shadows at their backs, fire glowing in their hearts. The chamber did not erupt in cheers. It merely bore silent witness to the birth of something new, something eternal.

# 5. Wings Of War And Oath

A sudden sharp beeping cut through the moment. Snjallt retrieved her sleek, arcane tablet, her fingers dancing across the interface. Her expression tightened. "We've got incoming," she said grimly. "D.E.T.A. agents heavy assault units. And Four Horsemen operatives."

The air thickened, Akhenaten remained composed, as if the chaos of war were merely weather. "Ah. I had hoped for more time. But it seems fate is impatient."

Verjast stepped forward, voice like steel. "Before we leave please. How can Orion regain his full power?"

Akhenaten turned to Orion, his eyes radiant with ancient knowing. "To reclaim your strength, you must face the Trials of the Old Ones. The Horsemen may wield terrible power but they did not take your gifts. You buried them."

Orion frowned. "Me?"

"The trauma. The guilt. The fear. It buried your connection to what you are." He paused, then gestured grandly. "Your journey begins with the Dogon an ancient tribe in Mali. They guard the path to your first trial. But beware... they do not welcome outsiders lightly."

As he spoke, he reached out and snapped his fingers. A pair of ethereal wings shimmered into existence on the table black and gold and silver, their feathers alive with flowing patterns of light and shadow. He stood, lifting them, and moved behind Orion.

"This... is my gift to you." He placed the wings against Orion's back.

Pain shot through him like liquid fire pouring into his spine, his bones shifted, muscles snapped and reformed. Wings burst from his back, feathers unfolding like blades. Orion screamed then gasped, the pain shifting to a rush of awareness.

Akhenaten pressed a hand to Orion's temple. Knowledge surged inward flight, combat, shielding, piercing. The wings weren't just beautiful. They were power incarnate. Orion stepped back, the wings unfolding fully majestic, fierce, balanced.

Their tips hummed with contained energy. Even the air shifted around him now, tuned to his will. He ran a hand along the feathers, awe in every breath. Then BOOM. The entire chamber shook. Dust and sand rained from above. Stone groaned. Everyone froze.

"It seems our time has run out," Akhenaten said, his voice steeped in the quiet gravity of ancient foreknowledge. "My strength wanes... but I will aid you for as long as I remain tethered to this realm."

The chamber trembled beneath their feet. Above them, the distant roar of descending aircraft grew louder thunder that announced the storm of war. Immediately, the group encircled Orion like a living shield. Weapons hissed from holsters, runes lit up along blades, and the polished steel of Verjast's hammer began to hum with gathering power.

"Eymd," Akhenaten said, his tone lowered but urgent. "A word. Alone."

She raised a brow, but obeyed without comment, stalking toward the towering Old One. He knelt beside her, and the others could only watch as ancient wisdom was passed through murmured words.

His hand touched her shoulder, once, brief. But whatever was said, it struck her hard. She nodded slowly, her posture taut not defiant, but transformed. When she returned to the group, Orion caught the flicker of something rare in her eyes: dread... and duty.

"What was that about?" Orion asked warily, narrowing his gaze.

"Shadow warrior business," Eymd muttered, tone clipped as she adjusted her belts and holsters.

Then, with forced levity: "You know how to use those shiny wings of yours yet?"

Orion folded them instinctively behind him. "I do."

"Then stay in the air. We'll handle the ground. Got it?"

Before he could answer, Akhenaten's silhouette loomed over them all, his form pulsing with golden light like a dying star. He extended both hands, drawing them into a tight formation with a magnetic pull.

"Stay close to me." The ground beneath them shuddered and then vanished.

The sanctum collapsed into blackness. They fell through the void, weightless, windless, breathless held together by Akhenaten's final act of divine power.

Then Impact.

They hit sand warm, coarse, blinding. The sun above them beat down mercilessly as reality snapped back into place. For one brief breath, all was still.

And then BOOM.

Explosions ripped through the air. Plumes of sand erupted like geysers around them. The sky cracked as D.E.T.A. drones screamed overhead, their black hulls flashing with red insignias.

"BY ORDER OF THE D.E.T.A.," a voice bellowed through a megaphone, cold and unmistakably cruel, "SURRENDER IMMEDIATELY OR FACE ANNIHILATION!"

Orion flinched. The voice was branded into his memory like a scar.

General Genevieve.

His gut twisted. Beside him, Eymd's eyes narrowed to slits.

Her hands clenched into fists.

"I knew I should've let the shadows take her when I had the chance," she muttered darkly.

Then, without another word, she was gone dissolving into black mist, vanishing between blinks. Only a single curl of shadow remained, and even that flickered out.

Verjast stepped forward next. His movements were measured, practiced. Liquid armour flowed over him like a second skin, moulding itself with ancient symbols of the Shadow Kingdom. The moment his helm sealed into place, the glow of his visor cut through the smoke like a lighthouse through storm clouds. He held his hammer out before him. It responded with a deep, resonating hum a war cry of old magic. His shield expanded with a sharp clang, unfolding like the wings of a predator.

He turned to Orion. "If the Shadow claims me today, know this" he said, his voice metallic but resolute, "it has been the highest honour to serve you, Sire."

Orion met his gaze, heart pounding, wings twitching at his back. Words failed him.

But Verjast nodded once, understanding everything that needed to be said. Then he charged into the storm, his hammer a blur of shadows and fury. The moments stretched into eternity as Orion and his two remaining companions stood in the shivering semi-darkness, tension coiled tighter than a bowstring.

Beyond Akhenaten's crouched form, the world had descended into chaos. Gunfire rattled like distant thunder, screams pierced the air, and mortars fell like the wrath of forgotten gods, shaking the very bones of the desert.

Akhenaten did not move.

Even as explosions peppered the sands around him, his colossal frame held firm. A serene smile played across his lips, incongruous against the backdrop of carnage. He knelt like a monument carved from eternity.

"When I stand, be ready," he said quietly, his voice carrying through the storm like a prophecy. "Orion ascend. Watch, learn. Do not be reckless."

Orion nodded once.

Then the sand around Akhenaten began to rise golden and shimmering like divine ash as he stood to full height. That was the signal. Orion launched into the sky, his wings slicing through the air with a thunderous beat.

Wind rushed past his face, burning his eyes, but he didn't slow. Higher and higher he climbed, piercing through clouds of smoke, until he could see it all. Below, Akhenaten moved like a divine storm. Mortars struck his body in flashes of light and fire, but each impact was absorbed with barely a flinch.

He reached down, grabbed a tank by its turret, and with terrifying ease, hurled it like a discus, sending it crashing through a D.E.T.A. gunship mid-hover. Both machines exploded in tandem a blossom of flame against the dusty canvas of war.

To the east, Rachel had shed her human skin. Her Martian form was a symphony of terror and elegance, long claws gleaming, eyes glowing like twin suns. She moved with liquid grace, slicing through a dozen soldiers in seconds. Bullets bounced harmlessly off her shifting defence field as she danced across the battlefield, a whirlwind of blood and motion.

Captain Aaron, relentless and unshaken, barrelled through the ranks like a desert gale. His pistols spoke death with every flash, and with each downed foe, he pressed harder toward his target General Genevieve. His jacket burned in places, blood streaked one arm, but his resolve was unwavering. He reloaded without looking, then flipped into a slide, taking down a sniper mid-dash.

From above, Orion could see the bigger picture. D.E.T.A. forces poured in from every direction, coordinated and ruthless. But the rebels, warriors, and guardians who followed him were holding the line with unimaginable ferocity. Then he heard it the low hum of something worse. A fleet of six enemy ships broke through the clouds, their sleek hulls painted in obsidian and scarlet, weapons glowing with unstable energy. They moved like vultures circling a fresh kill. The lead ship fired. A massive orb of purple plasma shrieked through the air, aimed straight at Orion. He twisted violently, dodging by inches.

The orb crashed into the sand below, erupting into a tidal wave of viscous, gravity-defying sludge, which pinned anything it touched to the earth in glowing amber binds.

"No time to hesitate," Orion muttered, and dove toward the enemy fleet.

The wind screamed as he tucked his wings, becoming a meteor of light and fury. Purple energy bolts zipped past, scorching the air, but Orion moved like a star reborn. Just before colliding with the lead ship, his wings expanded transfigured into blades of sharpened light. With a single, spiralling slash, he cleaved through the cockpit. The ship exploded in a geyser of shrapnel. He spun and banked hard, wings blurring as he tore through a second vessel, then angled for the third.

"I've got you!" came Eymd's voice.

She landed atop his back like a shadow given form, twin blades already drawn, her eyes glowing with anticipation. "Take me close," she whispered. "I'll make them wish they'd stayed in orbit."

Before Orion could respond, she dissolved into shadow, darting ahead. Within seconds, the hull of another ship bloomed with explosions from the inside. Screams echoed, and agents began leaping from the ramp like rats from a burning ship. Eymd's laughter followed them, dark and full of bloodlust. Orion veered to catch her but pain exploded through his left wing.

He looked back. The same purple goo had latched on, growing and hardening, locking his wing into a rigid, useless slab. His momentum failed. His body tilted violently.

"No no, no!"

He flared his good wing just in time, angling down and managing a controlled crash, hitting the sand in a crouch, knees shaking but intact. But he wasn't alone. He rose to find dozens of weapons aimed at his head.

General Genevieve stood in the centre of a tactical ring, her polished prosthetic arm gleaming beneath the desert sun. Her eyes burned with a kind of cold triumph. The blade on her left arm clicked out with a sharp, familiar snikt.

"You're done, filth," General Genevieve spat, stepping forward, her shadow stretching like a blade across the sand.

Orion stood tall, wings tucked neatly behind him, his brow damp with sweat and blood. Though surrounded, his eyes didn't waver.

"You assume I'll come quietly?"

"We have you surrounded," Enaquia snarled, venom flickering from her forked tongue. "And you're powerless."

"Oh, but I do have power," Orion said smoothly, bluffing.

His tone was calm too calm, and it set the agents on edge. The kind of calm that suggested something hidden. Something dangerous. Enaquia hesitated, her reptilian gaze narrowing. But Genevieve stepped closer, her voice dipped in ice.

"You preach peace," she sneered. "But your kind is chaos in disguise. Just like you. A walking bomb."

As the soldiers advanced, Orion's muscles tensed, his good wing twitching ever so slightly. He counted heartbeats. Steps. Angles.

"My people could have helped rebuild this world," he said. "We offered light. You chose darkness."

"Lies!" The General screeched, a snarl twisting her face. "No one being should possess such power! Your very existence is a threat to the balance of this world!"

The first soldier stepped too close. In a heartbeat, Orion moved. His wing snapped out like a blade, cleaving through two agents in one brutal arc. Blood sprayed across the sand. Screams erupted as the formation faltered. Bullets whizzed past him, barely missing his head.

Enaquia lunged, faster than lightning. Her claws clamped around his throat and lifted him off the ground like a rag doll. Orion choked, struggling as darkness swam across his vision. Her eyes burned with triumph.

"You're weak," she spat. "Just like your ideals."

Then suddenly she dropped him. He hit the ground hard, coughing, gasping for air. Enaquia loomed over him, triumphant.

"Without your powers, you're nothing."

But she was wrong. Akhenaten's voice echoed in his mind: Your powers are not lost. They are locked within. Believe.

Orion rose, slow and deliberate, wiping blood from his mouth. His chest heaved, but his eyes were clear burning with clarity and defiance.

"I am Orion I," he said, his voice cutting through the noise like a blade. "Son of Aurorina and Auren. Intenfli of my people. I carry the legacy of stars, of worlds older than your wars. And I stand to protect not destroy."

The ground shuddered beneath him.

The air shimmered. Sand began to swirl around his feet in spiralling rings, faster and faster. Enaquia's smile faltered. Then the sand exploded upward. A massive hand of earth and light burst from the dunes, grabbing her mid-step.

She shrieked in terror as the arm closed around her torso, dragging her down into the howling desert like a divine punishment.

"NO!" she cried, but the sand swallowed her screams.

Genevieve froze. Her skin paled. "H-how?" she stammered, stumbling backward. "You... you were powerless..."

Orion stepped forward, his silhouette crowned by sand and flame.

"The war is not yours to fight, General," he said. "The Horsemen bring only death. My people bring rebirth."

Around them, the remaining agents faltered. One by one, their weapons lowered. Fear crept into their eyes. Not fear of death but of revelation. Of truth.

Genevieve's hands trembled but then her rage boiled over. She screamed and raised her pistol. A deafening crack rang out as the bullet slammed into Orion's shoulder.

He screamed, the force knocking him to one knee. Smoke curled from the wound, and a sickly purple glow pulsed from the bullet's core.

Genevieve laughed. "Even gods can bleed."

But her victory lasted only a breath. Twin blades pierced her chest from behind, driving through her body with unrelenting force. Her gurgling laugh twisted into a gasp of agony. She dropped to her knees then crumpled, lifeless, into the sand. Behind her stood Eymd, blades dripping, eyes blazing.

"I've wanted to do that since the day I met her," she said, kicking the body aside. Then, turning to the trembling agents: "Tell your commander to stand down. Or you'll wish you had."

A shaken agent scrambled for his radio. Moments later, the distant sounds of gunfire fell into a chilling silence. Soldiers dropped their weapons. The battle was over.

But Orion was not. His legs gave out. He collapsed, clutching his shoulder as darkness crept along his veins.

"Eymd..." he rasped, "help..." She dropped beside him, panic flashing across her normally unshakable face.

"You're burning up hold on, my Intenfli. Just... hold on."

She ripped open his shirt, her fingers trembling as she extracted the bullet with surgical precision. The moment it hit the sand, it hissed like acid, melting through the grains.

"This isn't normal metal," she whispered. "This is... god-destroyer serum."

Orion's eyes widened in horror. "Can... can Akhenaten help?"

"I hope so." She disappeared into the shadows.

Seconds later, a golden cyclone swept across the battlefield Akhenaten arrived in a vortex of light and sand, cradling Orion in his massive arms.

"We're out of time," the Old One said.

Snjallt was already deploying a med-pod, her hands moving with terrifying speed.

Orion was placed inside, his body wracked with tremors. Akhenaten pressed a glowing red disc to Orion's chest.

"This will slow the spread. But it's not enough."

"What then?" Eymd demanded.

"I must put him in suspended animation," Akhenaten said, already keying in a code on the pod's surface. "It will preserve what's left until we find a cure."

Orion nodded weakly. He trusted Akhenaten. Trusted Eymd. Trusted fate.

As the pod sealed around him, a shimmering liquid filled the chamber. Panic clawed at him, but he kept his gaze on Eymd.

"Don't let me be forgotten," he mouthed.

"You won't," she whispered. The fluid thickened. His body stiffened. His breath slowed. And then, everything went still. Suspended in glowing silence, Orion drifted into sleep. A slumber not of peace but of war deferred.

The sky above crackled. The next battle loomed. And Orion, Son of Stars, was not yet finished.

# 6. A Spark In The Void

The warm scent of grass and campfires drifted through the air, stirring Orion from his slumber. He blinked against the haze, eyelids heavy with exhaustion, until the blur resolved into golden grass beneath him. A forest of impossible beauty surrounded the clearing purple trees stretching skyward, their canopies glowing under a constellation-drenched sky. No stars he recognised.

He sat up slowly, the ache in his shoulder dull but persistent, and brushed dust and dried sap from his tunic. This wasn't Earth, nor any known world. He turned toward the forest, following the faint murmur of voices.

A rustling noise made him freeze mid-step. From the underbrush emerged a strange, alien creature the face of a cat with the towering body of an ostrich, feathers shimmering like oil in the starlight. It padded past him silently, vanishing back into the thick, bioluminescent undergrowth without so much as a glance.

Orion exhaled and pressed forward, weaving through the vibrant vegetation toward the flickering lights ahead.

The forest opened into a wide clearing dotted with glowing crystals some jutting out like natural towers, others carved into rough shelters. Campfires burned in circles, their embers dancing across metal armour and polished weapons. Men and women of every race sat around them, laughing and conversing, but Orion's breath caught.

They were his guards the elite unit who once swore loyalty to him. Yet their uniforms now bore unfamiliar symbols: golden scales, and a silver quill.

He stepped forward. "Hello?"

The nearest group startled, leaping to their feet, weapons half-drawn.

"Sorry," Orion raised his hands. "I didn't mean to alarm,"

A towering blue-skinned woman stepped into view, her green tentacle-hair coiled tight against her six-eyed face. Her sword gleamed with etched runes, its tip now a hair's breadth from Orion's throat.

"Don't move," she barked. "Someone fetch the mistress now!"

Orion swallowed as one of the guards sprinted toward the massive crystal tent more palace than shelter. The blade before him pulsed with latent energy, and though his instincts screamed to act, he remained still.

"You don't need to threaten me," he said carefully. "Surely... you know who I am?"

Her grip tightened. "One more word, and I'll slice that tongue from your mouth."

Moments later, the guard returned followed by a figure cloaked in beige leather. A shawl masked her face, but her presence was unmistakable. The soldiers stood straighter, lowering their weapons as the figure approached.

"I recognise that face," she said, voice muffled but strangely familiar. "But the energy within you... feels foreign. Fractured."

Orion's brow furrowed. "Who are you?"

"Patience," she replied. "First, I must know that you are truly him."

She pulled off a glove, revealing a hand woven with stardust veins and glowing sigils. As she touched his cheek, gold and silver tendrils of magic erupted from his skin, intertwining with hers.

Recognition flooded him.

"...Aunt?" he whispered.

She lowered her shawl, revealing scarred cheeks, fierce golden eyes, and streaks of grey in her once-blonde hair.

"Yes, my nephew," she said softly. "You've dream-walked into my camp. But tell me... what pain brought you here?"

Orion's throat tightened. "I didn't mean to come. I just wanted to stop hurting."

She gestured toward a fire and led him to sit. The flickering flames cast dancing shadows across her face, revealing deep lines of war and wisdom.

"Then speak, Orion. I'll listen."

He spoke, slowly at first, then all at once the Great Four, Anton's death, the burning weight of failure. As he spoke, her face grew solemn. When he finished, her hand found his shoulder.

"You blame yourself for Anton. But his death was not your fault," she said gently. "The others Rachel, Eymd, Lillithan they live, but they are not safe. The one who holds them wields power that not even the Old Ones can see."

"Who could do that?" Orion asked.

She hesitated. "The New Order. A force older than war itself. They are the ones who reawakened the Horsemen. The Old Ones failed to destroy them eons ago... so they created you."

His breath caught. "Created me?"

"You are the fulcrum, Orion. The balance. But you are not yet whole."

His voice cracked. "I'll never be ready. I was just a kid trying to survive my father, survive school. I don't know how to be a saviour."

"You are not alone," she said. "The ones who fight with you they are not simply allies. They are your tether. Your compass."

He looked away. "If I show weakness, they'll stop believing in me."

Her eyes narrowed. "True strength is not in hiding pain. It's in sharing it. Leaning on your people is not weakness it's leadership."

He stared into the fire. "But what if I have to kill? What if becoming strong means becoming like them?"

Her voice dropped into steel. "You will face moments when the only way to save a thousand lives is to end one. Compassion is not weakness, Orion. But blind mercy in a time of war can be deadly."

"I won't become a monster," he snapped. "I won't."

She leaned in, her golden eyes sharp. "Then don't. But know this if you cannot make that choice when it matters, you may lose more than Anton."

Orion clenched his fists, trembling. "I feel like I already have."

She sighed and touched his cheek. "Anton chose to stand beside you. His death wasn't meaningless. He bought you time and that time can save worlds."

He shook his head. "I should've saved him."

"You are not omnipotent," she said. "Even gods fail. But the strength of a god lies in how he rises from failure."

"I don't feel like a god."

"No one ever does," she said softly. "But one day, you will look back and realise that was never the point. The galaxy doesn't need a perfect saviour. It needs someone who refuses to give up."

Silence settled around them, broken only by the fire's gentle crackle. Finally, Orion looked up.

"I don't know how to carry all of this."

"Then stop trying to carry it alone," she said.

The fire flickered. Stars wheeled above them.

"But what if I fail?"

She smiled, a flicker of pride softening the battle-worn lines of her face.

"Then you rise again. And again. Until the stars themselves burn out."

Orion let out a breath that trembled, a faint smile pulling at his lips. For the first time in what felt like lifetimes, the crushing weight on his chest began to lift.

"You sound just like my mother," he said.

Her expression turned wistful, distant stars glimmering in her golden eyes.

"Aurorina was always the wiser of us. She believed in you from the moment you took your first breath. She knew... you would be the one to change everything."

Orion met her gaze, the firelight dancing in his eyes.

"Do you?"

"I do," she replied without hesitation. "But it isn't my belief that matters it's yours. Trust yourself, even when doubt clouds your vision. You are stronger than you know, nephew."

She rose, the fire behind her flaring briefly, casting her in a radiant halo of light and shadow. With quiet reverence, she placed a hand on his head. Warmth spread through him, her magic seeping into his bones like sunlight through ice.

"I must go," she said, her voice tinged with sorrow. "But you will find me again, when the time is right." She began to turn, but paused. "And remember you are not alone. Lean on those who stand beside you. And never forget who you are."

"Thank you," Orion whispered, his voice cracking.

With a final flick of her finger, a shard of starlight struck his forehead, and the dream dissolved into a storm of light and shadow.

Her voice echoed in his soul:

"You are not a monster, Orion. You are a protector. Never forget the difference."

The sterile hum of the medical pod grew louder as Orion's consciousness clawed its way back to reality. He stirred, the warmth of the dream quickly fading into cold machinery. Voices drifted in and out like distant thunder.

"I told you already," Akhenaten's low voice rumbled through the nano headphones. "I consulted the Old Ones. We've contained the poison, but the final purge must come from him. It is his spirit's battle now."

"And you just expect us to wait?" Eymd snapped, venom sharp in her voice. "After everything he's done? This is why you lot are fossils because you sit in temples while people die!"

"Careful, shadow warrior," Akhenaten growled, his golden eyes narrowing like an eclipse. "Do not mistake age for impotence."

"Enough!" Verjast interjected, the calm weight of his voice silencing the room like a thunderclap. "We are on the same side. This is not the time for ego."

It was Verjast who noticed the flicker behind Orion's eyes. He turned, and in a low voice said, "He's awake."

Silence fell. The tension evaporated like mist, replaced by an overwhelming mix of relief, urgency and fear.

Akhenaten stepped forward, his expression softening.

"Young one," Akhenaten said, his usually stoic presence softened by something gentler concern, perhaps. "It's good to see you awake. I will begin the procedure soon, but you must know it will not be easy. It is dangerous, and there are risks." He hesitated, the weight of what he wasn't saying hanging in the air like smoke. "For now, I will give you some time with everyone."

One by one, they entered the room.

Rachel was first. She approached with hesitant steps, her face a fragile battlefield of hope and sorrow. Leaning over the stasis pod, her fingers trembled against the glass, as if trying to touch him through the barrier.

"You can't leave yet, Egg," she whispered, her voice raw with emotion. It was a name only she dared use soft, familiar, unshakably hers. "You're my best friend the only real one I've ever had. If something happens to you..." Her voice cracked, and for a heartbeat, it seemed like the room itself held its breath. She pressed a tender kiss to the glass. "Be strong, Egg." Then, like a ghost fleeing grief, she turned and hurried out, her muffled sobs trailing like echoes in a cave.

Next came Eymd. She dropped into the chair beside the pod with the grace of someone used to war zones, arms crossed and jaw clenched. For a long moment, she said nothing, simply studying him perhaps memorising his face.

"Well, I guess this could be goodbye," she muttered, her voice gruff but low, thick with something she wouldn't name. "But honestly? I doubt it. You're too damn stubborn to die. And besides..." Her lips tugged into a faint, rare smirk. "I still owe you a proper payback for all the times you nearly got me killed." Without another word, she stood and strode from the room, her shadow stretching behind her like a blade.

Twin wisps of smoke curled upward on either side of the pod. Verjast and Snjallt materialised in fluid silence, their robes shifting like smoke on windless air. They bowed deeply in tandem, ancient dignity in every movement.

"The shadows may not claim you today," Verjast said, his voice like the distant echo of thunder.

Snjallt followed, her tone warmer, almost motherly. "This will all work out. You'll see."

As silently as they had come, they vanished again, leaving only the scent of burnt incense and the faint ripple of star-magic in their wake.

Captain Aaron stepped inside, the harsh light behind him casting his figure in stark contrast. His uniform was torn, the corner of his mouth streaked with dried blood. One eye was swollen shut, his movements slow wounded, but still standing.

Aaron stood silently for a moment, the dim light of the med-chamber casting long shadows across the polished floor. The only sound was the rhythmic pulse of monitors and the low hum of the stasis pod. Within it, Orion floated in a hardened shell of stasis fluid crystalline, unmoving, preserving him like a figure encased in amber.

But his eyes were open.

Trapped inside the solid medium, Orion couldn't move, couldn't blink, couldn't speak. Yet the nano audio tech still embedded beneath his skin transmitted every word spoken in the room. He heard everything. Felt everything emotionally, if not physically.

Aaron stepped closer, hand brushing the cold surface of the pod. "I was told by the seer of my people that I'd spend my life with you," he said quietly, his voice stripped of its usual swagger, laid bare by raw honesty. "At first, I thought it was some old ceremonial metaphor. That it didn't mean anything."

He exhaled slowly, shaking his head. "But then I saw you broken, unconscious, locked away in St. Thomas' like some fallen star... and I felt it. Like I'd been holding my breath since birth and didn't know it until you were right in front of me."

Orion listened, frozen, helpless. His heart beat faster within the confines of the stasis cocoon.

"I asked to be your sentry, you know?" Aaron went on. "Told them I'd guard your room to keep you safe from stray enemies or spies. But the truth is..." He laughed softly. "I just wanted to be near you."

He reached into his pocket and pulled out a worn book tattered around the edges, the spine nearly cracked. "Every night, I'd read to you. The same stories I grew up with on my colony tales of silver deserts and dragons made of starlight. If you could hear whist you were in your coma, you probably would have thought they were childish. But they reminded me of home... and maybe I hoped they'd reach you, somehow. That you'd wake up."

Orion's eyes, frozen wide, burned with unshed emotion. He remembered the stories. Not from Aaron's world, but one's like them. Stories of courage, of love that spanned galaxies.

"I don't know if you can hear me," Aaron whispered, brushing his knuckles lightly against the glassy surface of the pod. "But I need you to know this: you're the one my heart belongs to. I don't care if it's strange, or sudden, or if you wake up and forget all of this. I love you."

He paused, then lowered his forehead gently against the shell that separated them. "And I'll keep loving you, even if you never open your eyes again."

Orion screamed inside the silence, his soul reaching across the glass. But his body remained motionless, entombed in light and stillness.

Aaron lingered one moment longer, eyes glistening. "When you come back, I'll be right here. And if you don't... well, I'll still be right here, anyway."

Then he turned, the echo of his footsteps fading as he walked out of the chamber, leaving behind the boy who could hear everything and say nothing.

Moments later, Akhenaten and Snjallt returned, the air around them charged with urgency. They moved like seasoned warriors before battle methodical, focused. The sterile hiss of protective gowns echoed in the chamber as they suited up.

Akhenaten stepped to the stasis pod tapped something on the screen and Orion felt the stasis liquid around his eyes receded.

"I need to know if you consent to this," he said gravely. "Blink once for no, twice for yes."

Orion didn't hesitate. He blinked twice, slow and deliberate.

Akhenaten bowed his head, accepting the answer as sacred. He turned to retrieve a strange metal syringe from a locked case its surface etched with alien script, its needle pulsing with an eerie, inner light that seemed alive.

"I must warn you," Akhenaten said, voice low. "You'll remain conscious during the procedure. It will not be gentle. But it is the only way."

He moved to the console and pressed his hand to the biometric panel.

"Reanimation protocol engaged," the pod's voice intoned. "Nano communication implants will dissolve. Oxygenated stasis fluid will now evacuate from the lungs. Discomfort may occur."

then.A sudden jolt shot through Orion's body like lightning. The pod's outer shell hissed and split, and the solid stasis fluid began to melt, sliding off him in heavy, viscous sheets. A metallic tube extended down from above, piercing the barrier and sliding gently into his nose. Heat surged through his chest as the fluid was sucked from his lungs, and then

Pain.

He coughed violently, gasping for breath as the last of the stasis liquid drained away, each inhalation feeling like knives against raw flesh. The pod cracked open with a hydraulic hiss, flooding the chamber with stale air and the scent of scorched metal.

Akhenaten was already there, looming over him like a guardian statue, the glowing syringe in hand.

"Brace yourself," he murmured. "This will hurt."

He plunged the needle into Orion's arm.

The reaction was instant.

Orion screamed.

It wasn't just pain it was fire incarnate, rushing through his bloodstream, burning away everything in its path. His back arched violently, muscles locking as his veins lit up like molten rivers beneath his skin. The serum was searching, hunting the poison that threatened to kill him and when it found it, the war began.

Snjallt gritted her teeth and threw her weight down across his chest and shoulders, holding him still as he thrashed against the restraints. Sweat beaded across his brow, then poured in rivulets, his skin gleaming under the harsh lights.

His cries turned to gasps, ragged and broken.

Akhenaten's own face was drawn with strain, beads of gold-flecked sweat forming as he directed the magic within the syringe. "He's fighting it," he said. "He's not giving in. Good. Good."

But Orion was slipping.

His vision blurred, edges darkening, and the fire inside him became too much. With one final, breathless gasp, his body seized and then fell utterly still.

# 7. The Librarians

Something had gone horribly wrong, Orion thought as he hovered in the ethereal void above his lifeless body. His transparent form was tethered to the physical shell below, unable to drift far despite his desperate attempts.

"So, I guess all that destiny stuff was rubbish," he muttered, his voice echoing endlessly in the emptiness surrounding him.

Below, Akhenaten and Snjallt worked frantically. Snjallt stirred a luminous blue potion in a rounded beaker, her brow furrowed with determination. Akhenaten stood hunched over Orion's body, his hands glowing with ancient magic as he sent repeated jolts of energy into Orion's chest. Each pulse struck the void like a gong, reverberating through Orion's incorporeal form.

The door to the medical chamber slammed open. Eymd stumbled in, her hand clutching her chest as if she'd been stabbed.

"I felt him die," she gasped, eyes locking on Orion's motionless form.

"Eymd..." Akhenaten began, his voice thick with sorrow.

"I'm afraid... we've done all we can," Snjallt said quietly, her voice cracking.

"Don't 'we've done all we can' me!" Eymd roared, grief twisted into rage. "Do your duty and save him! Now!" Black tears streaked down her cheeks, glinting against her dark skin like inked stars.

"I'm trying," Snjallt snapped, voice sharp with strain. She poured the glowing blue liquid onto Orion's chest, watching desperately as it disappeared into his skin. Nothing. No spark. No breath. Her expression collapsed into anguish. With a scream, she hurled the beaker against the wall. It shattered into a constellation of glittering shards.

Akhenaten bowed his head. "It seems we didn't awaken his powers early enough. I must consult the Old Ones."

Snjallt nodded, though her trembling hands betrayed her composure. Akhenaten pressed a glowing button above the pod. A thin sheet of glass descended, frosting instantly to seal Orion within. He murmured an incantation, golden sigils dancing from his fingertips, forming a protective barrier around the pod with a final, sombre flash.

Then he was gone, dissolving into golden sand.

Snjallt turned to Eymd. "Come, sister mine. We must inform the others."

"I won't leave him," Eymd choked out, throwing herself across the pod, her shoulders shaking. "I won't."

"Sister, this is not the shadow warrior way. We will mourn in due time."

When Snjallt tried to pull her away, Eymd snarled and drew a dagger. "I said I will not leave him!"

Snjallt sighed. "I'm sorry." She clipped a mask over her nose and threw a vial at Eymd's feet. Gas burst forth. Eymd crumpled.

Snjallt lifted her sister with practiced ease and carried her out, leaving the room silent. Empty. Frozen in time.

Orion drifted above it all, bitter. "So much for there being a light at the end of the tunnel."

"You're not dead," a crisp female voice said, startling him. "We had to intervene."

"Who's there? Why can't I see you?" Orion spun, searching the shadows.

"I am one of the Keepers of the Library," the voice said. "Entrusted to safeguard all that is, was, and will be."

"Our duty," a second, deeper voice added, "is to ensure that what the Writers have written comes to pass."

Orion frowned. "But this my death must've been written in my book, surely?"

"This was never meant to happen in this version of events," the female replied.

"Version of events?" he echoed.

"It's easier to show you," she said.

A vortex of swirling starlight exploded beside his body. From its heart stepped a tall, striking blonde woman in an immaculate white suit. She dusted herself off as if annoyed at the dust daring to exist.

"Honestly, Section 92," she muttered, snatching a medical instrument and pocketing it. "One job. They had one job."

Wings of golden light unfurled behind her, casting long, heavenly rays across the chamber. She smirked. "Oops. Clumsy me."

She peered into the hallway. "Incompetence everywhere." Then, with a dramatic spin, she finally looked up.

"Ah, there you are."

"You can see me?" Orion asked.

"Of course." She waved a hand, casual as brushing off lint. "Just a moment, sweetheart. I need to make a call."

She pulled a transparent disc from her pocket and tapped it with growing irritation.

"Section 92, how may I assist?" a croaky male voice answered.

"This is Librarian 19287. Verification Foxtrot Omega 7986. Get me your supervisor."

A pause. Then: "Supervisor 421 speaking. Why are you interrupting my lunch?"

"I'm reporting a failure to activate Holding Dimension 292. Fix it. Now."

"Done. You have 24 Earth hours. Do not contact me again," the voice snapped. The disc melted into a puddle of silver.

"Charming," the woman said, stepping over the sizzle. She turned back to Orion with a dazzling smile. "You can call me Vilantina."

"What are you?"

"The one tasked with fixing the mess others make." She winked. "Now let's get you sorted, shall we?"

She plunged her arm into her jacket's pocket her entire arm disappearing as though the fabric bent time itself and retrieved a shimmering, humming device shaped like a crystalline paint scraper.

"Hold still," she said. "This won't hurt. Probably."

She pressed a button on the scraper, and it emitted a low, rising hum that vibrated in the air like a warning. Orion tensed, his ethereal muscles coiling instinctively, unsure whether to flinch or brace. Before he could speak, the device made contact with his spectral leg. A ripple of energy jolted through him, causing his entire form to shudder and blur. The sensation wasn't painful, but it wasn't pleasant either. It was like being tuned to the wrong frequency.

"Just hang tight," Vilantina muttered, adjusting her grip. Her voice was calm but focused, her golden eyes narrowing as she scraped along the invisible tether binding him to his lifeless body. The link shimmered like spider silk in moonlight, resisting her efforts with stubborn elasticity. She grunted and pressed harder, severing the strand inch by inch.

As his leg finally came free, Orion felt an unearthly lightness, his body beginning to drift upward as though gravity itself had given up on him.

"Whoa, whoa not so fast!" Vilantina barked, grabbing his ankle with surprising strength. "We're not done yet. Stay grounded, will you?"

Piece by piece, she continued her meticulous work, moving from limb to limb before reaching his torso. Each tether she cut left him feeling simultaneously unburdened and bereft like sloughing off parts of himself he hadn't realised were still clinging to life.

Then came the final snap.

Orion shot upward like a balloon loosed into the sky, limbs flailing. Vilantina cursed, snatched something from her belt, and thrust a pair of jewel-encrusted silver rings onto his index fingers.

"There we go," she said, brushing spectral dust from her hands. "Anchors engaged."

Orion blinked in surprise as the rings pulsed gently. His once-transparent limbs shimmered, then solidified. His feet touched the ground again firm, real. For the first time since his near-death, he felt weight return to his body, strange and grounding.

"Better?" she asked, her radiant wings folding neatly behind her like a ceremonial cloak.

"Uh... I think so," he said, flexing his fingers. His voice sounded more present, more here. "What happens now?"

Vilantina clapped her hands, unleashing a cascade of sparks that swirled and danced like fireflies. With a practiced ease, she began tracing symbols in the air fluid, glowing glyphs of green energy that hovered and spun into alignment. With a final, decisive flourish, she pressed her palm to the pattern's centre. The air rippled and tore, revealing a doorway of pure white light that hummed with raw power.

"Now," she said, grabbing his arm, "we're going to fix this mess properly. Time to visit the library."

Before Orion could object, she pulled him through.

The other side hit him like a wave of wonder.

They emerged onto a vast, wooden pathway suspended in a sky of shifting colours auroras chasing each other through constellations that bloomed and wilted like flowers. Doors lined the pathway on both sides, each inscribed with glowing runes and symbols in languages Orion couldn't begin to understand. The air thrummed with unseen forces. Faint voices whispered at the edge of his awareness, a susurrus of secrets and songs.

"What is this place?" he asked, breathless.

"The Gods' Walkway," Vilantina replied casually. "From here, we can access any time, place, or dimension. Think of it as the highway of existence."

As they walked forward, the air thickened with noise a tidal wave of voices, countless and distinct, crashing into Orion's mind. He winced, clutching his head.

"Oh, right? The prayers," Vilantina muttered. She rummaged in yet another pocket, pulled out a small velvet pouch, and blew a shimmering cloud of powder into his face. Orion coughed, then sneezed once, twice, three times. With each sneeze, the voices softened, fading to a distant murmur.

"Better?"

"Much," he said hoarsely. "What were those?"

"The prayers of your believers," she said, grinning. "Get used to it, darling. Comes with the territory of being a god."

He stared at her, dumbfounded. The word god rang in his ears like a bell, impossible to ignore.

Before he could respond, Vilantina let out a sharp whistle. The wooden path beneath them began to shift, moving forward like a conveyor belt. They sailed past door after door, each one marked with glowing numbers and mounted screens that displayed glimpses into worlds some serene, others apocalyptic.

"This way," she said suddenly, pulling him onto a stationary landing before an unmarked patch of air. She knocked twice.

Slowly, a golden door materialised. In its centre appeared a glowing handprint.

She pressed her palm into it.

"Librarian 19287, authorisation confirmed. One visitor detected. Does the visitor require a wing set?"

"Yes," Vilantina replied, with a nod. "Full access, Omega level."

The door hissed open to reveal a softly lit chamber, walls lined with alcoves and floating tools. Vilantina strode forward, retrieving a Golden armband and a pair of intricately folded wings that shimmered like pressed leaves made of light.

She slipped the armband onto Orion's wrist. It clicked into place and tightened with a gentle pulse. Then she handed him the wings paper-thin, etched with spiralling designs that shifted when he touched them.

"These... are wings?"

"Library-grade," she said proudly. "Woven from the pages of the library's finest texts. Lightweight, self-healing, practically indestructible. Very chic."

He slipped them on, and they fused seamlessly to his back. The sensation was strange warm and organic, like being hugged by knowledge itself. They felt alive.

As she turned and leapt through the chamber's far exit, Orion followed.

His wings unfurled and caught the wind effortlessly, lifting him into the vast expanse beyond.

And that's when the déjà vu struck him.

"This looks... familiar," he murmured, glancing at the endless rows of glowing shelves below. "It's just like the library beneath the Sphinx."

Vilantina glanced back. "That place was modelled after this one. A fragment. A pale echo of what once was. This," she gestured to the shimmering realm around them "this is the original."

Below them, shelf after shelf stretched to the horizon some carved from obsidian, others formed from crystal, vines, or bone. Glowing tomes floated midair, orbiting columns of starlight. A warm current of unseen force kept them aloft, as if the knowledge itself breathed.

Above them, the sky turned like a slow-moving tide of stories waiting to be rewritten.

And Orion newly untethered, newly whole soared into it.

# 8. The Library

A low, resonant rumble filled the air, vibrating through Orion's very bones. His hand flew to his chest as the badge pinned to his tunic flared with an intense golden light, forcing him to shield his eyes. Murmurs drifted around him, indistinct yet strangely familiar, like the echoes of forgotten conversations. When the brilliance finally dimmed, he uncovered his face and froze.

The endless expanse of sky that had surrounded him moments ago was gone. Now he hovered just above an intricately polished oak floor, his wings instinctively folding tightly behind him. With a gentle motion, he descended, his boots making a soft tap as they touched the ground.

Slowly, he looked around, awe replacing confusion. This must be it the Library. The place Vilantina had described in reverent tones.

Bookshelves rose in every direction, impossibly tall, their heights vanishing into shadow. Each shelf brimmed with ancient tomes, their spines inscribed with glowing runes that pulsed faintly. Nearby, people in flowing white robes sat at gilded tables, engrossed in texts that dwarfed them. At the far end of the vast room, a group of ethereal figures sat at a pale desk, their forms wreathed in mist. Their hands moved fluidly above open books, which seemed to assemble themselves: pages fluttered into place, and covers sealed shut with a soft glow before the figures slid them aside and began anew.

"Right, sweetie, wait here for a moment," a familiar voice chimed at his side.

Orion nearly jumped. Vilantina stood beside him, her golden curls bouncing with each word. She flashed him a radiant smile before turning on her heel and striding confidently toward the pale desk. There, she engaged one of the mist-like figures in conversation. Whatever she said caused the figure to glance at Orion, an intrigued smile crossing its faintly discernible face. With a nod, the clerk dissolved into a streak of white mist and zipped down a shadowed aisle of shelves, the gloom retreating as it went.

Vilantina returned moments later, her expression light and casual. "He's fetching you a book to read while I get approval for you to visit the Librarian's Office," she said.

"Um, Vilantina..." Orion hesitated, gesturing toward the figures at the desk. "What are they?"

"They're the desk clerks," Vilantina replied, as though it were obvious. "The Father Superior Librarian crafted them from enchanted clouds. If you look closely, you can see the stardust and parchment woven into their forms."

Before Orion could respond, a soft tap on his shoulder startled him. He spun around to find one of the clerks standing behind him, its form now more solid. The figure bowed slightly, presenting him with a massive red book. Orion hesitated, then took the tome with both hands, instinctively bowing in return.

"You don't need to do that, Orion," Vilantina said with a sigh. "He's not your equal."

Orion frowned, cradling the book. "It's the right thing to do. Respect isn't about rank; it's about how we treat each other."

Both Vilantina and the desk clerk seemed caught off guard, exchanging perplexed looks. After a pause, the clerk inclined his head, acknowledging Orion's words.

"Thank you for the book... uh... sorry, I didn't catch your name. I can't just call you 'desk clerk,' can I?" Orion asked, looking up at the figure.

The clerk opened his mouth, then shut it, then tried again. His form flickered slightly, as if contemplating his next move.

"I don't think they can talk, Orion," Vilantina said. "They're made to serve, not,"

"Ma'am," the clerk interrupted, his voice deep and commanding, "please don't assume what the Father Superior made us to do. We simply choose to converse only with those who respect us."

Vilantina's cheeks flushed, and she looked away, scolded like a child. Orion, however, couldn't help but grin.

"Thank you for your respect, sir," the clerk said, his deep voice carrying a surprising warmth. "My name is Carmelo, First Desk Clerk to the Father Superior Librarian. I'll serve as your personal clerk during your stay."

Orion nodded. "It's a pleasure to meet you, Carmelo."

Carmelo's expression softened. "Likewise. A few rules for your stay: avoid the shadowed rows they are unsafe. If you need anything, come to the desk, and I will assist you."

"He's my guest, Carmelo," Vilantina interrupted, her voice sharper. "I just need to leave him here while I go upstairs to sign him in."

Carmelo turned his calm, steady gaze to her. "Head Librarian 001 has summoned you to his office immediately, ma'am. Until I receive further instructions, Orion is under my care."

Vilantina's annoyance melted at the mention of the Head Librarian, her posture straightening. "By the books... it must be important," she murmured. Turning to Orion, she gave him a quick smile. "I'll be back soon. Make yourself comfortable and start reading the book."

Orion watched her ascend a spiral staircase of shimmering quartz, her figure vanishing into the upper levels. Turning back to Carmelo, Orion nodded his thanks once more before taking a seat at a nearby golden chair. The massive red book rested on his lap, its worn cover inscribed with curling silver runes.

Orion's fingers traced the embossed silver lettering on the worn red cover before he carefully opened the book. The pages were thick and slightly rough, their edges gilded with an intricate pattern of celestial motifs. His breath caught as he read the title on the first page, written in bold, flowing script:

"In-Depth Training for Hybrid Gods,"

Written by Librarian Father Superior.

The ink shimmered faintly, as though it were alive, responding to the flicker of his thoughts. Intrigued, Orion flipped the page and found the dedication, written in a familiar hand. His eyes widened as he read the words.

Orion,

I know you feel lost at the moment, but things will get better. The path you are meant to walk will become clearer as you read this book.

Orion's hands trembled slightly, and he read the words again, his mind racing. This wasn't just a book it was a message. A direct communication meant specifically for him.

How could the Librarian Father Superior, a figure so distant and revered, know him? Know what he was feeling?

He glanced up instinctively, half-expecting to see someone watching him, but the library was as serene as before. The soft rustle of pages being turned and the occasional scrape of a chair being adjusted were the only sounds. Even Carmelo, stationed at the desk, stood motionless like a statue carved from mist and stardust.

Orion returned his gaze to the dedication. The words seemed almost to hum with resonance, as though they had been waiting for him to uncover them. He exhaled slowly, calming the knot of uncertainty in his chest. Whatever doubts or confusion he carried, this book had already begun to address them.

Flipping the page, he let his curiosity take over, eager to see what guidance awaited him.

Orion's confusion deepened with every page he read. How had the Librarian Father Superior known he would be visiting the library? Vilantina and the other librarians had shown no sign they were expecting him had they truly not known? Questions buzzed in his mind, but no answers emerged from the silent grandeur of the library.

He glanced up occasionally as people passed, each wearing variations of Vilantina's distinct suit, tailored in shimmering fabrics of various hues. At one point, a gentleman in a midnight blue suit strode past, pausing as his eyes met Orion's. The man offered a polite smile and inclined his head in a shallow bow. Orion nodded in return, but before the man could approach, a sharp cough sounded in the distance. The man froze, his face paling, then scurried off with a panicked expression. Orion frowned, puzzled by the man's abrupt retreat.

"Pardon me, Master Orion. I need you to follow me, please," a deep voice said from behind him, startling him so badly that the book tumbled from his hands onto the floor.

Carmelo, the desk clerk, stepped forward and bent gracefully to retrieve the fallen tome. Orion quickly stood, brushing himself off awkwardly, and followed Carmelo as the mist-like figure strode toward a door behind the main desk.

"Carmelo, where are we going?" Orion asked hesitantly.

"All in good time, sir," Carmelo replied, glancing over his shoulder briefly before opening the door. His tone left little room for further questions.

The hallway beyond was dim, lit only by faint, flickering lamps affixed to the walls. Framed portraits lined the corridor, each depicting a stern-looking librarian. Underneath each portrait was a plaque bearing the librarian's number and their department. The dark red carpet muffled their footsteps as they walked, and at the far end of the hall, a plain white door awaited.

Carmelo led him through the door, which opened onto a spiralling stone staircase. Orion followed in silence as they ascended. The climb felt endless, the circular steps winding upwards for what must have been twenty minutes. Finally, they emerged onto a small landing lit by two torches flanking a heavy wooden door. The flames cast a golden glow over the intricate carvings on its surface.

"When you enter," Carmelo began, turning to face him, "bow your head and wait for him to speak. If he offers his hand, you are to kiss the ring upon it. Do not sit unless invited and do not speak unless spoken to."

Orion hesitated. "Who am I?"

Carmelo cut him off with a stern look. "You'll see soon enough."

The desk clerk rapped once on the door, then opened it and stepped inside, his posture rigid and formal. Orion remained outside, his nerves mounting as he tried to remember Carmelo's instructions.

"Sir, His Royal Highness Intenfli Orion I, Admiral of the Fleet of Xerist, High Commander of the X1 Army and Stone Guard, Intenfli of the Xerist Galaxy, and son of Intenfli Auren and Intenfna Aurorina, is here to see you," Carmelo announced, his voice ringing out with clarity and precision.

Orion's breath hitched. He hadn't heard his full title spoken aloud in years. The weight of those words felt heavier than the galaxy they referenced. Carmelo stepped aside and gestured for Orion to enter. Swallowing his apprehension, Orion stepped into the room and bowed his head low, as instructed. The door closed behind him with a soft click, and he was alone.

"Come, boy, take a seat," a deep, authoritative voice said from somewhere ahead.

Keeping his head bowed, Orion shuffled forward, only to bump into a circular table. Wincing, he straightened slightly, glancing around the room for the first time. The office was small and intimate, the walls completely lined with shelves holding ancient books whose spines seemed to hum faintly with age and magic. A round table sat at the centre, flanked by two burgundy chairs and two velvet ones.

"Do you want tea or coffee?" the voice asked, now coming from somewhere behind him.

"Y-yes, please," Orion stammered, his throat dry.

"Speak clearly, boy. Which is it?"

"Tea, please, sir," Orion managed, his voice steadier this time.

Behind him, he heard the faint clink of china and the gentle rustling of fabric. He remained perfectly still, unwilling to risk offending the unseen man. A tray floated past his shoulder and settled onto the table before him, laden with an ornate teapot, two cups, and a plate of small pastries. As Orion stared at the tray, an elderly man stepped into view.

The man was tall and slender, with a face etched by centuries of wisdom. His silver hair was combed back neatly, and he wore a dark robe embroidered with golden symbols Orion couldn't decipher. A large ring glinted on his right hand, the gem at its centre catching the torchlight.

Orion bowed his head once more as the man seated himself across from him.

"Boy, stop looking at the floor," the man said, his tone softer now but still commanding.

"Yes, sir," Orion replied, lifting his gaze to meet the elder's.

The man sitting before Orion looked nothing like the awe-inspiring figure he'd imagined the Librarian Father Superior to be. Bald, with thick glasses that magnified his eyes into saucers, he wore simple brown robes reminiscent of monks Orion had seen in old books. Liver spots mottled his wrinkled face, and each breath came with a faint, wheezing sound. Yet, despite his frailty, there was an unmistakable power radiating from him.

"Enough with that 'sir' nonsense," the old man wheezed, waving a bony hand. "You're a smart boy. I assume you know who I am."

Orion hesitated. "I think you are the Librarian Father Superior, sir."

"That is correct," the old man replied, his thin lips curving into a sly smile. "Although you may call me Grandpapa." He reached for a floral teapot and began pouring steaming liquid into two delicate matching cups. His hands trembled slightly as he worked, yet the fluid never spilled.

"Why am I here, si Grandpapa?" Orion asked, correcting himself quickly.

"All in good time. Now, one lump or two?"

"Two, please," Orion said, watching as the Librarian Father Superior shakily dropped two sugar cubes into the tea.

With care, the elder picked up one of the cups and handed it to Orion, who accepted it gratefully. Orion added a splash of milk and took a cautious sip. The tea was unexpectedly rich and soothing.

"Apologies for my current appearance," Grandpapa said as he raised his own cup. "I'm waiting for this body to fail so I can move into a newer, younger one."

Orion nearly choked on his tea, but the old man's calm demeanour made the comment feel oddly casual. Grandpapa sipped his tea, smacked his lips in satisfaction, and peered over his glasses at Orion.

"You are here," he began, his tone now serious, "because someone has been tampering with my books. That meddling led to your death a mistake easily corrected, but it gave me the opportunity to meet you in person. And more importantly, to give you this."

The Librarian Father Superior extended his hand above the table. A brilliant light erupted from his palm, illuminating the room with an almost divine glow. When the light faded, an ancient book rested on the table. Unlike the pristine volumes Orion had seen elsewhere in the library, this one was battered and worn. Its cover was tattered, its binding frayed, and its yellowed pages looked as if they might crumble at the slightest touch.

"Keep this safe," Grandpapa said, sliding the book toward Orion. "No one but you must read it."

Orion picked up the book carefully. It felt oddly warm under his fingers, and the faint glow of the cover intensified slightly as he held it. The title was written in an unrecognisable script, and when Orion tried to open the book, its pages refused to budge.

"Why won't it open?" Orion asked, frustration creeping into his voice.

"All in good time, my child," Grandpapa said with a knowing smile. "Now, it has been a pleasure meeting you, but you must leave before time restarts."

Before Orion could ask what that meant, Grandpapa pressed a button on the table. A soft chime echoed outside the room. Moments later, the door opened, and Carmelo entered, bowing deeply.

"Sir," Carmelo said respectfully.

"Young Master Orion is ready to return," Grandpapa instructed. "See to it that Librarian 19287 fully understands the importance of her mission."

"Right away, sir," Carmelo replied.

Orion stood and extended his hand to shake Grandpapa's, but before their hands met, the old man winked at him a gesture so familiar it left Orion momentarily speechless. Then, Grandpapa vanished, leaving only a faint shimmer in the air.

Carmelo cleared his throat behind Orion, startling him back to reality. Grabbing the tattered book, Orion followed Carmelo out of the office. They descended the spiralling stairs and returned to the main library, where Vilantina sat at a golden table, tapping her fingers impatiently. When she spotted Orion, she sprang to her feet.

"I told you to stay in the library," she snapped, her voice sharp with irritation.

Carmelo stepped forward, holding out a thick brown envelope sealed with a golden emblem. "Librarian 19287, this is from the Librarian Father Superior," he said formally. "And the master requested an audience with His Royal Highness."

Vilantina's mouth opened, but no words came out. Her shock was evident as she glanced between Carmelo and Orion. Finally, she bowed her head toward Carmelo, a gesture of respect.

"It has been an honour, Your Highness," Carmelo said to Orion, a faint smirk curling at his lips. "Please don't be a stranger." With that, he turned and strode back to his desk, resuming his ethereal work.

Vilantina composed herself and turned to Orion. "I still need a few more books before we leave. You can wait here or come with me."

"I'll come with you, if that's okay," Orion said. "I'd love to see more of the library."

"That's fine, sweetie. Do you want me to put that book in my bag?" she asked, nodding toward the worn book in his hands.

"No, it's okay," Orion said, holding the book tightly

Vilantina strolled casually down one of the many aisles, her eyes scanning the shelves for the volumes she sought. Orion followed behind her, his attention wandering to the countless ancient books, tablets, and artifacts surrounding them. The air was thick with the scent of aged parchment and a faint hum of magic that seemed to emanate from the very walls.

As they moved deeper, a glint caught Orion's eye a shimmering tablet nestled among the other treasures. He paused, tucking the ancient book given to him by the Librarian Father Superior under his arm, and slid the tablet carefully off the shelf. Its surface gleamed faintly, and a single phrase was etched upon it in elegant, glowing script:

"Your destiny begins now, embrace it!"

The words struck a chord deep within him, sending a shiver down his spine. A small smile tugged at his lips as he returned the tablet to its place. But when he looked up, Vilantina was nowhere to be seen.

"Vilantina?" he called out, his voice echoing softly in the stillness. He hurried down the aisle to an intersection and glanced around. To his right and ahead of him, the aisles stretched empty and silent. To his left, a figure moved faintly in the dim light, retreating deeper into the shadows.

# 9. Between Shadows And Light

Forgetting the warning, Orion stepped into the gloom, his footsteps muffled by the plush carpet beneath him. The deeper he ventured, the more the enchanted light behind him dimmed swallowed by an unnatural blackness that clung to the walls and floor like living tar. It wasn't just the absence of light it was a presence. A hunger.

Soon, he couldn't even see his own hands.

Something shifted ahead. The silhouette was wrong. Disjointed. Its movements snapped from one pose to the next like a corrupted animation reel flickering through broken frames. A wave of nausea rolled through Orion, his gut twisting as primal fear settled into his bones.

"Vilantina?" he called out, voice brittle and echoing too loudly. Too alone.

The figure froze mid-step.

Then, with a voice like glass shattering beneath a frozen lake, it rasped, "Yes, sweetie. Come over here. I've found something... interesting."

Orion's blood turned to ice.

The voice wasn't hers. It wore her tone, stretched and warped like a dead thing pretending to live. He took an instinctive step back, heart hammering.

The figure turned.

Twin eyes molten coals snapped open, burning through the dark. Their glow lit a jagged grin: a maw full of glassy, knife-like teeth. Shadows bled off its form in smoky tendrils that writhed hungrily, licking at the floor like flames searching for kindling.

"There's no escape," it hissed. Its voice wasn't one voice it was many. Layered. Wrong. "You should have listened to the Librarian. You've wandered too far... into our domain."

With a piercing shriek, it lunged its body unravelling into a storm of claws and smoke.

Orion spun and bolted, adrenaline surging like fire through his veins. The corridor stretched around him like a nightmare maze, shifting with every step. Behind him, the creature howled its pursuit a chorus of screeching wind and scraping whispers.

The ancient book tucked under his arm slipped.

"No!"

It skidded across the floor, bouncing once then vanished, swallowed by the dark.

Orion reached for it but black tendrils beat him there, curling possessively around the leather cover before yanking it into the void.

"I told you..." the voice returned, now mere inches from his ear, "there's no escape."

Orion spun, swinging his fist

and hit nothing.

Then cold.

A black, clawed hand clamped over his mouth, yanking his head back. From the gloom, a face coalesced sculpted from shadow, its fanged mouth inches from his own. The heat of its breath stung like acid. Spit landed on his cheek and sizzled.

"I'm not here to hurt you," it lied, every syllable a dagger. "I just want your badge... so I can leave this cursed place."

Orion gave a trembling nod.

The hand slowly withdrew.

"W-who... are you?" he croaked.

The figure tilted its head. "I don't remember," it said wistfully. "I've wandered these halls for... millennia. Waiting. Always waiting for someone foolish enough to stray."

"Why do you want the badge?"

"It's the only way out. Or so the others say. Others like me."

It reached toward the golden band on Orion's arm.

The moment its fingers brushed the metal, a pulse of searing light exploded from it. The creature screamed, yanking its charred hand back as steam rose from the wound.

"Seems... it doesn't want to be taken," Orion muttered, forcing himself to stand tall.

Around them, the air thickened like coagulating blood. Then came the whispers millions of them rising in a ghostly chorus. A language older than nightmares. A dirge of lost souls.

"Give me the badge, boy, and you will not be harmed," the creature growled.

"And if I refuse?"

"You don't want to know the answer to that."

"Too bad," Orion said. "No."

The creature lunged.

Its clawed hand closed around his throat, lifting him like a rag doll. His legs kicked uselessly. Another hand reached for the badge.

"If you kill me," he gasped, "you'll never get it,"

"There are worse fates than death," it snarled. "Let me show you."

Its fingers melted into smoke, flowing into his ears, nose, eyes.

Pain detonated inside him.

He screamed his voice high and ragged as he dropped to the floor, convulsing. His hands clawed at his own face. Agony raced through his nerves like fire in oil.

The shadows drank in his cries.

"You are strong," the creature murmured beside him. "But you cannot resist forever. Give in. Submit."

"P-please..." Orion sobbed. "Let me go..."

"I said... GIVE IN!" the voice thundered inside his skull.

Darkness crushed him. His lungs screamed. His heart slowed. Vision flickered.

I'm dying...

And then light.

A golden blaze erupted above them, cutting through the dark like the sun rising over the dead. The creature screeched, flinching backward as the light seared into its form.

A wind followed warm, divine, and furious.

Vilantina descended in a halo of burning wings, her eyes glowing with wrath.

"I told you," she barked, landing in a storm of feathers and light, "Stay. Out. Of. The. Shadows."

The creature laughed and when it spoke again, it used Orion's voice.

"He is mine now, Librarian. Your light is nothing."

"Orion, fight him!" Vilantina shouted, kneeling beside him, wrapping her wings around him. "You can push him out. But you need his name! That's the key!"

"I can't!" he screamed, another wave of agony wracking his body.

"Yes, you can," she said, pressing her forehead to his. "Stop resisting and dive deeper. Find him. Own him."

Orion stopped fighting the pain.

He let go and dove into it.

The world fell away, swallowed in shadow. In the void, the creature waited.

"Yes... give in, boy," it whispered, looming. "I will start with your friends. Then your family. I will wear your skin and burn everything you love."

"No..." Orion whispered. Weak but unyielding.

"Bow to me."

The creature pressed a flaming hand to his forehead.

"I will not," Orion snarled through clenched teeth.

Shadows erupted, wrapping around him, binding him in agony. His thoughts cracked shattered

and then came Clarity.

He stopped struggling.

He smiled.

"Why do you smile?" the creature asked, its voice faltering.

"Because you should've searched my memories better," Orion said, rising within the dark. His voice rang like thunder. "Because now... I know your name."

The shadow's eyes widened, flickering with something Orion hadn't seen in it before fear. It began to retreat, its form unravelling like smoke in a gale. But Orion moved first. His hand shot out and seized the shadow's arm with unyielding force.

A shockwave of power surged through him vast, ancient, untamable. It wasn't just his magic anymore. It was the will of his bloodline, the legacy of stars and fire pulsing in his veins. The library trembled around him, books rattling, scrolls unravelling mid-air, as if the world itself recognised its sovereign.

Orion rose to his full height.

His eyes blazed like twin suns, light piercing the dark. Shadows shrieked and scattered, fleeing into the cracks of the old stone floor. Dust twisted into the air like ash, caught in the aura now radiating from him hot, golden, eternal.

The silence shattered under the weight of his voice.

"I am Intenfli Orion I," he declared, each word thunderous. "Bringer of Life. Courier of Death. And heir to the Throne of Xerist."

Trintani writhed, his form buckling under the command of royal power. The light stripped away his shapelessness, exposing the fragile echoes of his past. Vilantina bowed low, wings spread in reverence, her golden aura dimming in the presence of true authority.

"W-who are you?" the shadow rasped, its fire dimming to coals.

"Look again." Orion's voice crashed through the corridor, making the shelves tremble.

The shadows peeled back like retreating waves, revealing the creature's true shape small, hunched, ashamed.

"You," Orion said, stepping forward. "Are Trintani. Shadow warrior. Betrayer. Exile. Once sworn to defend the royal family, and cursed for breaking that oath."

Trintani fell forward, prostrating himself as much as his shifting form allowed. "I didn't know! I didn't remember I was lost please, my liege, forgive me!"

"Forgiveness?" Orion's voice turned cold. "No. What you've done echoes in the screams of children and the silence of ruined worlds. But death would be too simple a fate for you."

He raised a hand.

A bolt of lightning roared into life above his palm wild and hungry, laced with starlight. The ceiling of the library lit up as arcs of celestial fire raced along the stone, casting jagged shadows.

"You will live," Orion said, his tone final. "But your fate is no longer yours."

The bolt crashed down.

It struck Trintani's wrist, burning a circle of fire into his skin. He screamed once then stiffened, seizing violently. The brand flared, then transformed light becoming shape, shape becoming chain. A band of glowing red lightning coiled around his arm like a living serpent.

"And you will serve," Orion continued, his voice echoing with ancient authority. "From this day until the stars fall, you are bound body and soul to the royal line of Xerist."

The chain pulsed, reacting to the words like a living oath.

Trintani gasped and then collapsed.

Unconscious, his body limp in Orion's grip, twitching from the lingering charge. But the transformation had begun.

The red band glowed brighter, then began its crawl spiralling slowly across his body, inch by inch. His shadow form boiled away, peeled back by invisible hands. Flesh reformed where there had been smoke. Bones reshaped where there had been void. And the form that emerged was not the warrior he once was it was a mirror of those he had wronged.

His face twisted into a visage both alien and achingly familiar, bearing the features of a people long lost the last race he had betrayed before his exile.

The transformation was slow, grotesque, and painful even in unconsciousness. Muscles spasmed. Bones cracked like old wood. His skin, once void-like, was now pale and scarred. His eyes, once molten and cruel, fluttered closed beneath trembling lashes.

The chain receded, sealing itself beneath his skin. Its final pulse reverberated outward like a buried drumbeat one that would echo for eternity.

Orion bent down and lifted the now-human form of Trintani with ease. There was no satisfaction in his expression only resolution.

He turned.

Vilantina remained kneeling, golden wings drawn close, her head bowed low.

"Vilantina," Orion said, his voice calm, resonant.

She raised her head slowly, eyes wide with awe.

"Yes, Your Highness?"

"You don't have to bow," he said gently, stepping into the circle of golden light around her. "Not anymore."

She hesitated. Then slowly stood, wings folding back. Even upright, her eyes didn't meet his at first.

Orion noticed the change he had grown taller, his presence towering, his very skin glowing faintly with the swirl of stars. The celestial markings across his arms shimmered like galaxies shifting in orbit.

"You dropped this," Vilantina said, holding out the ancient book the Librarian Superior had entrusted to him.

"Thank you," Orion said, accepting the book in his free hand. Its cover shimmered briefly at his touch, the arcane runes pulsing in acknowledgment. He turned back to Vilantina, eyes narrowing, voice low and precise.

"Why will you not look at me?"

"I knew you were powerful," she said softly, still avoiding his gaze. "But what you just did... it surpasses even the greatest of Librarians. Your power is no longer measurable by our laws. It is... unparalleled."

Her reverence unsettled him.

Orion, who moments ago had felt untouchable, now felt alien even to those sworn to stand at his side. Even Vilantina the indomitable, the unshaken seemed afraid of him.

What had the Old Ones truly created?

"Will I be able to call Eymd here?" he asked, his voice threading hope and hesitation.

"She is paused in time," Vilantina replied carefully. "Caught between seconds. But with the force you've unlocked yes. If anyone can reach her, it's you."

Orion closed his eyes, slowing his breath. He pushed outward with his mind, past the crumbling boundaries of the Library, threading through time's fractured veil. At first only static. Cold resistance.

But then he forced his will through.

'Eymd. I need you. Now... please.'

Then silence. The link snapped back like a rubber band. He didn't know if it had reached her.

He opened his eyes and gently laid Trintani's unconscious form on the floor. The branded chain on his arm continued to pulse slower now, deeper anchoring him to the bloodline that cursed and spared him both.

Orion settled down beside him. Despite his seated posture, he still towered over Vilantina, who stood nearby. Wordlessly, he reached out and tilted her chin upward, forcing her to meet his glowing gaze.

"Have you read my story so far?" he asked.

"Yes, sir," she admitted, voice small.

"So," Orion said with a half-smile, "what part of my story makes you think I'm okay with being treated like some untouchable god-king?"

Vilantina hesitated, then slowly allowed herself to smile. She exhaled a breath she hadn't realised she was holding and folded her legs, sitting beside him on the Library floor.

"The Old Ones had no idea what they were making when they shaped you," she said. "The blood you carry... it may have passed through their hands, but its origin is older. Far older."

Orion's expression darkened with curiosity. "What do you mean?"

Her voice shifted calmer, more cautious. "This is not a conversation for now," she said quietly.

Her eyes flicked past him.

"We have company."

Orion turned.

From the shadowed end of the aisle, a figure staggered into view clutching her ribs, her expression twisted with confusion and rage.

Eymd.

Her storm-grey eyes found Orion, and something in her face cracked.

"You finally did it, didn't you?" she spat. "You killed me. I knew you'd go too far one day. And now here I am dead. Just like I always knew I would be."

"Eymd, calm down," Orion said, rising to his feet. "You're not dead. This is the Library."

"Liar!" she barked, pacing frantically, hands flaring with unstable shadow. "The Library is a fairy tale. A bedtime story for desperate archivists. This is just my punishment. My hell for failing you!"

Orion sighed, pinching the bridge of his nose. "I need you to do something for me."

"Oh great," she snapped. "Another task. Can't I just enjoy being dead for five seconds before I'm your errand girl in the afterlife?"

Before he could answer, Vilantina moved.

She was a blur across the space in an instant, slamming Eymd against a bookshelf with a gust of wing and fury. Her golden feathers flared, and in her hand materialised a quill-shaped blade, its edge hissing as it hovered against Eymd's throat.

"You will remember your place, shadow warrior," she growled. "You speak to the Heir of Xerist. Watch your tongue or lose it."

Eymd froze.

Her eyes, wide with sudden fear, darted to the gleaming edge of the blade. She swallowed hard, hands trembling at her sides.

"Vilantina, enough." Orion's voice rolled like thunder calm, but impossible to ignore.

The air shuddered.

Vilantina staggered backward, eyes wide. The quill-blade vanished in a flare of golden dust. Eymd gasped and sagged against the shelf, rubbing her throat.

"She cannot speak to you like that, my liege," Vilantina said quickly. "She,"

"I said enough," Orion repeated, gentler this time. "That's not how we do this. Eymd is being Eymd. You'll get used to it."

Vilantina bowed her head. "Forgive me. I lost control."

"And stop calling me 'my liege,'" Orion muttered with a sigh. "She and I have... a unique relationship. You'll see."

Eymd let out a breath, her balance returning. Her fingers traced her neck one more time, then she looked up.

"This really is the Library," she murmured. "You're... a librarian?"

Vilantina stepped forward, extending her hand. "I am Librarian 19287, but you may call me Vilantina. My earlier behaviour was... unacceptable. I apologise."

Eymd narrowed her eyes but slowly reached out. They clasped hands briefly before Eymd yanked hers back and vanished into the nearest shadow with a mischievous grin.

Moments later, she reappeared further down the aisle, already pulling books off the shelves like a child in a candy shop.

"She likes books," Vilantina said, watching her with a reluctant chuckle.

"She does," Orion said, smiling faintly. "But I need her to stop."

Eymd materialised beside him again, arms stacked with ancient tomes. Before she could dart away, Vilantina placed a hand firmly on her shoulder. Light shimmered from her palm, severing Eymd's link to the shadows in a silent flash.

"Hey!" Eymd snapped. "Why can't I phase?"

"It's temporary," Vilantina said smoothly. "Orion needs your attention."

Eymd let out an exaggerated groan. "What is it now?"

Orion gestured to the branded figure lying nearby. "I need you to take him to my stasis pod on Earth. Place him beside my body."

Eymd's brows furrowed. "Who is he?"

"It doesn't matter right now," Orion said. "He'll remain like this until the bond finishes rooting. But he needs to be protected."

Eymd tilted her head and studied the unconscious figure, noting the crimson band still glowing faintly beneath his skin. "He looks... unstable."

"He's bound to the royal line now," Orion said. "He can't hurt me. But I can't leave him here."

Eymd gave a low whistle. "You've been busy."

Then, with surprising care, she crouched and hoisted Trintani over her shoulder. He didn't stir. Moments later, Eymd reappeared alone, brushing her hands off like she'd just taken out the trash.

"All done. Anything else?" she asked, tapping her foot with exaggerated impatience.

"Yes." Orion handed her the ancient book the Librarian Superior had given him. Its cover still pulsed faintly, warm in his palm. "Hide this somewhere safe. Somewhere no one, not even I can find it."

Eymd raised a brow, then flipped the book over in her hands. Her sharp grin returned. "Dangerous. I like it."

With a flick of her wrist, she wrapped the book in shadows, then tossed it casually into the air. It vanished with a faint pop, like a soap bubble breaking.

"Done," she said. "Anything else?"

Orion chuckled. "You've got ten minutes. Explore. Just meet us at the main desk."

Eymd's grin widened like a child told she could have the whole candy store. In a blur, she snatched up her mountain of books and vanished into the Library's twisting aisles, shadows fluttering behind her like a cape.

Vilantina shook her head with a faint smile. "You might want to return to your normal form before we leave. The golden god-king look is... memorable."

"I don't know how," Orion admitted.

"Close your eyes," she said gently. "Picture yourself before the Library changed you."

Orion obeyed. Warmth surged over his skin, and as he exhaled, his cosmic glow faded. When he opened his eyes, he was back in his human form shorter now, eyes dimmed, skin no longer rippling with starlight.

"Better?" he asked.

"Much," Vilantina replied with a smirk. "Now, let's find our little book thief."

They entered the Library's vast foyer just in time to hear raised voices echoing across the polished marble.

"What do you mean I can't check out books?!"

"I'm sorry, ma'am," came a calm male voice from behind a polished obsidian desk marked CHECKOUT. "But only certified Librarians may remove volumes from the Archive."

Eymd stood at the desk, arms crossed, shadows twitching in irritation. "What kind of Library doesn't let people take home books?"

The receptionist, a silver-eyed man in a perfectly creased tunic, didn't even flinch. "Ma'am, if you'd like to read them, I can prepare a private reading suite"

"I don't want a private suite! I want these books!" Eymd snapped, gesturing at a towering pile of ancient tomes.

Vilantina stepped forward with a sigh and scanned the collection. "Some of these are... non-essential. Do you really need all of them?"

Eymd slid a protective arm around the books. "No. But books."

Vilantina chuckled softly. "Fine. I'll sign them out for you but I'll need form 2213."

Without a word, the receptionist handed it over.

"What's this?" Eymd narrowed her eyes suspiciously.

"It's a liability waiver," Vilantina explained. "If you damage any of the books, your soul belongs to the Library until the debt is repaid. One of these alone will cost you five thousand years of service."

"How many years total?" Eymd asked, intrigued.

The receptionist placed his palm over the stack. The document flickered with light numbers whirled up its surface, ticking like a slot machine before settling.

"One point five billion years," he said without blinking.

Eymd, equally unfazed, signed it with a flourish. "Right. Can I go now?"

"Of course," Vilantina sighed. "We'll meet you back on Earth."

Eymd gathered her mountain of books and vanished into the shadows.

The receptionist turned to Vilantina. "Have the edits been made to Orion's chronicle?"

"Yes," she replied. He handed her a thick leather tome, warm with power.

"The other books you summoned have been sent to your personal study," he added. "Is there anything else I can help with?"

"No. That's all. Thank you."

He nodded and pressed a bell beside his desk. A soft chime rang out and a door of radiant light shimmered into existence.

Orion and Vilantina stepped through.

The air warped around them, shimmering with unseen vibrations. The familiar hum of the Library's core resonated in Orion's ears. Each step felt like drifting, as though gravity had forgotten them.

"This won't take long," Vilantina said, her voice calm but edged with something anticipation, perhaps.

They walked the grand corridor toward the portal chamber, where the shelves themselves seemed to bow inward, acknowledging Orion's presence. Eymd's chaotic magic still lingered faintly, like a mischievous perfume on the air.

"I still don't understand how any of this works," Orion admitted, glancing upward at the impossibly high ceiling.

"Few do," Vilantina answered, her voice quieter now. "The Library doesn't obey mortal logic. It exists beyond time, beyond place. You've only glimpsed a corner of its design."

"Doesn't it ever get overwhelming?"

Vilantina smiled faintly. "It did. A long time ago. But I've learned to stop questioning and start listening. The Library knows where it's needed and who it calls. It chose you for a reason, Orion."

They reached the portal chamber an immense domed room lined with swirling columns of living light, each one flickering with the colours and signatures of different timelines, realities, and worlds. One column shone brighter than the rest, its centre a stormy blue-white swirl.

Vilantina gestured toward it. "This is your path. Your reality."

The light pulsed as they approached. Orion hesitated at its edge, his heart thudding. This wasn't just a doorway. It was alive buzzing with energy that called to the deepest parts of him.

"Step through with me," Vilantina said. "You'll feel disoriented, but it'll pass."

Orion nodded, steeling himself.

Together, they stepped into the storm.

It hit him like a tide.

Colour, sound, memory, sensation all crashing together. He was falling and floating all at once. Lights streaked past him runes, galaxies, fragments of thought. He saw glimpses of himself: younger, lost, glowing with power he didn't understand. Eymd training, her laughter sharp and wild. Vilantina standing alone in the Library, her eyes glowing as books circled her like planets.

"Stay focused," Vilantina's voice echoed, grounding him.

She walked beside him, unaffected. Her wings shimmered gold, her gaze unwavering.

"What is this place?" he asked, his voice distorted in the current.

"A bridge," she answered. "Between realities. You're seeing timelines. Echoes. You must not lose yourself here."

The images blurred into light then fractured.

Suddenly, something yanked them forward.

Orion stumbled, the ground disappearing beneath him. He felt a strange, floating weightlessness as if his soul were caught between gravity and dream as the tunnel narrowed into brilliance ahead.

And then

They emerged.

Disorientation hit him like a tidal wave.

The cold, sterile scent of antiseptic filled his lungs. His knees buckled, and he braced himself against a nearby wall, blinking rapidly as his senses reoriented. Machines hummed steadily. Monitors beeped faintly. Shadows stretched long and sharp across pale green walls.

He was back.

The hospital room. Dull. Finite. Mortal.

The contrast with the Library's infinite grandeur was brutal. The hum of magic was gone replaced by the clinical pulse of life-support machinery.

"This is it," Vilantina said gently, stepping aside. "Your reality. Your time."

Orion slowly crossed the room.

There on the bed his body lay motionless, pale and slack beneath a tangle of wires and tubes. He stared at it like a stranger, unease tightening in his chest.

Seeing his body from this distance this angle was surreal. It looked hollow. Abandoned.

He glanced at Vilantina, who now held a thick, leather-bound tome in her hands. Its worn spine glowed faintly, and as she opened it, golden script shimmered across the pages.

"What's that?" he asked.

"It's your story," she replied, her tone matter-of-fact, but reverent. "Every choice. Every breath. Every moment you've lived written here. It's how the Librarians track imbalance... and when needed, adjust the course."

She flipped to the most recent page.

"And what does it say about now?" he asked, voice tight with unease.

Vilantina's eyes scanned the page. Her brow furrowed. She didn't answer.

Instead, she said softly, "Go stand by your body."

Orion hesitated.

Then moved one step, then another until he was beside the bed. He stared down at himself, heart pounding. His form looked peaceful... but wrong. Like a painting of someone he no longer was.

"What happens next?" he whispered.

Vilantina closed the book and approached. Her fingers moved gently, reverently, as she slipped the two rings from his spirit-form hands.

The moment the second ring left his finger, something snapped.

An invisible force slammed into him pulling him downward like a riptide.

"Wait what's happening?!" he gasped, panic flaring.

"I'm sorry, sweetie," Vilantina said, her voice breaking. "This is the only way."

And then he was gone, dragged violently back into his body.

When he opened his eyes again, he wasn't in his body.

He was floating above it adrift once more, suspended in the sterile silence of the room.

Confusion and frustration surged through him. He turned sharply.

"Vilantina?"

No answer.

Across the room, a glowing portal shimmered just long enough for him to see Vilantina step through.

And disappear.

She was gone.

The portal vanished.

Orion clenched his fists. Below, his physical form remained still untouched, unmoved. Whatever the ritual was supposed to do... it hadn't worked. Or it wasn't finished.

A flicker of motion caught his eye.

He turned.

Trintani.

Still glowing faintly on the floor, his form spasming in slow, uneven pulses. The crimson chain around his wrist had expanded veins of energy crawling across his limbs like roots through stone. He twitched, convulsed unconscious but clearly enduring something profound.

The transformation wasn't over.

# 10. Meeting The Queen

Orion hovered, his ghostly form frozen in place, paralyzed by the weight of what he was witnessing. The twitching, glowing figure of Trintani on the floor pulsed like a heartbeat one that didn't belong to him, but to something older. Something inevitable.

Each pulse thudded in time with the rising dread in Orion's chest.

And then...

The stillness shattered.

The hospital ward door burst open with a crash, and Eymd stormed in, Orion's friends close behind, their expressions a blend of fear and desperate hope.

"See? I told you he was alive!" Eymd said triumphantly until her eyes landed on Orion's motionless body. Her voice faltered. "I don't understand... I was just with him. Look the person he told me to bring back is right there!"

She pointed to Trintani, still glowing on the floor, spasming with residual magic.

The others exchanged confused glances, gathering uncertainly around the bed. They looked to Eymd, then to the twitching figure on the floor, unsure whether this was a rescue... or something else entirely.

Then the air in the room shifted, growing heavier older.

A pulse of deep power rolled through the space like a distant drumbeat, and in the next moment, Akhenaten appeared beside the bed, emerging from a shimmer of gold-tinged light.

He stood tall, but time had pressed heavily on him. There was grace in his bearing, but also weariness. A man carved from legend and slowly hollowing.

He looked down at Orion's body, then to Trintani, then to the group huddled nearby. His expression was unreadable.

"Ah," he murmured, voice low, carrying the gravity of centuries. "Even in his suspended state, young Master Orion refuses to sit still."

A thin, bittersweet smile tugged at his lips, then faded.

"We have tried," he said, addressing the room without looking at anyone in particular. "The Old Ones those who remain we have poured all our strength, all our wisdom, into this. Into him. And still..."

He shook his head slowly, the words hanging in the silence like dust in air.

"We don't know how to bring him back. Not without consequence. Not without breaking something greater than ourselves."

Silence followed heavy, final.

Until it wasn't.

Suddenly, the room shuddered.

A boom cracked through the air like thunder striking inside the walls.

A portal tore itself open beside the bed, shimmering with layered light. From it stepped Vilantina, radiant in her white uniform, golden wings unfurling behind her like divine judgment. Her boots hit the floor with quiet precision, and in her right hand, the quill-blade burned faintly with starlight.

She didn't need to speak to command the room. She simply existed like a sword unsheathed.

"That is something I can help with," she declared, her voice smooth and sharp, echoing with power not of this world.

Akhenaten straightened, his posture stiffening instinctively at her presence. He turned to face her fully, ancient dignity rising to the surface.

"And who might you be?" he asked, cool and commanding.

Vilantina's eyes glinted. "I am one of the Great Librarians," she said. "Guardian of the continuum. Keeper of the unwritten. And you, Akhenaten, are but a relic of the first page."

Akhenaten's expression hardened. "There are no Librarians," he snapped. "They're myths. Fiction spun by fearful minds who couldn't grasp the gods."

His aura flared defensively. "I demand you reveal your true identity, pretender."

Vilantina's smile was razor thin.

She raised a hand and snapped her fingers.

Akhenaten's mouth sealed mid-breath. His eyes went wide with disbelief, hands rising to claw at his lips, but no sound came. His fury was silent.

"You Old Ones," Vilantina mused, circling him slowly, "so proud. So limited. You cling to divinity, but you were never more than a beginning. You are dust in the vault of creation."

She paused, letting her words settle. "I will unseal your mouth but only if you agree to listen."

Akhenaten glared at her, unmoving. Then, slowly, he nodded.

Another snap.

His lips parted with a gasp, breath shuddering.

"Now," Vilantina said, her tone shifting to steel, "the rest of you out. I must speak with the Old One alone."

Orion's friends hesitated, exchanging looks, but none dared defy her. Eymd lingered last, her eyes sweeping over Orion's body one final time before she turned and led them out.

The door closed behind them with a soft click.

Only three remained: Vilantina. Akhenaten. And Orion's spirit, unseen, floating silently in the corner.

Vilantina conjured a thick, rune-marked tome into her hands the book of Orion's life. It opened with a rustle like wind through time. She held it toward Akhenaten, who read in silence.

Line by line.

His brow furrowed. His hands began to tremble.

"This... this is the only way?" he asked quietly.

"I'm afraid so," Vilantina said, her voice gentler now. "It's the only course the Writers could find to preserve the weave."

"And after?" he whispered. "What comes next?"

She smiled small, honest. "What you never believed you'd live to see."

Akhenaten turned toward Orion's body and knelt beside it, his hand trembling as it brushed back a lock of Orion's hair. His face crumpled. Tears began to fall, silent and steady.

"He will know," he whispered. "He'll know what I gave?"

Vilantina didn't hesitate. "He's watching. But only I can see him."

Orion stared, breathless.

Then he understood.

"No. No, don't," he surged forward, his voice fractured with panic. "Vilantina, don't let him do this please!"

But she didn't respond.

Not at first.

Then: a whisper in his mind.

'It must be done, Orion.'

'I'm so sorry.'

He collapsed in midair, wracked with a grief he couldn't ground, couldn't release. He reached out to Akhenaten, to Vilantina, but his hands passed through both of them like vapor.

Akhenaten straightened, wiping away the tears that streaked his weathered face. His voice was steady, but quiet with finality.

"Then to sand I must return," he said.

He looked once more at Orion's still form then to Vilantina.

"Look after him for me."

"With my life," Vilantina promised, placing a gentle hand on his shoulder. "Farewell, Old One. May the Books forever look favourably upon you."

Akhenaten stepped closer to Orion's body, the glow from Trintani's twitching figure casting long shadows along the walls. Placing his hand over Orion's heart, he began to chant low and steady each word ancient and heavy with power. His voice seemed to reverberate through the room, bending the air itself.

Light shimmered beneath his palm, spreading into Orion's chest, his veins, his limbs. The light intensified with every word until, at last, he whispered the final line of the incantation and vanished in a burst of golden sand.

The sand lingered for a moment, dancing midair before settling on the floor like fallen starlight.

And then pain.

A searing pain tore through Orion's ghostly form as it was violently yanked back into his body. His vision twisted, everything spinning around him light, shadow, memory, heat and then darkness claimed him whole.

Orion's eyes fluttered open, stinging against the hospital's harsh ceiling lights.

Everything felt too bright, too real.

The world came into blurry focus and the first thing he saw was Vilantina, her eyes filled with relief and exhaustion, like someone who had just finished carrying an entire galaxy.

"Orion, wake up," a familiar voice murmured beside him.

He turned his head, slowly, achingly.

"Hello, sleepyhead," Rachel said with a watery smile, trying unsuccessfully to keep things light.

His throat burned. "Akhenaten?" he rasped.

Vilantina's gaze dropped. Her voice was low and soft.

"I'm sorry," she said, unable to meet his eyes.

Orion tried to sit up, but his limbs wouldn't obey. Sensing this, the bed whirred softly and shifted, lifting him into a more comfortable sitting position.

From this vantage, he spotted Snjallt and Verjast standing quietly in the far corner, their heads bowed. Around the bed, Rachel, Vilantina, and Aaron stood in a semicircle, faces etched with tension, concern... and relief.

Then a knock.

Soft. Polite.

Eymd pushed the door open, nose buried in one of the massive books she'd brought back from the Library. She didn't even look up.

"There's a guy out here who wants to talk to you," she said, flipping a page. "Says he's the replacement for that vile woman. Seems... nicer."

Orion sighed. "No rest for me, I guess."

Eymd stepped aside, holding the door open with her foot. A tall, sharply dressed man entered slim, composed, with neatly combed brown hair and a clean-pressed military uniform. He paused before Orion's bed, bowed deeply, and then dropped to one knee.

"Forgive the intrusion," he said, voice calm but laced with deference. "I know you're recovering from a very grave wound."

"Indeed I am," Orion replied, narrowing his eyes. "One inflicted by your predecessor, as it happens. I assume you're not here to finish the job?"

The man's eyes widened. "No, sir. Absolutely not. I come with apologies from the planetary council. Most of the leadership... only recently became aware of who you are."

Orion's brow remained furrowed. "And I'm supposed to believe this isn't some new trick?"

"We understand your skepticism," the man replied carefully. "But we ask only for a few minutes of your time. The world's leaders would like to speak with you via a secure link."

Orion exhaled through his nose. "Fine. But I need to wash up first."

"Of course," the man said, standing and bowing once more. As he turned to leave, his gaze caught Vilantina. He blinked.

"Pardon me... ma'am are you... an angel?"

Vilantina's expression turned to steel. "I most certainly am not," she snapped, her tone frosty.

The man blanched, nodded quickly, and retreated without another word.

"Can someone please help me get to a bathroom?" Orion muttered, frustration rising.

Snjallt stepped forward, already pulling a sleek, silver tablet from her satchel. "One moment, sire."

She tapped rapidly across its surface, then pressed it to an empty wall. A soft hum vibrated through the room, and an ornate door materialised, carved with unfamiliar sigils.

"There you are," she said cheerfully. "I added a dressing room, too."

"Much appreciated," Orion said, trying to push himself up again but his arms trembled and gave way.

"Are you all just going to watch me struggle?" he barked.

"Oh! Right," Snjallt said, hurrying to a nearby panel.

With a tap, a soft pulse of light rippled outward, and several humanoid figures began to materialise around Orion's bed. They wore flowing lilac robes, hoods drawn low over their faces, their movements fluid and serene.

They resembled the Kalligah Orion had seen at the palace but these felt gentler. Quieter.

Without a word, one of them leaned down and effortlessly lifted him into their arms.

Inside the chamber, they set him gently into a stone chair, then began undressing him with professional grace. Orion sank into a steaming bath, groaning as the heat soaked into his aching muscles. Three more attendants appeared, working in quiet coordination to wash him from head to toe.

When they reached the black spider-like mark on his shoulder, they paused. With deliberate care, they washed around it without touching the centre.

Orion tried to help by trying to lift his arms, but they flopped back uselessly each time. The attendants said nothing, simply working with precision and patience.

Ten minutes passed. The bath drained itself. Warm jets of air surrounded him, drying him head to toe in seconds.

Then came the robes.

Two attendants dressed him in ceremonial armour elegant, gold-edged, almost too grand for the moment. A royal sash was draped across his chest, and upon it gleamed three emblems: a system of revolving planets, a blue pyramid, and a quill resting atop parchment.

Orion blinked at his reflection as they held up a mirror.

"Are we sure this is mine?"

The lead attendant nodded solemnly, then placed a delicate circlet atop his head.

The transformation complete, they carried him still weak back into the hospital room.

But it was no longer a hospital.

The bed was gone, replaced by a raised throne, its high back carved with celestial patterns. Plush crimson chairs circled it, each occupied by his friends, their heads bowed.

Eymd leaned casually against one arm of the throne, nose still buried in her book.

Vilantina stood at his other side, quill-blade resting against the floor, head bowed in reverence.

The attendants lowered Orion onto the throne, then vanished without a word, dissolving into soft motes of light.

Orion looked around, bemused.

"...Okay," he said. "What's with all the formalities?"

"It was her idea," Eymd replied, not glancing up as she nodded toward Vilantina.

Vilantina straightened slightly, her posture flawless. "We cannot allow the world's leaders to see you in a weakened state, sire. Appearances matter."

Orion chuckled weakly. "Okay, but... they're not even here yet."

"It's about making an impression," Vilantina replied firmly, her gaze sharp and unwavering. "They must remember who you are."

"They're new allies, Vilantina," Orion said, his voice calm but pointed as he leaned slightly forward on the throne. "You need to relax a little."

"But,"

"Relax," Orion said again, this time with quiet authority. His tone left no room for further debate.

Vilantina hesitated, visibly holding back another objection. Then she dipped her head in a crisp nod. "As you wish. Shall we let the general in now?"

Orion exhaled slowly, resting his hands on the ornate armrests. "I suppose it's now or never."

With a sharp clap of her hands, Vilantina activated the door. It opened with a soft hiss, revealing three figures standing just beyond the threshold.

Two winged men stepped forward first tall and statuesque, dressed in perfectly tailored charcoal-grey suits that contrasted with the subtle shimmer of their silver feathers. Their movements were precise, synchronised, as if trained in both diplomacy and battle. They paused just short of the throne, bowed deeply, then moved with silent efficiency to flank Eymd and Vilantina, folding their wings neatly behind them.

Their presence was not decorative. It was ceremonial, calculated a message that this meeting mattered.

Then came the man Orion had spoken with earlier.

He entered alone, composed but visibly humbled by the atmosphere of the room. Gone was the tentative posture from before; now he carried himself with the solemn awareness of standing before something ancient and immeasurable.

Without a word, he approached the base of the dais and dropped to one knee, head bowed low.

His silence spoke volumes respect, recognition, and perhaps a trace of awe.

Unsure of the protocol, Orion glanced between Vilantina and Eymd, his unease flickering just beneath the surface. Eymd, still comfortably propped against the throne and buried in a thick tome, leaned toward him slightly without lifting her eyes.

"Tell him he may rise... and ask for his title," she murmured lazily, turning a page with a flick of her clawed thumb.

Orion swallowed and adjusted his posture on the throne. "You may rise," he said, his voice clear but hesitant, laced with the tremor of someone still growing into power.

The man stood smoothly, adjusting the lapels of his jacket. "Thank you. I am General Thomas Brownwater, representative of the World Council."

"Welcome, General," Orion replied, settling into the cadence of authority. "As you know, I am Intenfli Orion I. Please, take a seat."

With a faint motion of his hand, a sleek obsidian chair shimmered into existence behind the general, who blinked once in surprise before nodding and lowering himself into it with practiced decorum.

"May my technicians bring in the equipment necessary for the World Council to speak with you?" the general asked, his hands folding neatly in his lap.

Before Orion could respond, Snjallt cleared her throat gently from one of the surrounding chairs. "If I may, Your Highness?"

Orion nodded toward her. "Of course, Snjallt."

She rose gracefully, tablet in hand. "We would find it more efficient to conduct a holographic meeting with the world's leaders. The systems in this facility can be modified to handle multidimensional communications."

The general furrowed his brow. "I don't believe we possess that level of technology."

"That won't be an issue," Snjallt replied smoothly. "All I need is a few moments with your technicians to make the necessary adjustments."

After a brief pause, the general nodded, visibly intrigued. "Very well. Proceed."

Snjallt swept from the room, her crystalline braid swinging like a pendulum behind her, with one of the technicians trailing after her, muttering to himself in awe. The door slid shut with a soft click, leaving behind a silence that felt heavier than before.

General Brownwater shifted uncomfortably in his seat, his gaze flicking between Orion and Vilantina. When his eyes finally met Orion's, he offered a faint smile thin, unsure.

"If I may," he began, his voice tentative, "I would like to apologise for my predecessor's actions."

Vilantina bristled. Her wings rustled with subtle agitation, and the tip of her quill-blade tapped the polished floor like a metronome of judgment. Orion raised a hand calmly, forestalling her retort.

"It is kind of you to say," he said with measured poise. "I hope the World Council shares your sentiment."

"I cannot speak for all," the general admitted. "But I know Her Majesty the Queen wishes to rebuild trust and form an alliance with your people. She has not forgotten the assistance provided in the past."

Orion's brow creased. "Forgive me. My knowledge of my people's history is... incomplete. What do you mean by 'the past'?"

Before the general could answer, the door reopened. Snjallt returned, her expression neutral and efficient, the technician behind her blinking in stunned silence. She resumed her seat and gave Orion a small, affirming nod.

"Right," Orion said, exhaling deeply. "I suppose we should get this over with."

He clapped his hands once, and the hospital room dissolved around them. In its place, a grand circular chamber emerged, vast and luminous. At its heart stood a majestic throne of starlit obsidian, surrounded by a semicircle of high-backed chairs reserved for his council. Opposite them, an arc of smaller, dignified seats awaited the representatives of the World Council. Towering above the throne, a massive banner unfurled itself, bearing the royal insignia of the Xerist Galaxy flanked by three other crests: one depicting revolving planets, another a glowing blue pyramid, and the last a quill poised atop an ancient scroll.

General Brownwater's mouth parted in awe as he took in the awe-inspiring scene. His gaze lingered upon the royal banner, reverence blooming across his features.

"General," Orion said, politely drawing the man back to the present. "Are you prepared?"

The general blinked, gathering his composure. "Yes, Your Majesty. Forgive my momentary lapse. Might I make one small request? Could one of the chairs be replaced with a throne appropriate for Her Majesty the Queen?"

Orion nodded. "Of course." With a mere snap of his fingers, an identical throne materialised beside his own, positioned to reflect equality and mutual respect.

"When you are ready, General."

The general murmured into the communicator strapped to his wrist. When he concluded, he straightened his uniform with ceremonial precision and raised his voice.

"Introducing Her Royal Highness, Queen Alexandria II." He bowed deeply.

A regal figure shimmered into existence upon the newly summoned throne. Queen Alexandria sat poised in a dignified royal blue gown that glimmered like starlight. A modest, glistening tiara crowned her silver hair. Orion inclined his head respectfully, and his council followed suit, bowing with measured reverence.

The general approached the Queen's throne, bowing once more. "Her Majesty wishes to confer privately with Your Majesty before the remaining world leaders are connected."

"By all means," Orion said, gesturing with an open palm.

The Queen rose and crossed the chamber, every movement a study in measured elegance. She stopped before Orion's throne and met his gaze directly.

"Your Majesty," Orion greeted her solemnly.

"Your Majesty," she returned, her voice warm, with a tempered regality.

"It is an honour to stand in your presence," Orion said, his tone reflecting the quiet dignity he had come to master.

"The honour is mine," she replied. "And with it, I bring my sincerest apologies for the wrongs committed under the banner of my Crown."

Orion's voice remained even. "I believe those actions were those of your Prime Minister. Nevertheless, I appreciate your candour. My hope is that we may move forward toward an alliance that benefits both Earth and those under my protection."

The Queen's gaze flickered over his council Vilantina's serene strength, Eymd's silent defiance, Snjallt's composed intellect. She gave no outward sign of surprise, only a thoughtful nod.

"I believed it best to address this matter in person. Our peoples share more history than you may yet know."

"Forgive me, Your Majesty," Orion said, head tilting slightly, "but I am unaware of this shared past."

"Then allow me," she said with a gentle smile, "to enlighten you."

Snjallt rose from her chair and inclined her head politely. "Pardon the interruption, Your Majesties. If Her Majesty is willing, I can project the memory for all to witness."

The Queen considered for a moment, then gave a graceful nod. "Yes. Please proceed."

Snjallt made a delicate gesture, and the chamber dissolved into memory. The walls became bookshelves, the light dimmed to a royal study bathed in afternoon glow. A younger Queen Alexandria sat behind her desk. Across from her, a blue-haired man shimmered into being, seated with perfect stillness.

"Forgive the intrusion," he said, his voice resonant, deep with ancient wisdom. "I come only to request a moment of your time."

The Queen's hand moved instinctively toward the bell, then halted as her eyes met his. "How did you get in here without alerting my guards?" she demanded, her tone sharp with alarm.

"My race has no need for doors," the man explained. "What you see is a projection. My true self resides millions of your miles away."

"And who are you?" she asked, lowering her hand.

"I am Intenfli Auren I Admiral of the Xerist Fleet, High Commander of the X1 Army, and Stone Guard of the Eternal Seat. I sat at this exact desk with your father, King George VI."

"You've met my father?" she asked, astonishment overtaking caution.

"And his father before him. Four monarchs, in fact," Auren replied calmly.

"I assume this is not a mere courtesy call," she said.

"No, Your Majesty. I come with an offer of alliance continued protection of your realm in exchange for sanctuary for one not yet born."

As he spoke, a scroll-like document shimmered into existence before the Queen, hovering gently above her desk. She reached forward, took it with regal grace, and began to read. Her eyes scanned the elegant alien script that reconfigured itself into English as she looked on. Line by line, the nature of the proposed agreement unfolded mutual protection, shared knowledge, and a solemn vow of guardianship for a future child of Auren's bloodline. When she reached the final clause, she looked up slowly, her brow furrowed in thought.

"In exchange, you offer technology? Military protection?"

"Yes. Though we would freely give, our laws now require reciprocity."

"Why Earth?" she asked.

Auren's voice softened. "Because your world has long been under our care. And because nowhere else will he be safe."

The Queen stood slowly and approached him, studying his face with practiced insight. "I will consider your offer. My Prime Minister will want to weigh in."

Auren inclined his head, his expression serene. "Then I suggest you summon him without delay he is already expecting your call."

She lifted the receiver. "Connect me to the Prime Minister... Yes, about a visitor named Auren..." She paused, listening.

"I trust everything is in order?" Auren inquired, his tone courteous yet purposeful.

The Queen's gaze lingered for a moment, then she exhaled softly, placing the receiver back on its cradle. A silence stretched between them measured, thoughtful.

"Yes," the Queen said at last, her voice steady. "I must say, you are braver than I."

Auren tilted his head. "How so, Your Majesty?"

"I do not think I could send my only child so far away," she admitted gently, her regal composure momentarily slipping to reveal the mother beneath.

Auren's expression turned wistful. "The crown we bear is often a heavy burden," he said. "Be careful how you balance being a Queen, a wife, and a mother."

With those final words, Auren rose from his chair. His image flickered once, the blue shimmer of his projection dissolving into the golden light of the memory.

The royal study faded like mist at dawn, and the grand council chamber reformed around them its banners billowing faintly as if stirred by unseen winds.

The present-day Queen turned to Orion, her voice gentler now. "I should have heeded your father's words more closely," she said. "But I offer you the same wisdom now, and a hand of renewed alliance."

Orion straightened upon his throne, the weight of history coiling around his shoulders.

"Thank you, Your Majesty," he said. "It seems our destinies have been entangled longer than I ever imagined."

"Indeed," she replied, her voice carrying both gravity and grace. "And now, we must shepherd that destiny with vigilance. The world teeters on the brink fractured, uncertain its leaders seduced by the illusions cast by the Great Four. But where chaos seeks to divide, unity must rise to mend. Shall we speak with them, and remind them what true leadership demands?"

"Yes," Orion declared, his voice rich with regal command. "Let the world bear witness to what unity can restore.

# 11. The Council

The chamber shimmered, signalling the arrival of new participants. Across from Orion's throne, chairs lit up one by one with flickering holograms presidents, prime ministers, chancellors all garbed in formal attire, faces stern beneath the ceremonial calm. A low murmur swept through the hall as they took in the chamber's opulence... and the young ruler seated at its heart.

Orion sat straighter, disguising the strain it took. Moments earlier, Vilantina had handed him a slender walking stick carved from luminescent starwood and tipped with a stabilising crystal. "To make the rise less dramatic," she'd whispered, her voice half-mocking, half-concerned. He hadn't wanted it, but he hadn't argued. The hours since his resurrection had left his body frail, and pride alone couldn't support him.

Now, the stick rested lightly beside his throne, not a symbol of weakness, but of survival.

"Your Majesties, presidents, councillors, and esteemed leaders," the Queen began, her voice poised and clear, "I present to you Intenfli Orion I of the Xerist Galaxy guardian of a legacy that has safeguarded Earth across generations. Let us receive him not with suspicion, but with the gravity such history demands."

The murmurs stilled. All eyes turned to Orion. Though he felt the weight of their scrutiny, he met it with unwavering calm, regal and resolute.

"Thank you, Your Majesty," Orion said, inclining his head with grace before addressing the room. "To those who question my arrival, I say this: I did not come here seeking dominion, conquest, or control. In truth, returning to Earth was never my intention. But circumstances beyond my control forces older than even your oldest histories brought me back. And now that I am here, I choose to stand

before you in transparency, not subterfuge. My people have shielded
Earth from afar, asking only one thing in return protection for me."

Whispers spread through the gathering quieter this time, laced
with curiosity.

A middle-aged president leaned forward, his image flickering.
"Then why reveal yourselves now? If your people have remained
hidden all this time, what's changed?"

Orion held his gaze. "Because the world has already begun to
suffer. The Great Four are not distant myths or looming shadows
they have scorched worlds in their hunt for me. Cities lost, alliances
shattered, entire systems turned to dust as they seek to erase my
bloodline. Their wrath has now turned toward Earth, and your world
stands in their path. The Great Four are no longer approaching they
are here. My presence is not merely diplomatic. It is a warning."

Another figure a chancellor with cutting eyes cut in. "And yet
your timing feels... convenient. Earth is reeling from recent
devastation, panic spreads, and then a galactic heir appears offering
protection. Forgive my bluntness, but how do we know this isn't all
orchestrated? That you didn't bring these threats here yourself?"

Beside him, Vilantina shifted tense, ready but Orion gently
raised a hand, stilling her.

"I understand your doubt," he said evenly. "That's why I come
offering not commands, but partnership. An alliance. We bring
technology, medicine, energy systems advancements that could
elevate your societies by centuries. In return, we ask that Earth
becomes a sanctuary, not just for my people, but for any being in
need."

The Queen stood then, her presence commanding. "Let us not
forget the shared history between Earth and the Xerists. My
great-grandmother forged the first bonds of trust. Shall we now
abandon them, in humanity's hour of need?"

The silence that followed was deeper, the atmosphere thickening with unspoken tension.

The first president spoke again. "The Great Four what are they, exactly? And why should we believe they pose such danger?"

Orion straightened. "They are not nations, or armies. They are elemental forces harbingers of ruin who've dismantled civilisations more advanced than your own."

Another prime minister's voice rang out, cool and precise. "Then name them. Tell us what exactly we're facing."

Orion rose slowly, his voice low and firm.

"There is the Conqueror a force of relentless expansion, assimilating all in its path. The Harvester, which strips planets bare, leaving only lifeless husks. The Scourge, who exists only to destroy, sowing ruin for the thrill of collapse. And the Corrupter perhaps the deadliest of all. She undermines from within, turning nations against themselves until they crumble under the weight of their own rot."

A collective shiver moved through the room. A few holograms dimmed briefly, as if reflecting the unease of their occupants.

The skeptical president leaned forward again, his voice more cautious now. "These sound like myths. How can we know they're real? That Earth is truly at risk?"

Orion's gaze hardened slightly. "I wish they were myths. But their ships now orbit your world. The Old Ones tried to redirect a cosmic portal intended to cast me into a dying sun, a last resort to stop what was coming. But in doing so, they miscalculated. Their intervention hurled me here instead. Even they could not foresee where I would land. My arrival on Earth was never part of the plan. And yet, that accident has turned your planet into a target."

A chancellor's voice rang out: "And your people? What do they ask? What's the true cost of this alliance?"

Orion's response was steady. "No cost. Only cooperation. In return for sanctuary, we offer cures for your deadliest diseases, the end of hunger, the healing of your broken ecosystems. And above all, we invite Earth to take its place on the Council a seat among the worlds we protect."

A prime minister raised a skeptical eyebrow. "That sounds idealistic. Trust must be earned. How do we know this isn't... a veiled takeover?"

Orion met her gaze with quiet gravity. "You don't. Not yet. But I ask for a chance to prove my word. Watch what we offer. Judge us by our actions."

At that, the general from earlier stepped forward, voice like steel. "Then show us. Demonstrate what you speak of, Your Majesty."

Orion nodded. "Snjallt."

The room shifted as Snjallt glided forward, serene yet powerful. She extended her hand, summoning a glowing orb.

"This is a fondama," she said. "A device that transforms raw matter into what a community needs food, medicine, shelter."

She gestured, and the orb floated to the floor. In seconds, a medical clinic shimmered into existence clean, detailed, complete. Gasps echoed through the hall.

Snjallt continued calmly, "This is but one example. Imagine its use after earthquakes, floods, famine. We do not offer miracles. We offer solutions."

Now the room stirred with new energy. The Queen turned to Orion, a smile just touching her lips. "You've captured their attention, Your Majesty."

Orion gave the barest of nods. "Then let us begin the true discussion."

Voices rose not in anger, but in inquiry, collaboration. Snjallt continued her demonstrations. Eymd moved silently, noting tension points and allies forming in real time. Slowly, suspicion gave way to strategy.

A voice rose a president from a developing nation, her tone firm yet earnest. "And what of those like us? So often, when the world advances, the poor are left behind. Will this be any different?"

Orion leaned forward, eyes warm. "You speak truth. I vow that this partnership uplifts all. The Council I form will ensure voices like yours are not only heard but centred."

The woman nodded, faintly but sincerely. Around her, more leaders followed suit.

Finally, the Queen raised a hand. "The time has come. Shall we proceed with drafting a formal treaty?"

The answer came not in words, but in a cascade of nods reluctant from some, resolute from others, but united.

The general stepped forward once more. "Then we begin. Together."

And so, as hours passed, the treaty was written an alliance forged in desperation, but sealed in hope. Mutual respect, technological collaboration, and Earth's sovereignty formed its pillars.

Orion sat quietly for a moment, observing them not as a ruler, but as a guardian of possibility. And in the faces of these uncertain leaders, he saw the beginning of something rare:

Unity.

When the final draft was complete, the Queen rose with deliberate grace. Her voice, though calm, rang with historic significance. "The treaty is ready. Shall we proceed to the signing?"

Orion stood from his throne, the light glinting off his golden armour, catching in the fine etchings of celestial runes that shimmered faintly with power. "Let it be so," he said, his tone solemn.

A large crystalline table materialised in the centre of the chamber, humming softly with ancient magic. Above it hovered a rotating holographic projection of the treaty its glowing script shifting between languages, a symbol of universal inclusion.

Surrounding the chamber were floating orbs of light, each projecting a live feed of the proceedings to every major planetary station and broadcast network. The signing was being televised in real time, an intentional act of transparency meant to erase any doubt about the unity forming within these walls.

One by one, the leaders stepped forward kings, presidents, empresses each placing their hand over the projection. Their names appeared in radiant script, lingering in the air like constellations before fading into the pact itself. The chamber was silent but charged, the air thick with the weight of centuries of distrust now poised to give way to unity.

When the Queen approached, she turned to Orion with a look that held both steel and warmth. "Together, Your Majesty, may we build a better future."

She pressed her hand to the document. A pulse of light blazed from her signature, casting soft shadows across the chamber's grand walls.

Then Orion stepped forward, and the air seemed to still.

He placed his palm over the treaty. A surge of energy burst outward brilliant and golden rippling through the walls, through the very architecture of the chamber, sealing the accord not just in ink, but in essence.

"It is done," he declared, his voice low yet resonant, like thunder wrapped in velvet. "Let this alliance stand as a testament to what we can achieve when trust triumphs over fear, and understanding over division."

The chamber erupted in applause. Leaders rose from their seats, some visibly moved, others nodding with solemn approval. History had been made, and the whole galaxy had witnessed it.

As the holographic meeting dissolved and the chamber gently faded back into the muted tones of the hospital room, the weight of it all settled on Orion's shoulders. He slumped back into the throne-like medical chair, golden armour now feeling heavier with fatigue than glory.

Vilantina leaned toward him, eyes gleaming with a rare softness. "You handled that remarkably well."

"I had help," Orion murmured, casting a glance toward the companions who had stood by him through war, exile, and betrayal. His eyes briefly met Rachel's, then Eymd's. "This is just the first step. The real work... starts now."

Eymd crossed her arms and leaned against the edge of the room, a playful smirk tugging at her lips. "You'll be fine. Besides, you've got us to keep you in line."

Orion gave a dry chuckle. "That, Eymd, is what worries me most."

Laughter followed, light and fleeting but behind Orion's smile, his mind was already spinning. Earth's leaders had signed a treaty, yes, but paper and light were fragile things. Lasting peace would demand sacrifice, vigilance, and faith.

Still, for the first time in a long while, he let himself exhale. The door had opened. The journey toward unity had begun.

And in the quiet that followed, for just a moment, hope felt real.

The stars hung quiet and cold above London, pinpricks of pale fire set against a velvet sky. Their light barely caressed the half-rebuilt skyline, where skeletal towers pierced the low clouds like defiant scars. Only days before, this had been a charred husk: smouldering monuments to ruin, black ash drifting on a sulphurous breeze. Now, as Orion returned his first glimpse since their desperate flight he found the wreckage transformed. Xersist energy, liquid silver and violet, pulsed along girders and bridge cables, bathing steel and concrete in an otherworldly glow that shimmered against the night.

Reconstruction teams moved like a single organism across the expanse. Humans in steel-toed boots, sleek Xersist constructs with translucent joints, and hybridised Shadow drones with glinting carapaces laboured shoulder to mechanical shoulder. Sparks showered from welders' torches, illuminating dust motes that danced in converging shafts of light. Big Ben's clock face, shattered and forlorn, now bore a latticework of pale crystalline plating, its hands frozen in time yet crowned with refracted rainbows no longer a relic of the old world, but a beacon of what could rise from its ashes.

Orion stood amid the hum of generators and the hiss of pneumatic drills, shoulders slumped under exhaustion that burrowed into his bones. Three days ago this ground was a crater of despair, the air electric with hopelessness. Now drones zipped between scaffolded spires like silver insects; World Council engineers in cobalt vests directed operations through holo-displays that flickered with rune-like symbols. Each new circuit laid beneath concrete was a declaration: We will rise.

But inside him, something fractured. A dull ache throbbed beneath ribs still tender from the god-destroyer bullet wounds sealed in the healing pod, yet haunted by phantom pangs that crept like cold fingers over scar tissue. Every breath felt weighted, as if the air itself conspired to rob him of hope.

That morning, Snjallt had come to his bunk, her violet eyes heavy with regret. "You may never fully recover," she whispered, her voice softer than rain on glass. Fingers hovering above the jagged line etched across his side. "That weapon wasn't meant just to kill. It was built to erase. Part of you your light went with it."

He had offered no reply. Words tasted like ash in his throat. Yet beneath bone-tired grief, a faint ember of purpose glowed. The trials still awaited him the ancient rites Akhenaten had spoken of in half-forgotten prophecy, hidden within the star-temples buried beneath shifting dunes. Rites to purge, to awaken, to test an Intenfli's soul to its very brink.

He did not yet know the price they would demand. But he knew their purpose: for family, for those still lost to the Great Four's labyrinthine realms, for the mother whose name he'd barely breathed in weeks.

Behind him, holo-screens hovered like restless spirits. Johannesburg's southern ward pulsed with newborn power; Tokyo's vertical farms unfurled leaves beneath azure grow-lights. Even Detroit once a tomb of hollow towers now throbbed with revived transformers and humming cables. Across the globe, streaks of Xersist-lifted energy wove a lattice of renewal.

A new transmission lit the air with crystalline clarity. The Arctic Council proposed an intercontinental ecological restoration hub, and behind the speaker the World Council's emblem twelve luminous stars encircling a spiralling nebula, Earth at its heart glowed with solemn promise.

"The Council's pleased," Rachel's voice came, crisp as frost on metal. She joined him at the array, arms wrapped around herself against the chill. "They're calling this the Second Renaissance."

Orion let out a breath that fogged the holo-surface. "It's more than a renaissance," he murmured. "It's a second chance we never earned."

She tipped her head, frost glinting on her lashes. "But we'll take it, anyway. That's what survival looks like now."

Her gaze softened. "They want you to chair the next summit in Geneva, four days from now. You think you can manage?"

He stiffened, jaw clenched. "I'll be there. Even if I have to crawl across every continent."

A low hum resonated through the hangar bay as a craft descended. Its hull was burnished silver, wings folding like steel petals. Emblazoned on its flank was the new crest of Earth's defence: a phoenix spiralling through a ring of stars. No more D.E.T.A. They'd rechristened it at Rachel's insistence: the Earth Defence Accord. E.D.A. now stood for unity rather than fear a subtle shift that felt like prayer.

"I still can't believe they listened," Orion admitted, a half-smile tugging at his lips.

Rachel grinned, breath pluming between them. "You're an Intenfli. And Aaron's charm should be illegal."

Just then, Captain Aaron Cole stepped down the ramp, uniform immaculate, boots clicking against the deck. His presence was calm strength incarnate; his eyes immediately sought Orion's.

Rachel gave Orion a playful nudge. "Your date's arrived."

Orion's cheeks warmed. "Stop it."

She laughed and drifted away. "Have fun, Egg."

Aaron moved toward him with deliberate ease, as though gravity itself bent to his will. "You ready?" he asked softly.

Orion met his gaze. "Yeah. Somewhere quiet?"

A gentle smile curved Aaron's lips. "I know the perfect place."

They boarded the silver craft again, gliding north to a secluded cliff above the Welsh coast. The air here smelled of brine and damp moss; wind scoured the rock with salty hiss. The sky was bruised in twilight purples and molten gold, the sun's last embers seeping into darkening clouds. Below, breakers thrashed against basalt pinnacles, sending shards of spray into the air. Behind them, distant lights from a budding settlement flickered like fireflies homes and workshops rising on the wild land, lifeblood carried in veins of Xersist tech.

Aaron offered Orion a canteen of synthesised cider, droplets glinting in the fading light. They drank in silence, letting the hush of sea and wind settle around them like a cloak.

Finally, Orion spoke, voice low and trembling. "When I was in that pod... I could hear you."

Aaron blinked, heart stuttering. "What?"

Orion's gaze drifted toward the rolling waves. "You'd slip in at St. Thomas', thinking no one was listening. You told me stories tales of the seer, lullabies you hummed. Even in that emptiness, your voice stayed with me."

The air stilled. Aaron's hand, warm and steady, found Orion's. "I didn't know you heard any of it."

Orion turned to him, eyes luminous in the dusk. "I did. And... thank you. You helped bring me back."

Aaron's throat tightened. "I'm just glad you came back at all."

They sat side by side, two souls unadorned by rank or legend, listening to the ocean's slow hymn. Orion rested his head on Aaron's shoulder, eyelids fluttering shut as the wind whispered reassurance through pine and heather.

"I don't know if I'll ever be whole again," he murmured.

Aaron squeezed his hand. "Maybe not. But you're here. And that's enough for me."

Time stretched between them, filled only with breath, warmth, and the rhythmic crash of waves reshaping the shore.

When Orion raised his head, moonlight crowned his face in silver. "I wonder if my mother can see this from orbit."

Aaron's gaze followed the curve of the sky. "Do you think she's still watching?"

"I hope so. I hope she knows we're trying... that I haven't given up on her."

A breeze tugged at Orion's coat, carrying the distant cry of some woodland creature half wild, half familiar, as if the planet itself exhaled relief. In that stillness, a vow kindled in his chest: he would finish the trials, reclaim the power the Old Ones meant for him, and with that strength, scour every realm to rescue his family. No matter how deep the darkness, he would light the way.

And that promise, bright and unyielding, burned in his bones like a star come alive.

As the ship levelled out above the churning Welsh coastline, Orion let the silence stretch between them. Aaron had taken the controls again, but his eyes kept flicking toward Orion as if afraid to break the fragile stillness.

Outside the viewport, seabirds danced along the cliff winds, and waves roared below, battering the rocks in endless defiance. It was a world in motion, but here in this metal cocoon, time seemed to pause.

"I used to come here," Orion said suddenly, voice distant. "Before everything. Before I knew who I was. My foster dad would take us camping near here. Me and my brothers."

Aaron glanced at him, silent.

"There was this night... we'd stayed up late by the fire. Anton had fallen asleep with marshmallow in his hair," Orion's lips curled faintly, memory tugging at the corner of his mouth. "And Lawrence my foster dad he looked at me and said, 'You'll always be the one they follow. Just be sure you're leading them somewhere worth going.'"

The words hung in the air, carved from something deeper than nostalgia. Aaron didn't respond he didn't need to. He just reached over and gently clasped Orion's hand.

"I wish I could've known them," Aaron said softly.

"You will," Orion replied, eyes not leaving the window. "If I can bring them home."

Later that night, long after they'd returned to the heart of London, Orion sat on the jagged edge of a broken rooftop overlooking the Thames. The city, half-buried in scaffolding and radiant with Xersist scaffolding-glow, shimmered beneath a canopy of silver stars. Smoke curled in lazy spirals from distant fusion welders, and above it all, the night sky stretched wide and clear, the moon high and cold.

Behind him, the ship's soft lights glowed like a heartbeat, steady and persistent.

Snjallt emerged from the shadows without a sound, her arms folded, cloak whispering against the wind.

"You shouldn't be out here alone," she said, but there was no reprimand in her tone.

Orion didn't look back. "I can't sleep."

"Your body needs rest."

"My mind won't let it."

She approached, settling beside him. For a moment, they simply listened to the sea. Then, softly, Snjallt spoke.

"You remember what I told you... that you may never fully recover."

Orion nodded.

"I was wrong," she said, surprising him. "You might never be the same but I believe you will recover. You are becoming something new."

He turned to her, brow furrowed. "Something new?"

"Yes. That's what the wound did it didn't break you. It changed you."

She reached into her coat and withdrew a slim crystal, swirling with pale green light. "This is part of your next trial. When the time comes, press it against the Gate of Echoes in Mali. It will know your blood. It will open."

Orion took it, the crystal warm in his hand.

"I won't fail," he said quietly.

"I don't believe you will," Snjallt said, her voice lighter than he'd ever heard it. "But even if you do, you'll rise again. That's what you do."

Back inside, as Orion rejoined Aaron, Rachel, and Eymd in the map room projected Earth glowing between them there was a new fire behind his eyes. His voice was steadier. His back straighter. He pointed at the glowing triangle that marked the West African threshold.

"We leave for Mali at first light."

Eymd raised a brow. "You sure your body's ready?"

"No," Orion said, a grin tugging at the corner of his mouth. "But my spirit is."

Rachel crossed her arms. "And what if it's a trap? What if the Gate isn't just a door but a test?"

Orion locked eyes with her. "Then I pass."

Aaron gave a low whistle. "Remind me never to bet against you."

Rachel exhaled slowly, then tapped her comm. "I'll inform the Council that you won't be attending the Geneva summit. If they want answers, they can wait until you're done saving the planet."

The moment hung fragile, powerful.

And then, from above, the beacon lit red.

A transmission.

Aaron moved to the console, his face tensing as he scanned the message. "It's a World Council override," he muttered. "Geneva is under siege."

Everyone turned toward Orion.

His jaw clenched.

"They're forcing our hand."

Rachel stood. "Then let's remind them who we are."

Orion nodded. "Pack everything. Tonight... we fly."

# 12. The Geneva Siege

The Geneva skyline twisted against the dying sun's bruised gold, each turret and spire etched in molten shadow. Once a cradle of peace, the city now throbbed with a tortured heartbeat anxious tremors rippling through charred streets. Overhead, clouds curled like swelling wounds, veins of thunder and static pulsing through the air. Something ancient slithered toward them, as precise as a surgeon's scalpel and as inexorable as the void.

Orion crouched at the prow of the Shadow-class skimmer, the lake's icy breath lashing at his cloak. Frost clung to his gauntleted fingers as one hand gripped the frost-bitten railing; the other clasped the obsidian-black cane Snjallt had forged from star-shard. Its surface rippled with engraved runes, each glyph a faint pulse beneath the darkness, a silent heartbeat echoing his own. At its tip, the star-crystal gleamed like captured starlight, humming rhythmic and hypnotic with every ragged breath he drew.

"It'll anchor you," Snjallt's ember-low whisper had promised. "You can't call the stars, but you can echo their song. Let the cane carry you."

He had said nothing, mindful that his power remained scattered shards dying sparks that nonetheless could ignite apocalypse when willed.

Beside him, Rachel snapped the clasps on her armoured vest into place. The Earth Defence Authority crest gleamed across her chest like a stark warning. Her eyes, hard and obsidian-bright, never strayed from the battered horizon.

"Fray's forward units are online," she reported in clipped tones. She flicked a wrist, and a holo-projection shimmered into existence: a translucent overlay of rooftops and alleyways. "Snipers on perches. Recon drones combing the gaps. Civilians are being funnelled into evacuation corridors, but the grid's spiking comms are faltering under heavy interference."

"A Hand?" Orion rasped, voice raw with foreboding.

Rachel's jaw tightened. "No. Worse. An engineered spectre among assassins crafted for surgical eradication rather than brute force."

He nodded, lips thinning into steel. "A predator."

"And you're its prey," she replied softly. "But you won't face it alone."

The skimmer glided onto the lakeside platform like a great black cat padding toward its kill. Its doors hissed open, and E.D.A. agents poured out silhouetted sentinels in matte-black armour, masks blank and unreadable, plasma rifles vibrating with latent fury. They fanned out in silent columns, each movement precise as clockwork.

From the scorched ruins of a once-proud monument emerged Assistant Director Fray no longer the weary social worker Orion had known, but a tactician carved of iron and sacrifice. His eyes glittered like flint in the gathering gloom.

"Gamma through Kappa squads deployed," Fray intoned, and between them bloomed a three-dimensional holo-map of Place des Nations. A lattice of sectors glowed: six through nine marked in pulsing red. "Sniper nets active. Medic drones on standby along Avenue Blanc. Target displays no verbal cues already four kills, no discernible pattern, no warning."

Rachel nodded, a single crisp motion. "It's waiting in the square."

Fray's finger stabbed the air. "Thermal spikes every thirty-two seconds. It hunts with patience."

Orion's gaze swept the desolate plaza. The Broken Chair statue loomed like a fractured sentinel, ivory bones against ash-grey sky. Buildings slumped like wounded beasts, their walls blistered, windows splintered into jagged teeth. Silence pressed in a hollow void punctured only by the low thrum of emergency generators and distant drone rotors.

Then a scream shredded the hush, weaving through the air like poisoned silk. It did not crash in; it unspooled, thread by thread, until a figure emerged: a humanoid silhouette dressed in matte-black armour that seemed woven from pure shadow. Its limbs stretched at impossible angles, movements fluid and predatory. A smooth, featureless mask concealed its face, save for a single red slit that pulsed with lethal intent.

Blades slithered from its forearms sickle-curved, wickedly sharp, catching the dying light in sickly glints. It paused, head tilting as though savouring the moment before the kill.

"Hold formation! Evasive triangle ready!" Rachel's command cut through the chaos like shale.

Agents levelled their rifles, plasma bolts hissing earthward, but the assassin was faster than memory. It blurred through their ranks, a living shadow, and silver blades flashed in staccato arcs. Armour split, flesh rent; screams extinguished in metallic ruffles. Gunfire erupted, detonations mingling with agonised wails.

Fray dove behind a scorched security rig, eyes aflame with strategy. Rachel's wrist bloomed a rippling energy shield, each bolt of plasma sizzling against its surface. "Left flank, reposition! Funnel it this way!"

Behind cover, Snjallt lobbed three stasis grenades. They blossomed in cerulean rings, tendrils of ice spreading like frost on glass. The assassin flowed around them, undeterred, its lithe form slipping through azure mist.

Orion hesitated only a heartbeat before stepping off the skimmer's prow. "Not yet!" Snjallt's warning crackled through his comms. "You're not ready"

He planted the cane anyway. Underfoot, a corona of golden fire detonated. Scorch marks spidered across the plaza as celestial runes bled outward, each glyph aflame with raw starfire his true name inscribed in radiant fury.

The assassin reeled, its armour fracturing like black glass. Rachel's shout rang out: "Now!"

Fray's calm command followed: "Squad Delta, left pincer engage!"

The creature spun, blades arcing in a deadly dance, but in that frost-sharp instant its fluid grace faltered. A flicker of doubt an algorithm misread.

Orion lifted the cane high. Light siphoned up its shaft, fed by memories of blood and betrayal and loss: Akhenaten's bloodied sacrifice, Anton's vanishing shadow, every wound that had hollowed him. Grief and rage coalesced into a lance of golden fire that slammed into the assassin's chest. The mask spider-webbed; black ichor hissed like acid.

With a roar, Rachel vaulted onto the machine's back, her energy blade carving a white-hot gouge between its shoulder blades. It bucked, joints whining as steel shivered.

Fray advanced, rifle levelled, and a single nullifier round tore through its spine. Sparks danced as suppression tech bloomed in a crescendo of kinetic light.

Snjallt and Vilantina closed in, the cryo-prism blossoming around the assassin in fractal ice. Within heartbeats, its limbs were locked in crystalline stasis, tremors frozen in time.

Silence reclaimed the plaza. Steam spiralled from cracked stones; the acrid scent of ozone and singed metal hung heavy in the chill air. The cane's glow dimmed, embers guttering among the wreckage.

Orion swayed; Snjallt caught him gently. "You're burning yourself out a match masquerading as a star."

He stared at the immobilised spectre, chest heaving. "Then let me burn long enough to end this."

Rachel knelt, soot and adrenaline smudged under her eyes. "This was no random strike. It was a reckoning to gauge how shattered you truly are."

Fray stepped forward, eyes sweeping the bruised skyline. "They're watching. Not for your triumph, but to see if you'll break."

Orion wrapped his fingers around the cane's shaft like a talisman. Each breath hammered steel. "Then we'll show them I never will."

Above, the wounded clouds roiled, and distant stars pulsed in silent witness to the fire still burning in his veins.

# 13. Trial Of Guilt

The skimmer slid down through torrid air, its black hull absorbing the sun's blaze until it shimmered like molten night. The engines fell silent, and only the desert's lament remained: a swirl of wind and sand, whispering of ancient fires and buried memories.

On the rocky plateau, the ruined temple of Mali yawned like an open wound. Its spiral of sandstone steps cut into shadow, each tread polished by centuries of hidden truths. Along the lip, alien glyphs throbbed in a hesitant rhythm: at once a dare, a plea, a curse.

Orion stood at the ramp's mouth, cloak snapping in the heat-heavy breeze. His heart pounded, torn between dread and determination. Behind him, Aaron's hand rested on his shoulder: steady, warm, impossible.

"How are you holding up?" Aaron asked, voice tight with something between concern and restraint.

Orion forced a crooked smile, brittle as frost. "Terrible," he admitted. "But I stopped lying about it weeks ago."

Aaron stepped closer, eyes glinting with unspoken worry. "You don't have to pretend with me. Just come back."

Confusion churned in Orion's chest. He wanted to believe the words, to lean into that promise. Yet each breath carried the weight of every soul he couldn't save. "I'm not sure who I'll be afterward," he rasped.

Aaron's grip tightened, grounding him. "Then let us meet the future together. We'll find you in the pieces."

Orion's throat clenched at the raw hope in Aaron's tone, and at the fear that he might shatter if he let it in. "In the pod," he whispered, "when I thought I was gone, your voice was the only anchor."

Aaron brushed back a lock of Orion's hair, hands trembling. "Then let it pull you back again," he said. "Remember what Vilantina showed you, how each of them stood by your side, even in the dark. They never left you. None of us did. You weren't alone then, and you never have been."

They pressed foreheads, and for a moment the world stilled. No grand vows, just two souls refusing to drift.

Footsteps echoed behind them. Snjallt descended, her cloak a cascade of midnight wind. "It's time," she said simply.

Orion inhaled sharply. He lingered on Aaron's hand, its warmth defying fate, then turned.

Snjallt's eyes held no judgment, only truth. "You go alone. The temple tests souls, not strength. If you try to bring another, it will spit you out or worse."

He nodded, though terror and resolve danced bitterly within him. "How will I know if I pass?"

"You'll return."

He stepped onto the spiral, each tread a whisper of doubt beneath his boots. The light faded behind him, swallowed by the deep curve of the descent. A strange quiet claimed the air, as if even the wind outside dared not follow him here.

Ancient murals emerged from the dim: depictions of warriors, kings, and shadows that walked like men. One scene caught his eye, a being with starlight in its chest reaching out to a dying world. He recognised the gesture. He had made it.

The steps ended in a chamber shaped like a heart, vast and pulsing with dormant power. Crystalline walls arched inward, their surfaces entwined with star dust and Star magic, shimmering faintly as if breathing. They encased a mirror that floated in stillness. It radiated no heat, no light, only challenge.

The glyphs overhead pulsed once, slow and rhythmic, like a heart learning to beat.

"Face yourself," a voice intoned, old as the stars. "Or be consumed by your burden."

Orion approached. The air smelled of ash and something older, his past. As he stepped before the glass, it rippled, distorting, and then settled.

A figure stood across from him. It was himself, but wrong.

The reflection wore perfect armour, unmarred by battle or grief. Its stance screamed triumph. Its eyes held no sorrow, only judgment.

"I am you," it said, crystalline and cruel, stepping out of the mirror with fluid grace. The glass behind it rippled once more, then stilled, as though granting the illusion form and voice. "I never faltered. Never bled. Never lost."

Orion gripped his cane, its crystal tip pulsing with ancestral magic. He swallowed a tremor.

The reflection summoned a blade of fractured starlight. "Prove it."

They collided. The room erupted into light and force. The blows came fast, brutal. Each one dragged old wounds to the surface.

He blocked high, ducked low. Sparks flew from cane and blade. He struck back, but the reflection countered every move.

"You failed Anton."

The words landed like a punch. "I tried to save him," Orion growled, swinging his cane. "I would have given anything!"

"But not enough. You hesitated. You broke."

A vicious sweep of the reflection's blade caught Orion's arm, sending a shock of pain spiralling through him. Blood welled and glittered with tarfire. He staggered.

"You abandoned Earth," it hissed.

"I was a child!" Orion cried. "I had no choice."

"You had power. And you hid."

Orion's voice cracked through the haze of pain. "Because Earth didn't need me then, not in the way it needs me now. I was just a boy with Star magic in his veins, desperate for guidance, drowning in a heritage I didn't yet understand."

He fell to one knee. The room spun. The mirror showed more than the battle. It showed his worst memories: Genevieve's disgust, the blank stare of children he couldn't save, Anton's last breath.

"No more," he whispered.

A low hum built in his chest. He pushed to his feet.

"I am not perfect," he said, carving glyphs into the stone with light. "I am not whole. But I am real."

The reflection advanced.

"I carry failure," Orion continued. "And loss. And guilt. But I also carry their hopes. Their names."

He swung his cane in a wide arc, casting a shield of light. "I am their story."

With a cry, he drove the cane forward. It met the reflection's chest. Light exploded. Cracks spread across its form. It fell to one knee, gasping.

"You understand," it said, stepping forward with softened eyes. It embraced him, not as a conqueror, but as a part of himself long denied, regret, hope, and truth entwined. The moment their forms touched, the reflection shimmered and dissolved, melting into Orion like water returning to the sea.

Silence fell.

Orion stood shaking, heart pounding. His reflection was gone. The chamber was calm. The weight on his shoulders remained, but it no longer crushed him.

The ceiling split above. Starlight cascaded down, bathing him in fire and grace. The scar where the god-destroyer's bullet had struck glowed, then dulled. Not erased. Honoured.

He stepped back into the spiral stair, breathless. His limbs trembled. The desert light grew with each step until he emerged blinking into dawn.

Aaron ran to meet him. Orion collapsed into his arms, exhausted but free.

"You've changed," Aaron breathed.

Orion kissed him, slow and certain. A promise.

"I carry it all," he said. "But I'm not chained anymore."

The sky overhead turned pale gold. A single star lingered, defiant and proud.

Above the temple of Mali, hope had returned.

Orion sat beside Aaron in the sand, his back against a broken pillar that still hummed faintly with residual glyph-light. The desert wind was gentler now, threading through his curls like a whisper from the stars. He watched as the skimmer hovered silently in the distance, its hull still glowing faintly from the descent. It would be time to leave soon.

But not yet.

"I didn't think I'd come back up," Orion murmured, eyes fixed on the shifting sands. "Not truly."

Aaron didn't answer at first. He simply reached for Orion's hand and laced their fingers together.

"You came back different," he finally said. "But you're still you. Maybe even more so."

Orion leaned his head on Aaron's shoulder, eyes fluttering shut for a moment. For the first time in what felt like lifetimes, he allowed stillness to settle inside him, not the absence of movement, but the absence of fear.

In the distance, the sun crested higher, illuminating the broken temple in gold and blood-orange. Cracks in the stone caught the light, casting intricate patterns that danced like flame.

"I saw them," Orion whispered. "All of them. Anton. My brothers. Even Aurorina... in flickers. They're with me now."

Aaron turned to look at him. "Because you let yourself remember."

Orion nodded, eyes stinging. "Because I stopped running from it."

A glyph near the temple base flared once, then faded.

Far above, the lone star remained in the dawn sky, as if it too had chosen to linger, to witness a boy reborn not through conquest, but through courage.

And somewhere deep within, Orion felt it: the soul-forged truth of what he was becoming. Not just the heir of a forgotten world. Not just the wielder of Star magic. But the living bridge between legacy and tomorrow.

A quiet resolve settled in his bones. The temple had tested him. And he had returned.

Whole.

Later, aboard the sleek, gliding skimmer, Orion lay curled tightly on a narrow cot near the expansive viewing dome. The sky beyond had morphed into a deep, foreboding blue, punctuated by the sharp glint of early stars, like shards of diamond scattered across a vast velvet abyss. His eyes slowly surrendered, closing under the weight of an insistent slumber.

Sleep consumed him like a relentless tide, dragging him into a realm swirling with vivid dreams. He found himself striding through a corridor woven from burning threads of starlight, where the walls writhed between menacing shadows and fragments of haunting memory. At the distant end, a blinding archway yawned open into a vast, dark chamber, alive with flickering cages of ghostly light.

There they were. Lawrence, Aurorina, Jake. Their figures floated in spectral suspension, ensnared within transparent cells shaped like inverted teardrops. Each cell flickered fiercely, pulsating with the echoes of memories, casting a haunting glow in the oppressive dimness.

Orion's breath hitched sharply in his throat. He lunged forward, his fingers splayed against the unforgiving invisible barrier. "Dad?" he whispered, his voice a raw blend of desperation and longing.

Lawrence stirred feebly within his radiant prison but didn't awaken. Aurorina's lips moved in the silent rhythm of sleep, while Jake clutched something to his chest, a scrap of a drawing perhaps, held with the fragile tenderness of a cherished relic.

A soft, insistent whisper swirled around him, not menacing but charged with urgency. The dream space shimmered violently, like a mirage teetering on the brink of collapse. He wasn't truly there, yet his spirit had blazed its path.

"I see you," Orion murmured, his voice a fierce promise. "I'm coming."

And even as the dream began to unravel like mist under the unforgiving morning sun, he felt it, his magic stretching across the vast chasm of time and space, leaving behind an unbreakable thread of connection. A vow forged in intensity.

They would not be forgotten. And he would return.

The next morning, the skimmer coasted over the glittering ocean, a trail of radiant mist spiralling behind it. Orion stood at the prow beside Eymd and Snjallt, the wind tugging at his cloak as the waves gave way to rising columns of ancient stone. Beneath the surface, crystalline towers shimmered faintly like submerged stars.

"We're close," Snjallt said, her voice low with awe. "Atlantis breathes again."

The Lost City emerged from beneath the waves like a living machine of light and memory. Towers of translucent alloy shimmered into view, their sleek surfaces layered with responsive nano crystal skins that adapted in real time to the shifting tides and sunlight. Instead of stone, the city was sculpted from plasma-forged material interwoven with biotech tendrils that pulsed in rhythm with the ocean itself. The domes floated above magnetic lattices, suspended in midair, while spiral temples spun slowly like celestial gyroscopes, reconfiguring their shape with each passing moment. Glyphs projected as multidimensional holograms twisted and danced across the infrastructure, speaking a language that only the oldest bloodlines could feel. All of it responded to Orion's presence, not just as a visitor, but as a key unlocking the city's breathless return to life.

Aaron appeared beside him. "You sure you're ready for this one?"

"No," Orion admitted. "But I've learned that being ready isn't the same as being willing."

The city gates opened with a deep, resonant chime. The skimmer descended into an airlock of light. Inside, the Trial of Forgiveness waited etched into the very architecture of Atlantis, where history, heart, and hurt had been kept sacred beneath the sea.

Orion stepped forward, each pace echoing with memories and the weight of choices. This was not just about absolution from others.

This was about him learning to forgive.

# 14. Trial Of Forgiveness

The chamber into which Orion entered was unlike the others. Here the walls of Atlantis felt almost brittle, each surface humming with echoes of lives long past. Glyphs didn't just glow they murmured doubts and desires he couldn't yet name. Lights drifted along the curves of the stone as though they carried purpose, though he couldn't tell whether it was benevolent or cruel. This was no tribunal. It was a crucible, and he was already burning.

Alone, Orion stepped into the amphitheatre-shaped room. The floating tiers curved above him in concentric circles around a central, luminous disc. The platform beneath his feet rattled slightly as it rose, and a low vibration thrummed through his bones, tethering him to this place even as his pulse raced with uncertainty.

Then came the pulse.

The walls rippled. Reality fractured and reformed. He found himself in a battered Earth hallway fluorescent bulbs flickering overhead, grimy green tiles slick with old sweat and dust. The stench of bleach and blood hit him like a wave he hadn't been ready to face.

He was back at his old school.

Three boys loomed ahead, bigger, harder, their footsteps echoing like a promise of pain. Fury flared in his chest, mingled with a jarring echo of something older fear, confusion. He remembered folding in on himself then, not out of cowardice but because he didn't understand the power thrumming in his veins. He'd been a stranger in a uniform that cost more than his family could ever earn. A freak. A poor kid who didn't belong.

"Freak. Poor. Weak." Their voices slapped him, each insult a crack in the armour he'd built around his heart.

There was a punch to the jaw, another to the ribs. Hot pain blossomed, but more agonizing was the echoing question in his mind: Why didn't I hit back? Did I fear the monster inside me, or did I hate myself more?

Orion's voice surfaced, brittle: "What was the point in protecting myself?" He swallowed. "No one else ever did." The words rattled in the air before the scene tore open again.

In an instant, he stood in his childhood living room a cramped, damp caravan of a cottage redolent with yesterday's silence. His mother, gaunt and steely, turned from the window, arms crossed like a fortress. Her suitcase lay by the door. She'd made her choice weeks ago; today she simply executed it.

He'd whispered inside himself then: Fight for us. Stay. But her back receded without a glance. No sorrow flickered in the hard lines of her face only emptiness. He'd hated her, feared her, and above all, yearned for her to turn around. "I needed you to see me," he hissed now, stepping forward in memory. "To fight for us. Not walk away."

Her silhouette didn't waver. Love had cost her too much, or so he told himself. Yet as the image blurred, anger and grief tangled tight in his chest.

And then the final vision: the tiny kitchen, ten years old, crammed behind a splintered cupboard door, shielding his twin brothers with trembling arms. Above him loomed Lawrence his father's breath reeking of stale beer and bitter regret. Frustration had corroded into something close to rage.

"You boys were too loud," Lawrence slurred. "This house isn't built on magic." The belt cracked through the air before Orion could flinch. Each strike hammered truth into his bones: protection could hurt; love could hurt worse.

He tasted tears he could not shed, swallowed screams he could not utter. He thought then that maybe silence was safer than crying out. "I know now," he whispered, voice rough. "You were broken too. But I needed a father. I needed safety. Not survival."

All three scenes trembled and then crystallised around him bullies, mother, father eyes flickering from indifference to something resembling guilt. Their faces wavered, raw with recognition of the damage they'd done. Shame pooled in their eyes... or was it wonder at the boy who refused to break?

Orion's chest constricted. He stood at the centre of their remorse and hate and longing. His pulse thundered.

"I forgive you," he said, voice cracking like thunder over a stormy sea. Doubt rippled through him was he forgiving them, or himself? But the words rang out, jagged and necessary, shattering shackles he'd worn for decades.

In that instant, the glyphs lining the chamber blazed with renewed intensity. A surge of Star magic hammered through his veins, purer and fiercer than any power he'd dared to unleash before. His skin flickered with starlight, constellations mapping themselves across his arms in a trembling pattern of light and shadow. In that glow he felt both terrified and fiercely alive exposed as never before, yet known down to his fractured core.

His cane's crystal heart flared. He gasped as the ancient wound from the god-destroyer's bullet shivered awake. But instead of agony, warmth bloomed along the scar's edges. Pain receded and left behind a fine silver line: the mark of endurance, of carved-out hope.

The chamber rippled, steeped in golden calm. Glyphs spun like newborn stars, not warning him now but naming him. The Trial of Forgiveness had not tested his strength it'd forced him to reconcile every shard of grief, anger, and yearning held inside.

Above, the ceiling peeled back like a blossom in dawn's first light, revealing a sky streaked with rose and sapphire. Starlight gathered, drawn by him and for him, shaping itself into a future he'd scarcely dared imagine.

Orion stood taller, though a tremor of uncertainty still curled in his gut. The Star magic within him roared steady and sure, a promise and a question all at once.

He was healing. He was remembering who he truly was each star in his skin a story, each breath a thread of destiny rewoven.

He was becoming.

When Orion emerged from the chamber, the corridor outside pulsed with quiet light. The architecture of Atlantis responded to him now not just to his presence, but to his transformation. Panels of liquid crystal parted at his approach, revealing corridors of spiralling glass and magnetic lifts that floated like bubbles suspended in a dream.

Aaron stood at the threshold, eyes wide not with concern, but with reverence. "You look... different," he said.

"I am," Orion replied softly. "I finally let go."

Behind Aaron, Snjallt and Eymd waited in silence. Neither spoke, but something in their postures relaxed, grounded acknowledged what had occurred.

"Atlantis accepted you," Snjallt said. "It's already reconfiguring."

"What's next?" Orion asked.

Eymd glanced toward a glyph-glass interface that flickered with unfamiliar constellations. "The city's core is waking. It's showing us something... but we don't know what yet."

Orion stepped forward. "Then let's find out. I didn't come this far to stop now."

As the lift chamber opened, a faint hum filled the air deeper than before, threaded with something ancient.

The path ahead shimmered, and Atlantis opened its heart.

The lift descended, but not in any linear sense. It moved through layers of light, memory, and vibration. Orion felt it in his bones: a shift in gravity that wasn't physical, but spiritual. The air thickened with charge, like standing in the centre of a lightning storm.

They emerged into a vast subterranean chamber. Unlike the upper levels, this space was darker, older. The walls were alive with patterns of shifting light, as if the city itself were dreaming.

A massive sphere hovered in the centre of the chamber, suspended in stasis by magnetic currents and anchored with streams of data-light pouring from the ceiling and floor. Within it, constellations turned slowly mapped not in stars, but in living memory.

"What is this?" Aaron asked, stepping forward.

"The Heart of Atlantis," Snjallt whispered, her voice almost reverent. "A record of everything. Of every descendant who carries the Old Blood. Their pain. Their triumphs. Their betrayals."

Glyphs spiralled outward from the core, weaving around Orion like vines of light. Some brushed against his skin and lingered, transmitting sensations more than words: sorrow, exile, rebirth.

"It's showing me..." Orion trailed off, his eyes unfocused. "They knew. The Ancients knew what Earth would become. They left pieces behind. Messages hidden in bloodlines and buried cities."

Eymd stepped beside him, her brow furrowed. "So why awaken it now?"

"Because," Orion said slowly, "the timeline is shifting. Just like it did when I awoke. Something is coming. Something that was meant to stay buried."

A section of the wall melted into a holographic display: blueprints of Earth overlaid with unfamiliar energy signatures, pulsing like beacons. Some marked ruins. Others modern cities.

Aaron's face paled. "Those aren't just messages. They're warnings."

The Heart of Atlantis pulsed once more, and a voice not spoken, but embedded rang in Orion's mind:

"The remaining four draw near. You have passed Forgiveness. But your next path is one of birth, not battle. The Trial of Life awaits."

"You must learn to give life to restore what was broken without sacrificing your flame. Your Star magic must flow, not fade. Only then can the cycle mend."

Orion's fingers curled around his cane. The stars in his veins flared, not in defence but in anticipation.

"Then the next trial begins," he said. "And this time, I must learn to give... not just endure."

Later that evening, they slipped into one of Atlantis's most secret sanctuaries a glass-walled terrace garden suspended above a vast bioluminescent lagoon. The transparent panels framed a living tapestry of shifting blues and greens below, the water's gentle lapping echoing like distant chimes. Artificial twilight suffused the space with molten gold, assigning each leaf and petal an otherworldly glow. Luminous vines, thick as serpents and heavy with hanging blossoms, dripped phosphorescent nectar onto obsidian-stained walkways. Pools of radiant water reflected the arc of glowing blooms, pulsing in time with soft, unseen heartbeats. At last, Orion realised, no predator lurked beyond the glass no threat but the one he carried within.

He sank against a plush bench carved from pearlescent stone, his shoulders folding inward as exhaustion claimed him. The curling mist rising from a sculpted fountain swirled around his fingertips like silver smoke, and his eyelids fluttered shut against its hypnotic dance. Aaron settled beside him, the steady warmth of his presence a quiet reassurance. Their shoulders touched in a silent pact of solidarity. Nearby, Snjallt sat cross-legged on the polished floor, his eyes sealed in deep meditation. At the far end of the terrace, Vilantina and Eymd prowled between vine-wreathed columns, their silhouettes flickering in the golden gloom. Their voices, at first hushed, soon sharpened into verbal blades.

"I don't see why this is such a crisis," Eymd hissed, her tone brittle. The words snapped through the scented haze of night-blooming flowers. "Orion lived. He survived the trial. End of story."

Vilantina's dark eyes burned with suppressed fire. "Barely," she countered, her voice low and hard. "And don't pretend you weren't a phantom at his side. If you'd guided him if you'd cared enough to push him he might not have been on death's doorstep."

Eymd's lip curled in contempt. "I trusted him," she spat. "He's no child. Your constant hovering doesn't make you a saint."

"Caring," Vilantina shot back, "means standing firm when everything around you is in flames. You skulk away at the first spark, returning only to drape yourself in cynicism."

Eymd's arms folded across her chest like iron bars. "You're not his mother."

Her accusation cracked the warm silence. Vilantina's spine straightened as though braced by emotion, her voice growing distant. "No. But I know what it's like to scream for help and hear nothing but your own echo. I swore I'd never let anyone taste that loneliness least of all him."

A flicker of pain crossed Eymd's expression, raw and unguarded. Her voice dropped to a wounded whisper. "And what about me? You think I don't ache because I don't parade my scars for you?"

Vilantina's tone softened, but her eyes remained fierce. "You bury your ache beneath layers of sarcasm. But Orion deserves more than shadows and half-truths."

They held each other's gaze, the tension melting into something more complex: a fragile understanding. Eymd's shoulders slumped, her posture unguarding. "I lost people too," she confessed, voice trembling. "I... I just don't know how to keep what's left alive."

A single breath passed between them, thick with empathy. "No," Vilantina admitted quietly, "but I won't watch him slip through the cracks again."

Their words dissolved into the heavy warmth of the garden. Elsewhere, Orion felt the shift in the air and opened his eyes. He had heard every sharp barb and every tremor of care beneath the anger.

He said nothing, simply lifted his gaze to the vaulted ceiling where constellations of refracted light danced among the steel beams. The pale luminescence pulsed in time with his steadying heartbeat. Here, at the edge of silence and confrontation, friction felt less like threat than promise and for once, he welcomed it.

As twilight deepened into a soft indigo, slender glass tables bloomed around them, each set with dishes conjured by Atlantis's bio-synthesis engines. The steam curled in silver strands, dancing gently through the cold air, above bowls of opalescent grains that shimmered like star fields. Sea-fruit hissed on heated plates, releasing salty tangs that mingled with the sweet resonance of mineral elixirs glowing within crystalline goblets. The aroma was at once alien and deeply comforting, a symphony of brine and earth and light.

They gathered around a central table, the hush broken only by gentle clinks of cutlery and soft breath. Vilantina and Eymd sat opposite one another, the silent truce between them a taut thread above the amber glow of their meals.

Orion claimed the head of the table, permitting himself a rare, faint smile as Aaron leaned in, chuckling at Snjallt's quiet rumblings about cosmic manuscripts. Then Orion's gaze drifted to a lone, shadowed figure perched at the table's fringe.

"Trintani," he said his voice low, steady, unyielding.

At the name, the figure's crimson eyes snapped up. The binding glyph etched around his throat glowed with a dim ember-light, as though stoking the memory of some celestial fire. In the hush of the Celestial Library, amid voices of vanished ancestors, Orion had shaped that glyph not from chains of fear but from strands of living truth.

"Sit," Orion commanded, gesturing to the empty place beside him.

Trintani rose with a predatory grace, each muscle coiled beneath his sable skin. He lowered himself into the offered seat, silver armour plates gleaming against the garden's golden backdrop. His gaze flicked across the group over Aaron's watchful stance, Snjallt's composed calm, Eymd's still-held tension before fixing on Orion.

"You spared me," he rasped after a heartbeat, his voice a blend of bitterness and awe. "But mercy and justice are not kin."

Orion leaned forward, the lamplight sketching ten-thousand points of reflection in his steady eyes. "I'm not seeking vengeance. I want answers. You swore to defend the Shadow and yet you led their slaughter."

A muscle in Trintani's jaw twitched. "I was executioner, not protector," he admitted, voice hollow. "I turned my beliefs inside out, let my rage consume every oath. I razed sanctuaries, watched innocents fall, and told myself it was destiny."

Orion's expression hardened. "You butchered your own people."

"I cloaked my bloodlust in prophecy," Trintani confessed, shame and defiance warring in his tone. "I told myself I was chosen."

Orion's hand remained still on the table until, with a sudden flick, Trintani's fingers closed around a hidden blade. The steel arc glinted, aimed for Orion's unguarded heart.

But in the same instant, the glyph at Trintani's throat flared with incandescent starfire. Radiant chains of cosmic law snapped taut around his arm, freezing the blade mid-swing. Trintani's muscles spasmed under the invisible grip, pain blossoming across his features in white-hot pulses. The dagger clattered to the polished floor, echoing like a fallen star.

Orion rose with deliberate calm, his voice as unwavering as the glyph's light. "I didn't bind you in fear. I bound you in truth and the truth cannot be denied."

The glyph's flare softened to a steady pulse. Trintani sagged, sweat slicking his brow, eyes drained of defiance and filled with the hollow weight of remorse.

Beside him, Aaron leapt to his feet, sidearm drawn. Eymd's dagger gleamed at her hip. Vilantina remained poised, grief coursing beneath her silent vigil she had known Orion's will could hold, because reality grounded in truth carried its own gravity.

Orion returned his focus to Trintani. "Punish you? Your sentence is this: you remain. You bear witness to how leadership emerges from mercy and purpose, not hatred and blood."

He lifted his goblet in a solemn toast. Every weapon lowered, though tension hovered like drifting smoke. Aaron's finger hovered near his holster; Eymd's eyes glowed with residual betrayal; Snjallt studied the unfolding scene with the curiosity of a scholar discovering an ancient manuscript.

Vilantina's voice broke the hush. "Bonds alone won't heal him. Only truth can."

Aaron shifted in his seat, glancing from Vilantina to Orion. "You really believe he can change?"

Orion studied Trintani's broken silhouette, the glyph's beat still dimly lighting the guilt etched into his features. "I don't know," he admitted, voice gentle as starlight, "but galaxies shift one choice at a time. Even the darkest celestial bodies were born in the light."

He met each face around the table Eymd's restrained fury, Aaron's cautious hope, Snjallt's inquisitive calm, Vilantina's unwavering faith, and the silent questions swirling in the eyes of those yet unnamed. These were his constellation now each star scarred yet luminous.

Trintani spoke not a word. The silence that settled over him was no longer armour but the heavy hush of a man finally hearing his own remorse an echo that might, at last, be the first step toward dawn.

# 15. The City That Remembers

The city was stirring to life like a great leviathan waking from slumber. Orion lingered at the rim of the glass-encased terrace. The dawn light refracted through the crystal panes and painted his silhouette in pale aqua glimmers. Below him, Atlantis, ancient and vast, a dormant mind of stone and starfire, awoke with a low, omnipresent murmur: a pulse of memory long sealed in vaults of coral-tinted obsidian. The ferment of awakening rippled through the city's halls like breath rekindled in a body frozen for millennia.

The air itself quivered with resonance, as though the city exhaled a sigh of recognition. Veins of Star magic glittered along the walls and crystalline pillars. Liquid silver kindled constellations that had slept uncounted ages. Far beneath the terrace, the bioluminescent lagoon glowed with phosphorescent blues and greens. Its light danced in ripples across the dome overhead, flickering like dormant stars snapping into being. The faint scent of wet stone and ozone drifted upward, heavy with the promise of power and memory.

As if beckoned by an ancestral summons, Orion stepped forward. Each footfall echoed against polished stone floors that registered his presence not just physically, but spiritually. He placed his palm against the largest panel of the wall, smooth obsidian inlaid with swirling silver filigree. It felt cool, steady, and faintly vibrating, like the spine of some slumbering god. Expectation thrummed in the air around him.

The moment his skin touched the surface, the response was instant. A surge of starlight erupted, shooting outward in molten arcs of electric pale gold. Lightning of pure radiance threaded through conduits and veins in the walls, setting crystalline runes alight. Deep beneath him, ancient gears groaned back to life, echoing through hidden corridors. Overhead, the terrace ceiling split open into fractal hexagons of shining rock. Petals of stone folded back to reveal a latticework of dormant machinery now humming with renewed purpose.

At the centre of the terrace, a command platform rose on silent pistons. It was forged of polished alloy that glowed with inner radiance. Its surface shimmered with star-script: maps of planets, swirling grids of gravitational waves, and real-time trajectories of satellites and defence outposts around Earth. Holographic whorls of data spun in midair. Each symbol hovered like a miniature galaxy.

The hum of new power stirred the guardians of Atlantis. Down stony corridors carved into living bedrock, statues of obsidian and crystal cracked open. Eyes dulled by time ignited with prismatic fire. The Stone Guard emerged from shadowed alcoves. Hulking forms of humanoid symmetry, their mirrored visors were alight with cosmic embers. Circuits of stardust traced their armour plating, and pages of the Celestial Library were sculpted into geometric motifs across their broad shoulders. They moved with solemn purpose, stepping onto the terrace in measured procession. Their armour breathed with pent-up star energy.

Orion, unmoved by their silent majesty, lifted his hand in greeting. The nearest guardian knelt with a grinding of stone and crystal. Its voice rumbled like tectonics beneath the ocean floor.

"You bear the power of the Old Ones, yet transcend them. You are inheritance and divergence woven into one."

At a thought from him, massive defence pylons burst from hidden wells around the terrace's rim. Runes cascaded down their columns in spiralling patterns of gold and jade. Above, a dome of shimmering shield unfurled. An incandescent canopy of warming light curved over the city like the wings of a forgotten god. Pulse cannons whirred and locked into position. Their barrels tilted skyward in precise arcs. The atmosphere crackled with living potential, every molecule thrumming in tune with Atlantis's reawakening.

A crystalline chime rang out. It was a note as pure and ancient as the first song of creation. From the heart of the command platform rose a voice both mechanical and oddly tender.

"P.I.L.S.S. online. Personal Intelligent Life Support System reboot complete. Orion, your code enhancements from millennia past remain intact and have been optimised. Welcome back. Last synchronisation: 273 days ago."

Light cascaded along conduits like liquid starlight. Atlantean glyphs unfurled in dancing ribbons of script, the ancient tongue merging with modern code. The city yielded to him. Every corridor and chamber acknowledged the heir returned. A pulse of warm reassurance throbbed beneath his skin. Atlantis remembered him not merely as lord, but as catalyst.

Soft footfalls approached from behind. Orion felt the presence before he saw her, grounded and familiar, imbued with countless shared memories. Rachel joined him at the terrace's edge, her breath caught in the hush of revelation. Beneath her gaze, constellations of Star magic shimmered across the crystalline pillars. They clustered like bright thoughts.

"You did it," she whispered, voice trembling with awe.

"No," he corrected softly, firm as starlight. "It did. It remembered."

His eyes, bright as comet-forged gemstone, turned to her.

"Rachel, contact the World Council at once. Tell every nation Atlantis has reactivated. From this moment, it is our new base of operations."

Her eyebrows rose. "All of them?"

He nodded once, sure and unyielding. "Every government. Every leader. This is no longer negotiation. It's a transition."

"And the Earth Defence Authority?" she asked, her tone steady despite the weight of their charge.

"Inform Assistant Director Fray," Orion replied, gaze drifting back to the rising command core. "The E.D.A.'s operations will relocate here, fully integrated. Atlantis is no myth. It's our shield and spear. Soon, the galaxy will remember why."

Rachel's fingers flew across her console, dispatching encrypted pings to the surface. Around them, the runes and star-veins pulsed in cadence with Orion's resolve. It was intentional, purposeful, and inexorable.

Beneath their boots, Atlantis's heartbeat grew stronger, resonant and sure. The Stone Guard remained arrayed around him like silent constellations come to life. One figure, slightly taller than the rest, stepped forward. Its chest plates were etched with a denser webbing of cosmic circuitry. Its voice rolled out in low thunder.

"We are the Echo Wardens, bonded to the First. We stood vigil when Earth's divisions tore at the heavens. Now we rise again for you."

Another Warden's voice glinted like a chime in the deep. "Our memory flows deeper than time's breath. We serve only one touched by the First. You bear that essence, but there is more than even the First foresaw. As Atlantis awakens, so too do we."

In unison, the Wardens struck fists to chest. A gesture solemn and exacting. At that moment, a torrent of golden starlight leapt from Orion's heart-space, spiralling across the terrace. Where the runes and armours intersected, a radiant emblem blazed into being. A phoenix wrought of living flame. Its wings arced in eternal ascent. Beneath it, a quill and parchment crossed like keys, and a guiding sword poised like a compass. The mark imprinted itself upon each guardian's breastplate, forging a covenant older than any oath.

The lead Warden inclined its mirrored helm in reverence. Its voice softened by awe.

"Welcome home, Intenfli Orion."

A soft tone chimed from the command platform.

"Connection to Earth's orbiting channels established. Incoming: World Council secure line."

Above the console, the faces of presidents, premiers, monarchs, and defence chancellors flickered into view. Their images wavered for heartbeats before stabilising, alight with alarm and curiosity.

Chancellor Yurev's clipped voice broke the tension. "Our sensors detect a planetary-scale energy bloom. Are we under threat?"

Queen Alexandria II leaned forward. Her countenance was inscrutable. "Is that... Atlantis?"

Rachel stepped slightly forward, her voice steady as blade steel. "No threat. You stand at the cusp of history. Atlantis has returned. Orion has returned."

Orion rose from the platform's glow and addressed the council.

"I am not here as conqueror, but protector. This city is Earth's inheritance, a nexus of starborn knowledge, memory, and defence. Henceforth, it will serve as our planetary capital. For humanity. For the E.D.A. For the future we must defend."

A restless murmur rippled through the assembly.

One delegate's tone sharpened. "Who granted you this authority?"

He met the question with unflinching calm.

"Not tradition or ceremony, but sacrifice and trust. I've bled and died for this, and Atlantis chose me. Under our treaty, I offer this city not as dominion, but as unity. As hope. Let it belong to all of us, not rulers but guardians. Our survival depends on togetherness."

Silence fell. It was weighty and expectant. A delegate of the Pan-Eurasian Alliance rose. Her steel-edged voice challenged him.

"You awaken a myth, rearm ancient weapons, and demand the reins of Earth's defence? We were not consulted. There was no vote."

Orion, bathed in the golden glow of the shield dome, advanced one step.

"Remember. It was your urgency and trust that placed me at this post. I did not come to crown myself. I came to forestall an ending. Atlantis once sank itself because Earth lost its way. Now it rises not for a ruler, but for a shared future. Let us not repeat past mistakes."

Queen Alexandria II inclined her head once, measured and sovereign.

"Then let history unfold. Tell me, Orion. Will there be space for royal residences? I suspect we'll need more than a lagoon view."

He allowed a small, wry smile to brighten his features.

"Atlantis is alive. It adapts. Each district can be shaped by intention. Your Majesty, you'll have a kingdom carved from memory and magic."

A ripple of laughter, tentative but genuine, swept the chamber.

The Prime Minister of the African Confederacy leaned in. "What of resources? Medical facilities? Civilian housing?"

Orion gestured to the holographic schematics dancing at the console.

"Infrastructure is modular. As your delegates arrive, the city will reconfigure to your people's needs. Nothing here is static. That is Atlantis's magic."

President Moreno of the South American Union nodded slowly. Awe softened his stern countenance.

"We aren't merely witnessing a new capital. We're invited to build it with you."

"Exactly," Orion said. "This is not my empire. It is our legacy."

The King of the Oceanic Coalition chuckled. "Then I claim first dibs on a district of hot springs and sky gardens."

Warm laughter rose among the delegates. Orion lifted a hand in benediction.

"The first wave of Atlantean transports departs momentarily. Coordinates are linked to your grids. Prepare your teams. Welcome home."

He turned to the console and issued his final command.

"P.I.L.S.S., open secure channels to all incoming representatives. Query their needs: medical, housing, defence. Modulate Atlantis accordingly."

"Affirmative," the voice replied, smooth as liquid metal. "Initiating intake requests and structural modulation based on projected parameters."

Orion paused, gazing up at the living city whose heartbeat pulsed beneath his feet. He drew in a steadying breath. The terraces and towers stretched around him in crystalline affirmation. Then, voice low with purpose, he murmured:

"Send the shuttles. Let them remember where we began and what endures."

# 16. The Age Of Unity

The first pale fingers of Atlantean dawn curled over the city's crystalline spires, igniting them in opalescent fire. Light danced like prophecy upon the ancient skyline as transport shuttles descended in silence from Earth's orbit. Their engines traced golden ribbons through the pearlescent haze, unfurling across the heavens like celestial calligraphy. Above, the great dome, woven from translucent lattices of force and memory, peeled back with reverent grace, revealing the metropolis below: a living jewel of motion and mind, thrumming in anticipation.

Verdant gardens hovered between the quartz towers, laden with dew-soaked orchids and trailing vines that shimmered with unseen pollen. Silk-smooth waterways curved like galaxies in miniature, threading through bridges of onyx and meteoric iron, pulsing with energy older than language. At the city's heart stood the command terrace, white marble steps etched in constellations that shimmered underfoot like stilled starlight, awaiting the arrivals fated by more than diplomacy.

Each shuttle bore the proud heraldry of Earth's fractured unity: the Pan-Eurasian Alliance's sun-flanked eagle in molten gold, the Oceanic Coalition's silver crescent embracing cobalt wave, the African Confederacy's emerald flame burning against a midnight field. One by one they descended in solemn procession, each landing reverberating like the toll of ancient bells across Atlantis's Grand Concourse.

On the receiving steps, Orion stood beneath the awakening sun, flanked by Rachel and Assistant Director Fray. Eymd stood motionless, serenity and latent danger braided into her stance. Vilantina radiated calm light beside the silent form of Trintani, his newly anchored body shimmering with tempered starlight. Behind them, Verjast loomed like a sentinel forged from myth, Snjallt unreadable in a flickercloak of frost-dusted shadow. The Stone Guard stood unmoved, obsidian bodies veined with golden light, while the Echo Wardens' luminous helms caught the dawn like divine mirrors.

Orion's armour was ceremonial yet alive, celestial white and void-black, traced in golden star-maps that shifted in rhythm with his breath. His expression was quiet, but within his stillness stirred the gravity of alignment. His presence did not command; it invited.

The first to descend was Queen Alexandria II, her silhouette wreathed in dawn light. Her gown, woven of moon-silver and memory, rustled like whispers of forgotten oaths. Jewels glinted in her diadem, catching rays as though responding to Atlantis itself. Beside her, Crown Prince's in gilded regalia, the young Princess Elenora with eyes wide in wonder, and Lady Margaret's poised grace completed her cortege. President Moreno followed with bronze resolve, Chancellor Yurev bearing the calm of storms past. One by one, they stepped into the plaza, the air thick with unspoken history.

Orion's voice flowed across the space like a rising tide. "Welcome. You stand on ground once walked by those who built your skies and lived alongside you. This city does not demand allegiance. It invites courage."

A breathless stillness followed, an echo of recognition, not fear.

Rachel stepped forward, her voice crystalline. "Each delegation will be guided to its district. Atlantis has adapted its infrastructure to your environmental, medical, and security specifications. The city listens. It learns. It evolves with you."

Beneath their feet, strands of ancient light awakened, runes of sapphirine and emerald spiralling into luminous pathways. They pulsed with each delegate's presence, syncing with heartbeats and intention. Marble softened beneath the weight of arrival. One by one, radiant lifts rose like starlit breath, carrying them to their quarters in silence.

Queen Alexandria lingered. The silk of her gown curled like mist in orbit. "And what of the throne room, Your Majesty? Will there be a seat for each of us?"

Orion met her gaze. His starlit eyes held no claim. "There will be a circle. No thrones. No crowns. Only voices."

Her lips parted in a small smile, and she stepped onto her lift. The breeze caught her cloak like a banner.

Fray exhaled beside him, ozone lacing his breath. "You sure you want to share that much power?"

"It was never mine to keep," Orion murmured. "Only to protect."

High above, the dome realigned with the rising sun, fracturing its light into kaleidoscopic mosaics across the spires. As the final shuttles vanished into the radiant cityscape, Orion turned to Rachel. "Begin integration."

She nodded, steel behind her serenity. "The age of Atlantis has begun."

"No," Orion replied, eyes sharpening on the horizon. "The age of unity has."

And as if summoned by that very declaration, reality tore.

Beyond the shimmering bounds of the city, a ripple moved through space like memory awakening, and from that breach, a second wave emerged. Ships not of Earth, nor Xerist. Their hulls were forged from shadow-metal and twilight matter, their edges drifting in tendrils of soft starlight. They made no sound, yet the air shifted, aware.

Rachel froze. "They're not human, but how did they bypass the Great Four's blockade?"

Fray's brow darkened. "Not Earth. Not Xerist. No known configuration."

Orion remained still, the pulse of the city threading through his bones. The Atlantean systems grappled with the newcomers' energy patterns, no threat, no signal, only something remembered.

The lead vessel descended without propulsion, unfolding a seamless ramp of obsidian glass. A figure stepped forth, tall, otherworldly. Its skin shimmered like mercury under moonlight, robed in shadow braided with solar flame. Around its head, twin rings of motes drifted in orbit, like memory-stained halos.

Stillness gripped the plaza.

The figure raised a hand and spoke in soundless unity, echoing through every mind.

"I am Enthis. Echo of the Pactum Aeterna. We come not in judgment, but in remembrance."

A collective gasp rippled through the delegation. Even Orion's heartbeat stumbled at the weight of that ancient name.

Rachel whispered, "What is the Pactum Aeterna?"

Enthis's throat glowed with inner dawn. "It is memory made manifest. A covenant forged across galaxies, older than your oceans, older than your sun. Once, it bound the strong to shield the rising, and the rising to remember the stars from whence they came. We return because Earth has forgotten. The pyramids, the ziggurats, the great stones of the north, they were never raised alone."

Another figure emerged, flickering with constellations that swirled like dreaming thought. Its voice shimmered like starlight across still water. "We passed not through your sky, but through your memory. The Great Four saw nothing. They guard the now. We walk the was and the will be."

Enthis turned to Orion, gaze piercing. "You are more than an heir. You are divergence incarnate. The Pactum Aeterna, once broken, stirs again because of you."

A third being, a youth cloaked in spiralling galaxies, stepped forward, voice reverent. "We walked with Ilustrnad, beneath triple-moon skies. He forged the first pact when Earth still dreamed of unity. Your line carried it forward, none more boldly than Intenfli Auren I, who reforged it amid the crucible of the Great War."

Orion's voice was a breath drawn from the marrow of stars. "And I am?"

Enthis bowed, motion shimmering. "You are the fulcrum. Not above the Pactum, but its living axis."

A lone Echo Warden dropped to one knee, voice tremulous. "God-born. Child of star and will."

Orion said nothing. Yet within, his skin blazed with constellations of light. Visions pierced him: Ilustrnad beneath a golden pyramid, arms outstretched to the stars; Intenfli Auren I circled by alien allies, forging sigils in fire; the Great War ripping across the cosmos, betrayal, unity frayed. And finally, himself, standing alone yet unbowed beneath a silent sky.

Each vision was a legacy. Each a summons.

The alien vessels began to hum, casting golden filaments that kissed Atlantis's pylons. The city answered, glyphs reigniting, towers glowing like the veins of a living titan.

Enthis's voice rang like a prophecy. "The Pactum Aeterna was a promise between equals. Now, it must bind the divine and the fractured. The protector and the awakening child."

Orion stepped forward, voice ringing with finality. "Then let the pact be reforged. Not as a treaty, but as truth."

The alien ships pulsed with golden accord. Enthis bowed once more, radiance cloaking them.

"The Pactum Aeterna stands with Earth."

# 17. The Pact Rekindled

The council chamber was no throne room.

It unfurled like a great bloom at the core of Atlantis, suspended above a yawning void of light and echo. There were no walls, only arched spires of translucent crystal that curved toward one another without touching, channelling the wind and light of the upper city. The ceiling shimmered as though submerged in water, reflecting stars that no longer burned in Earth's sky, constellations drawn from forgotten epochs.

Beneath its floating canopy, the gathered leaders stood on platforms of levitating marble, each etched with fractal inscriptions in languages lost to time. They were drawn inward into a perfect ring. Between them, radiant threads of energy wove the air into a living constellation with Orion at its axis. He stood at the centre on a raised disc, his armour dimmed now to a matte glow, as if allowing the moment to speak louder than his form. The silence around him thrummed with restrained power, and his breath crystallised slightly, touched by the chamber's living presence.

Queen Alexandria's voice was the first to cut through the hush, clipped and resonant. "You've invoked a promise older than our nations, yet none here recall forging it. Are we meant to honour oaths we never made?"

Orion's voice was calm but carried the depth of ancient tides. "You may not remember, but your bones do. Your ancestors stood beside mine when the sky was still young. They carved stone by starlight and built wonders with hands guided by something greater. They looked up and recognised themselves not in conquest, but in connection. And that memory lives on, even if buried."

President Moreno tilted his head, eyes narrowed. "And if this is manipulation? A ploy for control under the guise of celestial reunion?"

Before Orion could respond, the very air shimmered. A ripple passed through the chamber like the surface of disturbed water. Enthis appeared once more, not walking but unfolding from a pillar of light, like a thought given shape, their form limned in glimmers of gold and violet.

"We do not bind. We remind," they said, their voice a multilayered harmony, like music composed by gravity and breath. "You stand not beneath a god, but beside a fulcrum. If Earth wishes to remain apart, it may. But the storms beyond your sun do not ask permission. They consume."

Chancellor Yurev's voice followed, laced with steel and skepticism. "Then speak plainly. What do you warn of?"

Rachel's eyes narrowed, her voice tight with rising unease. "Are you saying Earth's survival depends on rejoining this Pactum?"

"No," said Orion, his tone steady as a blade's edge. "Earth's survival depends on remembering who it is and what it has already survived. The Pactum is not salvation. It is solidarity."

From behind him, Vilantina stepped forward into the growing light. Her wings flared slightly, their golden luminescence catching the crystalline chamber's resonance like a chorus of bells. "Let them choose, not as kings or queens, but as stewards of their peoples. As those who dare to stand between what is and what must never be."

One by one, the world leaders glanced toward their delegates. Tension spiralled across the ring suspicion, hope, fear, and the unbearable weight of possibility. Whispers turned to murmurs, then to silence once more.

Then, from the youngest among them, a voice clear as the first light of dawn. Princess Elenora. "If we remember... can we still shape what comes?"

Orion turned to her, eyes warm and luminous. "That is the only reason to remember."

Suddenly, light surged through the chamber, not blinding but embracing, as though the city itself had exhaled. The floating platforms glowed faintly. The leaders hesitant, resolute, trembling stepped forward. Not all with surety, but all with choice.

The Pactum Aeterna pulsed anew. Not with history. With promise. A promise rekindled not in fire, but in will.

Outside the chamber, Atlantis shifted.

The crystal towers resonated with rising harmony, glyphs awakening along their facades like veins of light responding to the pact's renewal. The waterways brightened, and the air carried a deeper stillness, a reverent hush as if the city itself had heard and approved.

Within the command centre, Rachel's voice spoke low into her comm. "P.I.L.S.S., begin syncing planetary defence arrays to Pactum alignment protocol. Prepare for reclassification of threat vectors focused on the Great Four and their master."

"Confirmed," came the serene voice of the AI. "Integrating ancient defensive schema and cross-referencing Atlantean archives. Estimated readiness in five minutes."

She turned to Fray, her expression unreadable. "It's not just a pact. It's a signal. Across Earth. Across space. Anyone watching knows we've awakened something older than empires."

Fray gave a single nod, then gestured to the viewscreen. "Then we better be ready when they come looking."

On the screen, above Earth's atmosphere, the last of the Great Four's lingering constructs began to shift.

They had felt it.

Far beneath the city, where starforged vaults thrummed with awakening energy, the sanctum of the Stone Guard surged to life. Columns of crystal light ignited in sequence, pulsing through the chamber like a heartbeat returning to a slumbering god. Ancient mechanisms ground open with tectonic resonance, revealing deep alcoves carved into the obsidian walls. From each recess, new Stone Guard's began to emerge, sculpted forms rising from beds of stardust and stone.

Their bodies formed in slow, reverent pulses of light and matter, veins of golden energy threading through fresh obsidian skin as ancient forging sigils etched themselves across their armour. Each construct bore a different constellation across its chest, marking its celestial purpose. The chamber filled with the sound of awakening metal shifting, runes locking into place, power returning.

The Stone Guard were no longer few. Atlantis was preparing for war.

Their duty, long dormant, had begun again. Yet they did not march. They waited, silent as mountain roots, for the command that would awaken their purpose. Not just any command. They waited for the new Intenfli, heir to the ancient bloodline, the one whose voice bore the weight of creation. Only then would their blades be drawn, not in wrath, but in remembrance.

Back in the council chamber, the final echoes of energy clung to the crystal arches like vapor, then dispersed into stillness, sharp, sacred, and complete. Orion stepped forward once more, his presence drawing the weight of the room around him like a cloak. The Starborn Vanguard advanced with him, Rachel's stance poised and alert, Eymd's eyes aglow with silent focus, Verjast exuding barely leashed power, Snjallt shifting with quiet calculation, Vilantina radiating solemn grace, and Fray's gaze cool and sharp.

"There is more you must understand," Orion said, his voice low and resonant, like the toll of a starbell. "This is not an ending. It is the ignition of what must come. I am bound to another trial, one woven into the Pactum itself, into the bloodline I carry, and into the unseen currents shaping our fate."

Gasps broke the silence like glass. Delegates leaned in, drawn to the gravity in his words.

"Atlantis will stand as your shield," Orion continued, his tone now firm with command. "P.I.L.S.S. is awakened. Its protocols are ancient, tested in the crucibles of extinction. The Stone Guard stir not for conquest, but for guardianship. They will not move until I call them, but in their stillness lies your safety."

Rachel lifted her chin, her voice cutting cleanly through the room. "The E.D.A. will hold the line. Across cities, skies, oceans we will defend what we have reclaimed. But to endure, we must share the burden."

Vilantina's wings unfurled with a pulse of radiant force. "Orion will not walk alone. But the journey is his to complete. Only by reaching its end can any of us hope to survive the storm on the horizon."

Fray stepped forward, voice clipped and precise. "Atlantis is fortified. The Earth is not yet broken. The world watches. Let them see our strength."

Orion's gaze swept the chamber, lingering on each delegate. He saw hesitation, awe, resolve, and something deeper: belief kindling into flame.

"I do not go to abandon you," he said, and his voice carried like sunrise over ruins. "I go because I must ascend. Because the world you dream of cannot be defended by memory alone. It must be reborn in motion."

Later, in the stillness of his private quarters, Orion stood alone. The walls shimmered with faint constellations, pulsing gently as if breathing with him. A low chime echoed through the air, followed by the soft hiss of a hidden panel sliding open.

From within, a sleek mannequin emerged, cloaked in shadow and starlight. Upon it rested a new set of armour deeper in colour, forged from Starwoven Alloy, a living metal born of collapsed stardust and ancestral resonance, veined with lines of white-gold energy. The chest plate bore a stylised starburst sigil pulsing with faint blue light. It was not ceremonial. It was alive.

A voice resonated in the room, smooth and warm.

"Orion," said P.I.L.S.S., "your new interface has been completed. Forged in accordance with your biometrics, ancestral frequency, and command lineage. Shall we connect again, as we did during the fall?"

Orion stepped closer. The armour seemed to hum at his presence, not with mechanical readiness, but with recognition as though some part of it remembered him.

"Yes," he whispered.

As he reached out, stardust-laced tendrils of light unfurled from the armour and wrapped gently around his wrist. In that instant, a cascade of data streamed across his mind not numbers, not code, but memory. Visions flared behind his eyes: maps of the city's hidden layers, echoes of ancient battles, P.I.L.S.S.'s dormant grief, and the memory of Atlantis bleeding light into darkness.

"Welcome back, Intenfli," P.I.L.S.S. said, reverently.

Orion exhaled, shoulders squaring.

The armour responded.

The plates of Starwoven Alloy shimmered, then liquefied with eerie grace. They lifted from the mannequin in swirling ribbons, wrapping around Orion in graceful arcs. Each segment hissed as it bonded to him, flowing over his limbs, spine, and chest like molten constellations. The metal was warm, breathing, syncing to his pulse. He gasped as a momentary surge of celestial power pulsed through his bones, his thoughts interwoven with the living alloy.

The final layer coalesced at his chest, forming a luminous starburst sigil that pulsed once then again with harmonic resonance.

And somewhere deeper, beneath words and light, the city sighed.

"I'm ready," Orion said, his voice newly weighted by destiny.

# 18. The Trial Of Life

The Intenarii alongside Orion assembled like a storm beneath the vaulted ribs of Atlantis's upper docking tier, where graceful Atlantean arches arced overhead like drawn blades and banners of the sacred vow snapped in a manufactured gale. Each silk pennant, stitched with silver runes, quivered into life as if gasping for breath. Beyond the yawning bay, the city pulsed, a living constellation of crystal spires and etheric filigree throbbing to the planet's clandestine heartbeat, like a slumbering deity stirred by prophecy.

Before them crouched their ship: a crescent-winged leviathan, half-Atlantean, half-Xerist, forged in silence and storm. Its hull shimmered with burnished plates laced by bioluminescent veins, its engines glowing like the embers in a god's breath. The deck trembled beneath their feet, a promise of velocity, a sanctuary forged in fury.

Rachel cinched her prototype gauntlet tight, the unstable blue core pulsing with jagged light. Each throb kissed the air with the taste of thunder, as if the gauntlet hungered for confrontation. Beside her, Fray hovered like a hawk, luminous fingers darting across a hovering holo-display, reading data like prophecies.

Captain Aaron stood apart in silence, his figure carved in shadow and intent. The ship's glow traced the harsh angles of his face, but it was the tension in his posture that betrayed the storm inside. Around him, the others prepared in their own quiet rituals: Eymd whispered to her curved blades, their edge humming like grief. Verjast weighed a vial of liquid galaxies in his palm. Snjallt traced glyphs in the air with blue fire. Vilantina, motionless and radiant, simply waited her breath in rhythm with the cosmos.

Orion stepped forward, his presence anchoring them all. "The Cradle waits. I will face it alone, but your purpose carries me to the threshold."

Rachel's voice rang like tempered crystal. "Then we walk with you to the edge."

Without further word, the Intenarii ascended the ramp, the ship sealing shut with a breathless hiss. The engines roared a creature waking from eons of slumber and the vessel plunged not into sky, but into stone.

They dove beneath Africa's oldest bones. Layers of history peeled away, replaced by veins of pulsing crystal and walls etched with Atlantean harmonics coded frequencies that sang in lost tongues. Through tremors and molten veins, they were led by the Earth's memory.

At last, the vessel emerged into a vaulted subterranean cathedral, carved by tectonic whispers and the patient hands of time. Spires of refracted crystal arced into the cavern's dome, and monoliths drifted like ancient thoughts, wrapped in coils of forgotten light.

The Cradle of Life.

Fog glimmered across a causeway of living stone. Orion stepped forward, his breath catching. The hum of creation beat beneath his soles.

Then movement.

Figures emerged from a mirrored treeline. The Xal'thane: tall, otherworldly, skin like prism-glass etched in runes, robes flowing with stardust. Their eyes held starbursts frozen in ice.

Rachel's gauntlet sparked. Aaron's fingers twitched near his sidearm.

But the air thickened. One guardian stepped forward, slow and deliberate. It placed a hand over its jewelled sternum and spoke, its voice resonating like tectonic pressure:

"You tread where life was first whispered. We are the Xal'thane Guardians of Life. Earth chose us to defend its spark. If you falter, we do not forgive. We end."

Orion's reply was a calm flame. "We seek the trial."

The Xal'thane bowed. "The Cradle has chosen. One alone may pass. The rest remain under our gaze."

The guardians parted. A gate opened pulsing, alive. The Intenarii formed a ring of silence as Orion approached.

Rachel pressed a hand to his arm. "We'll hold the edge."

Aaron stepped in, his voice cracked but strong. "I don't care about stars. I care about you. Come back."

Orion touched his cheek. "Then I will."

No kiss. Only truth. Only fire.

He turned.

And crossed into genesis.

The chamber bloomed around him. Its walls rose like lungs breathing starlight and history. Constellations shifted above like memories drawn in motion. The floor rippled, a mirror of forgotten skies.

A voice, ancient and intimate, coiled through him:

"You have endured guilt. You have embraced forgiveness. Now, you must master genesis."

Mist swirled. A black dais rose. On it absence. Not emptiness, but potential.

"Creation is not sacrifice," the voice said. "You have bled. Now, give nothing and create."

He stepped forward. The chamber shifted.

A child emerged faceless, weeping, woven of shadow and light. "Give me your light."

He trembled. The storm within called to unleash. But instead, he knelt.

"What do you need?"

"To be seen."

He looked, and that was enough. The child dissolved, smiling.

A world appeared, dying. Fire and silence.

"Restore it."

He did not raise his hand. He remembered. Not just the sound of rain, or the breath of growing things but the moment he had conjured Promendium in the heart of despair. How he had shaped a substance from will and memory, fusing forgotten alloys and starlit essence to give birth to something that had never existed. He recalled the feeling: not of power, but of presence. Of aligning with the rhythm of the universe, and letting it flow through him like breath returned. The sound of rain. Of breath. Of seeds.

He believed.

And life answered.

From the ashes of the broken world, forests unfurled like dreams reborn. Rivers carved new paths through memory. The sky shed its veil of smoke and sang in azure clarity. At the centre of it all, light danced pure and radiant.

Then came more.

His breath deepened, and the chamber listened. Mountains sprouted where none had stood, veined with crystal rivers. A flock of winged creatures burst from the newly grown canopy, feathers glinting with the hues of dusk and dawn. Trees bore fruit laced with golden threads, their leaves singing faint, harmonic tones. Amphibious beings slithered from hidden pools, blinking with innocent wonder. Every spark of life flowed from thought not as command, but as an offering.

The chamber pulsed, not with approval, but with awe.

This was not replication it was revelation. Life that had never been. Songs never sung. Faces never imagined. He did not give a part of himself to make it he allowed creation to rise through the space he held.

It pulsed not with power, but with presence not born of command, but of communion.

Then the mirror. Tall. Obsidian. Within, himself: crowned, broken, silent.

"What do you create when the creator is empty?"

He stepped close, every breath a quiet storm.

"I create space for voices not yet heard. I create silence for truth to bloom. I create trust in the promise of what will come."

The mirror shattered, not with violence, but revelation. Light didn't just pour out it sang.

And from the shards rose Orion reborn in radiance, eyes ablaze with starlit conviction. But this time, something deeper stirred.

Galaxies wheeled open, constellations whispered in tones only he could now hear. Every star was a syllable. Every flicker, a breath.

Star magic flooded him, but not as a gift it recognised him. He was not its master. He was its reflection, its axis. The force he once summoned now pulsed in his bones like memory. He had become the language of creation.

"You are no longer the vessel," the voice whispered. "You are the magic itself."

The stars bowed not to a king, but to kin. Orion stood no longer separate from the cosmos. He was its will. Its dawn.

The Cradle did not simply end the trial it crowned the truth.

Orion rose not as a boy reborn, but as the seed of genesis unbound.

The chamber expanded. The walls dissolved into galaxies, and the dome above became an ocean of constellations. Star magic once a tool, once a mystery now coursed through him not like a river through a channel, but as his very blood, his breath, his being.

"You are no longer the vessel," the voice whispered. "You are the magic itself."

The stars bent toward him in silent reverence. No longer did he wield power. He was power alive, aware, infinite.

The Cradle did not simply end the trial. It had revealed the truth: Orion's journey had not led him to power. It had returned him to what he had always been.

Orion rose no longer bound by memory, but as genesis incarnate. As the chamber of stars pulsed around him, his form began to shift no longer bound by the dimensions he once knew. His body stretched skyward, rising beyond the frame of his former self. Muscles realigned, not in bulk but in balance, forged with the harmony of galaxies. His frame elongated until he stood over seven feet tall, a living monument of starborn inheritance.

His skin shimmered with layers of cosmic flux like stardust painted over galactic stone and pearl. Lines of radiant stardust glyphs etched themselves along his arms and collarbone, marking him as both the wielder and the weave. His hair glowed faintly with silver threads, not unlike the aura that surrounded him when he had first awakened in the Library's archive, but now it crackled with sovereignty.

He was not cloaked in magic he was the cloak. The air bent around him. Gravity slowed its grip. The chamber recognised him as a returned son.

This was not a transformation. This was an unveiling.

The Old Ones had whispered it when he had spoken to them that the stars did not simply grant power, they remembered those they once called kin. And now they remembered him fully.

The chamber stirred. Light twisted in arcs around Orion as if testing the limits of his new form. A flash sharp and sudden cut through the space before him. A beam of compressed starlight, faster than thought, shot toward his chest.

Orion moved.

Not with effort, but with instinct. His arm swept up, fingers flicking outward in a counter-motion that dissolved the beam before it touched him. Another followed, curving from behind, its energy cloaked in darkness. He pivoted, fluid and precise, a blur of cosmic grace. The attack vanished in a ripple of golden shimmer.

He did not falter.

The chamber began to accelerate, glyphs swirling around him in spirals of shifting colour. Platforms of light rose and fell, spinning like the rings of distant worlds. He leapt no, glided across them, his motions elegant and absolute. He did not command the chamber's rhythm. He became it.

Each test was not to challenge him but to affirm him. That his body, now vessel and source, was no longer bound by hesitation or fear.

He landed at the centre, light surging around his silhouette.

Orion flexed his fingers. The air hummed in reply.

And for the first time, he smiled not in triumph, but in understanding.

Far beyond the chamber, in the crystalline vale where the Intenarii stood among the Xal'thane, the air trembled. The monoliths pulsed in synchronous light. The guardians stirred, tilting their heads as if listening to a celestial chord only they could hear.

Rachel felt her gauntlet vibrate in silence. Snjallt froze mid-chant. Aaron's breath caught. The ground beneath them briefly shimmered with light that resonated in the bones, not the ears.

One of the Xal'thane turned to the Intenarii and bowed deep, reverent.

"It is done," the guardian murmured. "He has remembered what he is."

Above them, the arch to the chamber unfurled like the petals of a cosmic bloom. And from its heart, a figure emerged taller, radiant, cloaked in a living aura that shimmered like the horizon of a star.

Orion had returned.

Not as the boy who entered.

But as the being the stars once trusted with their name.

He looked at his hands no longer fragile, but forged in memory and fire and felt the silent truth ripple through him.

"I am almost whole again," he said softly, his voice layered with stardust and certainty. "Almost."

Rachel staggered back a half-step, breath stolen. Her gauntlet dimmed and sparked, momentarily overwhelmed by the radiant field emanating from him. Tears welled in her eyes not of sorrow, but recognition. She whispered, "You really did it."

Aaron's hands clenched, then opened slowly. A reverent smile curved his lips. He didn't speak. He didn't need to. His gaze locked onto Orion's, pride and love written in every line of his face.

Eymd dropped to one knee in instinctive homage, her blades crossed over her chest. But more than awe stirred within her she felt it deep in her bones, in the star-forged fragment of Orion's heart she carried. It pulsed in unison with him now, not as a remnant but as a tether. Her breath caught as her heartbeat synced with his new rhythm, a resonance not of memory, but of becoming. "You walk with the breath of stars," she murmured, voice trembling with reverence.

Verjast's vial slipped from his grasp, hovering in mid-air, suspended by Orion's aura. He stared in awe, voice caught in his throat.

Snjallt clutched her bandolier of potions, eyes wide behind her lenses. "It's not just magic," she said, barely above a whisper. "He's... become part of the source."

Vilantina bowed her head, golden wings unfolding behind her in silent acknowledgment.

Even the Xal'thane, ancient and unreadable, lowered themselves onto one knee. Their leader pressed a fist to their heart and spoke in the language of stars.

"Welcome, Child of the Infinite. The wheel of light moves again, and with it, all destinies shift."

The guardian's voice deepened, its crystalline tone edged with gravity. "But know this: the light cannot rise without passing through its shadow. There is no light without darkness. You have mastered genesis, but the balance is not yet whole."

Another guardian stepped forward, eyes pulsing with threads of dark flame. "What is born must one day fall. The Trial of Life is but the first star in a constellation of becoming."

A silence swept the vale as their words hung heavy in the air.

"You must next walk the path no light dares tread," the leader intoned. "The Trial of Death awaits you, Orion. Not all who step into that night return. Prepare your soul."

After the guardian's words faded, the vale did not return to silence. Instead, the Xal'thane beckoned Orion and the Intenarii toward a tiered crystal platform where a bizarre yet elegant meal had been laid out.

Dishes floated above the surface, shifting in shape and hue as if tasting thoughts. Spherical fruits pulsed with inner light, shedding mist that curled like smoke around glass blossoms filled with violet nectar. Coils of translucent root-meat twisted midair, rearranging themselves with every breath. A shimmering pool of silver broth steamed at the centre, reflecting faces not as they were but as they might become.

Rachel hesitated, then reached for a fragment of sun-fruit, biting into it. Her eyes widened.

"It tastes like home... and something I've never known," she murmured.

Verjast sipped from a floating petal, blinking as if it had whispered a secret to him.

The Xal'thane sat among them not speaking, but radiating a low harmonic that hummed through the bones of the earth. It was not a feast. It was communion.

Orion, silent still, descended the final step of the chamber's threshold and moved toward the gathering. The others parted instinctively, making space as he approached the crystalline platform.

With a quiet nod, he took a seat between Aaron and Eymd, the light of his aura gently dimming as if in deference to the moment.

Eymd passed him a dish an iridescent spiral that changed colour in her hands. Orion accepted it, the food shifting form as if recognising him. He tasted it. It was unlike anything he had known: at once starlight and soil, memory and prophecy.

Aaron looked at him, wide-eyed but calm, and offered him a pale slice of something that glowed faintly blue. "I think this one's safe," he said, a small smile breaking through his awe.

Orion chuckled softly and took the piece, savouring its strange, silken sweetness.

Around them, the meal continued bizarre, surreal, sacred. A communion not just of flesh, but of becoming.

As Orion chewed thoughtfully, his gaze flicked to Eymd beside him. Without moving her lips, she spoke directly into his mind a gentle, familiar rhythm.

"I felt it happen," she whispered across their bond. "When you changed... the piece of your heart inside me changed too. It surged. It sang. It was like I was being rewritten while still breathing."

Orion met her eyes, a quiet flame dancing in his own. "You were never just a carrier, Eymd. That piece of me it brought you back, yes, but it doesn't belong to me anymore. My heart has mended itself... and yours carries that spark now. It's become yours. But between us, it still hums. A living bridge. A reminder. Always."

"You moved like the stars were inside your bones," she thought, her voice reverent. "You've become more than I was told you would become. You're becoming the song the stars once kept hidden."

He smiled not outwardly, but through the current that bound them. "I may have changed, but I'm still me, Eymd. Still the same heart just closer now to what it was always meant to become. Let's keep walking. Let's see where the adventure takes us."

# 19. The Trial Of Death

The next morning, the mist over the Cradle of Life swirled with the whisper of farewells. As Orion and the others stepped from the crystalline vale, leaving behind the echoes of genesis, the ship's hull shimmered with anticipation.

A chime pulsed in Orion's mind the signature tone of P.I.L.S.S.

"Orion," the AI said, its voice deeper now, laced with reverence, "while you walked the chamber of genesis, a transmission reached me scattered, ancient. It originated from the uncharted heart of the Amazon Rainforest. The lost tribe residing there spoke of the final trial. They were expecting you."

Orion turned slowly. "How would they know?"

"They always have," P.I.L.S.S. replied. "They are not bound by time as we understand it. And... there's more."

A pause.

"The one you captured Enaquia of the Great Four. She was taken from Earth's custody. I have tracked her signal. She was delivered... to the Trial of Death."

Orion's breath stilled.

"I forgot her," he admitted quietly. With everything the trial, the transformation, the pulse of stars singing in his veins her presence had slipped from his thoughts. Not out of indifference, but sheer overwhelm. He had changed so much, and in that vast redefinition, some truths had scattered like dust. Only now, with P.I.L.S.S.'s words, did the memory resurface sharp, urgent, undeniable.

"No," P.I.L.S.S. answered. "You remembered her now. That is enough. Memory returns to those willing to carry it."

As the weight of the revelation settled, Orion stood motionless at the helm. The hum of the vessel deepened, and coordinates shifted guided not by maps, but by fate. Below them, the crust of Africa slowly gave way to sky. They rose above the verdant Earth, not in triumph, but in quiet knowing.

Then southwest. The ship curved in silence toward the great green lungs of the world. Toward the forgotten interior of the Amazon Rainforest, where myths still breathed and light seldom touched.

There, cloaked in memory and shadow, the final trial waited.

Not a battlefield. Not a throne.

But death itself.

And of all the trials, this was the one Orion had feared most. Not for lack of courage but because it stood in opposition to everything within him. He who had created, who had healed, who had given pieces of himself to restore others he did not want to take life. The concept itself jarred against his soul like discordant notes in a song of harmony. It reminded him of Strixium, how he had chosen to bind that terrible force in stone rather than end him. But with the loss of his powers during his fall, that seal had likely fractured. He had forgotten Enaquia, yes but perhaps, on some level, he had wanted to forget the truth of what was coming. Yet deep down, he knew: to walk through death was to understand it. And understanding did not always come without loss.

As the ship descended through a veil of mist into the emerald cathedral of the Amazon, the air thickened with memory. They passed beneath canopies that had never known satellite eyes or human names, where vines curled like sleeping serpents and the scent of blooming secrets lingered.

Then they saw them.

At the edge of a cliff wrapped in cloud and moss, the tribe appeared neither startled nor aggressive, but still as stone. Their skin was inked with constellations, some glowing faintly beneath their chests and eyes. Their garments shimmered with leaves interwoven with filaments of gold and ancient tech. Atop their heads, some wore crowns of woven light.

They had no weapons. But the way they looked at Orion the way the jungle itself stilled around them was more threatening than any blade.

The leader stepped forward, taller than the rest, with a gaze as endless as the river behind him. He did not speak aloud. Instead, the words pressed into Orion's thoughts like heat from the sun.

"You have come late, but you have come. Death does not wait, child of stars. And we do not suffer pretenders."

Around the leader, more of the tribe emerged, their eyes glowing with quiet judgment. The canopy groaned as if the rainforest itself breathed in unison.

Rachel's fingers tensed near her gauntlet. Aaron stepped closer to Orion. But none moved.

Then the leader gestured not with hostility, but with finality.

"The Trial awaits. And the jungle does not lie."

He turned then not to Orion, but to the others who stood ready to follow.

"You must remain aboard your vessel until the Trial is done. The land of death does not welcome those who do not walk it alone. If you set foot where the soul must journey unburdened, the jungle will not be kind."

His voice, though silent, pressed heavy against their hearts less a warning, more a truth. Even the birds above seemed to pause, as if the trees themselves agreed.

Without another word, Orion turned and walked toward the edge of the vessel's ramp. He did not say goodbye. No parting looks. No whispered vows. His silence was not cold it was sacred.

The moment his foot touched the moss-covered earth beyond the threshold, the air thickened and shimmered.

And in an instant, his form rippled tall grace vanishing in a breath. The towering vessel of star-magic condensed, folded inward. His hair shortened, his stature shrank. The glow dimmed. What remained was a boy.

Orion before the Cradle, before the stars, before destiny's crown.

The jungle had stripped him of power not in cruelty, but in challenge.

Here, in the land of death, he could carry no godhood's mask.

Only the truth of himself.

His power still thrummed beneath the surface, hidden but intact. The jungle had stripped his celestial form, not his essence. In this place, only the raw soul mattered not the radiance that cloaked it. His strength remained, folded tight like starlight behind cloud cover, waiting.

The jungle stirred in answer.

Vines tightened across the canopy above, leaves shimmering with sudden iridescence as if reacting to the echo of the starborn power now veiled within him. Trees leaned inward, groaning softly with wooden breath. Birds did not sing. Insects did not stir. The land had noticed.

And so had the tribe.

The leader, still standing at the cliff's edge, narrowed his eyes. One hand lifted palm out, as if to measure the unseen. He said nothing, but his gaze shifted, not with contempt, but wary reverence.

"You wear the skin of a child," he said, voice pressing into Orion's thoughts like thunder in fog, "but you are not small. We feel what walks beneath your silence."

Around him, the tribe began to chant not with joy or malice, but with a rhythm older than language. Their voices rose in low, resonant harmony, vibrating through the moss and stone. The sound echoed through the forest, awakening vines that curled inward, revealing a veiled passage cloaked in a drifting haze of luminous spores, as if the jungle exhaled memory itself.

The entrance to the Trial of Death had revealed itself not by force, but by recognition.

The jungle opened, and the silence that followed was not absence. It was an invitation.

"The jungle sees," the leader added, "and it does not forget."

Orion stepped forward, alone. As his body passed through the veiled passage of luminous spores, a quiet pressure enveloped him neither hostile nor warm, but aware. The spores clung to his skin like dust from forgotten stars, illuminating his every breath. Each step shifted the colours around him blues deepening into void-black, greens flaring into sun-gold.

The trees thickened. Their trunks coiled upward in impossible spirals, bark etched with symbols that pulsed faintly with life. Vines drooped like silk tendrils, brushing against him, tasting his presence. The deeper he walked, the quieter the world became, until even his footsteps seemed swallowed by moss and memory.

Time unravelled.

The path beneath his feet flowed not stone, not root, but something in between, a living conduit guiding him forward. Shadows rippled along the edge of vision, some humanoid, some not. None approached. They watched.

Above, the canopy parted briefly to reveal a sliver of sky blood-orange and swirling with celestial wind. Orion felt a heartbeat that was not his own echo through the forest.

He was not merely in the jungle.

He was inside death's breath.

A clearing opened ahead, round as a pupil, and in its centre stood a figure tall, cloaked in tattered black-veined white, their face veiled in shimmering mist.

It turned, slow and soundless.

"Welcome, Orion," it said not in words, but in memories he had buried.

The trial had truly begun.

And the jungle deepened around him.

The trees no longer stood as mere sentinels they bent inward, twisted by ancient design. Their leaves wept with dew the colour of dusk, and their roots coiled like serpents into glowing patterns that pulsed with spectral memory. Bioluminescent fungi bloomed from hanging branches, whispering secrets in pulses of light. Some resembled eyes; others, mouths half-formed in moss.

The air itself thickened, tinged with the faint scent of petrichor and decay, as if every breath he took was borrowed from something older than the Earth itself. Strange birds of lightless plumage watched from perches unseen, their eyes flickering like candle flames. Insects the size of coins moved in geometric formations, weaving webs of energy that shimmered between the trunks like constellations spun too low.

Sound unravelled. His footsteps made no echo, and the rhythm of his heart seemed to reverberate against the undergrowth, each beat answered by something vast and waiting.

Orion could feel it now not just death as a force, but as a presence. A spirit woven into every branch, every flicker, every silence.

And still, the path wound forward beckoning.

Orion moved toward the cloaked figure with slow, deliberate steps. The ground softened beneath his feet, not yielding, but accepting. The deeper he stepped into the clearing, the more the veil of mist surrounding the figure began to shift threads of memory unravelling in silence.

He could feel the air condense around him, a hush so complete it seemed to press against his skin. His pulse steadied, his thoughts sharpened. The spores clinging to him dimmed, as if respecting the gravity of the moment.

Each stride was a conversation between him and the unknown.

And still, the figure did not move.

Orion came to a halt a few paces before it. The distance between them pulsed not space, but meaning.

The figure raised its head slightly, and though its face remained hidden behind a veil of drifting silver light, its presence struck like the whisper of thunder.

"Are you ready to learn what it is to become wielder of death itself?" it asked in a bone-chilling voice.

And Orion, no longer a god nor a boy, but something between, nodded once.

The mist between them trembled, and with a gesture like the fold of a dying leaf, the figure extended one hand. Within its palm hovered a memory not seen, but lived.

Orion gasped as it consumed him.

Enaquia's hand seized him by the front of his armour, lifting him effortlessly into the air. Her eyes burned with cruel delight as she held him suspended, his feet dangling above the ground. Time slowed to a crawl as the battlefield blurred around them.

"Goodbye, Orion," she hissed.

Her fist glowed with burning energy, and when it struck, the world exploded. He was flung backward. Pain carved him open as the pull of the collapsing portal yawned behind him.

And in that final moment before he vanished, he saw it Anton.

His brother turned just as a fireball, searing and immense, struck him in the chest. He crumpled, flames consuming him, and Orion's last glimpse before blackness took him was of Anton's body falling, still and silent.

"Why show me this again?" Orion whispered.

The figure's voice drifted through the memory like a cold wind. "Because you still believe you failed him."

"I did," Orion said. "He died because I wasn't fast enough. Because I chose wrong."

"No," the figure said. "He died because it was time. His thread was written. Even your light could not rewrite what was sealed into the breath of the stars."

The image flickered, slowing. Orion saw something he hadn't before Anton's final glance. Not panic. Not fear.

Peace.

"He knew," Orion murmured.

"Yes," the figure replied. "Because sometimes death is not defeat. Sometimes it is design."

The vision faded, leaving only the quiet breath of the jungle.

But the figure was not finished.

It raised its hand once more, and a second vision bloomed another reality, one where Orion had reached Anton in time, pulled him back through the portal by sheer force of will.

Yet even there, death came.

A sickness in Anton's veins, a collapse on a later battlefield, a final breath whispered in a moment of peace. Again and again, no matter the path, Anton's thread ended.

Orion staggered under the weight of it.

"There are deaths you cannot save," the figure said. "Because they are not yours to hold back."

It gestured gently, and the multiple endings faded into starlight.

"This is the truth you must bear. Death is not always a consequence. Sometimes, it is a calling."

From the swirling mist, voices echoed softly whispers layered with age and sorrow, as if the jungle itself was speaking through them. "Some threads end no matter the hand that holds them," they murmured. "Some songs close even as others begin.""

"You are not here to undo death," the figure said, voice now softer, older. "You are here to learn to carry it. As you give life, so too must you be its counterweight. You are not just a bearer of light but the courier of endings, the one who must know when to let go, and to help others find peace in that letting go.

The figure turned once more, and the mists curled tighter, thickening into a new vision.

Orion watched himself again, this time showing the stone guards marched forward, dragging the shadowy figure of Strixium, whose once defiant demeanour had dimmed. Shadows coiled like vipers around the edges of Orion's memory. Power surged at his fingertips, sharpened by judgment.

"You are accused of genocide and the murder of a royal family member. How do you plead?" Orion demanded, his voice a blade.

Strixium's laughter echoed, manic and defiant. "Foolish boy. My master will come for me."

Orion's lips curled into a smirk. "Your master? Do you truly believe she will rescue a failure? Think, Strixium. You've served her poorly."

The realisation struck Strixium like a blow. His confidence wavered. "I... I acted in her name! Please... show mercy."

"Mercy?" Orion's tone darkened. "I find you guilty of all charges. For your crimes, I sentence you to live the rest of your days encased in stone. And I strip away your powers."

Before Strixium could protest, dark tendrils erupted from Orion's hands, striking the condemned man. Strixium screamed as his magic was torn from him, leaving only a trembling husk. Orion stepped forward and pressed his palm to Strixium's forehead, releasing the sealing spell. Stone erupted over his limbs and face, freezing his final scream in eternity.

A flash of light marked the spell's end. And when it faded, a statue stood before them a twisted image of Strixium's last breath, immortalised.

Now the vision shifted.

Orion wounded, drained lay unconscious after the Fall. The encased figure of Strixium's seal cracked like old ice.

And then the other three came.

Enaquia, Lucandr, Josnan the Great Four, reunited stood at the edge of the stone prison. With power, fury, and vengeance, they shattered what remained.

Strixium rose freed not by fate, but by the cracks in Orion's mercy.

"You chose mercy," the figure said.

"And mercy has its cost."

The mist boiled violently, and another vision surged into view Strixium, no longer chained, stood over a hologram projecting images of Orion's remaining family. The twisted grin carved into his face was almost inhuman.

"You should have killed me, little star," he hissed. "Now look what you've given me more toys to play with."

He stepped forward in the vision, raising a hand as if to caress the projection. The images shifted faces Orion knew and loved, his mother Aurorina, his father Lawrence, his remaining brother Jake and Lillithan.

Strixium's voice echoed with venomous delight.

"I wonder whose screams will be the sweetest. I've waited a long time to return the favour."

The vision snapped closed like a jaw.

The figure watched Orion silently, allowing the weight to settle. "This is the legacy of spared wrath. Mercy without vigilance invites ruin."

Orion trembled.

The cold fury rising in his chest was not born of vengeance, but of revenge. His breath hitched as the faces of those he loved his mother, his father, Jake, Lillithan flashed through his mind, twisted by Strixium's mockery.

He clenched his fists, fingernails biting into his palms. For all his power, all his starfire and promise, he had let Strixium live. He had hoped mercy might be a cure.

Now that mercy had teeth.

"I should have ended him," Orion said, voice hoarse, barely above a whisper.

The figure said nothing.

"But I didn't," he continued. "Because I wanted to believe there was something left to save. Something even he could still become."

His shoulders shook, not with fear but with the weight of understanding.

"And if they suffer because of that mistake then I will carry it. All of it."

The jungle fell utterly silent, and the hooded figure vanished as if swallowed by the fabric of the Trial itself.

Then came the shift slow, seismic. The sky blackened as if a dying star had cast its last breath across the heavens. The air thickened into a suffocating shroud, every particle charged with ancient judgment. The ground beneath Orion's feet cracked into black ash, pulsing with veins of red light. Trees ignited from within, burning silently, their branches writhing like skeletal limbs in agony.

At the far end of the clearing stood Enaquia.

She did not flinch. Her eyes shimmered with contempt, her smile the cruel crescent of someone who believed herself eternal.

Orion stepped forward. His aura seethed not with rage, but with absolute clarity. The air around him split into fractures of light and shadow, the resonance of something godlike and final.

The trial was over.

Judgment had come.

"I am the wielder of death," Orion said, his voice low, gravelled by stars.

Enaquia laughed, the sound like glass breaking underfoot. "You think you can claim death, Orion?" she sneered. "You couldn't even kill my brother. You sealed him in stone like a coward and called it mercy. And now he's free. What makes you think you can do any better with me?"

"No," he replied, his voice sharper now. "I let your brother live because I believed in redemption. I showed mercy when I should have delivered justice."

He stepped forward, the shadows and starlight around him coiling tighter. "I won't make that mistake again."

He lifted his hand, and stardust unfurled like a halo of knives around his fingers. Not fury. Not vengeance.

Certainty.

"Like you ended Anton," he said, each word sharp as law, "I am ending you."

Stardust flared in his eyes. The heavens above wept solar fire. Time slowed to a crawl as the world held its breath.

Then, with a sudden tremor in the air, the ground before Enaquia split open. From the fissure rose a figure hulking and terrible, sculpted from dusk-hued stone laced with stardust veins. Its eyes burned with silver fire, and across its chest was etched the sigil of the Final Rite. This was no ordinary Stone Guard it was Death's Warden, the end made manifest.

It stepped forward in silence, and with one great hand, seized Enaquia by the arms. She snarled, a shriek of rage twisting from her throat. Her body writhed, attempting to break free, tendrils of violet flame surging from her hands only to be extinguished upon contact with the chains. Her expression warped from contempt to disbelief, then to pure panic as the Warden's grasp tightened with finality.

Her feet left the earth. Her body arched against the bindings, every muscle flaring in defiance but the more she struggled, the more the chains constricted, feeding on resistance like a beast long-starved. Chains of starlaced bone and ash coiled upward like ancient verdicts, rising up from the ground, pulsing with a cold, alien rhythm, latching around her limbs like the judgment of time itself.

She was caught not by Orion, but by the will of death incarnate.

And in that moment, Orion raised his hand.

"I unmake you. I erase you from time itself. All that you could have become will be no more. There will be no redemption or rebirth after this just an empty void where you used to be."

The words rang like divine verdict.

The instant they left his lips, the air shattered like glass under pressure. The sky roared. The world trembled.

Enaquia's scream tore through the silence but was not heard, only felt as her form twisted violently, unravelling in spirals of light and ash, pulled apart by the laws she had defied.

She did not die.

She ceased.

And far away, in the deep infinity of the Library of All That Was, the moment echoed like a chime in eternity. A single book bearing her name began to tremble upon its shelf its bindings creaked, its spine split, and then, with a sigh of finality, it withered into ash. Its pages curled into glowing cinders. No echo. No title. No trace. Even the index that once listed her presence rewrote itself in silence.

Where once stood a Horseman of Ruin, now there was only absence.

Death had a new hand.

And its name was Orion.

In the stillness that followed, the air around Orion pulsed once and then again as if the world were relearning his shape. The shadows that had cloaked him peeled away, and his true form emerged. No longer veiled in childhood nor cloaked in divine glamour, Orion stood tall restored not just in height, but in essence. His body stretched upward, limbs lengthening, his stature rising to over seven feet. Stardust coursed visibly beneath his skin, constellations flowing like rivers across his arms and collarbone.

But something had changed.

Where before there was the luminous radiance of life, now there was also the chill grace of finality. Etched along his spine, new sigils glowed with shifting hues symbols of both genesis and end, bound in harmony. His eyes shimmered with mirrored galaxies, one dark as a collapsed star, the other bright as newborn flame.

From his back unfurled wings vast and ethereal woven from starlight and dusk. Each feather shimmered with duality: one side a radiant white that pulsed with life's essence, the other a shadowy silver, heavy with the solemn weight of death. They moved not with wind, but with thought, casting halos of twilight wherever they stretched. In their quiet rustle echoed the breath of galaxies born and the silence of worlds ending. His voice, when he exhaled, resonated not only in air but in the soil, the wind, and the hearts of those nearby.

Somewhere, far above the clouds, the stars pulsed once acknowledging their kin.

And in that moment, the last of Orion's fragmented connection to the stars fused together. The bond, once frayed by death and grief, was whole again.

The Star magic did not return to him.

He became it.

Far above, aboard the waiting ship, Eymd gasped.

She clutched her chest not in pain, but in recognition. The piece of Orion's heart that beat within her pulsed with sudden brilliance, a surge of warmth and power threading through her veins like liquid dawn.

"He's whole," she whispered, eyes wide.

Aaron turned sharply. "What do you mean?"

"I felt him... become," she said, voice barely a breath. "The part of him in me his gift it shimmered. He's no longer just connected to the stars. He is the stars."

The others gathered close, silent.

Even Vilantina bowed her head.

From the edges of the jungle canopy, a low hum resonated distant yet distinct. As if the land, too, had sensed his rebirth.

Below the ship, in the sacred glade, the tribe began to stir. The once-still elders raised their heads as one, eyes wide, their glowing tattoos pulsing in synchrony with the energy rising from the earth. Children fell silent. Birds that had hidden since Orion's descent emerged from shadowed nests, wings twitching, feathers aglow with refracted starlight.

The tribal leader stepped forward and dropped to one knee, touching his brow to the mossy earth. A murmur rippled outward prayer or reverence, it was impossible to tell. One by one, the others followed, a great circle of beings bowing not in submission, but in recognition.

"The cycle is complete," the leader whispered to no one and everyone. "He is not merely death. He is the balance."

Above them, the vines swayed despite the still air, and the jungle exhaled a sigh that was not wind but memory itself.

"He's coming back," Eymd said, not as prophecy, but as certainty. And he did.

The veiled passage of the jungle unfurled once more, luminous spores cascading outward like a breath held too long finally released. Light shifted through the trees, casting layered shadows like celestial runes across the mossy ground.

From that corridor of memory and mist, Orion emerged.

Each step he took resonated with the jungle's pulse. The air shimmered around him heatless, electric. His wings, still outstretched, seemed to gather the light and shadow of the forest into their wake.

He was taller now, broader, but what struck the watching tribe and his companions most was not his form it was the presence that preceded it. The harmony of contradiction: power and peace, creation and closure, star and stone.

The tribal leader rose slowly, awe painting his ancient features. The others followed, falling into a hush deeper than reverence.

Aaron was the first of the Intenarii to step forward. "Orion?" he asked, voice tight with something between hope and fear.

Orion's gaze turned to him bright with recognition and deep understanding. "I'm still me," he said simply, voice soft and vast.

# 20. The Balance Starts To Return

The moment Orion stepped from the veiled passage, time itself seemed to hesitate.

His presence rippled across the jungle, through leaf and stone, across bark and breeze. Every thread of the rainforest-sentient and slumbering-responded. The trees leaned forward. The sky parted. Even silence itself felt reverent.

He walked slowly, not with hesitation but with weight. As if each step carried the echo of every death he had accepted and the power of every life he had yet to protect.

His wings arched high behind him, casting twin shadows of light and dusk across the moss-strewn clearing. The tribe knelt again, not from command, but awe.

The Intenarii moved without a word.

Rachel stepped forward first, her gauntlet dimmed in her hand. She searched his face, lips parted.

"You..."

Orion met her eyes and nodded, a playful glint softening the gravity in his gaze. "The trial changed me," he said, then smiled. "But I'm still egg."

Snjallt followed, cautious but curious. She circled him once, then exhaled sharply. "Your magic, it doesn't flow. It radiates. You're no longer drawing from the stars. You are the current."

Eymd stepped closer, her gaze unfocused as if listening not with her ears, but with her heart. "The piece of you that lives in me... it stopped humming. Then it pulsed, like it knew you'd come back whole."

Orion placed a hand gently over hers. "It's still yours, Eymd. What I gave doesn't return. But we're bonded forever."

She nodded, fighting a sudden burn of tears.

Verjast, silent as always, lowered his massive form to one knee and said nothing. But his eyes shone crimson and bright with respect.

Then came Aaron.

He crossed the distance slowly, every muscle tense, every breath shallow. "You said you'd return."

Orion's voice was soft. "I meant it."

Aaron reached for him, not as a soldier, but as a boy who had watched someone walk through death and return as more. "What did it cost?"

Orion looked to the sky, then back to him. "Only the parts I was ready to lose."

He paused, searching Aaron's eyes. "But now that I'm whole again... do you still feel the same?"

Aaron's brow furrowed, but his gaze didn't falter. He stepped closer, resting a hand over Orion's chest, just above the slow pulse of starlight.

"I don't love parts of you, Orion. I love you. Whether scattered or complete, god or ghost. I didn't wait for who you'd become, I waited for you."

They stood in stillness, the jungle stretching like a cathedral around them.

The tribal leader approached, his staff striking the stone softly with each step. "The land knows you. The breath of death no longer follows you, it walks beside you. We will tell your story here, so the forest remembers."

Orion bowed his head.

Rachel looked to the sky. "And now?"

He turned toward the ship. "Now we finish what we began. But not alone."

The Intenarii fell into step behind him. Above them, the vines parted. And the rainforest, for the first time in living memory, sang, a sound like wind, stars, and memory woven into harmony. The song carried beyond the canopy, beyond the continent. Across oceans and cities, deserts and mountains, the world paused to hear it. A melody older than language, newer than hope, echoing the name of the one who had become both end and beginning.

The reunion was complete.

The storm was coming.

But this time, the balance had a name.

Orion.

And across every land and ocean, in every beating heart and silent stone, something stirred. Every creature, great and small paused. A memory not of the mind but of essence itself surfaced. The song that echoed through the trees resonated in them all. They didn't know why they listened. They only knew they must.

Because somewhere within them, they remembered that song.

In a village nestled on the slopes of the Himalayas, an old monk raised his eyes to the sky and whispered a name he hadn't spoken in decades.

In the glowing depths of Atlantis, ancient conduits flickered to life, humming with resonance that matched the new rhythm in the waters.

On the streets of New Tokyo, traffic stilled as citizens turned instinctively toward the rising pulse overhead, their breath catching in unison.

In the ruins of Cairo, the surviving children of the last siege stopped playing and stared upward as if called by a voice older than memory.

And in the high council chamber of the World Alliance, silence fell as every delegate, regardless of creed or nation, felt their pulse echo a beat not their own.

Some wept. Some knelt. Others simply listened.

Because they all knew, something immense had returned.

And the world would never be the same.

In a quiet cave beneath the Scottish Highlands, Vilantina's sister long thought lost to a realm of silence, looked up from her meditation, the star-shaped scar on her palm glowing faintly.

In the moonlit gardens of the Lunari Monastery, Grand Keeper Nahlis dropped her staff mid-prayer and wept openly, whispering, "He's returned. The Child of Starlight lives."

Deep beneath the waves, among coral towers of bioluminescent wonder, the aquatic guardian Aruvel, half-human, half-xenith spread his luminous fins and let out a slow, reverent cry that rolled through the ocean like a hymn.

And on a distant lunar outpost orbiting Mars, the exiled Shadow Scribe Tilver, once loyal to the Xerist Empire, felt his ink well boil dry. The words he tried to write vanished mid-stroke. His final message: "Balance walks again."

In the crystal throne chamber of the Shadow Empire, High Matriarch Elskar stood before the flame of prophecy an ancient living pyre that pulsed only when the tides of fate shifted. It now roared high, casting fractured light across her veiled face. Her attendants fled in fear, but Elskar remained.

"He has returned," she said, voice steady, eyes like twin eclipses. "The thread has been restored. And the endgame... begins anew."

With a single wave of her hand, she extinguished the flame. Darkness fell again, but it trembled with waiting.

Later, as twilight bathed the Elders clearing, Orion sat cross-legged among the elders of the jungle tribe beneath a canopy of woven leaves and softly glowing fruit. The fire at their centre crackled with blue flame, its light dancing across the weathered faces of the gathered guardians.

The tribal leader stirred the embers thoughtfully, then spoke, voice like bark softened by rain. "You ask why we vanished. Why we let the world forget us."

Orion nodded, his wings folded and eyes intent.

"It was not we who forgot the world," the elder said. "It was the world who forgot itself. Its harmony. Its duty to the breath of life. Greed and noise drowned the old songs. You call it progress. We called it a storm."

Another elder, her face marked with silver veins, added, "We remained here, in silence and stewardship, so when the balance returned, we would still be listening. Still be ready."

Orion bowed his head, then looked up thoughtfully. "There's no harm in progress," he said. "Growth, innovation they're not the enemy."

The tribal leader's smile faded, replaced by a solemn weight. "There is when progress forgets its place," he replied. "Their cities grow tall, but their roots poison the soil. Their machines soar, but leave the skies choking. Weapons built in the name of safety now tear holes through the earth. What you call advancement, we have watched become erosion."

The tribal leader smiled faintly. "Now the world has remembered the song. But it must choose whether to sing it or silence it again. Will they take the lessons from your race and build technology that works with the planet, not against it? Or will they once more drown the roots of wisdom beneath towers of glass and steel?"

Orion's gaze lingered on the fire. "Only time itself will tell," he said softly. "But opinions can change and humanity, for all its flaws, is capable of listening. Especially to a people who have walked this world since its first breath. Maybe that's the key. Maybe it's not just about teaching them, but reminding them of what they once knew."

The tribal leader nodded slowly, his eyes reflecting the flicker of the flame. "Then let us remind them together. If the world is to change, it must do so with memory and meaning."

Orion's expression softened, touched by the offer. "It already has one reminder rising from the deep." He met their gazes with quiet intensity. "Atlantis has awakened. Its towers breathe again. And its voice our voice will speak for the Earth."

The tribal leader closed his eyes for a long moment, then opened them with quiet wonder. "We felt it. When the ocean pulled back and the old lights flared once more, our roots trembled. The stones sang. Atlantis is no myth to us it was a promise, sleeping beneath the tides."

Another elder murmured, "We whispered to its bones even in dreams. We wondered if we would live to feel it rise."

Orion nodded slowly. "Then let it be more than memory. Let it be the bridge between what was, and what must be."

He looked across the circle, his voice lowering but gaining intensity. "I would ask that some of you come with me. Join us in Atlantis. Take your place in the Global Council. Let your wisdom shape the path forward, not from the shadows, but from within the halls of power."

The elders exchanged glances, murmurs rippling like wind through leaves.

"It is time the world remembered who its first stewards were," Orion continued. "If balance is to return, it must include those who have lived in harmony with the land since the dawn."

The tribal leader placed a hand over his chest, nodding once. "Then we shall walk with you, Child of the Stars. Not as relics, but as roots deep, unseen, and strong."

At dawn, the skies above the Emerald Reach shimmered with the quiet roar of the waiting ship. Its hull caught the rising light like a blade carved from sunrise. The elders chosen for the journey stood adorned in ceremonial garb woven from leaf, bone, and light-infused thread as the tribe gathered to offer their blessing.

Orion led the procession, his wings folded, his gaze steady. Eymd and Aaron flanked him, while Rachel and Snjallt secured the passage, guiding the elders with respectful care.

As they boarded the ramp, the forest stirred winds whispering songs through the trees, animals calling in rhythmic tones that echoed ancestral farewells. The jungle seemed to weep and sing in one breath.

Before the hatch sealed, the tribal leader turned back, raising his staff to the sky. "Let this be the season of remembrance," he called. "Where the Earth speaks, and all listen."

The ship rose with silent grace, disappearing into the clouds.

Hours later, as Atlantis's crystal towers came into view, the elders leaned forward in reverent silence. What had once been a myth returned now as monument.

The city's domes pulsed in time with the Earth's core, and as they descended into its heart, the elders whispered among themselves. "It lives."

And indeed, it did.

Atlantis welcomed them home.

As the ship touched down and the crystalline platforms extended to receive them, Orion raised his hand to the glowing air. "P.I.L.S.S.," he said calmly, "initiate development of a new district designated the Emerald Reach. Let it mirror the Cradle. Let it bloom with the breath of the Amazon."

The voice of P.I.L.S.S. echoed softly across the ship's interface. "Acknowledged. A new district shall be grown within Atlantis, calibrated to reflect the flora, atmosphere, and harmonic biofield of the Amazon rainforest. Integration underway."

The tribal elders exchanged glances of quiet amazement.

When they stepped into the Grand Hall of the Global Council, the chamber fell into an immediate hush.

All eyes turned not just to the elders but to Orion.

Gasps gave way to stunned silence.

He moved with the gravity of something not born, but shaped etched by fire and memory, trial and triumph. His wings stretched behind him, not angelic, but elemental half light, half void casting moving patterns on the polished crystal floor. Where he stepped, the floor pulsed beneath his feet, echoing the heartbeat of Atlantis itself.

The room swelled with reactions.

A delegate from the Eurasian Territories backed away instinctively, whispering a protection charm under his breath. A woman from the Western Crescent clasped her chest, tears streaming from wide eyes. Others dropped their gaze entirely, unable to bear the intensity of his presence.

And yet Orion stood still. Alone but not abandoned. Changed but not lost.

He caught fragments of the whispers fear, awe, wonder. The awe-struck like lightning. The fear like frost.

And for a moment, behind all the divine presence and the celestial transformation, he simply stood there, afraid.

He had become what they needed. But he wasn't sure they would still love who he was.

Would they still see Orion?

With a breath, he let the glow beneath his skin dim slightly. The towering presence softened. His frame shrank just enough to echo the boy they once knew leaner, closer, more familiar. He tucked in his wings, though their shimmer still remained.

He chose not to speak yet, but in the shift of his shape, he spoke volumes.

I am still me. I just carry more now.

And they saw it.

The same delegate who had whispered a charm lowered his hands, blinking in confusion. The woman who had wept now smiled faintly through her tears. Whispers softened, reshaping themselves from fear to recognition.

"It's him," someone murmured.

"He's still Orion."

The room exhaled. Not all at once, not completely but enough. He had not only returned. He had chosen to be seen.

He didn't speak.

He didn't need to. Delegates from every continent turned to see the new arrivals. Adorned not in power, but in reverence, the elders of the lost tribe walked beside Orion as equals.

One of the council heads rose. "And who are these that walk with you?"

Orion stepped forward. "They are the voice of Earth's memory. They are its breath, its roots, its oldest guardians. And today, they take their seat in this circle not to beg, but to guide."

A murmur swept the chamber, then silence. And slowly, as if time itself nodded, a chair of woven light emerged beside Orion's own.

The tribe had returned. The council would listen.

As the final murmurs settled and the elders took their place, a crystalline sigil on the ceiling above pulsed with Atlantean light. The high chancellor of the council leaned forward. "With the remaining Great Four scattered, and their armadas withdrawn from Earth's orbit... we have a window."

Orion nodded. "A chance to rebuild. Not as you did before, but better. The war left scars, yes but also revealed truths. Your cities must rise not just in steel and stone, but in symbiosis with the world they inhabit."

Rachel stepped beside him. "We've seen what's possible. The new technologies derived from Xerist memory-thread, the living architecture of Atlantis, the biological integrations that P.I.L.S.S. now cultivates... Earth can heal through them."

An elder added, voice steady, "Only if the builders remember the roots."

Orion looked across the chamber. "Let us rebuild cities that breathe. Structures that grow. Let every beam and foundation echo the truth that we serve the planet not the other way around."

A new resolution formed among them not in ink or decree, but in intention. Rebuilding would begin not from blueprints, but from balance.

And for the first time in generations, Earth's council spoke not just for its people, but with its soul.

A hush fell over the chamber once more as Orion closed his eyes.

The polished crystal beneath his feet pulsed not with the engineered rhythm of the city, but something deeper. Older. Primeval.

Then, he heard it.

Not a voice in the air, but in his head deep and resonant, as if the thought had become thunder.

"You have awakened the tower, Starborn. But do you hear me now?"

Orion's breath caught as he replied "I do."

The chamber blurred at the edges, the walls dissolving into a warmth both vast and intimate. Beneath it all, a gentle thrum the heartbeat of the planet. A voice not in words, but in essence.

"They built upon me. They bled me. But you... you remember."

Tears stung Orion's eyes. Yet in that moment, beyond the grief, beyond the weight of all he had become, there was joy quiet, aching joy. For the first time since he woke in the hospital, he could hear again. Not just the stars. But a world. A home. A planet alive.

He remembered what it meant to belong.

"What would you make, Child of the stars?"

He whispered aloud, "A beginning."

The vision faded, the council still watching.

Orion turned to them, steady now, filled not just with resolve but with reverence. "The first project will begin here," he said. "In the shattered rim once known as the Old Belt. It won't be built. It will be grown rooted in memory and guided by the planet itself. A sanctuary where nature and progress walk side by side. Where what we create gives back, not takes."

The council sat in thoughtful silence.

Then, slowly, they began to nod.

Earth had spoken.

And Orion its son, its servant, its listener had answered.

Beneath them, Atlantis rumbled.

A low vibration shivered through the crystal floor, growing into a harmonic tremor that echoed across the city's towers. Lights flickered in cascading pulses as ancient systems stirred, not with alarm but anticipation.

"Structural displacement detected," P.I.L.S.S. intoned calmly. "Uplift sequence initiating."

With a breathtaking surge, Atlantis rose.

The domes shimmered, the city's roots detaching from the ocean floor. It climbed skyward not to escape, but to reveal. The clouds parted in awe as it lifted high above the Earth's crust, floating just beneath the threshold of low orbit.

From their new vantage, the council turned in wonder.

Below, in the vast oceanic basin where Atlantis had once slumbered, the planet shifted. Plates folded and parted. Light burst upward like seedlings of magma and memory.

A new landmass emerged.

Green and wild, wreathed in mist and promise, it bloomed from the sea as if Earth herself had offered her next chapter.

And all across Atlantis, the city breathed as one.

It had risen.

And Earth had made ready.

The council chamber erupted not in chaos, but in collective wonder.

Some delegates gasped audibly, others rose to their feet to peer through the crystalline walls now shimmering with real-time projections of the shifting world below. The representative from the Oceanic Coalition placed a trembling hand to his heart, tears forming in the corners of his eyes. "A new land," he whispered. "A gift from the Earth itself."

One of the elders from the Cradle stood with quiet dignity. "Not a gift," she said. "An invitation."

The Western Crescent's envoy, long skeptical, turned toward Orion with new light in her eyes. "You heard her. The planet. You spoke with it." Her voice trembled, not with disbelief, but something deeper an awe wrapped in the weight of confirmation. "I've spent countless hours poring over the archives beneath Atlantis. The fragments, the echoes left in crystal memory... they all hinted at a return. A reckoning. And a voice waiting to be heard again."

Orion gave a slow nod, his voice soft but resolute. "She remembers. And now, so must we."

And with that, the future found its footing not in monuments of stone or steel, but in the heartbeat of a world once silenced now rising to speak again.

# 21. Between Star And Skin

Atlantis thrummed beneath him like a living heartbeat, yet Orion lay awake. He rose from his silken mattress and crossed to the alabaster balustrade of the terrace overlooking the Emerald Reach. There, night glimmered in soft indigo under a canopy of bioluminescent leaves, each a lantern and a lullaby for the restless city. Behind him, crystalline towers arced into the sky, faceted spires that caught distant starlight and fractured it into silent rainbows across polished walkways.

Below, the jungle city pulsed with life: vines climbed living walls in emerald spirals, lantern-fruits glowed like lazy fireflies in synchronised beats, and the scent of jasmine and wet earth drifted upward on humid breezes. Harmony reigned, Yet its rhythm failed to soothe him.

Orion pressed a hand to his chest, where stars blazed under his skin a constant, insistent thrum of cosmic awareness. Even in perfect stillness, the universe roared through his veins. He hadn't eaten for days not from forgetfulness, but because each morsel dissolved into starlight the moment it touched his tongue. He let out a hollow chuckle. Hunger had abandoned him, too.

Soft footsteps approached behind him. He didn't turn.

"You're brooding again," said Captain Aaron's low voice, edged with quiet concern.

Orion exhaled. "I'm... adjusting."

Aaron stepped beside him. From this height, the coral-blue arc of the ocean glimmered under a sky thick with stars. "You haven't slept in four nights."

"Sleep doesn't come easily anymore." Orion's gaze drifted to the lights below. "And when I do close my eyes, I don't see my dreams. I see strangers cities burning under alien suns, dying stars collapsing into themselves, whole civilisations passing like sand in an hourglass. As if the cosmos insists I catch up on everything I missed."

Aaron shifted his weight on the smooth stone floor. "Is it painful?"

Orion considered. "Not painful. Perpetual. Like standing in a wind that never stops sometimes soothing, sometimes tearing at you. But always there."

They stood in silence, broken only by the city's distant murmur. Then Orion whispered, "I don't laugh like I used to."

Aaron turned to him. "You still smile."

"Yes." Orion's voice cracked. "But it's not the kind that rattles your ribs like the ones Anton used to pull from me. That part feels buried."

Aaron's jaw tightened. Orion reached out, brushing Aaron's wrist, finding warmth. "I miss it the wild laughter that was mine alone."

Aaron closed his eyes. "You haven't lost it. It's just covered by deeper roots. Still feeding the same heart."

Orion leaned into the words. "Sometimes I wonder if I'll ever be just Orion again."

Aaron pressed his forehead to Orion's. "To me, you always are."

They stood like that until a new voice stirred the air.

"You should share these thoughts with the council." Rachel's silhouette appeared in the softly lit archway. Her hair fell loose around her shoulders; the ornate gauntlet she once wore lay on a nearby pedestal, its runes dormant.

Orion sighed. "Would it matter? I'm their symbol now a god who walks. Vulnerability breaks the myth."

"But truth forges legends stronger than myth," Rachel said, stepping forward. "They need to understand what it costs, otherwise they'll try to claim it and burn."

Aaron nodded. "She's right."

Orion gave a tired smile. "You two are exasperating."

Rachel smirked. "We strive for excellence."

She stood beside him. "I'm not afraid you'll lose yourself to power," she said softly. "I'm afraid you'll stop letting us help carry it."

The silence that followed was full of meaning. Orion looked at Aaron, at Rachel his anchors.

"Then help me remember," he said. "Not who I was. Who I still am."

He reached out. They took his hands. Above them, stars traced lazy arcs. Below, Atlantis dreamed. And in that stillness, the god within the man found rest.

Dawn came wrapped in rose and gold. In the upper gardens a platform suspended over the city and draped in vines heavy with golden pollen Aaron insisted on breakfast. The table gleamed with local fruits marbled in jewel tones, dense seed cakes, and steaming tea brewed from blossoms native to the Emerald Reach.

Morning light painted Aaron's face in lilac and honey. He looked younger here like the boy Orion had met among shipwrecked survivors and starless hope.

Orion regarded the feast with wary fascination. Aaron nudged a fruit toward him. "Try this. P.I.L.S.S. tweaked it. No stardust."

Orion's hand trembled as he picked it up. Its skin was cool, with a floral aroma. He bit. The flesh held sweet and sharp, mingled with memory. Juice ran down his chin, and he laughed bright and unbound.

Aaron's grin widened. "Told you."

"It tastes like summer in my grandmother's garden," Orion whispered. "I never noticed how sweet the air could be."

"Memory seasons reality."

They ate in easy silence, every bite a rediscovery. The tea warmed him; the cakes crackled like dry leaves. Above, the sky rippled with morning light. For the first time in days, Orion felt grounded not a guardian, but a participant.

When they finished, Aaron leaned back. "You going to do it?"

Orion nodded. "Rachel's right. They need to know not just what I am but what it's cost."

Aaron reached for him. "Then speak. Not for them for you."

That afternoon, the council gathered within the crystalline dome of the High Hall. Delegates arrived in silence, their steps softened by woven-light carpets and their voices hushed by the vastness of the space. Constellations shimmered across the glass ceiling real-time reflections of the skies above Atlantis.

Rachel stood near the dais, flanked by tribal elders from the Emerald Reach, each dressed in ceremonial garb. Aaron waited just behind, eyes trained on the entrance. A quiet tension thrummed through the chamber respectful, but brittle.

Then Orion entered.

He moved with deliberate grace, the soft pulse of starlight beneath his skin dimmed to a gentle glow. His wings were folded, the shimmer of their trailing light subdued. Not cloaked in power, but presence.

Every gaze turned. The chamber fell into complete stillness.

He stepped onto the dais and paused. For a moment, he said nothing.

Then:

"You've all seen what I've become. But you haven't seen what it's taken."

His voice, low and clear, travelled without amplification. It needed none. The silence leaned in, listening.

"This form this power it didn't arrive with celebration. It came with loss. It cost me laughter. Sleep. Simplicity. I can't eat without the food turning to stars. I can't rest without hearing the grief of worlds I've never known. I no longer dream my own dreams."

He glanced at Aaron. "I still smile. But it's different. Lighter on the face. Heavier in the heart."

The room didn't move. Even the crystalline panels overhead dimmed slightly, refracting only the softest glow.

"I don't speak today to ask for sympathy. I speak so you understand: I am not here to lead through reverence. I stand before you not as a ruler but as a reminder. A reminder that power is not the same as peace."

He turned slowly, addressing every corner of the dome.

"I need your limits. Your logic. Your challenge. Your contradiction. I need your humanity to tether what I am becoming. Because without it, I risk becoming something none of us will recognise."

One of the Western Crescent delegates bowed her head. A tribal elder placed his hand over his heart. Others stood, wordless but moved.

Rachel exhaled slowly.

Aaron stepped forward, placing his hand on Orion's arm. The message was clear.

They heard you.

Orion nodded once.

He stepped down from the dais not exalted, not deified but understood.

And in the quiet that followed, something unspoken shifted.

A symbol had spoken as a man.

And the council... had listened.

Atlantis stirred around him its crystalline veins pulsing with low, harmonic resonance, like a planet breathing in sleep. Orion stood at the edge of a high atrium, morning mist curling through the arches. Behind him, the city shimmered in hues of opal and pearl. Before him, the open hangar waited.

A ripple of light coalesced beside him.

"Good morning, Orion," came P.I.L.S.S.'s voice, smooth and faintly amused. "You've received a gift. From Atlantis herself."

Orion turned. "What kind of gift?"

A section of the hangar wall unfolded like petals, revealing a sleek vessel suspended in humming stasis. Its frame glimmered with starsteel and living coral, woven together in elegant curves. It looked like a creature carved from memory its silhouette unmistakably reminiscent of the great Manta ship, though smaller and refined, meant for a tighter bond between captain and crew.

"Your new ship," P.I.L.S.S. declared. "Forged in the Deep Forges of the Starforge Temple. A smaller cousin to the Manta vessel. Designed for you... and the Intenarii."

Orion stepped closer.

The ship shimmered as it sensed him. Bioluminescent veins sparked across its hull, syncing with the light beneath Orion's skin. The cockpit unfurled like wings opening in slow reverence. Within, six seats shaped from polished rootstone and curved crystal awaited. It was not just a ship. It was a shrine in motion.

He laid his hand on the hull. Warm. Alive.

"A ship of guardians," he whispered.

"It responds to your resonance," P.I.L.S.S. added. "And has already named itself."

Orion blinked. "It has?"

"Yes. It chose the name: Seraphel."

The name echoed like a breath between stars. He didn't ask how or why. He simply nodded.

"You'll take her to the Cradle," P.I.L.S.S. continued. "The elders await you. You're to enter meditation. Deep communion. Before your next steps, you must root yourself in stillness... or risk losing the thread between who you were and what you're becoming."

Orion exhaled slowly. "Then let's go."

# 22. Sacrifice And Song

The journey began in absolute silence, heavy as a withheld confession. Seraphel glided through the cosmos like remembrance made flesh each movement supple and deliberate yet Orion's pulse pounded with unease, as if the void itself watched him, waiting for a misstep. Far below, Earth spread out in reverent obeisance: jagged mountain ridges bowed like sentinels weighed down by secrets; rivers snaked across plains, glinting like uncertain reflections of the heavens. When the vessel dipped low over an age-worn valley, the air seemed to hold its breath and so did Orion, torn between awe and the nagging fear that this stillness concealed something unspeakable.

Without warning the hull softened, and they slipped beneath Africa's deepest bones. Layers of ochre rock peeled away like forgotten memories, revealing veins of pulsing crystal prisms of lavender and emerald throbbing with Atlantean harmonics.

Seraphel's landing felt like a silent benediction too perfect, too complete. A ramp unfurled with such reverent calm that the echoes seemed reluctant to stir. Orion stepped onto the hallowed ground and felt it quiver beneath his boots, as if judging him. The air smelled of dew-laden vines sweet as promise, sour with unspoken cost. Tendrils of foliage swayed like dancers with hidden ambition, blossoms unfurling as though they knew more than he did. Every blade of moss hummed in time with a pulse he did not fully trust.

From the mirrored reflections of a crystalline treeline, the Xal'thane emerged. Statuesque and lithe, their opalescent skin gleamed with filigreed runes. Their robes shimmered with drifting stardust, each step shedding motes of pale light. Their eyes burned like frozen supernovae beautiful, distant, and terrifyingly precise. In a silent choreography, they encircled a shallow pool at the chamber's heart and raised a unified gesture. Orion's throat tightened. He was both chosen and afraid.

The water in that vessel was the deepest indigo, liquid night rippling with pinprick galaxies. A veil of mist hovered above its surface, expectant as a question. Orion understood without words. His soul wrenched with conflict as he peeled off cloak, armour, boots every layer of protection until he stood bare and vulnerable in the sacred hush. He stepped into the pool. Cold seized his calves, then welcomed him as though it had been waiting. He knelt, water rising to his waist, and closed his eyes. In that instant the pool ceased to be mere liquid; it became a portal. Beneath the glassy surface, stars stirred and shifted, as if waking from some dread dream.

He breathed deep and sank inward. Instantly he was adrift no ground beneath, no sky above only the sonorous hum of creation stretching infinitely. He was weightless, unbound, yet each moment felt like standing on the edge of something vast and unreasoning. Doubt gnawed at him.

Then they came. The Old Ones appeared around him as formless swirls of starlight and sorrow, their shapes magnificent and mournful. Woven from cosmic fire and memory, they pressed upon him like a tidal wave of ancient longing. Their voices did not speak to ears but rattled his very marrow:

"You were born of sacrifice kindled in longing, shaped by sorrow. A spark of us placed in flesh, drifting between stars."

Orion's tongue failed. In that silent concert he remembered his first awakening the gentle voice in the dark, the ember of warmth that had pulled him from oblivion. And now before him was that same presence, colossal and remorseless.

"We gave the cosmos breath," they intoned, melody rising like storm-lit waves. "But even breath can scorch to storm. You stand as the bridge and bridges must choose their anchors."

Visions flared: worlds blossoming like jewelled flowers and unmaking into ribbons of dust; children's laughter echoing through starlit groves then silenced by cosmic ruin; titans crumbling into void. He saw himself in the Hall of Dawn pillars of light, the starseed pulsing in his chest, Aurorina's cry haunting his heart and Anton's sacrifice cutting through his calm.

"Remember," the Old Ones sang, "you are not the end. You are what remembers the beginning."

From the dark swirl before him emerged a form bearing his face, rendered in bone-white hair and eyes blazing with galaxies. Wings of constellations unfurled behind it. Its mouth opened and from that abyss spilled a miniature sun of utter darkness.

Orion recoiled. The figure drifted close. "This is the shadow of forgetting," it whispered, voice both his and not his. "This is what you become if you sever your roots."

It pressed a spectral hand to his chest. Pain exploded in his mind: fire and ice in collision, memories fracturing into shards. He saw city-worlds consumed by flame, empires reduced to dust; Aaron crushed beneath a tumbling moon, Rachel's scream lost in collapse; the Intenarii scattered like leaves, Eymd fading into starless night.

Then a sudden stillness. The agony dimmed, replaced by a single voice tender, coaxing:

"But if you remember..."

New visions bloomed: children dancing beneath silvered trees, Earth vibrant with song; Aurorina laughing, the Intenarii reunited; galaxies not overwhelmed but healed. The phantom form softened, its features human. "To be a god is hollow. Your sorrow, compassion, hope that is your strength. Never sever it. Only a soul in balance can carry both ancient reign and new beginning."

The void quivered, then cracked with silent tumult. Orion gasped, lungs drawing him back to the cold pool. He broke the surface with a single breath that rippled through the still air.

When he opened his eyes, the Xal'thane elders stood before him, hands pressed over hearts not in worship but in recognition. He had ventured inward seeking not dominion but equilibrium and he had returned, fractured and whole.

The indigo waters cleared to crystalline transparency, revealing the polished floor beneath. The cavern no longer shimmered with mystery but glowed with living truth. The eldest elder a woman with bark-textured skin and eyes like dying twilight stepped forward. In her hand she held a stone veined with silver fire.

"Rise, Orion," she intoned, voice low as distant thunder. She pressed the radiant stone to his chest. It dissolved in a cascade of light, and upon his flesh bloomed a symbol: a flame clasped by roots, encircled by dancing stars.

"This is your sigil," she whispered, "not a crown, but a compass. Follow it, even when doubt twists your path."

Around them the crystal pillars pulsed once with warm resonance. A gentle breeze stirred the vines overhead. From deep within Seraphel, P.I.L.S.S.'s calm voice echoed: "The world stirs, Orion. The Intenarii await."

He lifted his gaze toward the cavern's yawning mouth, where clouds parted to reveal constellations watching him. Somewhere on the horizon, change gathered like a storm. Conflict roiled in his chest, but beneath it simmered a fragile resolve.

He exhaled, voice steady despite the turmoil. "Then let's return."

With that, he turned and walked back toward the ship carrying within him a light tempered by doubt and hope alike.

As Seraphel's ramp sealed shut behind him with a final, metallic echo, the gentle thrum of the ship enveloped Orion in a welcoming embrace, a soothing hum that vibrated with familiarity. The chamber within pulsed gently, its rhythm in harmony with his newly etched sigil a subtle, invisible resonance that echoed through the starsteel walls, resonating with an ancient, unspoken song. He sat in contemplative silence, eyes closed, as the vessel ascended through the majestic cathedral of crystal and stone, parting from the Earth's oldest memories like a gentle breath released into the cosmos.

Above, the endless heavens awaited, a vast tapestry of stars and possibilities. In the command cradle, P.I.L.S.S. flickered into existence, his holographic projection cast in a cool, dusky blue that shimmered like twilight.

"Vitals stabilised. Emotional patterns conflicted but aligned," he noted in his calm, analytical tone. "I dare say you have returned changed, Orion."

Orion opened his eyes, revealing a gaze filled with newfound clarity. "I must never forget who I am!"

A pause lingered, longer than usual, as if the air itself was holding its breath. "Do you wish to speak with the Intenarii?"

"Not yet, let them sleep. I need to see Earth first from above. I want to know if I can feel her voice again."

With a subtle shift, Seraphel tilted slightly, ascending beyond the cave's reach. As the veil of rock and memory fell away, the ship broke into the upper sky, where the brilliant tapestry of clouds parted like curtains, unveiling the majestic curve of Earth in its entirety.

But this time, Orion didn't merely see the planet; he heard it. A soft murmur a deep, ancient whisper, like roots remembering rain reached out to him. It wasn't in words or language, but in presence. A greeting from the heart of the world.

"I hear you," he whispered, his voice tinged with awe.

P.I.L.S.S.'s form tilted his head inquisitively. "What does she say?"

"That the new land she raised isn't just soil and stone. It's an offering a beginning. A sanctuary born from her grief and longing."

He paused, his eyes misting with emotion.

"She wants me to seed it with hope. To guide its growth, not as a god, but as a guardian. For all life. For all species. A place where past wounds can heal and new roots can grow."

The lights on the panel flickered in warm agreement, glowing softly in the dim chamber. Then a chime sounded, breaking the reverent silence.

"Message incoming. The Intenarii are assembled. Rachel reports movement in orbit an unknown signature has breached the outer perimeter."

# 23. When Shadows Kneel

Orion stood, a storm settling behind his gaze. "Plot a course to high orbit. Tell Rachel to keep the Intenarii on Atlantis. I will face this alone."

Seraphel climbed higher, in the command cradle, P.I.L.S.S. spoke again. "Incoming vessel: Shadow Empire design. Large. Defensive posture minimal. Purpose unknown."

"Hold." Orion raised his hand, palm forward. Starlight rippled through his fingers like heat over water. Invisible threads of force unfurled, wrapping the enemy vessel in gentle stillness. It didn't shake. Didn't flinch. It simply... paused.

"This is no threat," Orion murmured. "This is a message."

The great ship drifted closer. Its hull shimmered with voidglass and dusk-metal, an echo of a dying star's bones. Orion lifted his hand again. Energy shimmered like silent lightning along his arm.

Then came the voice: "This is Elskar, Matriarch of the Shadow Empire. I come in peace. I seek only to speak with the one who holds the Flame."

Orion inhaled deeply. "Prepare for docking. Align us with their main port. I'll go to her."

The two ships met like the clasp of old friends wary of memory. As the corridor sealed behind him, starlight surged.

A Stone Guard appeared at his right, sculpted from alloy etched with drifting constellations. An Echo Warden unfolded at his left, cloaked in shadowlight that shimmered like fractured futures. No words passed. No orders given. Just presence.

Together, they entered.

The Shadow Empire cruiser was carved from majesty and silence. Metallic violet arches crowned the halls. Glyphs shimmered like secrets half-remembered. Shadow Warriors lined the halls, silent and watchful. One stepped forward, his movements fluid and precise, and without a word, turned and began to lead Orion and his companions deeper into the heart of the ship toward the throne room.

The throne doors opened.

Elskar stood at the atrium's centre. Columns twisted with shadow-glass. Braziers burned with inverted fire. Overhead, stars pulsed in mosaic, a sky only her kind remembered.

Her armour shimmered with dusk-metal plates trimmed in etched gold, capturing faint glimmers of starlight with every movement. Her hair, a cascade of silver curls, drifted behind her as though stirred by unseen tides. Her cloak whispered with layered fabric that shifted like twilight shadows over still water. One eye burned emerald bright, the other blood-red and unreadable twin lighthouses that seemed to search for cracks in the soul.

Orion took a measured step forward, his voice calm but edged with gravity. "Why have you come, Elskar?"

She tilted her head slightly, the firelight reflecting in her mismatched eyes. "To speak of what must come. The Great Four and their master pose a greater threat, and my Empire will no longer stand apart. The Flame showed me what you did when you unmade Enaquia. It showed me your strength, your judgment, and your sorrow. The Shadow Empire has never been one to forgive or show mercy but perhaps, for once, it is time we change. You have proven yourself worthy of our allegiance, Orion. We will fight beside you."

Orion's expression remained unreadable, but something in his stance eased a subtle shift from confrontation to acceptance. The mention of Enaquia echoed in his memory, not as a triumph, but as a wound that still hummed beneath his skin.

"I didn't want to unmake her," he said quietly. "But the path she walked led only to ruin. I offered mercy. She chose defiance."

Elskar's gaze did not falter. "And still, you mourned her. That is what convinced the Flame. Power alone does not sway it. Only purpose tempered by pain. We are not a people known for mercy or forgiveness, Orion but perhaps that is what makes this moment matter. Change must begin somewhere, and you carry both the weight of sorrow and the will to do better."

She stepped forward, one slow, deliberate pace. The braziers flickered, casting mirrored shadows across the chamber floor. Then, in an act that defied the unbending pride of her kind, Elskar slowly bent the knee. Her head bowed low, silver curls spilling forward like starlight pouring from a cracked moon. It was a gesture never seen in the annals of the Shadow Empire not just submission, but a vow. And in the wake of her gesture, her guards followed suit, one by one falling to their knees in silent, stunned reverence. It was not Orion's power that demanded it, but the weight of his purpose, the clarity of his path, and the hope he embodied. In this act, the unthinkable became truth: the Shadow Empire knelt not before a conqueror, but before a future reshaped by empathy and unity.

"You are not the god we feared," she continued. "Nor the boy we doubted. You are something older... and something still becoming."

The Echo Warden stirred beside Orion, as if acknowledging her words.

Orion's voice dropped to a murmur. "Then let it be known the god I am becoming does not seek worship or dominion. I walk with those who choose to stand beside me. The Shadow Empire will have its place in this alliance, but only if that unity is forged through truth, respect, and purpose."

He extended a hand toward Elskar. His gesture was quiet, unforced. A simple offer to help her rise.

She accepted it without hesitation.

"Come," Orion said, his tone now tempered with a warmer strength. "Let us sit and speak of terms."

They seated themselves opposite one another beneath the mirrored sky. Elskar's eyes gleamed with unreadable intensity. "There will be terms of my own," she said. "You ask for unity. I ask for"

Orion's voice cut through, sharp and commanding. "No."

The word echoed off the chamber walls like a stone cast into still water.

"But" she began.

He leaned forward, gaze unwavering. "You do not get to make demands of me, Elskar. Not here. Not now."

A ripple of tension spread through the chamber. One of the Shadow Warriors standing nearby stepped forward abruptly, hand flashing to the hilt of his sword. The blade cleared its scabbard, its edge humming with dark energy.

In the same breath, the Echo Warden at Orion's side flicked a single finger. A ripple of unlight surged forward, silent and absolute. The Shadow Warrior dissolved into nothingness erased from existence as if he had never drawn breath.

Gasps echoed across the chamber.

Elskar's expression flared with shock and restrained fury. "Was that truly necessary?" she demanded.

Orion's voice was cold steel. "The Echo Wardens do not show mercy. Their purpose is singular: to protect me without hesitation. Their power has evolved with mine. They act before intent becomes a threat."

Elskar slowly nodded, gathering herself as the silence stretched between them. "Very well," she said, voice tempered and calm. "Then tell me, Orion what are your terms?"

Orion met her gaze. "First, Eymd, Verjast, and Snjallt are to have their titles and honours reinstated without delay. Second, you are to treat Eymd with respect no more of what passed between you before. Third, you will treat the other council members as equals. Here, Elskar, you are not above them."

Elskar held his gaze, the weight of his terms settling over her like a slow-burning truth. For a moment, silence reigned once more. Then she leaned back slightly, her voice softer than before but no less firm.

"So be it," she said. "You ask for much... but perhaps not more than I deserve."

Her fingers drummed once on the carved armrest of her seat before curling inward. "Eymd, Verjast, and Snjallt will have their honours restored. I will not treat Eymd as I did. And the council" she paused, as if tasting the words on her tongue "will be treated as my equals. I will abide by your terms, Intenfli. Not because I am forced... but because the fire within me demands I evolve."

She looked toward the empty space where the warrior had once stood. Orion paused, casting a glance toward the same spot. With a breath drawn deep into his chest, he raised his hand. Starlight spiralled around his fingers, and from the void shimmered the shape of the fallen Shadow Warrior whole, breathless, and kneeling.

"It was not his time," Orion said quietly. "Let this act be understood as goodwill, not weakness."

Elskar's gaze flicked between Orion and the restored warrior. "The Shadow Empire does not bend. And yet... we bowed. That truth will echo for generations."

Then she turned back to Orion, her eyes gleaming with something rare: humility.

"You are reshaping more than alliances," she said quietly. "You are reshaping legacy."

Orion inclined his head. "Then let us build on that legacy. Would you accept a seat on the Council? A district upon Atlantis, where your people may stand as equals in this new era?"

Elskar's eyes narrowed not in suspicion, but in calculation. She studied Orion as one might study a star long hidden behind clouds, now burning with a light no lens could measure.

"To sit among your council..." she said slowly, almost tasting the words. "To hold a district in Atlantis... For the Shadow Empire, such a gesture would once have been seen as surrender."

She paused, then shook her head.

"But no longer. Not after what I've seen. Not after what the Flame showed me. This is not surrender it is alignment. And we would be fools to turn away from a future carved by such conviction."

She stood, her posture still regal, but the edge of defiance now tempered by understanding.

"I accept," she said. "I will take the seat you offer. Not as ruler, not as conqueror but as a voice willing to listen, to challenge when needed, and to shape what must come. My people will walk beside yours... not behind them."

She stepped forward, and for the first time, offered a formal Shadow Empire salute right fist over heart, then a slight bow.

"And this district," she added, her voice softer, almost reverent, "shall be a symbol. Not of shadow's dominion, but of its place in the balance."

She reached beside her throne, producing two crystal flutes filled with a violet-hued liquid that shimmered like dusk. With a silent nod, she extended one to Orion.

"A toast," she said. "To the forging of something greater than fear."

Orion accepted the glass. "To unity shaped by will, not by war."

They drank, not as adversaries, but as architects of a new age.

As the last light settled in the chamber, Orion set down the flute and stepped forward. "When you're ready," he said, "I invite you to Seraphel. Come with me to Atlantis. Let your presence there mark the beginning of this alliance."

Elskar inclined her head in silent agreement, the weight of generations shifting beneath her cloak as she prepared to follow.

# 24. Return Through The Light.

The sky above the open sea shimmered like a polished obsidian mirror, reflecting dawn's pale violet and rose as the Atlantean transport skimmed just inches over the water. Each bow wave broke in whispered sighs of foam, beads of spray catching the first light. The ship's hull was a carved tapestry of glowing filaments, delicate, twisting lines of luminescence that pulsed softly in time with Orion's presence at the helm. With every faint flutter of his pulse, those filaments brightened and dimmed like living constellations set free from the night sky. The sea, the hull, the horizon, all of it responded to the rhythm of his stardust heart, as if Atlantis itself had learned to breathe with him.

Across from him sat Elskar, draped in a midnight-black cuirass and mantle, her armour etched with silver runes that caught stray beams of sunlight and held them in cool reflection. She looked every inch the unassailable warrior queen, her posture rigid, shoulders squared, but the slight hitch in her breathing betrayed the echo of a war barely left behind. Elskar's throat tightened. Home. It had been a word etched in blood and rebellion until now. Her eyes, burnished gold-rimmed orbs, never ceased to roam the horizon, seeking both the familiar towers of home and something just beyond her grasp.

Orion himself was a study in silent power. His robes trailed starlight, each fold brimming with the ghostly shimmer of distant galaxies. He sat motionless, yet the air around him hummed, a vibration too vast for mortal form. Every gesture he made left a soft afterimage, whorls of pale blue and silver, like brushstrokes on an unseen canvas. His right hand rested on the armrest of his seat; the metal there glowed with a warm, molten gold pulse, as if it were a heart unto itself.

"P.I.L.S.S.," he murmured, each letter precise, falling like a sacred syllable.

A voice answered, neutral and harmonic, its tone drifting through hidden speakers in the cabin walls. "Yes, Intenfli?"

Orion's gaze remained fixed on the horizon where the spires of Atlantis rose, crystalline and proud. "Initiate construction of a new district within the Atlantean ring. Shadowtech compatible. I want living quarters, power grids, transit lines. This one is for the Shadow Empire."

Elskar's golden eyes flicked toward him, measuring, curious and unthreatening. She inclined her head slightly, the runes on her armour glinting. "You honour us."

He turned to her at last, his expression calm but unreadably deep. "No," he answered simply. "I welcome you home."

Below them, the city's towers caught the nascent sunlight and fractured it into a spectrum of dancing halos. Each pinnacle seemed carved of living light, rose and sapphire, emerald and amber swirling in living breath. As they banked toward the docking bay, the city's radiant façade felt less like an ending than the soft promise of a new beginning.

Moments later, as the ship docked and calm prayer songs thrummed beneath the veil of Orion's awareness, he did not hear words so much as a chorus of anguish, an undercurrent of suffering echoing through the fabric of reality. It was not pleas but raw pain woven into the cosmos, distant wails bent by time, voices shattered, longing for sight and salvation. They did not utter his name, yet every anguished vibration carried his essence: "See us. Save us. Bring us home."

Before footfall touched the gantry, Orion's gaze had lifted skyward, distant and unblinking. The shimmering arches of Atlantis dimmed around him; the world hushed itself, bracing for what would come next. Within his skin, the stars brightened, tiny suns waking from slumber.

"They're calling," he whispered, as though confessing to the morning sky. "They've been calling."

Elskar opened her mouth to speak, but a crackling tension filled the cabin, divine and undeniable. Orion rose, not as a mere man but as myth incarnate. Light pulsed from every edge of him, pressure lingering in the air like the gravity of a newborn star. He lifted his hand, not in command, but in celestial invitation, as though asking the stars themselves to part.

Reality rippled. The space ahead of him peeled back like silk torn aside, and a portal blossomed, its edges void black, rimmed with argent flames that flickered with silver sparks. Inside, a fractured emptiness pulsed rhythmically, a wound in the tapestry of space.

Elskar's lips parted in reverence. "Where is it that calls you?"

Orion's voice dropped to a reverent hush. "I don't need to fight. I remember who I am, and where they've kept the ones I love."

He held her gaze a heartbeat more, then turned toward the shimmering aperture. Its edges curved toward him, as though in recognition of their master. "It calls me to where the stolen light waits," he added, softer but unwavering. "Tell Eymd, Aaron, and Rachel I'm sorry. And tell Eymd she must not follow. I have sealed that path."

In the pregnant silence that followed, the cosmic ache, the prayers etched into starlight and sorrow, tugged on him like a living thread of purpose. With a final measured breath, he stepped forward and vanished into the silvery maw.

He descended into a realm both still and storm-wracked: a corridor of obsidian sky flecked with distant suns frozen in mid-blink, strands of halted time twisting like silver rope. The air hung thick with despair, metallic, like blood left too long on stone. The very walls seemed to pulse in slow agony, breathing memories that had long since forgotten mercy. Faces flickered in the dark, some screaming silently, others frozen in infinite weeping. Chains without origin snaked along the edges, binding nothing, yet radiating the presence of things long damned.

Each step Orion took sent shockwaves through this haunted domain. His light clashed with the oppressive weight of centuries of torment, not just revealing the horrors, but daring them to move. Shadowy forms, twisted silhouettes of memory and pain, sought to coalesce, only to recoil at his presence, disintegrating into wisps of mournful ash.

No chain could hold him. They disintegrated at his touch. Rusted iron crumbled to dust, spectral bindings snapped apart in silent undoing. Cries of terror stilled, replaced by gasps of wonder and hope.

Row upon row of stasis pods flickered along the chamber's edge, glass coffins bathed in faint red light, flickering like dying stars. Orion's gaze swept across them, recognition dawning in his golden eyes. Without hesitation, he extended both hands. Starlight surged outward in ribbons, gentle yet commanding, and each pod responded in turn.

The seals hissed and evaporated. Frosted glass dissolved into mist, and restraints blinked out of existence. The prisoners within slumped forward, caught mid-moment between unconscious torment and awakening grace.

Orion moved from pod to pod, placing a hand over each and whispering their names like sacred verses. One by one, they stirred, not to panic, but to peace. His presence cradled their minds as surely as his light warmed their bodies.

Only when the last seal broke and the final figure breathed anew did Orion allow himself to kneel beside the one he had sought most.

There, in a stasis-field prism, lay Aurorina, his mother, collapsed in exhaustion and restraint. Her crimson gown, once regal, hung in tattered folds around her shoulders, the fur trim dulled by dust and time. Copper-gold curls framed her gaunt face. He dropped to his knees, voice thick with awe. "Mother..."

Aurorina's lashes fluttered open. Her whisper was ragged, but filled with recognition. "My star..."

Warm tears blossomed on her cheeks and glowed into golden motes that drifted away like fireflies. He brushed her cheek with a tender hand, and each tear that fell vanished into light. For a moment, neither of them spoke. Words would have only cheapened the gravity of their reunion. Instead, they clung to the silence, eyes locked across an eternity lost and reclaimed. In her touch, he felt the lullabies she used to sing, the scent of jasmine oil from nights long gone. In his, she saw the boy she once carried now returned as a god reborn.

Lawrence followed next, ragged but unbowed, rising to embrace his son. For a heartbeat, they only stood there, forehead to forehead, breath mingling between them. His arms trembled, grief and relief warring in his voice. "I failed you both..."

Orion wrapped him in a firm embrace, not as a son receiving comfort, but as a beacon offering it. A forgiveness passed between them without the need for speech, heavy, unspoken, but complete.

Jake emerged from another shard of stasis, taller, haunted, yet at Orion's side he only grasped his hand, finding lifeline in the brother he had missed. The grip tightened, and Orion pulled him into a brief but fierce embrace. "I never stopped thinking about you," Jake muttered, voice cracking. "Every day."

There was a pause, and then, more brokenly, "I saw him fall, Orion. Anton... he didn't stand a chance."

Orion's breath caught. The mention of Anton, fiery, loyal Anton, tore through the moment like a silent scream. His eyes burned not with light, but with the ache of memory. "I know," he whispered. "I saw it too. I carry him with me."

Jake nodded, tears streaking through grime. "He would've wanted this. For us to make it home."

Orion nodded, forehead resting against Jake's temple. "We're together now. That's all that matters. We'll carry him forward in every step."

Lillithan rose in shattered silk and grit, bowing low as though greeting long-lost prophecy. "We knew," she whispered. "I told them you would come."

Vando, battered sentinel, limped forward, service crown askew, grin split by bruises and spit of blood. "By the stars, about time."

One by one, Orion's earliest comrades emerged, their eyes rekindled with fierce light. Each carried wounds, scars etched in spirit and skin, but their faces lit with awe as they looked upon him. Lillithan's breath hitched when their gazes met again, the memories of laughter and firelight rushing back. Vando's half-limp turned into a full sprint for two steps before he caught himself with a wheezing laugh. Their reunion was more than sentimental. It was spiritual, soul-deep, the mending of a broken constellation.

He said nothing. Words were unnecessary. His glow alone healed, restored, consecrated freedom.

With a sweeping gesture the prison cracked asunder, not with violence, but with hushed acknowledgment that its time had passed. Light fanned outward, and Orion gathered his lost family as though cradling the dawn itself: Aurorina tucked into his arm, Lawrence braced beside him, Jake clinging to his robe, Lillithan and Vando drawn close by bonds of shared sacrifice.

He turned once more toward the portal and spoke, his voice a distant solar storm. "Strixium. Lucandr. Josnan. I know you watch. Your reckoning comes." The void held its breath. Even shadow dared not move. The void below trembled; somewhere within those black depths, ancient wills stirred but dared not speak.

Then, with promise fulfilled, Orion led them into the portal's silver-fire light, and vanished, a living star returning home.

# 25. Ashes Beneath The Gold

The portal unfolded on the steps of Atlantis. Orion emerged first, his glow dimmed slightly but still awe-striking, and behind him came the family he thought lost each one clutching the edge of hope as they stepped into the dawn of a new life.

"P.I.L.S.S.," Orion said calmly as they descended the final steps. "Prepare emergency medical teams for intake. Priority level: divine trauma and stasis extraction. Direct them to the East Pavilion."

"Confirmed, Intenfli," replied the harmonic voice through the city's quiet systems.

"Also," he added as they walked, "refit my quarters. Expand to accommodate Aurorina, Lawrence, and Jake. I want them close. Design each space for healing and privacy. And connect them all to mine."

"Understood. Construction schematics initiated."

Orion stepped into the Atlantean breeze. The crystalline towers above shimmered with morning light, but the reunion he walked into was anything but warm.

Eymd stood with her arms folded, eyes burning with restrained fury. Her expression didn't soften as she approached every inch of her vibrating with betrayal.

"You severed the shadow-path," she snapped, stepping into his path. "You locked me out."

Orion stopped. "I did."

"You had no right," she continued, her voice cracking with more than betrayal. "And you left me with her. You left me with Elskar."

Orion's gaze flicked briefly to the side, where Elskar stood silent. "She is your mother," he said.

"She is a stranger," Eymd snapped. "You know what she did to me. To all of us. And still, you trusted her before you trusted me."

"I had every right," he answered quietly. "Because you would've followed. And you would've died."

The moment hung between them. Elskar, silent at Eymd's flank, looked on with measured calm.

Aaron stepped up next, jaw clenched. "You could've told us. You went alone. Again."

Without waiting, Orion moved. He ran to Aaron not with grandeur, but with the urgency of someone remembering the weight of a heart. His arms wrapped around the captain, fierce and wordless.

Caught off guard, Aaron stiffened, then slowly returned the embrace.

As their chests pressed together, Orion's towering form shimmered. The starlight flowing through him calmed, his celestial glow receding inward like the tides pulling from shore. His limbs shortened, his golden veins dimming, skin shifting and cooling. In the span of a breath, the god receded and the man returned.

By the time he pulled back, Orion was once again eye-level with Aaron, his form wholly human, but his eyes still bore galaxies.

Orion looked at him, the light in his gaze softened. "I know. And I'm sorry."

Aaron didn't answer at first, but nodded sharply, tension easing just slightly.

Rachel, quiet in the background, stepped forward last. She didn't speak right away, only looked at him with eyes that carried centuries of secrets. She simply said, "You brought them back."

Orion gave a small nod. "I had to," he said quietly, the weight of it threading through his voice like starlight through silk.

"That's enough," she whispered, though her eyes shimmered with something more than forgiveness. It was understanding, and grief, and the echo of all the choices that had brought them to this fragile stillness.

The halls of Atlantis echoed with restrained motion as Orion walked beside his family and those he'd rescued. Medical teams in white and violet robes descended with gentle urgency, scanning the group with glowing instruments, murmuring assessments into transparent tablets as they directed stretchers, healing pods, and salves warmed by solar light.

Aurorina, still swaying slightly, paused at a wide archway rimmed with pulsing blue veins of crystal. Her hand tightened on Orion's forearm. "This place... it remembers me."

"It should," he said softly. "You helped shape it."

Behind them, Lawrence walked with his head held high, but his steps were slower, more deliberate. Jake hovered close by, alternating between awe at the grandeur and glances toward the others who had joined them. Even as the medical teams moved in, he never drifted far from Orion's side, a silent shadow of loyalty and a lingering fear of separation.

He lingered near Orion's side, as if uncertain whether to speak. Orion noticed and turned, his expression softening.

"I didn't think I'd see you again," Jake murmured, voice wavering.

Orion didn't respond with words. Instead, he pulled his brother into a firm embrace, one hand cradling the back of Jake's head. Jake tensed for a second, then melted into it, a sob catching in his throat.

"I was so scared," Jake whispered. "When they took us when Anton... when you vanished I thought it was over."

"I know," Orion said, voice thick. "I felt you calling. I heard you, even through the stars."

Jake pulled back just enough to look him in the eye. "You really heard me?"

Orion smiled, brushing a tear from Jake's cheek with his thumb. "Every day. And I swore I'd bring you home."

For a moment, time seemed to still around them. The grandeur of Atlantis faded into the background. It was just two brothers one forged in fire, the other in hope finding each other again.

"I'm not letting go again," Jake said fiercely.

"You won't have to," Orion promised.

Orion turned to the lead medic. "I've done what I can. Prioritise Aurorina and Lawrence for full diagnostics. Deep neurological recovery. Use starfield immersions and harmonic cleansing. Jake just needs stabilisation. The others start the usual protocols."

The medic bowed. "As you will it, Intenfli."

Before moving on, Orion crouched to speak softly to Jake. "I'll need to meet with the others. But I want you close. Stay by me."

Jake nodded quickly, brushing his sleeve across his eyes. "Try and stop me."

As the group dispersed under guidance, Orion stood for a moment in the centre of the transit chamber Jake still beside him, refusing to step away. Then he exhaled and stepped through a glimmering archway that led upward.

"P.I.L.S.S.," he said aloud as he walked. "Do we still have contact with Promendium, Zanek, and Alexi?"

There was a brief hum before the system responded. "Promendium remains contactable and is currently with Zanek and Alexi on Yimmana. All three are under the protection of the Stone Guards you deployed during the uprising chronicled in your Awakening. Their status is secure."

Orion exhaled a breath he hadn't realised he was holding. "Good. Keep a channel open. I'll need them soon."

Together, Orion and Jake ascended to the next tier, stepping into the chamber beneath the Sky Garden where his closest allies waited. Vilantina stood with hands clasped before her, golden wings slightly furled. Snjallt paced slowly by the far wall, blue hair catching glimmers of crystal light, while Verjast leaned silently against a column, arms folded and crimson eyes unreadable.

They looked at him not with awe, but with expectation. Jake lingered behind Orion, quiet but watchful, his presence grounding the moment with a sense of brotherhood reclaimed.

Snjallt spoke first. "So. You've returned. With your family."

Orion nodded. "Yes. They're not the past. They're my foundation. And we don't have the luxury to stand alone anymore."

Verjast's voice rumbled low. "We felt the shift. Whatever prison you shattered it rang through the deep places."

"I didn't just bring back blood," Orion said. "I brought back what was taken from me what was taken from all of us. They are not relics. They are my family. And through them, I've reclaimed myself."

Vilantina stepped forward. "Then we must prepare the world. All of it. The Council grows restless. Rumours have reached every surviving capital. They will demand answers."

Jake stepped forward beside Orion, his voice quiet but firm. "They deserve answers. But they also deserve hope."

Snjallt tilted her head. "Is this the boy you never stopped talking about?"

Orion placed a steadying hand on Jake's shoulder. "This is Jake. My brother. I didn't just find him I found the piece of me I'd forgotten. The part that still remembers why we fight."

There was a pause then Verjast gave a single nod of respect. Jake returned it, his shoulders squaring just slightly.

"Then we give them answers," Orion replied. "But we do it on our terms. I will speak before the World Council tomorrow. And they will see what stands before them now."

He turned, the starlight beneath his skin flickering once more as he faced the towering glass window overlooking the heart of Atlantis. Beneath him, the city gleamed like a dream reborn.

"Today, we return. Tomorrow, we rise."

There was a beat of silence in the chamber after Orion's words settled into the crystalline walls. Then Vilantina stepped forward, her wings brushing the floor as she approached.

"We will stand ready," she said, her voice resolute. "But you must rest, Intenfli. Even stars burn out if they do not pause between rises."

Orion gave her a tired smile. "Rest will come. Once I know they're all safe."

Jake tugged gently at his sleeve. "Then let's check on them together."

Snjallt gave a small, uncharacteristic grin. "A good plan. For once."

As they left the Sky Garden chamber and descended through curved glass corridors filled with warm light, Orion noticed how Jake kept glancing at the city's wide expanses, jaw slightly ajar.

"It's beautiful," Jake breathed. "But it feels... like something's holding its breath."

"It is," Orion replied. "Atlantis remembers too. It waits for the choice we make next."

They reached the healing wards, where Aurorina rested in a bed of hovering starlight filaments. A soft halo surrounded her, pulsing in tune with her breathing.

Orion approached and knelt beside her. Jake lingered behind, arms crossed tight.

"I still don't understand how she stayed alive," he murmured.

"Will," Orion answered. "And the part of her that believed I would find her."

Lawrence sat nearby, more alert now, nodding faintly as he met Orion's eyes. "You kept your promise, son."

Jake stepped forward and took his father's hand, fingers tight. "We thought you were dead."

"We were," Lawrence replied. "In all the ways that mattered until today."

The room swelled with quiet understanding. No grand speeches. Just presence.

Later, as Orion watched his family rest, Snjallt appeared at his side again, this time with a clear vial glowing a faint violet.

"Energy stabiliser," she said. "For you. You're running on sentiment and starfire. One of those burns out faster than the other."

Orion took the vial with a soft laugh. "Thanks."

"You don't have to carry it all," she added quietly.

"I know," he replied. "But I will."

They stood there in silence for a time, watching the rhythm of the healing pods pulse like breath across the chamber. Jake had fallen asleep beside Orion's mother's bed, curled into the curve of a low chair, one arm still resting protectively on Aurorina's blanket.

"He hasn't changed," Orion murmured.

Snjallt followed his gaze. "No. But you have."

Orion turned to her slowly. "Is that a good thing?"

She considered it. "You walk more like them now. Less like a weapon. More like a man."

He looked back to his brother, then his father, then their people. "Maybe that's what we need right now."

Snjallt leaned against the doorframe. "When you speak to the Council tomorrow, do you think they'll listen?"

"They'll have to," Orion said. "Or they'll fall behind. The galaxy won't wait for them to catch up."

Snjallt nodded. "Just don't forget this room when you stand in that one."

"I won't," he promised. "Everything I say tomorrow starts here."

Orion approached his father's bedside again. He lowered himself into the chair beside him, the silence stretching just long enough to say what words couldn't.

"I need to say something," Orion began quietly. "About Anton."

Lawrence turned to him, brows furrowed but patient.

"I should've protected him. He was with me when it happened... and I couldn't stop it. I saw it coming and still..." Orion's voice cracked. "He trusted me. I failed him."

Lawrence's gaze didn't waver. "You didn't fail him, Orion. Anton made his choice, we all did. to stand beside you and fight."

"I know," Orion whispered, voice heavy with guilt. "But knowing that doesn't make it easier."

Lawrence reached out, resting a calloused hand over Orion's. "You carry him with you. That's all any of us can do. And because of you, the rest of us are still here. Anton would've been proud."

Orion bowed his head, his shoulders slumping with the release of a burden he hadn't even realised he was still holding.

"I just wish he could see this," he said.

Lawrence nodded solemnly. "He does."

# 26. The Reckoning Approaches

The Council chamber had changed.

No longer a room of hushed agendas and veiled politics, it now hummed with purpose. Sunlight streamed through the high crystalline arches, casting long patterns of refracted brilliance across the floor where leaders from across Earth and beyond had gathered. Every seat in the vast amphitheatre was filled: governors, warlords, empresses, scientists, and envoys, all waiting.

At the centre, Orion stood cloaked not in divine radiance, but in the quiet gravity of one who had seen the end and chosen to return.

Jake stood behind him, a silent anchor, while the murmurs of the chamber settled like dust.

"I convened this meeting not to speak of peace," Orion began, voice measured and firm, "but to prepare you for war."

Gasps flickered across the assembly. An archbishop leaned forward. Someone dropped their data slate. A general clutched the edge of her seat. Even the solar banners above seemed to sway, as if bracing against the truth.

"The final three of the Great Four, Strixium, Lucandr, and Josnan will come," Orion continued. "They are not hiding. They are not scattered. They are regrouping, and they are making their way back to Earth."

The words settled with the weight of prophecy.

"They do not come to conquer. Not this time. They come for me."

He let the declaration hang, silence stretching taut.

"I am the one they marked. I am the one they fear and the one they blame. And so I will stand before them." He took a breath. "Alone."

A flurry of protest rippled through the room. Voices raised. Chairs scraped.

"Alone?" General Kamala of the Eastern Accord surged to her feet. "You would face them alone and leave the world exposed?"

"No," Orion replied, calm but unwavering. "I do not abandon Earth I shield it. Their war is with me. I will not let your armies be decimated for a vengeance they do not understand."

A queen on the upper dais leaned forward. "And if you fall?"

Orion's gaze met hers without blinking. "Then you rise. All of you. Together."

He stepped forward, light catching the edges of his robes, the stardust in his skin flaring briefly. "But I do not intend to fall."

He looked to Vilantina, who stood at the edge of the platform, wings folded but tense. She gave him a single nod.

"To those who still wish to fight beside me, your courage is not forgotten. But know this: I will go first. I will meet them where they land. I will end what they began."

Jake's voice rang out, younger but steady. "We won't let you face it alone, brother. Even if you must stand at the front... we'll be right behind."

Orion gave him a quiet smile. "I know."

And then he turned back to the chamber.

"I will call my allies those still hidden in the deep reaches, and what remains of my army. They will answer. They will stand guard over Earth, not just for this battle, but until the end of time."

He paused, then added with sober honesty, "But it may take some doing. For one, I must ask Yimmana yes, the living world itself to shift. To relocate somewhere nearer to Earth. If it agrees, we will not stand alone. We will have a fortress at our back and a sanctuary beyond the stars."

"Prepare your nations. Ready your people. This is not the end, but the proving. What comes next will test everything we've built. But we do not face it as factions. Not as scattered survivors. We face it as one world."

For a long moment, silence ruled. Then murmurs rippled like waves, first uncertain, then firm with conviction. A minister from the Arctic Coalition whispered to his neighbour, then stood with a solemn nod. The Empress of Sol'Tharan placed a hand to her heart and rose. Then came the unified leaders of the Saharan and Amazonian alliances.

General Kamala, still standing, raised her voice. "Then let them come. If they seek one man, they will meet the will of many."

An ambassador from the Tethys Colonies added, "If Yimmana answers, we will extend them our alliance. If not, we will become the fortress ourselves."

Even the Arch-Chronologist of Aegir Prime, long known for silence, spoke at last. "Time remembers those who stood. Let it remember us."

Then, slowly, figures rose one by one until the whole of the council stood in unity.

The war had not begun. But the world had chosen its side.

Later, when the chamber had emptied and the echoes of agreement faded, Orion did not rest. Instead, he made his way to the upper vault of the Atlantean stronghold, where the Star Council Chamber lay hidden its domed ceiling carved from celestial-forged stone, a fusion of starlight-forged alloy and living crystal, threaded with celestial light and ancient constellations that shimmered like living runes.

He stepped into its centre, the air thick with quiet reverence. There was no council here now, only memory and potential. With a breath, Orion activated the command node at the heart of the chamber.

"P.I.L.S.S.," he said into the dark.

"Yes, Intenfli?" came the soft reply, reverberating gently through the walls.

"I want you to re-establish contact with the council I formed when I became Intenfli. Every surviving member. Every world that once answered when I first called."

A pause.

"Locating their last known frequencies and quantum signatures now. Some links remain active. Others... will require deeper tracing."

"Do what you must," Orion said. "Tell them I'm calling them here."

Moments later, beams of starlight cascaded from above, forming an array of translucent thrones. Holographic traces shimmered into form familiar faces taking shape across the space.

For a heartbeat, no one spoke. Many of them had not expected to see him again. When Orion had vanished into the portal swallowed by the chaos of war and starlight most believed him lost. Whispers of his demise had lingered in the edges of their systems for months. Yet here he stood.

Lord Sanjen appeared first, seated in his grand hall on Pinaxir. His voice wavered with genuine reverence. "My lord... I am honoured to hear your call. The Pinaxir system is ready."

Next, Lady Valoria, with white eyes glowing faintly, inclined her head slowly from within her crystalline chamber. "We thought you were gone. Lignorium mourned you. But now... we stand once more."

Lord Jandavinr gave a deep, formal bow, the royal crest on his chest catching the ambient light. "Quirtiam remains loyal and grateful. Your return is a spark we thought forever extinguished."

Then came Lady Kirand, regal in gold and silver, a rare softness in her voice. "Cousin, so nice to see you again. Fortanda never stopped watching the stars for a sign."

A youthful woman stepped forward in the projection next, her eyes sharp, red and gold dress shifting with astral motes. "I am Lady Untria. Comparni lives and we will not falter. Not now."

Finally, a deeper pulse of energy resolved into the image of Zanek. His form remained composed, but something flickered behind his gaze. "We feared the worst. Yimmana prepared to mourn you. And yet... here you are. Yimmana listens. And so do I."

Orion stepped closer to the central light, his expression grave but resolute. "Before we begin, I must ask you plainly: are you still loyal?"

He let the question hang in the celestial air, the constellations above flickering like watchful eyes.

"I am not the boy I was," he continued. "I have crossed realms. I have seen the truths buried in the stars. I am no longer only your Intenfli." His voice deepened, a quiet thunder beneath his calm. "I am a god now, and if you pledge yourselves to me again, know this is not a vow made in passing. It will echo across time, binding through light and legacy."

The chamber remained silent for a breath, and then Lord Sanjen stood from his throne and placed a hand to his heart.

"Then let our loyalty be eternal."

As each pledge rang out, the constellations above glowed brighter threads of starlight pulsing in rhythm with every oath.

Lady Valoria followed. "We pledge, not out of fear, but out of hope."

Lord Jandavinr inclined his head deeply. "We are yours. In life, in shadow, and in light."

Lady Kirand smiled, her voice steady. "Cousin, we never left you. Our oath only deepens."

Lady Untria's eyes shone. "Comparni swears to you anew. Let the stars witness it."

Zanek was last. His voice did not rise, but its weight carried through the room. "Yimmana does not kneel, but we stand with you. Always."

Orion's eyes passed over each of them, the resonance of their words settling deep within him. He raised a hand, and the constellations above shifted once more, now forming a single radiant nexus.

"Then I ask more," he said, voice calm yet rippling with celestial intent. "Join me. Not in symbol. In presence."

He extended his arms toward the command node, and pulses of star-forged glyphs spun through the air. "I will open star portals, stable, sovereign. One for each of you. Let them guide you to Earth, where you will take your rightful seats beside me."

The thrones brightened in acknowledgement, light reflecting in the eyes of each projected figure.

"Earth will be the heart of this convergence," Orion continued. "And I will not stand as its guardian alone. Your presence here will speak louder than fleets."

Lady Valoria inclined her head. "Then we shall come."

Zanek's image crackled with force. "Yimmana's root will answer. And I will walk through your gate."

One by one, the council affirmed, and the chamber pulsed with renewed purpose.

The stars had not just remembered, they had returned.

Still, two tasks remained. Orion stepped back from the command node, closed his eyes, and reached beyond the chamber walls beyond Earth itself. He opened his mind, focusing not on a name, but on a presence. One vast, ancient, and living.

"Yimmana," he whispered telepathically, casting his thoughts into the void, carried by Star magic and memory.

At first, there was silence. Then a slow, warm presence stirred in response a planetary consciousness vast and serene, like a great tree awakening from deep slumber.

"Intenfli... child of the constellations. You return to me now?" Yimmana's voice was both wind and gravity, sorrow and strength. Her presence pressed gently against his senses, like deep roots stirring beneath the soil, a song of warmth and vast age resonating in his bones.

"Yes," Orion answered silently. "I ask not for protection alone but presence. Will you come closer to Earth? Move through the stellar stream? The time of reckoning nears, and I need your sanctuary and the Stone Guard by my side."

There was a deep pause, filled with the creaking of old stars and the echoes of ancient roots.

"I have not moved since you revived me," she replied slowly. "But for you, and for what rises... I will stir again. My Stone Guard are ready. Give me the signal, and I will begin the shift."

Orion bowed his head, heart heavy with gratitude. "Thank you, old friend. Soon, the stars themselves will witness your arrival."

And across the cosmos, Yimmana turned.

Orion remained still for a breath, then shifted his focus once more. With a gentle touch of Star magic, he initiated another link this one seeking a presence more familiar, more mischievous, and utterly grounded.

"Promendium," he sent out telepathically.

A heartbeat later, a crackle of laughter echoed across the connection.

"You always pick the most dramatic moments, Orion."

Orion smiled. "I need to ask you something. Will you come to Earth?"

"I already heard you ask Yimmana," Promendium replied, his voice carrying both humour and resonance. "Kind of hard not to, when you're speaking across the roots of a living planet?"

Orion raised an eyebrow. "So you heard everything?"

"Every word. I'm helping her people balance their nature-tech harmonics. You might say I'm part of the landscaping committee. Or" he added with a teasing grin, "have you forgotten that I'm part of a planet's heart now?"

"Never," Orion answered with quiet fondness. "Still, I need you. Your voice. Your mind. Your magic."

Promendium's reply softened. "Then open your portal, Friend. I'll step through when she finishes shifting her roots."

"It will be done," Orion promised.

And high above, stardust danced as two old allies prepared to meet again.

Across the void, old alliances stirred and with them, the last light of a unified defence.

# 27. Arrival Of The Stars

Above the capital's great plaza, beneath towers of living crystal and sun-bathed banners, the very air held its breath. Citizens, diplomats, and defenders gathered, eyes fixed on the sky. The ground pulsed with a steady rhythm, a heartbeat shared with the cosmos itself.

Then the first portal opened.

It shimmered into being, a vertical ring of constellated starlight rotating with quiet dignity. From within it stepped Lord Sanjen, tall, broad-shouldered, his cloak embroidered with storm glyphs and the swirling colours of the Pinaxir system. Gravity drones orbited behind him in solemn silence, each one bearing his sigil and flickering with electric-blue authority.

Gasps echoed through the plaza. A wave of energy passed over the crowd, not oppressive but charged, Sanjen's very presence was planetary.

Another portal bloomed, like a veil drawn through frost.

Lady Valoria emerged in gliding silence, her white eyes alight with ghost-fire. Mist curled at her heels, and her gown flowed like liquid crystal. Around her, spectral birds of light circled and vanished. She gave no speech, her gaze alone quieted the plaza.

The third portal crackled open in a burst of amethyst geometry.

Lord Jandavinr strode forth, his purple skin luminous beneath a crown-like turban. Behind him, rotating star-maps hovered like living history. His voice echoed through the silence:

"Quirtiam has returned to the heart."

The fourth arrival came with fire.

Lady Untria descended on spirals of solar flame. Her red and gold dress trailed embers, her feet never quite touching the ground. She raised one hand and the flames parted around her like respectful dancers.

Then came the golden storm.

Lady Kirand emerged amid a cascade of mirrored feathers. Her gown was woven from sunlight, and wings of gold and silver unfurled as she touched down. "I never miss an entrance," she said with a smile that broke the tension.

And last, rising from a breach in the very earth, was Zanek. Stone and vine swirled upward, coalescing into a platform as he stood tall and silent, eyes glowing with deep emerald light. A fragment of Yimmana's own root curled beside him like a protective serpent.

The Star Council had come, Lord Sanjen, Lady Valoria, Lord Jandavinr, Lady Untria and Lady Kirand, summoned from their worlds to stand once more at Orion's side.

Orion stepped forward, flanked by Jake, Vilantina and the rest of the Intenarii. The plaza bowed not from command, but from awe.

He turned slightly, addressing the people of Earth with a voice both firm and clear. "Behold, the Star Council, our ancient allies and sovereign defenders of the realms beyond."

He gestured as he spoke, each name given the gravity of ceremony.

"Lord Sanjen of Pinaxir, whose strength steadies stars and storms. Lady Valoria of Lignorium, whose sight pierces time and mist. Lord Jandavinr of Quirtiam, keeper of the sky's archives and celestial memory. Lady Untria of Comparni, whose flame defends the innocent. Lady Kirand of Fortanda, regal in both wit and wisdom. And though she is not present, we honour Lady Alexi of Iskatar, guardian of the dawn tides."

He looked to the council and spoke only once:

"Welcome all. Lord Sanjen, where is Lady Alexi?"

Sanjen inclined his head. "She sends her apologies. She cannot attend. Lady Alexi is currently with child."

Orion tilted his head slightly, his tone curious but concerned. "And she was comfortable with you attending in her stead?"

Sanjen allowed himself the barest hint of a smile. "She insisted. Besides, you forget, this child is ours. She said I'd only get in the way pacing around her chambers."

A soft murmur swept through the gathered crowd. Even among the Star Council, the news carried a weight of legacy.

Orion's expression softened, the corners of his mouth lifting ever so slightly. "She honours us, even in her absence. Her child will be born into a world worth protecting."

Lady Valoria placed a hand to her heart in silent tribute. "May the child be strong in the light and steady in the shadow."

Lord Jandavinr added, "And may they never know the kind of war we have known."

Orion inclined his head with solemn respect. "We carry her with us. And her future."

He turned once more to face the assembled Star Council, the people of Earth watching in reverent stillness.

"We stand at the edge of all things," he declared. "The Great Four gather. Their return will not be whispered, it will arrive in flame and shadow. But we are not what we once were. Today, Earth is not alone."

He raised his right hand, and from the stone of the plaza bloomed radiant pathways of light, guiding lines that arced toward the skies above.

"These are the convergence points. Each of you will be given one. You are not only here to honour alliance, but to prepare with us. Your wisdom, your technology, your magic, we will weave it into Earth's defence."

Zanek stepped forward, his voice low and steady. "Then let us begin."

Lady Untria summoned a flame between her fingers. "Let them find us ready."

Vilantina moved beside Orion, her wings unfurling slightly. "Orders will be distributed. Coordinates relayed. We have work to do."

The crowd stirred, not in fear, but in purpose. Earth was no longer a single world. it was the heart of a gathering storm, and the galaxy had answered its call.

Orion held up a hand once more, his voice ringing clear. "Two more guests remain. One walks among Yimmana's living forests, a scholar of stars and spirit. The other is the world itself."

He turned to Zanek. "Is she ready?"

Zanek gave a slow nod. "Yimmana listens. And she moves."

A hush fell over the plaza.

"And Promendium?" Orion asked aloud.

A shimmer of laughter echoed from a distant platform as a swirl of shimmering petals spiralled down from the air. Promendium materialised from the arc of light, hands tucked behind his back and a playful smirk already dancing on his lips.

"You didn't think I'd miss this, did you?" he called. "I heard every word. You do remember I'm living on the surface of a sentient planet now, right? It's hard to avoid these things."

Orion chuckled, shaking his head. "Of course."

Promendium rushed over to Orion and hugged him tightly. "She's nearly here. And so am I."

He stepped back only slightly, his hands still on Orion's shoulders. "I missed you, you know. It's not often I say that, but stars, it's true."

Orion met his gaze, voice quiet but resolute. "I missed you too, Promendium."

Promendium grinned, hair shimmering molten gold in the sunlight. "You know I prefer to be called Pro."

Orion opened his mouth, beginning to speak, perhaps an apology, perhaps something deeper, but Pro cut him off, eyes widening.

"Oooooo, she's here."

With a sound like the pop of a collapsing star, the air above the horizon shimmered and folded inward. The heavens rippled, space bending in a slow, spiralling unfurling. In the distance, just beyond Earth's curve but luminous and unmistakable, a second world emerged into view.

Yimmana appeared not with violence or thunder, but with breathtaking majesty. Her surface shimmered with iridescent jungles and starlit lakes, veins of crystalline circuitry pulsing gently beneath living forests. She moved gracefully into Earth's periphery, not too close, not too distant, close enough to be seen, to be felt, to be revered.

Yimmana had arrived, her colossal form radiant with biomechanical beauty, haloed by rings of living crystal and luminous vines. She did not threaten Earth's orbit. She circled gently, like a guardian keeping watch.

A voice bloomed in Orion's mind, as warm and vast as the stars themselves.

"My Intenfli, it is a pleasure to be close to you again and have you gaze upon my surface. The two planet-protector Stone Guards you created are on their way, but they do not have the same grace I do in travel."

The words echoed with affection and ancient patience, filling him with a quiet sense of reverence.

Orion tilted his head, murmuring under his breath, "P.I.L.S.S., is it possible to project her voice, so the Council can hear her as I do?"

The AI responded immediately, gentle and harmonic. "Yes, Intenfli. Routing Yimmana's telepathic signature through the resonance lattice now."

A shimmer passed through the plaza as the air itself subtly shifted, tuned to the presence of the planetary mind soon to speak aloud.

Orion turned once more to the gathered crowd and Council. "Before she speaks, allow me to properly introduce two figures vital to our future."

He gestured toward Promendium. "This is Promendium, though he prefers 'Pro', he was created when I remade a broken planet and told it all my hopes, fears and dreams. In doing so, he became a part of me."

Pro gave a short, mock bow, his molten gold hair catching the light. "Charmed, I'm sure."

Orion then extended his hand toward the vast shape of Yimmana in the sky. "And above us, now within reach once more, is Yimmana, living world, ancient guardian, and planetary mind who stood with the Old Ones and now stands again with us."

A hush rippled outward as the plaza held its breath. Then Yimmana's voice filled the space, carried through the resonance lattice, no longer confined to Orion's mind, but now echoing in the ears and hearts of all who listened.

"Greetings, Council of Stars, and children of Earth. I am Yimmana. Long have I watched the galaxy spin, but few moments shine so brightly as this reunion. My Intenfli walks among you, and so I walk closer too. Let my presence remind you: even worlds can choose where they stand."

"I bring no threat, only allegiance. And though my guardians are slower than I, they will arrive soon. When they do, know this, our bond is ancient, and we will defend this home until the stars fall still."

Even as her words echoed through the plaza, the sky behind her rippled once more. From the same fold in space where Yimmana had emerged, two immense figures began to form, taller than planets, their silhouettes forged of black stone veined with glowing gold, eclipsing distant stars as they moved.

The Stone Guards had arrived.

Each one drifted through the cosmic rift with slow, thunderous grace, gliding into place beside the planet Yimmana. Their bodies glistened like living starstone infused with drifting stardust and etched with constellations, massive forms dwarfing moons as they took position in orbit. Their armour, an elegant fusion of celestial and Starforged craftsmanship, gleamed with radiant lines of power. One bore a colossal spear that crackled with starlight, the other wielded a shield so vast it cast shadows across the clouds below.

Gasps rippled through the crowd. Even the Star Council stilled in their places, momentarily taken by the awe of these divine creations.

Yimmana's voice softened as they reached their place in the sky behind her.

"The Stone Guards are here to watch and to protect. They are bound to your will, Intenfli, and by extension, to the survival of Earth."

Orion looked skyward, his expression grave but resolute.

"Then Earth is no longer undefended," he said quietly, yet the weight of his words carried through the plaza like the toll of a great bell.

Lady Kirand stepped forward, her mirrored feathers catching the starlight. "I have seen many forces rise to challenge the void," she said, voice smooth and powerful. "But never have I seen a planet summon such allies."

Pro chuckled beside her. "That's what happens when you give your dreams to a world, and she dreams them back into being."

The crowd stirred, voices rising in hushed awe and disbelief.

General Brownwater pushed through the assembled Earth command, stepping toward Orion. He looked up at the Stone

Guards, then toward the gathering of cosmic beings. "My Intenfli," he said formally, "the world is watching. What shall we tell them?"

Orion stepped forward. "Tell them this: the stars have not abandoned Earth. We are not alone in the dark. The Great Four are coming, but so are we. So are the worlds that believe in us."

Yimmana's voice, now gentle and mothering, whispered once more through the lattice.

"And if the stars must fall to keep your world from burning, then let us fall like blades."

Silence returned.

Then Jake, still near Orion's side, spoke up, his voice young but steady. "We're going to win this, aren't we?"

Orion placed a hand on his brother's shoulder. "We're going to stand. That's what matters."

# 28. Edge of the Storm

The days that followed were filled with movement, strategy, and reverent awe.

The newly risen continent, formed during Orion's celestial resurgence, spread like a radiant crown along Earth's equator. Its terrain shimmered with fused stone and crystal, infused with Star Magic at its core. Lakes of starlit water rippled under foreign skies, while mountains pulsed with ancient energy veins. Towers of bioluminescent glass grew where no cities had been, rising in spirals shaped by thought and will.

This was Intenara, a land born of unity, memory, and power.

Each member of the Star Council wandered its wild beauty with reverence.

Lady Valoria moved through the crystalline forests, reading the vibrations in the leaves like pages from time. "This land sings," she whispered. "It remembers every sacrifice Earth has made."

Lord Jandavinr sketched maps mid-air with a flick of his fingers, chronicling this newborn world. "A land built by starfire and faith," he murmured. "It deserves to be known."

Lady Kirand stood atop a high cliff overlooking a valley of swirling light. "This will be the place I defend," she said. "They will not take it."

Meanwhile, Promendium wandered barefoot through glowing meadows, hair alight with joy. "This is what happens when Orion dreams and inspires," he told a bemused Jake. "You get wonder and impossible architecture."

Preparations began in earnest.

Zanek and Vilantina coordinated supply corridors and dimensional fortifications. Elskar, alongside Eymd and Verjast, trained elite units in shadow and flame. Snjallt brewed elixirs that shimmered with planetary resonance, each vial humming with latent defence.

At Elskar's request, a fleet of Shadow Warrior ships pierced the veil of the upper atmosphere, their sleek hulls etched with black sigils that shimmered with starlight. They descended in perfect silence, taking up positions around Intenara. Crews of disciplined, dark-armoured warriors emerged, bowing first to Elskar, then to Orion, ready to defend the world that now stood as their own.

Evenings in Intenara became moments of silent preparation. Council members watched the stars not for guidance, but for signs of war. Celestial charts were redrawn, magical flows realigned. Ancient prophecies, once thought dormant, were reinterpreted by scholars from Yimmana and Earth alike. The barrier between science and magic blurred until both were part of the same breath.

The Earth Council, once fractured and uncertain, began to heal in the presence of the Intenarii and the Star Council. Their sessions, once tense, now resonated with shared resolve. Representatives from every continent walked the shining bridges of Intenara, side by side with interstellar dignitaries.

Queen Alexandria spent hours at Orion's side, learning not just of battle plans but of the histories that had forged his rise. She was regal yet inquisitive, and her quiet questions revealed deep understanding. One evening, they stood on a balcony overlooking a valley of golden mist.

"I've read about your past," she said softly. "But I never imagined the weight of it. How do you stand beneath so many stars?"

Orion glanced at her, his expression gentle. "I don't. Not alone. I never could."

She placed a hand on his arm. "Then let us carry some of it with you. Earth has walked blindly for so long, we see now. We stand with you."

Their bond, once ceremonial, deepened into something more grounded, an alliance of hearts as well as thrones.

In the central chamber of Intenara, an open-air spire of starlight and stone, Orion convened daily with the Council, forming strategy and intent.

"The Great Four will not strike all at once," he said, fingers brushing holograms of shifting threat signatures. "But they will strike with focus. And they will aim here."

He tapped the heart of Intenara.

"This is the symbol. The beacon. Earth will not fall while this stands."

Lady Untria raised a hand, flame crackling at her fingertips. "Then we burn bright enough that even death fears to tread here."

Above them, the Stone Guards drifted in the upper atmosphere, silent sentinels whose presence bent the sky.

And from the depths of the ocean, a presence long forgotten rose.

A figure emerged upon the shores of Intenara, tall, graceful, and resplendent in armour that shimmered like moonlit tides. His skin bore the luminous markings of the Xenith, yet his eyes held the warmth of humanity. Gills flexed at his neck before receding into his skin. A trident of coalesced sea-light hung at his back.

"I am Aruvel," he announced, voice like waves against a sacred shore. "Son of two worlds, half-human, half-Xenith. I come to stand with Orion, as my ancestors once vowed."

Orion stepped forward and embraced him without hesitation. "Your timing is perfect. We need every heart that still dares to hope."

Aruvel's arrival stirred not only curiosity, but hope. Children of both land and sea gathered near him, their questions boundless. He taught them to listen to the ocean's pulse, and in return, they taught him how Earth had changed. In the depths of night, his songs joined with the whale-chorus, a harmony that lulled the coastline to sleep.

And beneath the silver moon of Earth, as plans continued and allies arrived, another bond quietly rekindled.

Aaron found Orion alone in the garden of shifting stars that now crowned the heart of Intenara. The air glowed with pale light, and the silence was soft.

"You disappeared again," Aaron said, folding his arms.

"I needed a moment," Orion replied. "Before all of it begins."

Aaron stepped closer, his voice quieter. "Next time... take me with you."

Orion looked at him fully, something vulnerable breaking through his calm. "I thought I had to protect you by keeping you away."

Aaron shook his head. "I'm not here to be protected, Orion. I'm here to stand with you. I always was."

A pause. Then Orion reached forward and pulled him into an embrace, one hand resting against Aaron's cheek.

"I don't want to lose you," Orion whispered.

"Then don't," Aaron said, eyes locked with his. "Because I'm not going anywhere."

They sat together afterward, overlooking the crystalline terrace. Orion's fingers laced with Aaron's as they watched lightships soar across the twilight sky.

Aaron rested his head on Orion's shoulder. "Do you think they know? The Great Four. That you're not the same person they once faced?"

Orion's gaze didn't waver. "The remaining three know, and so does their master."

And under the flickering starlight of their own making, they stood together, unspoken promises between them stronger than any spell.

The world prepared, not just for survival, but for defiance.

As the final stars faded into morning mist, Orion summoned his core circle, the Intenarii, into the Heartstone Pavilion, a crystalline chamber carved from starlight and anchored to the core of Intenara itself.

Here, beneath a vaulted dome of ever-shifting constellations, his chosen stood waiting. Snjallt leaned against a translucent pillar, arms crossed and eyes sharp. Verjast stood like a mountain, silent and still, his hammer resting at his back. Eymd adjusted the blades at her waist, glancing toward the sealed horizon as if she could feel the distant storm brewing. Vilantina knelt in quiet reverence. Aruvel entered last, still sea-damp, his presence as fluid as it was focused.

Aaron and Rachel stood on either side of Orion. Together, they completed the circle.

The air inside the chamber thrummed with ancient energy. Celestial runes drifted overhead like fireflies, and the floor pulsed faintly with each word spoken.

"Thank you all for coming," Orion said, his voice resonating through the crystalline space. "This world is no longer the same. And neither are we. The Great Four will come. But they will not face the man they cast through the void. They will face the Intenarii."

He looked to each of them in turn.

"I need your wisdom, your skill, your courage, but most of all, your unity. Earth stands because of us. And Earth will endure because we stand together."

Snjallt rolled her eyes, but her smirk was fond. "We didn't come this far to let some prophecy-fuelled nightmares ruin the décor."

Verjast gave a slow nod. "We hold the line. Let the storm break."

Eymd stepped forward, her red eyes fierce. She reached into her cloak and pulled free a weighty, rune-marked tome, its cover gleaming faintly with shadow-bound energy.

"You gave me this in the library," she said, offering it to Orion. "For protection. But it's been calling to you from the shadows ever since. It wants to return to your hands."

The moment her fingers brushed his, the book pulsed with recognition. A gentle hum rippled through the chamber, and the constellations above rearranged themselves, casting the room in a tapestry of ancient light.

Orion accepted the book solemnly. As his fingers closed around it, the runes flared with silver light, recognising their rightful bearer. He held it close for a moment longer, eyes narrowed as the echoes within began to whisper to him once more.

"Then it is time I answer," he said, his voice low with purpose.

Aruvel placed his trident against the floor, the motion echoing like a distant tide. "Then let the oceans rise with us."

Vilantina unfolded her wings. "Let the heavens watch. We will not fail."

Rachel raised her voice at last, steady and calm. "The cost has been great. But what we're building here, this alliance, this hope, it's worth everything."

Aaron reached for Orion's hand beneath the table. "Then let's finish what we started."

Orion turned to face the starfield above. A final image solidified within the dome, three looming shadows against a field of light.

Strixium. Lucandr. Josnan.

"And so we prepare," Orion said. "Not for battle. For victory."

For what was coming next would shake galaxies.

# 29. Echoes Of Light, Roots Of Flame

Orion sat in solitude beneath the boughs of a silver-branch tree near the outskirts of Intenara, the tome Eymd had returned resting across his lap. The pages no longer turned by hand. Instead, the book pulsed faintly in his palms, resonating with a rhythm like a heartbeat, his own, yet older, deeper. The runes on the cover shifted and flowed, reconfiguring themselves with every breath he took.

He closed his eyes.

And it spoke.

Not in words. In memories not his own. In visions carved from starfire. In futures glimpsed through the lens of destiny.

His body remained rooted to the ground, but his consciousness unfurled like stardust swept into the upper reaches of the cosmos. He felt himself ascend, not physically, but through strata of time and truth, each layer peeling away illusion. Space folded inward. Reality thinned.

A crown appeared, not fashioned of gold or jewel, but braided from the strands of creation itself, woven from living light and shadow so profound it swallowed thought. It pulsed with purpose, not power. Then came wings, not metaphor, but real, vast beyond imagining. One wing dark as a dying star, matte and endless like a void without memory. The other, radiant as the birth of suns, glimmering with the hues of new galaxies.

The firmament bowed as they spread.

Galaxies spiralled around him, not in orbit, but in awe. Each shimmered with recognition. He heard his own voice then, not from his throat, but echoing through the cosmos, a sound so primal, so resonant, that creation itself seemed to hold its breath.

It wasn't language. It was command. It was arrival.

And the stars... the stars listened.

He gasped as the vision receded, breath ragged. The tome snapped closed with a finality that made his skin prickle.

It had not taught him anything in the way mortals learn.

It had reminded him of who, what, he was becoming.

And it was not yet time to know it all.

With quiet reverence, Orion lifted the tome in both hands. The runes across its surface shimmered, pulsing faster now, as if sensing its final purpose. He whispered a word in the ancient tongue, one that came not from memory, but from deep within his essence, and hurled the tome into the air.

It did not fall.

Instead, it rose higher, higher still, spinning gently as it ascended. Light wrapped around it like the embrace of a star being born, its pages unfolding one last time in radiant bloom. Then, with a burst of silver fire, the tome expanded, becoming a radiant celestial body. Where once it had rested in Orion's hands, now it hung in the heavens, glowing beside Earth's moon.

A second moon, forged from knowledge and legacy, now watched over them all.

He rose slowly, grounding himself in the now. In the scent of starlit grass. In the soft breeze that carried salt from distant oceans.

Later that day, he found Aaron watching the horizon from a quiet balcony carved into the highest spire. The wind tousled his blonde hair, and the twin moons glinted in his eyes.

Orion hesitated.

"We've never talked about it," he said at last.

Aaron turned, brow raised. "Talked about what?"

"Us."

A smile crept across Aaron's face. "I was wondering when you'd bring it up."

Orion exhaled. "I know we've been close. Since I woke up. Since you stayed by me. But I never asked properly."

He stepped closer, gaze unwavering.

"Would you like to date? I mean, formally. As more than just two souls orbiting the same flame."

Aaron didn't speak right away. He closed the distance and took Orion's hand.

"I thought you'd never ask."

Their foreheads touched briefly, a silent vow passing between them in starlight.

Later still, Orion gathered his family, Aurorina, Lawrence, Jake, and Lillithan, within the Garden of First Light. The leaves shimmered gold and violet, and constellations danced in the sky above.

Aurorina sat regal yet weary, her arm looped through Lawrence's. Jake hovered close to his brother, still carrying the boyhood awe he'd never outgrown. Lillithan, ever composed, held a gentle smile.

A long table had been laid out beneath the glowing boughs, bowls of rice and peas, curried goat, sweet fried plantain, jerk vegetables, macaroni cheese pie, creamy coleslaw, golden roast potatoes, and sorrel drink lined the length of it. The air was rich with the warmth of spices, the tang of familiar sauces, and the comfort of culinary heritage passed down through generations.

"I want you to meet someone," Orion said then, beckoning Aaron forward.

Aaron gave a respectful nod, then bowed slightly. "It's an honour."

Aurorina looked him over with eyes that had once commanded empires. "So you're the one who stood vigil beside my son."

"I tried," Aaron said. "But he didn't need saving. Just waiting for."

To everyone's surprise, she stood and embraced him. "Then thank you. For being patient with him, he's carried enough. If you help him remember who he is beneath the stars... then you're already family."

Jake stepped forward, studying Aaron with curiosity. "You're the guy with the dual pistols, right?"

"That's me," Aaron replied with a grin.

"Cool," Jake said, then glanced up at Orion. "He's cool."

Lawrence extended a hand, firm and warm. "If Orion trusts you, that's enough for me."

Lillithan said nothing, only smiled and inclined her head, her approval quiet but clear.

Orion stood at the head, watching the scene unfold. "It's what we would have cooked back home. Before the stars. Before everything."

Jake's eyes lit up. "You remembered?"

"I never forgot," Orion replied, passing him a spoonful of curry. "This is how we reclaim what matters."

As laughter and warmth filled the garden, shadows curled gently at the edge of the lanternlight. Then, with a shimmer, Eymd stepped from one of them, hands on her hips, eyebrows arched.

"You thought you could keep food this good away from me?" she said, mock offence colouring her tone.

Orion laughed. "I was wondering when you'd appear."

Eymd helped herself to a plate with practiced grace. "You'd better believe I felt that aroma in the shadowways."

Jake offered her a plate with an arched brow. "Shadow warrior or not, you'll have to fight me for the last piece of macaroni pie."

Eymd smirked, her cloak of dusk fluttering faintly. "Challenge accepted, tiny human."

Then came the faint hum of teleport signatures, and moments later, the members of the Star Council appeared at the edge of the garden path, Lady Valoria, Lord Sanjen, Lady Untria, Lord Jandavinr and Lady Kirand.

"We sensed a gathering," Lady Kirand said, her smile playful. "And something about roast potatoes."

Orion laughed warmly, setting down his cup of sorrel. "I'm just glad I made a lot more than needed. Seems I've accidentally summoned half the galaxy with my cooking."

The Star Council members joined the others around the table, plates soon filled, stories shared, and bonds deepened under the soft canopy of glowing leaves.

Moments later, more footsteps echoed along the starlit path. Elskar, Vilantina, Snjallt, Verjast, and the rest of the Intenarii approached hesitantly, accompanied by Queen Alexandria herself. Each of them wore an expression somewhere between reverence and apology.

Alexandria gave a sheepish smile. "Forgive the intrusion. We followed the scent... it was too good to ignore."

Vilantina nodded, already eyeing the macaroni pie. "We didn't mean to disrupt such a personal moment."

Orion gestured to the empty seats at the table with a wide grin. "Then it's doing exactly what it's supposed to. Caribbean dinners are meant to bring people together."

Chairs scraped gently as the guests joined, laughter spilling over the dishes and glasses clinking in celebration. The garden of First Light glowed brighter, warmed by the joy of found family and chosen kin. Overhead, the canopy of leaves shimmered in soft pulses, almost imperceptibly in time with Orion's heartbeat, as if the trees themselves were listening, remembering.

Whatever the shadows still held, he would meet them with light, and with the ones who stood beside him.

And above him, high in the skies of Intenara, the runes on the sealed tome pulsed once more.

# 30. The Soulmoon Rises.

The stars above Earth shimmered with uncanny precision, each pinprick of light suspended in velvet darkness as though the sky itself had paused to listen. A hush draped over the city like a brocade cloak, soft and weighty, the kind of silence that crackles with expectancy. Where moments before the feast had raged, laughter tumbling through marble halls, music thrumming from gilded amphoras, the air now held only memory, as fleeting and cool as a breath exhaled into winter air. Dew clung to the silver-leafed trees of the Garden of First Light, each droplet refracting moonbeams into shards of pale sapphire. Beneath the arching branches, petals folded inward, as though in slumber, while even the wind tiptoed through the boughs, its exhalations gentle as a lullaby.

Orion stood sentinel beneath that vaulted canopy, shoulders squared though his gaze was drawn heavenward. Overhead, the second moon, the transformed tome, hung in silent vigil, a softly glowing orb of carved runes and starlight, its surface shifting like living marble. It moved in stately arc around Earth's familiar companion, their twin orbits a whispered promise of renewal and remembrance. Pale shafts of lunar radiance painted Orion's features in washed-out silver, the faint luminescence tracing the lines of determination and doubt alike.

His chest rose and fell in a slow, deliberate cadence, as if each inhalation were an anchor dropping deep into the well of his purpose. Within him, ambition and anxiety churned like molten metal in a forge, sparks of memory scattered with every breath: the lessons learned under frost-lit skies, the visions that danced behind his eyelids in half-woken dreams, the sacrifices worn like scars beneath his skin. All of it had led him to this hushed moment beneath sentinel trees.

Footsteps approached on the soft carpet of moss and fallen petals. Aaron emerged from the shadows without a word, his stride measured, respectful of the stillness. He settled at Orion's side, close enough to offer warmth but distant enough to preserve the sanctity of his thoughts.

"You're holding something back," Aaron murmured, voice as low and steady as the slow drip of dew from leaf to ground.

Orion did not shift his gaze. "The tome offered only fragments, flashes of what I am to become."

Aaron's eyes, dark with concern, followed Orion's silent vigil of the moons. "Must you face it all on your own?"

Orion's shoulders tightened. He exhaled, long, ragged. "I never wanted to be alone in this. But the burden chose me. It begins here, within me." He paused, voice dropping to a whisper. "I can't lose anyone else, Aaron. Not again." He turned, silver light revealing the rawness in his expression. "My earth mother... she slipped beyond my reach. I tried to open a portal to her essence, to feel her heartbeat in the aether. But it's like she was snuffed out, gone from every fold of magic I know." He swallowed, his throat bobbing. "And Anton... I watched him burn. The fire took him so fast. I wasn't quick enough to save him." His voice cracked. "If I, I lose anyone else I love, I'm afraid I'll shatter completely."

Aaron's hand found Orion's, calloused fingers closing around delicate ones. "You will not stand alone," he vowed, eyes bright. "I... we stand with you."

Orion drew a shuddering breath, the tension in his shoulders easing. "Then let us share the breath." His voice was scarcely more than a breeze through the branches.

At dawn, the Star Council Chamber gleamed like a crystal dawn. Translucent arches of pale quartz formed domes overhead, their facets catching the newborn light and scattering it as prismatic ribbons across starmetal columns. The air was cool, scented faintly of ozone and polished gem. Ancient runes floated above the central table in slow spirals, each symbol glowing like a firefly poised on the verge of song. Around the table sat representatives of Earth and Intenara: Lady Valoria in robes of storm-grey silk, Lord Sanjen with his ironbound staff carved in comet-iron, Lady Untria's eyes shining like dew-lashed petals, and the rest of the Star Council, each face set in solemn expectation. Along the walls, holographic panels flickered with vistas of allied star systems, constellations pulsing in time with distant beacons.

Orion stood at the chamber's heart, robed in deep violet trimmed with threads of burnished gold. Under the fabric, his skin shimmered faintly, as though the moonlight itself had seeped into his veins. He lifted his gaze to the assembly.

"The remaining three of the Great Four have begun their approach," he declared. His voice, clear and unwavering, carried through the hall like a blade of light. "They come not to conquer but to obliterate. They see me as the unravelling of the old order. They intend to unmake the future."

A ripple of chill swept the chamber. The runes dimmed, their glow retreating to ghostly embers.

Queen Alexandria leaned forward, obsidian hair spilling over her shoulders like molten night. "You've charted their course?"

Orion inclined his head. "Their path terminates at Earth."

Lady Valoria's gaze hardened, steel in her eyes. "And your plan?"

He inhaled, the crystal floor catching the rise of his chest in prismatic streaks. "I will confront them alone. Offer them one final chance to abandon this devastation. If they refuse, let the blame rest on me, not a planet, not an entire galaxy."

Silence answered him, weighty and expectant. Then Aaron stepped forward, the hem of his tunic whispering across the floor. "You do not go alone."

Eymd's jaw set, the crystalline pixels of her projection shimmering. "You severed the shadow-path once to save me. I will not stand idle."

Orion met their eyes, Aaron's fierce loyalty, Eymd's unwavering resolve. "I ask not for suicide, but for readiness. If I fail... safeguard what we have forged."

A crackle of static heralded Zanek's voice through the chamber's crystal speaker. "Then do not fail."

Before the echo faded, the room trembled. A low hum rose from the runes, as if awakened by a hidden drum. Outside, the second moon pulsed in solidarity, and a wave of soft azure magic washed through the hall, stirring hair and drifting robes like a sudden breeze.

At the chamber's far edge, space itself rent open. Threads of starlight and night sky wove together, forming a jagged tear in the ether. Through it stepped a figure draped in shifting colours, blues bleeding into purples, then black so deep it swallowed the light around it. Her hair flowed like liquid dusk; her eyes burned with runes that circled and danced like newborn stars.

Gasps rippled around the chamber. Even Aurorina, poised on the edge of her seat, could not hide the astounded inhale that caught in her throat.

"I am Kytherae," the stranger announced, her voice like wind passing through canyons of crystal. "From the Starlit Fold, a realm cradled between moments. We have watched the threads of fate weave and fray for too long."

She stepped onto the chalcedony floor, boots silent as falling snow. "Though few, we bear the oldest bonds, older than galaxies, older than time's first breath. We stand with the Intenfli. We stand with Earth."

At her words, the tome above the planet pulsed once more, a gentle chime of approval resonating through the chamber like a clarion call.

Orion inclined his head in reverent greeting. "Welcome, Kytherae. Your arrival honours us."

Her lips curved in a slow, knowing smile. "And unites us."

Lady Kirand's golden eyes narrowed with a mix of caution and awe. "We've heard of watchers who slip between realms, but never one bold enough to step into the light."

Kytherae's gaze swept over the assembly, steady and serene. "There are truths carved in the breath between stars, truths even your enemies have forgotten," she said. "But you... you were written into them before you were born, Orion."

That night, Orion returned to the upper gardens, where lanterns hung like captive fireflies among silver-leafed branches. A warm breeze stirred the air, carrying the scent of night-blooming jasmine and ancient stone. The grass was cool beneath his fingers as he lowered himself beside Aaron on a velvet cushion of moss.

Above them, Earth's moon and the newly born tome drifted in silent tandem, twin orbs of pale light that seemed to pulse with every beat of Orion's heart.

"You need not become something beyond reach to protect us," Aaron whispered, his breath soft against Orion's shoulder.

Orion turned, eyes reflecting the twin moons like liquid silver. "But I already am," he admitted, voice hushed. "Now I must learn to come back."

Aaron brushed a strand of dark hair from Orion's forehead, fingertips warm as candlelight. "Then let us be your anchor. Me, Jake, everyone who calls you family. We will hold you in this moment while you guide us forward."

Orion's eyes glistened. He interlaced his fingers with Aaron's, the simple touch a tether to the present. "Thank you, for reminding me I don't have to stand alone, even when every instinct tells me I must."

Aaron hesitated, then leaned in closer. "You say you're afraid to lose us," he murmured, voice thick with feeling. "But I'm afraid too. Afraid you'll ascend so high I can't reach you anymore."

Orion turned to him fully, brushing a thumb along his cheek. "Then stay with me. Anchor me. And if I rise, I'll take you with me."

A sacred hush settled around them. The lanterns flickered, casting roving shadows across the grass. Far below, buried in the city's heart, the runes of Intenara thrummed like a great dragon stirring from slumber.

And high above, the second moon watched, patient, luminous, waiting for the moment to reveal what would come next.

Later, as they descended into the quiet halls, Aaron glanced up at the glowing orb. "People are already calling it the Soulmoon," he said softly. "Says it brings dreams they don't remember, but they wake up crying from. Like it's reminding them of something too old to name."

He paused, the reflection of the moon painting his face in silver hues. "I had one of those dreams last night," he added. "I couldn't tell you what it was about. Just... sorrow. And love. Something ancient. It felt like it wasn't even mine. Like I was remembering for someone else."

Orion studied him quietly, the weight of the moon mirrored in his own eyes. "Maybe that's what the tome is. A bridge, not just to what's lost, but to what still matters. The emotions left unsaid, the connections frayed by time."

Aaron's hand found his again. "Then maybe it's doing what you hoped the tome would, reminding us we're all part of something greater. That we're not alone."

# 31. The Breath Before.

Dawn tore across Atlantis in opalescent fire, setting every tower, every spire aglow with trembling light. Orion pressed his palms against the carved marble balustrade of the Soulmoon balcony as though the cool stone might tether him to sanity in this moment of waking reckoning. The horizon bled from bruised violet into furious rose; crystalline pinnacles below erupted in prismed conflagrations that danced like living embers, each flash a promise of salvation, and a harbinger of ruin. Bioluminescent vines quivered along the tower walls, their cerulean veins throbbing with a desperate light that ebbed only at dawn's unyielding claim. All Atlantis inhaled sharply, held in that suspended instant between triumph and abyss.

He had not slept. Night after night stretched out like a cold, suffocating shroud, his mind a tempest of dread and resolve that barred any escape into dreams. A soft exhalation of silk announced Aurorina's arrival, her silhouette slipping into the dawn like a spectre of comfort against his storm.

"You used to drift to sleep watching this sunrise, before they tore you from us," she whispered, each syllable warm as molten honey, weaving through the crisp morning air. Her midnight-velvet gown shimmered with stardust motes that trembled as if alive; pale jasmine petals clung to her hair like fragile memories. Grief and resolve etched deep valleys beneath her eyes, as though she carried the world's heartbreak in her gaze.

He turned, desperately seeking answers in her expression.

"Did you see something, remember?" His voice was thick with hope and fear intertwined.

She tilted her chin to the rosy sky, her breath trembling.

"Not with clarity," she admitted, voice threaded by uncertainty. "Last night I wandered a hall of fractured mirrors. Each reflection warped me into a dozen selves, until I saw you, unmoving amid a tempest of roaring flames, scorched but unbowed. And I heard the Old Ones whisper: 'Only when he walks willingly into shadow will the stars yield their light.'"

Orion drew a jagged breath; her words slashed through him like steel.

"Always cryptic," he rasped, though the sting of omen clung to him.

Aurorina's hand found his chest, heat pulsing through layers of doubt.

"Perhaps they speak truth," she said, steady and clear. "Whatever awaits, remember who you are, not what others carve from your fate."

For a fleeting heartbeat, mother and son stood locked in dawn's fierce promise, their bond tangible as the rising sun. Then Eymd's tall silhouette filled the doorway, runic tattoos blazing like living constellations across her skin. Her wry grin was gone, replaced by a blade of urgency.

"Dress now, star prince. The Council will brook no delay."

In the heart of Atlantis, the Grand Chamber thundered with raw power beneath its vaulted crystal dome. Gilded filigree caught stray shafts of light, fracturing them across projected constellations that drifted overhead, dreams spun into reality. Holographic star maps floated above, emerald evacuation corridors winding towards distant refuge worlds, amber nodes marking every teeming city on Earth. Each flickering point was a cry for help. Footage shimmered alongside the map, tidal waves swallowing coastlines, ash clouds cloaking cities, columns of evacuees crossing through Nexus Gates with nothing but children in arms and relics clutched to chests. Children slept beneath sirens, unaware of the sky's betrayal.

Robed delegates of the Star Council, Intenarii, and Earth Council arrayed themselves in a riot of colours too vivid for mere royalty.

Orion stepped forward, his robe a void of deepest midnight that swallowed light whole, only the starburst crest over his heart gleamed defiantly, like a lone sun defying night. Verjast rumbled first, his basalt flesh carved as if by primeval mountain gods.

"Deploy civilians and volunteers through safety portals to worlds beyond the shadow's reach! Evacuation is our first command."

Kytherae glided up next, her diaphanous gown swirling in ghostly trails. Her eyes shone with impossible knowledge.

"I have peered through the Fold at the coming war, it bleeds from more than our realm. Dimensional rifts tear open reality's seams! Time itself will knot and snap beneath their onslaught!" Her voice trembled, then steadied. "The last time the Fold bled, we lost seven moons. This is worse. The boundary isn't just fraying, it's screaming."

A wave of alarm passed through the assembly, a collective intake of breath that trembled the very air. Orion lifted one unyielding hand, palm outward like a challenge hurled at despair itself.

"Then we do not merely defend Earth, we anchor it. Should the Great Four unleash their fury, we shall meet them united, unbroken!"

Snjallt's slender fingers danced across the central star map, and crimson veins of fracture pulsed over London, Geneva, and beyond.

"Activate Stone Guard to shield London's ramparts! Dispatch Echo Wardens to Geneva's canals, our wards will hold the tears at bay, if only for a heartbeat!"

Orion inclined his head, determination ablaze in his eyes.

"Before the battle," he said, voice a vow of steel, "I must stand at the Soulmoon shrine."

Below the balcony, glowing roots wove around the shrine like living veins. Wind chimes crafted from starlit shells and woven glass swayed gently, their tones ringing like whispered blessings. The hush was broken only by the murmur of leaves and the rhythmic pulse of the Soulmoon's roots, a heartbeat of light echoing through the shrine.

At its heart lay offerings left by whispering pilgrims: river stones etched with prayers, dawn-tangled garlands, shards of coloured glass trembling in morning gales. A shallow pool mirrored the lingering moon, its surface rippling under dew's caress. There, perched with legs dangling above the earth, sat a solemn child, his wide eyes glinting like distant stars peering from a pitch-black sky.

Orion knelt before him. Tears stung his eyes. Fierce. Silent.

"You're the one the sky spoke of, aren't you?" he asked, voice hushed.

Orion answered as the boy looked up at him.

"I am."

The boy drew a tiny wooden star from his pocket, each facet spiralled with live runes that pulsed warm in Orion's hand. The carvings shimmered faintly, like the mirrored flames from Aurorina's vision. The same heat. The same promise.

"For you," the child said, voice steady, "to keep safe."

Orion bowed his head.

"Thank you. What's your name?"

"Matteo," came the soft reply.

"And I believe in you."

Orion closed his eyes.

"Then I will not fail."

He rose, the rune-star clenched in his palm like a promise.

In the palace observatory, brass consoles winked alive beneath the shifting constellations. At the centre hovered P.I.L.S.S., its cobalt core pulsing like a heartbeat on the brink of war.

"Initiate Protocol: Starborn Rally!" Orion's command cut through the dark like a blade.

"Broadcast to all allied systems. Awaken the outer rim, unseal the ancient tomes, ignite the satellite relays. Summon our allies in the void!"

"Affirmative," P.I.L.S.S. replied. The observatory roared to life. Golden beams exploded outward, racing through long-abandoned channels, torrents of light reclaiming the stars. Across Yimmana and Pro, cloaked satellites stirred. Old fleets rose. Dormant portals cracked open.

Rachel slipped beside him, her silhouette carved by starlight. Arms folded, eyes solemn.

"You've called them all, even those who swore they'd never return."

"I had no choice," Orion said. "Some won't make it."

She met his gaze, fierce and unwavering.

"Nor will we, unless we stand together."

They stepped onto the balcony. Above them, a thunderhead of bruised clouds rolled in, tendrils of shadow snaking across the sky. One by one, stars winked out.

Orion gripped the rune-star. It pulsed in his hand like a second heartbeat, warm, rhythmic, waiting.

The Great Four were coming. And as the last stars blinked away, all Atlantis held its breath, for the light that would only come when shadow was faced willingly.

# 32. When The Veil Breaks

It began with a sound. Not thunder. Not metal, something deeper, a subterranean groan as if the sky itself cracked open along some primeval fault. Above Cairo, the Fold pulsed like a bruised heart, then ripped in two with a jagged seam through low-hanging clouds. Beyond the rent, a churning sea of starlit ink unfurled. Gravity convulsed sideways. Screams climbed before sound could follow, a ragged chorus ripped from frozen throats.

For a heartbeat, the world faltered. People squinted, thinking an eclipse, then stared dumbstruck as time shuddered. Children stood mid-stride, their laughter caught in the air. Cars hovered over asphalt, engine idling in suspended silence. A man's coffee cup cracked on the sidewalk; steam curled upward in frozen tendrils. In a narrow alley, a woman sprinted only to loop back on herself again and again, a macabre dance in endless replay.

From the heart of the Fold, a coil of black flame unfurled, sinister as smoke caught afire, gouging the atmosphere like claws through silk. The very fabric of reality quivered.

In Geneva, klaxons shrieked, drowning out the electric crackle in the sky. Echo Wardens, obsidian sentinels flecked with living constellations, stepped into formation, shields raised against the shimmering tide. Across every frequency, P.I.L.S.S.'s crystalline voice reported: "Breach convergence in multiple quadrants, Geneva, Cairo, northern Pacific. Temporal instability confirmed."

Far beneath Atlantis's mirrored domes, Verjast leaned over a holo-map, his stone jaw set in immovable lines. "They're testing the seams," he growled, breath echoing off runic walls. "They're not coming, they're already here."

No sooner had the words fallen than the skies flared again, this time with molten gold. Crescent-bladed ships of Yimmana descended in perfect auroral arcs above Cairo. Their hulls, forged from solar-forged alloys, shimmered with living light. From each craft, warriors draped in glimmering solar silk leapt down, scorching arcs of flame that wove across ruptured time, stitching reality's tears closed just long enough for panicked crowds to flee.

In Geneva, as a century-old monument buckled under dimensional strain, the canals sighed. Columns of water rose in sinuous spirals, glistening like liquid crystal. From their swirling crests stepped the Proxari, tall, silver-skinned beings whose bodies glowed from within. They moved as though born of the currents themselves, erecting translucent shields that linked with the Echo Wardens' dark bulwarks, reinforcing Geneva's last stand.

Above the northern Pacific, where the rift yawned like an open wound, a gargantuan vessel emerged, a fortress of interstellar bone and midnight iron. The Umbrael Guard, thought lost in the starless depths, unfurled an aurora barrage so brilliant it scorched the heavens. Rifts quavered, then stilled.

In the mirrored observatory of Atlantis, Orion inhaled, the weight of every battlefield and broken world reflected in his storm-grey eyes. One by one, the allies had come. Not all would survive. But they had answered.

Lights flickered, then died. The centre holoprojector sparked, shimmering lines coalescing into a face of smoke and hunger, Strixium. His form resolved into crimson shadow, eyes flecked with violet fire. He lounged in the projection like a dark king atop a throne of void, his voice a silk-tipped dagger.

"Orion, Starborn child of whispers and defiance. You gather insects and call it resistance. How quaint."

A murmur rolled through the council chamber as the hologram flooded every node. Orion stepped forward, fingers curled into taut bronze.

"Strixium. I wondered when your stench would reach my door."

The shadow smiled, a rift of burning malice.

"Doors are for mortals. I walk through worlds. You think old fleets and broken kings change what's coming? You will kneel."

Orion's voice rang like a sword unsheathed.

"No. Not here. Not ever."

Strixium's grin fractured.

"Then let the galaxy watch your fall."

Orion leaned into the holo-light, his cloak brushing carved marble.

"Enough threats. We end this where humanity was born anew, Aetherion Crater on Mars. I'll come alone."

Strixium tilted his head, violet embers dancing in his eyes.

"Alone?"

"Only the Stone Guard and the Echo Wardens still bound to Atlantis shall walk with me. The rest remain."

Silence crashed through the chamber. Strixium's shadows writhed.

"Then I shall not come unaccompanied. Josnan and Lucandr join me. We shall see if your starlight burns when faced with true oblivion."

Orion's jaw clenched.

"A graveyard for your pride, then. I accept."

The projection shattered in a shower of sparks. An uproar followed. Councillors shouted. Aurorina leapt up, face pale but fierce. "You cannot go alone! You're not a sacrificial pawn, Orion!" Delegates from Earth wept or clenched fists. Even Snjallt, ever icy, cracked: "This is madness!"

Orion raised both hands, calm and resolute. "I do not intend to die. I will stop them. If I fail, Earth must stand. That is why you remain. We split their focus, we do not hand them the heart of the resistance."

A hush fell, heavy as falling stone. The western gate's ancient hinges groaned. Light spilled through.

From the shadows emerged a woman in golden robes, voice soft as dawn. "He will not go alone." She dropped her hood, revealing features identical to Aurorina's, sharp cheekbones, storm-grey eyes, yet she glowed with the quiet certainty of ages. Aurorina gasped. "Sister... Velastra."

Velastra's gaze softened for a breath. "I felt the Fold tremble and answered. You called me across the stars, even when you didn't know it."

Aurorina's tears glimmered. "I thought you were lost."

"I was," Velastra murmured, "but your lullabies remembered me." She turned to the council, voice resonant. "I come as Seer-Marshal of the Sisterhood of the Veiled Sight. It was we who foresaw Orion's journey, and his return at the end of the age."

Mothers and sisters embraced in solemn silence. Then Velastra stepped back. "Orion goes guarded. Blood calls to blood." Twelve figures in ancient battleplate emerged, moving as one, a silent tip of spears, hammers, and shields etched with a sigil of starlight.

The last guardian knelt. "We are yours again, Intenfli Orion."

Orion inclined his head, reverent but unbowed. "No. You remain. Your duty is to protect what keeps me tethered: family, home, hope. Under no circumstance pursue me. Only the Stone Guard and Echo Wardens beside me, that is my command."

A taut stillness followed. The lead guardian bowed, voice rumbling like bedrock. "Then we hold the line, Intenfli Orion, until the stars burn clean."

The ground trembled. A low groan vibrated through Atlantis's foundations. With a grinding roar, the Vault of Atlantis, sealed since eternity, began to open. Obsidian doors peeled back in layers, unveiling a vast chamber pulsing with molten light.

From the darkness they emerged. The Stone Guard: towering figures of stardust-veined obsidian, etched with golden constellations. Each bore a weapon born of cosmic fury, comet-spears, sun-hammers, gatesized shields. Behind them, the Echo Wardens glided forward, crystal visors alight like prisms, runic armour humming with quiet power.

Hundreds filled the courtyards and steps of the Soulmoon plaza, silent as carved monuments.

Just before Orion stepped onto the marble floor, a low growl echoed across the plaza. From the eastern archway bounded a golden Labrador, scruffy, tongue lolling, eyes bright with knowing joy. Cries of confusion and surprise rippled through the crowd, for few recognised the beast in this humble form.

But Orion knew. He froze, chest tight. "Pragor?"

The Labrador barked once, tail wagging, and then shimmered.

Golden fur rippled like water. Bones stretched, muscles expanded. Astral veins ignited beneath his skin. The transformation unfurled in a radiant burst, his body elongated into its true form: leonine and majestic, crowned with a mane woven from starlight and fire. Wings of radiant mist unfurled from his shoulders. His eyes, once doglike and eager, now burned with cosmic intelligence.

Orion stepped forward, awe and laughter mixing in his throat. "You cheeky thing. You've been watching me all this time."

Pragor rumbled in amusement and lowered his massive head. Orion pressed his forehead to the creature's. "Then burn with me, old friend. One last blaze."

Pragor growled, a promise of loyalty that echoed like thunder.

As Orion turned and stepped onto the marble floor, Pragor fell into stride beside him, his claws clicking like ceremonial drums against the stone. The great army knelt.

"We are yours to command, Intenfli," they intoned, a living mountain range of voices rolling across the plaza.

At their head, Thael, the Echo Warden entrusted to Orion at Atlantis's rebirth, stepped forward, bowed low, then stood sentinel, visor gleaming beneath the Soulmoon's glow.

Orion met Thael's gaze, voice a tempered ember. "You interfere only at my word. You are my shield, not my sword."

Thael's nod was an iron vow. "Understood, Intenfli. We stand and wait, until your word calls the stars to move."

Orion turned, eyes sweeping over his family, his council, the silent soldiers beyond. "Everyone not of the Stone Guard or Echo Wardens," he commanded, "cover your eyes. Now."

In a crescendo of urgency, heads bowed, visors snapped shut, hands covered startled faces. The air hummed, pregnant with expectancy.

Orion inhaled as the Soulmoon flared. Golden radiance pulsed from his skin in blinding waves, cascading like supernova fire across the plaza. His frame convulsed, expanding with divine purpose, curls erupting into silver-gold flames, stubble dissolving into runes aglow along his jaw. With a thunderous crack, twin wings burst forth, one incandescent as newborn stars, the other an abyssal black that drank every flicker of light. His armour liquefied and reforged itself into overlapping plates of cosmic energy, each rune older than memory.

As the divine surge enveloped the plaza, Pragor lifted his head beside Orion, howling a deep, echoing roar that shook the marble beneath them. Golden light spilled from his chest, his mane fanning wide with streaks of starlight and fire. His body expanded in tandem with Orion's, bones stretching into titanic proportions. Wings of plasma and wind burst from his back, wide enough to eclipse towers. Runes blazed across his hide, ancient and wild, as though etched into his very soul by the Old Ones.

Pragor's eyes locked onto Orion's, and in that silent bond a sacred truth passed between them.

They would rise as one.

The god-form of Orion, Starborn Phoenix, and the ascended form of Pragor, Celestial Fang, stood side by side, twin avatars of hope and fury.

Their presence was cataclysmic. A storm and a promise. Retribution and shield.

Silence fell. Even the stars held still.

Orion lifted his gaze to the sky, voice layered with celestial resonance. "Earth, you were my sanctuary, my proving ground, my healer. You sheltered me when I bled and reminded me who I am. For that, I will protect you. I will burn brighter than the end."

He flexed his wings and launched skyward in a comet of living fire, parting clouds like woven curtains. Beside him, Pragor soared in a spiral of howling light, fangs bared, mane trailing embers.

Behind them, the Stone Guard rose in thunderous unison, forming an obsidian-and-gold ring. The Echo Wardens followed, lifting like silent sparks drawn to a blazing core, forging a second circle of radiant defence.

Together they spiralled upward, a celestial phalanx bound for Mars and the war to come.

# 33. Red Reckoning On Mars

The air above Mars shimmered, thin and bitter, the ghost of an atmosphere that still remembered fire.

Aetherion Crater stretched vast and hollow before Orion, its jagged lip scorched by ancient wars, its centre littered with timeworn remnants of rebellion: broken banners, shattered armour, half-buried monuments to the first Earthborn uprising. It was here, centuries ago, that humanity had earned its right to rise. And now, it would be tested again.

Orion descended like a comet, golden fire trailing from his wings. Beside him, Pragor landed with a bone-rattling impact, his celestial form cracking the crust. Behind them, the sky churned with thunder and power as the Stone Guard and Echo Wardens, celestial warriors etched in cosmic armour and radiant crystal, descended in a perfect spiral, forming silent phalanxes across the crater rim. They stood immobile, divine sentinels awaiting only one thing, Orion's command.

Dust settled.

Stillness held.

Then, with a hiss like a knife through silk, the Fold tore open again.

Three figures emerged through the bleeding sky. Strixium came first, a roiling pillar of crimson shadow, flames licking from his shoulders, his void-born eyes locked on Orion. To his left, Lucandr floated slightly above the ground, his stitched face split in a grin too wide for any human mouth. And to Strixium's right stood Josnan, the blind giant whose coiled beard whispered with serpentine motion, his great limbs trembling with contained violence.

They did not speak.

They did not need to.

Strixium's grin twisted into something almost admiring. "So you wear your true form so openly, Starborn. It would be rude not to match."

His body erupted in a blaze of crimson and shadow, expanding outward like a solar flare gone wrong. Horns burst from his head, curling like molten obsidian, while his arms split into tendrils of smouldering ether that lashed the air. His eyes blazed brighter, deepening into vortexes of violet fire. He towered over the crater now, a god of death and mockery.

Lucandr laughed, a jarring, multi-tonal cackle, as his form warped grotesquely. His stitched body split and reknit in waves, growing taller, broader, until his limbs ended in clawed gauntlets of blackened bone. A second face emerged from beneath his jaw, grinning with teeth of glass. "I always liked the old shape better," he whispered in echoing voices.

Josnan let out a low, guttural snarl. Without flourish or announcement, his body stretched and cracked, sinews thickening as his scaly hide spread wide. His beard of coiled serpents writhed into a halo of wriggling dread, and wings, torn and ancient, unfurled from his back. Though blind, his empty eyes glowed with ruin.

Strixium spread his arms wide, voice a rolling mockery. "You thought yourself divine, Intenfli? You are not the only one who can shed a mask."

The sky darkened, unnaturally swift, as if the sun itself recoiled in fear. Lightning split the heavens in threads of red and violet. The very air began to tremble, each breath thick, like inhaling sorrow.

Orion narrowed his eyes, the divine flare of his armour pulsing in synchrony with his heart. He could feel the ancient power radiating from them, raw, wild, the kind that bent galaxies into ruin. But it wasn't fear that gripped him.

It was memory.

He had seen this once before. In a vision. In the eyes of a child who handed him a wooden star.

Pragor stepped forward, his mane bristling with divine fire, and growled low, a sound that cracked stone and silenced wind. Behind them, the Stone Guard and Echo Wardens remained still, unmoving statues of war, awaiting the command that had not yet come. Their weapons gleamed, but not a single blade rose.

For a moment, no one moved.

Then Strixium's laughter returned, sharper now, almost fraying at the edges. "You feel it, don't you? The unravelling. The last threads of your fate tugging loose."

Orion raised his hand slowly, fingers shimmering like forged starlight.

"No," he said. "I feel the end of yours."

With that, Orion slammed his fist into the earth. The crater exploded in a burst of white-gold energy, shockwaves rippling outward in rings of raw force. The sky shattered in streaks of colour.

Strixium's roar split the air, but he did not move. Instead, he lifted one hand lazily, as if conducting an orchestra of annihilation. "Go," he commanded, voice laced with contempt and fire. "Show him what happens when stars defy the void."

At his word, Josnan launched skyward and Lucandr reappeared in a shriek, his limbs distorting into blades and hooks. Strixium remained still atop a raised slab of scorched stone, arms folded, watching with the predatory amusement of a god who had seen empires burn.

Josnan launched himself skyward, wings beating hurricanes across the battlefield before plummeting like a meteor toward Orion.

Orion caught the descent with both hands, locking Josnan in midair. The impact cracked the land beneath them, sending shards of red rock flying. Sparks erupted across his god-forged armour as claws tore at celestial plate.

Josnan snarled, a sound more earthquake than voice, and lunged forward with a flurry of strikes, each swing heavy enough to fell a mountain. Orion ducked beneath one blow, twisting with winged momentum as he countered with a radiant punch to Josnan's ribs. Divine light exploded on contact, sending ripples through the serpent-beard giant's chest.

But Josnan didn't flinch. Instead, he twisted his head sharply, and the serpents within his beard uncoiled, striking out like whips of bone and muscle. They wrapped around Orion's arm, attempting to yank him down into the dirt.

Orion gritted his teeth and summoned his inner fire. "I do not fall to beasts born of rot."

With a burst of celestial force, his wings snapped wide and unleashed a shockwave that tore the serpents free and hurled Josnan backward. The crater floor split as Josnan dug in, claws gouging trenches through molten stone. He charged again, eyes unseeing but locked on Orion's aura.

Their fists collided mid-air, a boom of cosmic fury flattening nearby ridgelines. The echo rang across the atmosphere.

Josnan lashed out with a tail Orion hadn't seen, a scaled club tipped with volcanic starmetal. It struck his side, sending him crashing through a jagged ridge. He tumbled, rolled, then rose amid smoke, armour glowing and cracked.

Orion lifted a hand to his brow and narrowed his eyes.

"Come then, brute. Let's finish what your kind began."

And once again, he launched skyward, blazing into Josnan like a living meteor.

Their clash lit the Martian sky like the birth of a new star. Orion's fist crashed into Josnan's jaw, snapping the titan's head sideways with a thunderous crack that sent tremors spiralling for kilometres. But Josnan countered instantly, his massive hands slammed together, trapping Orion in a bone-crushing grip of scaled force. He roared, lifting Orion like a banner of defiance before driving him into the crater wall.

Dust and rock geysered skyward. The ground screamed.

But even buried, Orion's glow did not fade.

From the rubble, a blinding lance of light erupted, Orion's wings slicing outward in twin arcs of burning divinity. He burst forth, wreathed in stormfire, his body a conduit of celestial rage. With a single beat of his wings, he blasted skyward, then reversed in a spiral and drove his heel down onto Josnan's skull.

The blow dropped the giant to one knee, dust swirling in orbit around his broken form.

Josnan snarled, head jerking upward as the serpents of his beard struck again. But this time, Orion was ready. He caught them mid-air, hands glowing with runic fire, and twisted, severing them with a slash of raw energy that shrieked through the void like a torn veil.

Josnan screamed. For the first time, pain, true pain, flared in his blind eyes.

Orion floated above him, glowing like a wrathful nova.

"You will not break this world," he said, voice a bell tolling at the end of time.

And then he dove, a streak of vengeance and glory, into the wounded colossus once more.

The impact cratered the earth beneath them, a rupture of red stone and golden light. Josnan roared, his voice a cathedral of rage collapsing inward. He swung upward with his remaining strength, landing a glancing blow across Orion's side that would have shattered lesser gods.

Orion grunted, skidding across the battlefield, but stayed aloft, his wings flaring wide. Sparks flew from the crack in his chestplate. He winced, but there was clarity in his eyes now. Not fury. Not vengeance. Purpose.

He called, not with words, but with will, summoning the harmony of Earth's memory, of all who still believed. The rune-star gifted to him by the child Matteo pulsed at his side, its warmth threading through the chaos like a whispered prayer.

Josnan staggered upright, blood, dark and smoking, dripping from his mouth. His serpents gone, wings tattered, the ancient giant braced himself for one final charge.

"This ends with you," he growled.

Orion raised his hands skyward. Starlight gathered between his palms. "No," he answered, "it begins with me."

He brought his palms together, and the light between them flared into a spear of truth, forged from faith, pain, and a thousand broken tomorrows. He hurled it with the weight of every promise he had made.

The spear pierced Josnan's chest with a scream that split both sky and soul.

The giant froze, eyes wide. Light poured from his mouth, his wounds, his empty gaze.

Then he fell. Backward. Into dust.

And did not rise again.

Orion hovered above the fallen titan, his breath steady but wary. The crater was silent but for the hum of lingering power.

He narrowed his gaze. "I've fought too many ghosts to believe in easy ends."

Raising his voice, Orion turned toward the crater rim. "Thael! Korrin! Bind him, now."

Two Echo Wardens stepped forward, wings of crystal shimmer and dusk unfolding behind them. Without hesitation, they descended into the ruin. Runes lit their gauntlets as they approached the collapsed form of Josnan, arcane manacles forming from bands of starlight and obsidian.

They worked swiftly, reverently, chaining his limbs and sealing him in a containment glyph as large as a temple floor.

Orion didn't look away. "If he so much as twitches, restrain him with force, but do not kill him unless there is no choice. I want them together, bound and accounted for when this ends. No loose shadows."

Pragor pounced on Lucandr, the two titans tumbling in a cyclone of fire and shadow, fangs and flame colliding in a blur of god-beast and darkborn horror.

Lucandr twisted mid-roll, his limbs warping into jagged scythes that tore across Pragor's flank. Sparks and golden blood fountained from the wound, but Pragor responded with a roar that shattered stone and bit down hard on one of Lucandr's many shifting arms. Shadow screamed.

They separated in a burst of force, Lucandr slashing with his multi-faced grin gleaming, Pragor circling with wings outstretched, tail lashing.

"Beast," Lucandr hissed. "What are you but a pet given teeth?"

Pragor's only reply was a snarl of such raw intent that even Lucandr faltered.

Suddenly, a radiant spear streaked between them, Orion descended like a falling star, crashing beside Pragor with light searing through the dust.

"I don't recall giving you permission to insult my familiar," Orion said coldly.

Lucandr's smile grew impossibly wide. "Two for one? Delightful."

"Then scream your delight to the end," Orion answered, summoning twin blades of coalesced light and shadow.

Together, god and beast lunged at the monster stitched from nightmares.

The crater burned anew.

Lucandr twisted his body mid-leap, morphing into a bladed vortex. Each appendage shifted into jagged weaponry, scythes, saws, and serrated tendrils spinning like a hurricane of razors. He tore through the crater with unnatural speed, aiming to split them apart.

Orion and Pragor separated instinctively, one soaring high, the other plunging low. As Lucandr struck, Orion intercepted a blade with his crossed swords, sparks flying in every direction. The force drove him back, heels skimming across the shattered earth.

Pragor struck next, launching himself at Lucandr's exposed flank with a roar. His jaws clamped down on the enemy's midsection, wings battering the air. But Lucandr flexed, his body melting and re-stitching itself mid-grapple. He emerged behind Pragor in a blink, his clawed fingers digging toward the beast's spine.

Orion dove, intercepting the blow. Their blades clashed again, but this time Lucandr's grin twisted. "You bleed, Intenfli. Soon, you'll beg."

"Try me," Orion growled, then blasted Lucandr with a point-blank burst of pure starlight. The stitched monster screamed, thrown across the battlefield in a plume of burning shadow.

Orion landed beside Pragor, chest heaving. "No more dancing."

Pragor growled in agreement, smoke curling from his nostrils.

Together, they prepared to charge, but the air shimmered with sudden urgency. A flickering blue projection surged to life beside Orion's head. He felt it before it even spoke, a disturbance beyond the battlefield.

P.I.L.S.S.'s voice, usually calm, now crackled with strained precision.

"Intenfli Orion," it said, "The Great Four's armada has begun its assault. Earth is under attack."

Orion froze, just for a breath, as the weight of the message settled over him. Then he ducked under a spinning blade from Lucandr, countering with a rising arc of light that carved through shadow.

He shouted over the chaos, "P.I.L.S.S., can they hold?"

Pragor snarled beside him, intercepting Lucandr's strike with his wings, flames erupting along the beast's back.

P.I.L.S.S. responded, its voice pulsing through the combat din. "The planetary defences have engaged. Queen Alexandria, your mother and Elskar are coordinating with the Intenarii, the E.D.A and the shadow warriors. But the fleet is vast. Resistance is holding, for now."

Orion gritted his teeth, sparks flaring from his shoulders as another of Lucandr's blades scraped past.

# 34. The Planet's Answer

The sky above Earth fractured in veins of fire.

From the upper thermosphere down to the lower stratosphere, war raged in silence. The Great Four's armada cut through orbit like a plague of steel and shadow. Their vessels, forged in the void, resembled monstrous insects, jagged wings of metal, glowing cores of red and violet, and tendrils that lashed out like hungry limbs. They broke through Earth's planetary defences with terrifying precision.

But Earth did not fall quietly.

Queen Alexandria stood atop the Royal Citadel's command dais, her emerald gown replaced with battle armour of Atlantean alloy. Beside her, Elskar coordinated the movement of celestial glyphs across a glowing tactical sphere. Holograms flickered, Earth's planetary shield rippling, then stabilising again under pressure. Behind them, the council chamber had become a war room, the walls alive with communications from across the globe. Auroriona stood near the rear, silent but resolute, her presence a steady beacon.

"Forward Intenarii regiments to the Eurasian shield barrier," Elskar instructed sharply. "They must hold sector twelve."

Alexandria nodded, voice steel wrapped in calm. "Deploy the second echelon. Evacuate civilians below zone four. And Elskar, activate the Skybound Protocol. I want the outer sentries charged."

The three women, Queen, Seer, and Guardian, stood united in purpose.

"I know this plan will hold," Auroriona said. "Because it was born from Orion's hope and fortified by all of ours."

A pulse of power shimmered through the tactical sphere.

The Star Council, gathered at the centre of Atlantis, turned toward them. Lord Sanjen's gravity drones stilled in respect, and Lady Valoria's spectral birds circled once before vanishing.

"We are aligned," said Lord Jandavinr. "Earth stands not alone. This council does not simply witness, we intervene."

Lady Kirand offered a sharp smile. "Let them taste celestial retribution."

From orbit, the Great Four's capital dreadnought loomed.

And from its bow, something stirred.

But Earth answered.

A searing bolt of golden light carved through the clouds, shattering a swarm of enemy vessels before they could reach London's inner perimeter. The skies parted, not from retreat, but from arrival.

Pro descended like a meteor of divine intent.

Wreathed in armour laced with stardust and fire, his form hit the Earth like judgment itself. Shockwaves rippled outward, turning advancing shadowbeasts to ash mid-screech. His eyes, two suns behind obsidian brows, burned with the fury of an ancient force awakened.

He rose from the crater, cloak billowing like a banner of vengeance.

"This planet is not yours to take," Pro said, voice resonating in every living soul nearby.

As he spoke, the Earth beneath him responded.

Roots of light unfurled from the soil, tracing across scorched ground and crumbling stone. Pro placed a hand against the earth and closed his eyes. A pulse of consciousness surged upward, ancient, planetary, alive. Earth's spirit was with him.

They did not speak in words, but in knowing.

"Together," the planet whispered through pulse and wind.

"Until the stars fall," Pro answered.

Together, they merged.

All across Atlantis, runic gates flared into being, humming with ancestral power. Each one pulsed with a distinct celestial seal, their resonance tied to the planetary core.

The Star Council stood together one final moment at the heart of the city, gathered around Elskar, Auroriona, and Queen Alexandria. No speeches. Just a nod shared between powers.

Lady Valoria was first. Her portal bloomed with crystal and lightning. With a flick of her wrist and a soft flash, she stepped into the rift and vanished.

Then Lord Sanjen entered his, a vortex of oceanic pressure and thundering clouds. His gravity drones followed like moons in orbit.

Lady Untria's gate ignited in a spiral of molten dust and flame, Lord Jandavinr's opened through frozen starlight and drifting constellations. Zanek was last, his portal blooming from bark and stone. Before stepping through, he bowed his head, kissed the carved ring on his finger, and whispered a silent vow to come back home to Alexi and their child.

Each gate closed behind them with a harmonic pulse.

Their destinations: key regions across Earth. Places under siege. Each Council member had chosen where their presence could shift the tide, Valoria to the ruins of old Osaka, Sanjen to the shattered sea-wall of Greenland, Untria to the scorched sands of Sudan, Jandavinr to frozen Siberian fields, and Zanek to the trembling Amazon.

Back in the Atlantean war chamber, Elskar stared at the now-closed portals.

"They have taken their positions," she whispered.

Alexandria stepped forward, her voice rising with fierce command. "Then we hold."

She tapped a crystal node on the dais. "All units, this is Queen Alexandria. Our celestial allies are engaged across the world. Engage with full force. Earth does not kneel today."

In the streets below, civilians and soldiers alike looked skyward as the heavens erupted with colour and light. Hope surged.

On the ground in Geneva, Aaron rappelled down a rope and landed beside Rachel.

"They're here," he said.

Rachel's emerald eyes flared, her Veilshard spinning into its dual-blade form. "Then let's help them."

Above them, the tide began to shift.

The war for Earth had truly begun.

At the base of the newly risen Halcyon Spire, Earth's nascent planetary heart, Pro stood at its edge, his gaze sweeping across a horizon drenched in fire and shadow. The wind carried cries of both despair and defiance, but beneath it all, he could feel the beat of the planet's soul, strong, steady, awake.

Golden veins of starlight traced across his forearms as he extended both hands, kneeling. The spire pulsed beneath him.

"They fight," Pro whispered.

The ground beneath him vibrated, and though no words came, he felt the planet's response. "And we rise."

Together, they began.

Pro pressed his palm to the surface. Across the globe, sleeping nodes buried in deep tectonic folds awakened. From jungle roots and desert stone, from seafloor vents and mountain hearts, Earth answered. Energy unfurled like breath held too long. The planet was no longer a passive battleground. It had become a living force.

"Let me be your voice," Pro said aloud. "Your guardian. Your blade."

From the core of his being, starlight erupted upward, joining with the golden lattice of planetary essence. The Halcyon Spire lit like a beacon, casting arcs of radiance into the storm-filled sky.

Atlantean towers reacted, resonating, amplifying the pulse. In New Avalon, old temples cracked open. In the ruins of fallen cities, buried sigils reactivated, casting protection over survivors. The land itself warped to protect the innocent, forming walls, redirecting fire, turning terrain against the invaders.

Pro rose slowly, transformed yet again, not in form, but in presence. He was not just a child of Orion's hand. He was Earth's will made flesh.

And Earth, for the first time in eons, was speaking back.

"Let them come," Pro said, stepping into the light.

High above the burning plains of Sudan, Lady Untria carved spirals of flame across the battlefield. Her gown of solar fire lashed like a comet-tail as she flew through squadrons of winged wraiths, each one disintegrating with a shriek of molten shadow. The ground beneath her steamed and cracked as long-dormant lava veins ignited, summoned by her every gesture.

She wasn't alone.

Shadow Warriors from the western provinces fought beside her, reborn exiles who had answered the call when Earth itself stirred. At their front, a young warrior in gold-threaded armour raised a banner stitched with ancient glyphs of flame. Behind them, supply carriers and plasma turrets surged to life as her power awakened the region's long-dormant sunforged relics.

Untria landed atop a crumbling obelisk, eyes scanning the horizon.

"They come in numbers. Let them learn fire has memory."

From the east, a shadowbeast of monumental scale rose from the sands, part insect, part starved leviathan. It roared, spitting corrosive bile across the battlefield.

Untria raised both hands, her palms glowing.

She whispered a phrase only the sun understood.

A ring of flame erupted from her feet, expanding outward in a shockwave. The sands melted into glass. The creature screamed as its limbs scorched and splintered, crashing to the earth with a quake that rattled distant dunes.

Below, warriors cheered.

Untria turned to the sky and whispered, "Your light still answers me, old friend. Let's burn their lies away."

Elsewhere, far from the Atlantean gates and crumbling cities, the jagged coastline of the broken Norwegian cliffs pulsed with shadow and steel. Here, Eymd led the charge.

She stood at the forefront of a fractured ridge, twin swords drawn, eyes burning with defiance. Her blood-red hair whipped around her in the wind, armour scorched and scuffed. The Echo Wardens flanked her, silent, crystalline visors aglow, their cosmic armour glinting under dim skyfire.

Behind them, Orion's elite guards formed tight phalanxes, shields raised, spears gleaming with starlight. These were the champions who had stood beside Orion, and now they stood for Earth.

"Formation Theta," Eymd barked.

The soldiers responded without hesitation. Shields locked. Star magic surged.

A roar thundered from the canyon beyond, monsters made of nightmare and scrap metal charged, twisted remnants of shadowtech summoned by the Great Four. They surged like a wave, screaming with static and hunger.

Eymd didn't wait.

She launched herself forward, slicing through the first wave with the fluid grace of a dancer born to war. Her blades became ribbons of starlight. Behind her, the Echo Wardens ignited their spears and marched into the fray, a wall of silence and celestial vengeance.

One Warden fell, dragged down by a beast with five spines and a plasma maw, but a second split the creature in half with a single hammering blow.

Overhead, Orion's elite vanguard descended with jet bursts and blades drawn. The enemy broke against them like waves against midnight stone.

Eymd struck again, this time decapitating a shrieking warlord of the enemy's command brood. "Hold this ridge!" she shouted. "For Earth! For Orion!"

The response was a thunderous battle cry, one that echoed up the cliffs and into the sky above.

And in that sound, Earth fought back.

Far beyond Earth's surface, in the silent gravity wells of orbit, the last two ancient protectors of Yimmana stirred once more.

As a new wave of shadowbeasts poured from the dreadnought's underbelly, winged, fanged, and rippling with entropy, the Stone Guard moved.

One raised a hand, and a spear of crystallised starlight formed mid-air before launching with thunderous precision. It struck a beast the size of a fortress, vaporising it in a sun-bright flash.

Another Guard brought down a colossal mace, crushing a host of voidspawn that had clustered too close to one of Earth's orbital stabilisers. Their destruction rippled with silence but echoed with meaning.

These two sentinels moved with divine grace, orbiting Earth not just as protectors but as judges. They were living relics of a time before time.

And they remembered.

They positioned themselves into a celestial arc along Earth's upper atmosphere, an unyielding wall of cosmic justice. Their constellated armour pulsed in rhythm with the Halcyon Spire below.

Above the chaos, the heavens bore witness.

And the void, for the first time in an age, hesitated.

# 35. Orion's Stand

The crater still smoked.

Dust spiralled in slow eddies as Josnan's chained body lay dormant beneath celestial bonds. The Echo Wardens stood vigil over his defeated form, their weapons lowered but hands never far from readiness. The golden containment glyphs carved into the red Martian stone pulsed in rhythmic intervals.

Above it all, Orion hovered.

His armour was cracked, his breath shallow, but the fire in his eyes had only grown brighter. Each beat of his wings sent streaks of radiant light down the crater's edge. He watched the battlefield not with exhaustion, but with sharpened focus. He knew what was coming next.

A jagged shadow tore across the far ridge. Lucandr.

The stitched monster hadn't fled, only regrouped. Now, he emerged once more, wreathed in writhing tendrils and wearing a face that wasn't entirely his own. Blades jutted from every joint; laughter peeled from his many mouths.

"You always were the dramatic one, Intenfli," Lucandr hissed, voice echoing like metal dragged across bone. "Burning light, noble speeches, and yet, still mortal."

Orion gripped his blades tighter.

"Mortality isn't weakness. You should know. You lost yours long ago."

Lucandr's grin stretched impossibly wide. "And what did it get me? Freedom. Power. Purpose."

He lunged.

Their blades met mid-air. Sparks screamed into the Martian sky. Lucandr spun mid-strike, morphing into a bladed vortex, but Orion flipped beneath the onslaught, wings folding to avoid the scything arc. He struck back with twin arcs of searing light, carving deep into Lucandr's torso.

The creature howled. Shadow and fluid spilled from his wounds, only to re-knit moments later.

"You're stalling," Orion growled.

Lucandr's many eyes glittered. "And you're bleeding."

Orion touched his ribs, blood shimmered on his fingertips.

From behind, Pragor streaked down in a comet of flame and fang, his roar splitting the sky. He slammed into Lucandr with divine fury, biting deep into the shadow creature's side. Lucandr shrieked, warping his body to escape. His form unravelled, then reassembled twenty feet away.

"I tire of this," Lucandr said. "Shall I show you what I've become?"

He tore the stitched mask from his face.

What lay beneath made the sky itself flinch.

And Orion knew, the real battle was only just beginning.

Lucandr lunged again, this time faster than before, his limbs fracturing into jagged chains of sinew and shadow. The air cracked with each strike, his limbs moving in impossible directions, weaving traps of black entropy that snapped and hissed. Orion was driven back, his wings tearing through the vortex just in time to avoid a strike meant to skewer his heart.

He roared, the sound shaking the crater walls.

A burst of starlight erupted from his shoulders, a flare of solar-white that shattered Lucandr's chains midair. Orion twisted, driving his heel into the creature's chest with such force that the ground cratered anew. Blades clashed again, every strike now a collision of titanic forces, steel, shadow, and ancient power.

Lucandr's body warped, doubling in size, bones cracking outward as a mouth split across his chest, screaming in three languages long extinct.

"Enough!" Orion thundered, his voice amplified by the very planet beneath him.

Where steel failed, he summoned raw will, an orb of compressed starlight igniting between his palms.

With a cry, he released it.

The orb detonated on impact, sending shockwaves that hurled Lucandr backward. The shadow creature screeched as his form splintered, chunks of stitched limbs flung across the crater. For a moment, he wavered, unstable, struggling to reform.

Orion didn't hesitate. He surged forward, slamming a glowing fist into Lucandr's chest.

"P.I.L.S.S.," he muttered through gritted teeth, even as divine energy surged from his strike, "status update, Earth, the Spire, the Council?"

The AI's voice flickered to life in his ear, crisp despite the chaos: "Defensive lines holding. Queen Alexandria and the Star Council are active across all sectors. Promendium has stabilised the planetary core and activated long-range terra-shields. The Halcyon Spire is resonating in harmony with your energy. Earth stands, for now."

With his other hand, he carved a searing sigil into the air, a mark of judgment, passed down from the Old Ones.

The sigil flared, branding itself onto Lucandr's writhing skin. Smoke poured from the wound, and Lucandr screamed, a sound torn from every soul he'd devoured.

"You carry the screams of the fallen," Orion said, eyes alight with cosmic fire. "Let them rise against you."

Around them, the crater stirred.

Orion's magic had awakened more than just light. Echoes from the Martian stone, memories of rebellion, sacrifice, and hope, responded to his call. The spirits of the ancient Earthborn uprising stirred, their essence rising in waves of golden flame.

Orion let out a roar and channelled them, his form now surrounded by a storm of ancestral power. His weapons grew brighter, his strikes faster. He moved with a rhythm that echoed across centuries.

Lucandr twisted in rage, forming bladed limbs and spewing corruptive void in every direction. But the light would not yield.

With one mighty sweep, Orion cleaved through Lucandr's arm. A second blow severed a leg.

Lucandr collapsed, reforming rapidly, his laughter now tinged with desperation.

"Even if you kill me," he gasped, "you cannot stop what's coming."

"I don't intend to stop it," Orion said, his wings flaring wide. "I intend to rewrite it."

He lifted both blades and crossed them before his chest. Starlight pooled at the tips, then exploded outward in a wave that lit the entire sky.

Lucandr screamed as he was hurled backward into the jagged ridge, his form folding and fraying like torn cloth.

Orion gave chase, wings igniting with fresh propulsion. He didn't let Lucandr breathe, he drove forward with a relentless fury, blade meeting claw in a whirlwind of fire and shadow. Every blow from Orion now carried echoes of a thousand souls, his strikes thunderous with celestial momentum.

Lucandr fought back savagely. His body warped again, erupting in voidglass spikes, one impaling Orion's shoulder. Blood, golden and searing, splashed across the air. Orion roared, gritting his teeth as he twisted free, answering with a strike that sundered Lucandr's side and split the air in two.

"I AM THE LAST LIGHT YOU WILL EVER SEE," Orion shouted, his voice booming with layered resonance, carried by the memories of fallen worlds.

Lucandr tried to shape-shift again, tried to vanish.

But Orion grabbed him mid-fade, burning starlight coursing through his arms like divine chains.

"Not this time."

With a blinding pulse, he slammed Lucandr down from the sky, the impact sending tremors through Martian bedrock, forming new canyons around the crater.

The heavens flashed.

And the crater became a crucible.

Orion hovered, breathing hard, body glowing with purpose.

This fight wasn't over.

But for the first time, Lucandr looked afraid.

He tried to flee.

Tendrils of shadow snaked toward the fractured ridge, desperate to slip into the folds of broken stone, but Orion gave chase like wrath incarnate. A lance of radiant energy burst from his palm, pinning Lucandr mid-escape. The creature roared, twisting his form in protest, but his limbs were already failing.

Orion dove, slamming into him with celestial force. The ground ruptured beneath the impact, and Lucandr crashed into the Martian bedrock in a mangled spiral of limbs and shadow.

His fractured mouth opened to retaliate, but Pragor was already there.

The divine beast descended like a falling star, his paws erupting with molten flame. He crashed into Lucandr's chest with unstoppable force, snarling as he bit into the creature's shoulder. Lucandr shrieked, black ooze spilling from the wound, but Pragor drove him deeper into the earth, wings flared, claws searing.

"Echo Wardens!" Orion's voice rang across the battlefield. "Now!"

From the crater's rim, beams of gold and white streaked downward. The Echo Wardens arrived as a divine phalanx, armour aglow, movements flawless. Their staves shifted into radiant shackles, their visors flaring with purpose.

Lucandr thrashed, each motion ripping through the dirt like tectonic spasms, but it was too late.

The Echo Wardens formed a perfect circle. Incantations in a language older than stars spilled from their lips. Chains of pure Star magic erupted from their hands, binding every limb, muzzle, and bleeding edge of Lucandr's fractured core.

He screamed. The air fractured.

And then,

Pragor released a final exhale. A wave of golden fire rolled from his chest, washing over the bound monster.

Lucandr's body spasmed once... then stilled.

The final seal clicked into place.

Lucandr, the stitched mockery, was caged in divine light.

Orion hovered above them, battered but unbroken.

"Take him to the pit beside Josnan," he commanded. "If either twitches, I want every Warden on high alert. They're not corpses. Not yet."

The Echo Wardens bowed silently and began the extraction.

The crater pulsed with residual power.

But for now, it was quiet.

# 36. Showdown With Strixium

The quiet didn't last.

Above the crater, crimson lightning arced across the fractured Martian sky. Strixium had never left. He had watched from his perch, silent, still, certain. And now, with Lucandr and Josnan fallen, he moved at last.

The last of the Great Four descended not like a god, but like a sentence. A towering figure of flowing shadow and flaring crimson, his body dripped with molten rage. Horns crowned his head like jagged thrones, and wings of bleeding smoke fanned wide enough to blot out the sun.

Orion turned slowly.

He didn't speak. He didn't posture. He simply raised his blade.

Strixium landed without sound, but the force of his presence cratered the earth. Where he stepped, stone turned black and ash peeled away into nothingness.

"You burn so brightly," Strixium said, voice calm but poisoned. "And yet you flicker."

Orion's wings unfurled, divine energy surging through his veins. "I've faced your kind. I've endured worse than you."

"Not worse," Strixium corrected. "Only earlier."

He raised one hand, and the world screamed.

The sky turned crimson as meteors of cursed flame fell from the heavens, each one birthing monstrous forms of pure chaos, warped giants, howling beasts of corrupted starlight. The Echo Wardens instinctively moved to defend, forming a perimeter around the crater's edge.

But Orion didn't look away from Strixium.

He launched forward, starlight trailing behind him like a comet. Blade met claw. Heaven met Hell.

The force of their clash flattened entire ridgelines.

Strixium's laughter was cold. His blows thundered like cataclysms. But Orion met each one with the might of a resurrected world. His armour cracked again, light bursting from the seams, but he did not fall.

Pragor roared and leapt into the fray, biting at Strixium's wings, but the dark titan flung him aside with a backhand that sent the beast crashing into a distant mountain.

Orion gritted his teeth and drove both blades into Strixium's chest.

The Great One didn't flinch.

"I AM DEATH'S FAVOURITE SONG," Strixium whispered.

But Orion, half-shrouded in flame and fury, met his gaze and replied, his voice low, steady, infinite:

"No. I am Death now. And you? You're no song, Strixium. You're static, discord drowned beneath something far greater."

Strixium's body convulsed. The air vibrated with an unnatural pitch as molten runes erupted across his skin. His form twisted, doubling in height, skeletal wings erupting with solar flares of shadow. Eyes burned violet, one for each world he'd helped destroy. He was no longer a god of death. He was death unbound.

Then he exploded.

A sphere of pure annihilation erupted outward, swallowing the crater.

The blast was no mere detonation, it was a scream of uncreation, a roiling tempest of entropy that devoured matter and memory alike. Mountains vaporised at the edges. The crater's walls folded inward like paper igniting at its centre. The air itself became unsteady, vibrating with the cry of worlds once consumed by Strixium's will.

Orion was at the centre of it all, arms outstretched as the void tore at him. His Star magic flared violently, a radiant net trying to hold together the fabric of what should not exist. Every heartbeat risked obliteration. Every breath resisted the call to oblivion. His body screamed. The marrow in his bones boiled, Star magic burning hotter than it was ever meant to. Doubt crawled at the edge of his mind, was this too far? Had he finally reached a limit even he couldn't break?

Strixium advanced within the storm, wading through destruction like a god of endings. His body regenerated endlessly, every lost limb reshaped, every torn shadow reformed. He raised both arms and called down a second strike from the fractured heavens: spears of ruin, void-made lightning that rained across the battlefield.

But Orion answered.

He inhaled deeply, and the storm responded.

His wings ignited anew, brighter than any star. He beat them once, and time stilled. With a flick of his wrist, he summoned a wheel of ancient Star magic behind him, its spokes inscribed with language older than gravity, turning with a slow, thunderous hum.

He hurled it forward.

It struck Strixium mid-charge, embedding itself into his chest. The force stopped the crimson titan mid-air, and the wheel began to spin, grinding down his regeneration, unravelling his borrowed immortality, severing him from the Well of Endless Hunger.

Strixium shrieked, not in rage this time, but in something worse. Doubt.

And Orion vanished into fire.

For a breath, all was silence.

Then the fire parted.

From within the heart of the annihilation, a pulse of golden-white erupted, pure, divine, sovereign. It was not survival. It was domination. Orion rose, wings flaring with twin arcs of brilliance that defied the smoke and shadow. His armour reformed in radiant layers, infused with streams of living Star magic, primordial energy whispered into being at the dawn of existence.

From his chest, a ring of light pulsed outward. It struck the edges of the blast zone, halting the encroaching entropy. The crater held.

Strixium reeled.

Orion raised one hand, and the sky answered. Spears of celestial fire rained down like judgment, tearing through the abominations Strixium had summoned.

"Let me show you," Orion said, his voice echoing through bone and soul, "what true finality feels like."

He vanished, then reappeared behind Strixium, driving both blades into the demon's back with a burst of divine momentum. Crimson lightning shattered across the heavens.

Strixium roared, not in mockery, but in pain.

Orion twisted, unleashing a pulse of starlight directly into the wound. Flames erupted outward like wings.

"I am not your ending," Orion said, voice breaking through the screams. "I am what comes after."

Strixium howled, and the Martian sky fractured anew. But Orion would not yield.

He launched upward into the storm of blood-red clouds, drawing all light toward himself. His wings stretched wide, and from his palms he conjured a sphere not of fire, but of memory. The echoes of every soul lost to the Great Four shimmered within it, names, lives, moments. Starlight wept through its surface.

With a single motion, he hurled the sphere downward.

It struck Strixium's chest and exploded, not in heat, but in remembrance. For a heartbeat, the stars themselves wept. Orion saw a boy, barefoot in a ruined hallway, clutching a wooden star. He saw Anton. Aurorina. Earth. Every loss forged into a single truth: he had become more than an heir. He was legacy incarnate.

A force that unravelled illusions and stripped away shadow. Strixium staggered, pieces of his twisted form peeling off, screaming as the light of truth devoured every lie he'd built his power upon.

"No more death without memory," Orion growled. "No more fear without name."

Strixium lashed out, talons sweeping in an arc of burning shadow. Orion caught the blow on crossed blades, absorbing the impact with a grunt. His Star magic surged in response, flowing from the fractures in his armour, transforming pain into radiance.

"YOU CANNOT UNMAKE ME!" Strixium bellowed, wings flaring wide.

"You were never made," Orion answered, voice calm as the stars. "You were absence pretending to be form."

He plunged one blade deep into Strixium's heart, the other into his throat.

The sky turned white.

The explosion of light faded slowly, revealing the wreckage of battle, dust, ruin, silence. And Strixium, on one knee.

For the first time, the Great One bled.

Black ichor spilled from his wounds, steam rising from the seared gashes torn by Orion's blades. He looked up, a twisted grin flickering across his cracked obsidian lips, but the arrogance had fled. What stared back was something primal. Cornered.

Orion hovered above, his wings seared but steady, starlight dripping from his body like a molten sun.

"Echo Wardens," he called, his voice iron.

The divine sentinels moved without hesitation. From the edges of the shattered crater, they descended in spiralling formation, twelve warriors of crystal helm and Star magic-veined armour. Their staves reshaped into radiant manacles.

Strixium roared and lunged one final time, talons seeking anything to kill,

, but Pragor struck.

With a flash of motion, the beast slammed into Strixium's side, tackling him back into the ground. Claws dug deep into shadow flesh, wings beating with thunder. Strixium snarled, eyes wild, but Pragor held him fast, jaws clamped on his shoulder.

The Echo Wardens moved in.

Chants filled the air, old words, pre-creation syllables drawn from the well of cosmic law. Chains of Star magic bound Strixium's limbs, his wings, his burning core. The ground trembled beneath the effort.

He thrashed once, twice, then stilled.

A final ring of containment locked into place around him, glowing with energy older than suns.

Strixium, the Crimson Harbinger, was bound.

Orion landed beside him, gazing down in silence.

"No more endings," he said softly. "Only reckonings."

He turned slowly and raised his hand to the heavens. High above, stationed just beyond the Martian skyline, the remaining Stone Guard watched from the void, their celestial forms immobile, silent.

Orion's voice rang out like a bell forged from the soul of the universe itself.

"Stone Guard," he commanded. "Retrieve them."

There was no question who he meant.

"Bring all of them. Josnan. Lucandr. Strixium. Their trial begins now."

From orbit, the void shimmered. The two massive sentinels moved at last.

They descended like titans reborn, massive, stardust-veined arms reaching into the crater. With divine care and precision, they lifted Josnan and Lucandr's bound forms from their containment glyphs and stood behind Strixium's restrained body.

Three of the Great Four, silenced and subdued, now loomed like fallen idols beneath the Martian sky.

Orion looked to the stars.

"Prepare the Circle," he said. "Judgment is coming."

Then, summoning power from the core of his being, Orion raised both arms to the sky. His voice carried not through comms or channels, but through resonance. It rippled across frequencies, echoed through the thoughts of every living being, both ally and enemy, amplified by the Star magic still crackling across Mars and the remnants of the Fold.

"This is Intenfli Orion," he spoke, voice steady as bedrock. "The Great Four have fallen. Josnan, Lucandr, and Strixium are bound. Their judgment begins now."

A hush fell over the battlefields scattered across solar space, ships disengaged, weapons lowered, as the words continued to ring out like cosmic decree.

"To all forces, stand down. There is no glory left in this war. Lay down your arms and witness what justice truly looks like."

He paused, eyes burning.

"We are not broken. We are the force that rises from ruin, shaped by fire, tempered by memory."

# 37. The Trial Begins

The skies above Mars remained scorched and silent.

But Orion did not linger.

With one final glance toward the crater where the Great Four had fallen, he rose.

Wings of divine starlight unfurled behind him, and he ascended into the void, leading a procession unlike any other. The Stone Guard followed in his wake, cradling the bound forms of Josnan, Lucandr, and Strixium in fields of pure containment. Behind them, the Echo Wardens flew in ordered formation, their staves now transformed into spears of justice.

The passage through space was brief, but solemn. The portal shimmered open ahead, and Orion passed through first, the atmosphere of Earth bending to allow him entry. He did not land in silence.

Thunder echoed over the Atlantean capital.

Civilians and soldiers looked skyward as the heavens parted. Orion descended with authority, light trailing from his form like a comet of judgment. Behind him, the captured titans followed, chained, humbled, and defeated. The Stone Guard's immense silhouettes cast divine shadows over the domes of Atlantis.

The Council Chambers were already prepared.

As Orion landed, the great atrium's Star magic-laced floor ignited beneath his feet, mapping constellations in motion.

With a breath, he let the divine form recede. Light peeled from his body like falling veils, his stardust shimmer dimming to flesh and blood. His wings dissolved into his back, his eyes cooling from golden suns to storm-grey resolve. He stood once more as a man, whole, mortal, and unwavering.

Beside him, Pragor lowered his head with a deep, rumbling growl. His massive form shimmered, folding inward, shrinking until fur replaced flame and fangs. In his place stood a majestic lion, broad-shouldered and gold-maned, his eyes still carrying the fire of a divine beast. The tall crystalline spires of the hall reflected the glow of his return, while the air shimmered with expectation.

Queen Alexandria stood at the base of the dais, flanked by Elskar and the Star Council members, Lady Valoria, Lord Sanjen, Lord Jandavinr, Lady Untria, Lady Kirand, and Zanek. All eyes turned toward him as he stepped forward.

"The prisoners are secured," Orion announced, his voice filling the chamber. "And the Circle has been called."

With solemn grace, the Stone Guard placed the Great Four into containment pillars at the chamber's perimeter, each one marked by a symbol of the world they had ravaged.

The starlit dome overhead dimmed, then began to cycle through images of war, Earth ablaze, the battle for Mars, the fall of the Fold.

Orion turned toward the gathering.

He lifted his hand and looked to both the Star Council and the Earth Council, his gaze steady. "I ask each of you to bear witness, not as rulers or commanders, but as representatives of your people. This judgment goes beyond law, beyond alliance. It was never meant to rest in your hands."

He stepped forward, voice quiet but undeniable. "You are here to witness what must be done, not to influence it."

He turned back to the imprisoned titans.

But before he could continue, murmurs broke into open protest.

A member of the Earth Council stepped forward, his voice edged with concern. "With respect, Intenfli Orion, Earth has laws. No matter how powerful the enemy, we are bound by principles of justice. Even monsters deserve a trial."

Lady Kirand of the Star Council nodded in agreement. "We have witnessed atrocities. But justice must be transparent, not divine fiat.

If this judgment is final, should it not be earned through process, not pronouncement?"

A wave of tension rippled through the chamber.

Orion's expression hardened, not in anger, but in the gravity of memory.

"I showed them mercy once," he said, voice quiet but searing. "I held back the fire. I believed in redemption. And that mercy led to Anton's death... to Earth's near-collapse... to your skies torn open and your people hunted like prey."

He looked from council to council, his gaze unwavering.

"I am not bound by the laws they sought only to break. I carry the weight of what followed. You stand here because I survived what they did. I won't allow history to repeat itself under the guise of civility."

He drew a slow breath.

"I can take them to another world, one bound by my rule, outside the confines of Earth law. A world shaped by the will of the Old Ones, where judgment is more than ceremony. If that is what's required."

Before anyone could speak, Queen Alexandria stepped forward. Her emerald cloak flowed behind her, battle-worn and regal.

"I stand with Orion," she said. "He carries the burden no one else could. His justice is not ours to question, it's what kept Earth from falling."

A silence fell.

Orion nodded once, solemn.

"This is not vengeance. This is reckoning. We stand now not just for Earth, but for every world they tried to silence."

The Circle of Judgment glowed into being.

As the chamber held its breath, a soft chime echoed through the air, P.I.L.S.S.'s voice materialising like crystal wind.

"By command of Intenfli Orion, the Intenarii are recalled."

Moments later, golden runes shimmered in the air, forming concentric spirals. Portals opened in staggered rhythm across the chamber's periphery, and through them stepped the true Intenarii, Orion's chosen six. Eymd, eyes sharp and twin blades strapped at her back, moved with predator grace. Verjast followed, his colossal hammer across his shoulders, expression unreadable behind glowing red eyes. Snjallt's blue hair flickered like cold fire as potions clinked along her bandoleer. Rachel arrived next, her Veilshard weapon holstered but glowing faintly, emerald eyes locked on Orion. Captain Aaron strode beside her, Xerist-tech pistols gleaming, his blue eyes resolute. And last, Vilantina descended with wings folded in, radiant and composed.

These six marched forward in silence.

When they reached the centre of the chamber, every one of them dropped to one knee, heads bowed low, weapons sheathed in a symbol of deference.

Their presence was not one of dominance, but of unity, pledging loyalty not to the law, but to the spirit of justice Orion now embodied.

Only then did the trial begin.

Orion stepped forward, his eyes sweeping the chamber. The murmurs faded as he raised his hand once more.

"Let there be order," he said.

The words carried a resonance that stilled even the flickering lights above.

The members of both the Earth Council and the Star Council slowly took their seats, the tension in their movements evident, but their deference clear. Each one settled into the curved gallery that ringed the Circle of Judgment, their gazes focused on Orion, on the prisoners, and on what was to come.

The chamber grew silent again, heavy with anticipation.

Then Orion turned to face the bound forms of Josnan, Lucandr, and Strixium, and the first true silence of justice fell over Atlantis.

"P.I.L.S.S., initiate chamber seal," Orion commanded.

The crystalline walls shimmered, and a translucent field of layered Star magic rippled into place, sealing the chamber in a lattice of energy. Glyphs spiralled in the air, locking every portal and channel. The field thrummed, not with aggression, but with divine certainty.

P.I.L.S.S.'s voice responded, calm and precise: "Containment field activated. Internal resonance harmonised. Escape probability, zero."

At Orion's signal, the Echo Wardens stepped forward. With practiced motion, they released the full bindings from the Great Four, but luminous cuffs of starforged alloy remained on their wrists and ankles, each pair tethered to a Warden standing behind.

The three prisoners, though no longer encased, were surrounded by power far more absolute.

The trial had truly begun.

Strixium was the first to speak.

His voice cut through the silence, low and mocking. "So this is how it ends? A room of frightened mortals and a fallen heir playing judge?"

Lucandr chuckled, a discordant sound that echoed unnaturally. "You always did love a stage, Orion. But tell me, when this is done, who judges you?"

Josnan remained silent for a moment longer, then turned his blind gaze toward the chamber, his voice gravelled and strange. "You cannot contain what you do not understand. You chain rot and call it cured. This... is not justice."

Orion stood unmoved, eyes burning like tempered steel.

He took one step forward, and his voice rang with divine command.

"I am His Royal Highness Intenfli Orion I, Admiral of the Fleet of Xerist, High Commander of the X1 Army and the Stone Guard, Intenfli of the Xerist Galaxy, son of Intenfli Auren and Intenfna Aurorina, starforged child of the Old Ones, and a god of the new age."

His words echoed through the chamber like thunder.

"You will all speak," he said. "And the galaxy will listen."

He turned first to Strixium, eyes unwavering. "You led the charge against Earth. Begin."

Strixium smirked, unfazed. "I did only what was necessary to cull weakness from the stars."

The moment the lie left his lips, the chamber responded. The Star magic field pulsed and struck Strixium with a sharp arc of radiant energy. He gasped, not from pain, but from surprise. The cuffs binding him flared.

"A lie," Orion said. "This field is bound to truth. Try again."

Strixium's smirk faltered, the first crack in his arrogance. The chamber waited, glowing softly with judgment.

Lucandr chuckled darkly. "So, we're playing by your truths now?"

"You will speak truth, or the chamber will take it from you," Orion said, voice cold as stars.

He turned back to Strixium. "Continue."

Strixium's lips curled, not in defiance this time, but with something closer to resignation.

"Our master brought us back," he said. "Not for conquest. Not for chaos. But for you."

His voice deepened, tinged with something ancient and cold.

"You, Orion. Everything we did, every planet razed, every blade drawn, was to prepare the stars for your fall. You were my masters threat. The one who threatens my masters prophecy. We were just the harbingers."

The chamber dimmed at his words, the light in the dome flickering with unease. Even the Echo Wardens behind him shifted subtly, their grip tightening.

Strixium exhaled a long breath. "Our master wanted you broken before you ever reached them. And we failed."

Orion let the silence stretch for a moment, the weight of Strixium's words settling over the gathered council. Then he turned, eyes narrowing on Lucandr.

"Your turn," Orion said, his tone precise and cold. "Why did you betray the accords of Quirtiam? Speak truthfully, or the chamber will know."

Lucandr's smile widened. "Betrayal is such a mortal word," he said, voice laced with layered tones that unsettled the air. "I merely... reinterpreted destiny."

He turned his mismatched eyes on the council, each orb glinting with a different shade of malice. "They called it treason when I saw what the future could be. A future without boundaries. Without your quaint laws and brittle treaties. I gave the galaxy a mirror and told it to look."

The chamber pulsed, registering distortion. A warning shimmer flared around his cuffs.

"But you already knew that," Lucandr continued, unfazed. "This isn't about the accords. It's about fear. You fear what I understand. What I am."

The Star magic field flickered again, rejecting his partial truths. A pulse of force slammed into Lucandr's back, silencing him mid-sentence.

Orion's eyes narrowed. "No riddles. No illusions. Say it plain."

Lucandr coughed as the force settled, the light in his cuffs still flaring. His smile returned, but it no longer reached his eyes.

"I fractured the accords of Quirtiam," he admitted, his voice now stripped of theatrics. "Because they threatened our influence. Unity breeds resistance. A united galaxy is harder to bend."

He looked toward the Star Council gallery, his gaze lingering on Lord Jandavinr. "We sowed chaos to create silence. We dismantled trust so our master could reshape the stars without opposition."

The chamber grew cold. Even the light seemed to recoil from his words.

"We were the opening act," Lucandr said bitterly. "The curtain hasn't fallen yet."

Gasps echoed among the gathered councils. Lady Valoria's hand tightened around her blade of light. Lord Sanjen leaned forward in his seat, storm flickering at his shoulders. Elskar narrowed her eyes, starlit glyphs dancing across her fingers in silent preparation.

But Orion did not flinch.

"Then we will see who remains standing when the curtain finally closes.

Orion turned his gaze on the final prisoner. "Josnan. You have seen more than most. Speak your truth."

Josnan raised his massive head, his blind eyes glowing faintly. "I have no need for riddles," he said, voice deep as tectonic plates shifting. "We followed because we believed in rebirth through ruin. I tore down your cities not for pleasure... but because life grows best from scorched soil."

The chamber pulsed. No lie registered.

He continued, voice steady, unrepentant. "We were the scythe before the storm. Our master sowed the winds to see who would survive the harvest."

Josnan leaned slightly forward, serpents of his beard twitching faintly. "You grew strong, Orion. You thrived in pain. That was the point."

A murmur moved through the gathered councils. Vilantina's wings flexed behind her seat, and Aaron's hands twitched toward his pistols, eyes narrowed.

Orion remained still. "So you broke the world to test me."

Josnan nodded once. "And now we know."

The trial chamber fell into silence once more.

Then, unexpectedly, Lucandr tilted his head and laughed, not the wild cackle from before, but a low, knowing laugh that sent a chill through the chamber.

"Do you want the real truth, Intenfli?" he asked. "We were more than harbingers. We were horsemen, four horrors riding across galaxies, not out of duty... but because we enjoyed it. The ruin, the screaming stars, the collapse of empires, it was beautiful."

He leaned forward, eyes gleaming. "The Old Ones stopped us once. Imprisoned us in chains forged before time had a name. We thought it was over. We thought we had been forgotten."

His smile twisted, serpents of shadow flickering across his cuffs. "But then our master broke the seals, not for mercy, but with one command: finish what we started... and when the last world burns, bring him the ashes of the godling who threatens everything."

The Star magic chamber flickered, not with punishment, but with fury.

A voice rose from the Star Council gallery, Lady Untria, eyes alight with solar flame. "You admit it freely then, your joy in destruction. Your crimes are not born of war, but of indulgence. You revel in suffering."

Lord Sanjen stood beside her, storm glyphs crackling at his shoulders. "What possible judgment could balance this?" he growled. "No prison could contain it. No exile undo it."

From the Earth Council, a representative stood, Councillor Duvane, voice tight with fury. "You speak of ruin like poetry. But we buried the dead. We held the mothers as they screamed. Don't you dare call this beauty!"

Even Lord Jandavinr, usually the most reserved, clenched his star map staff. "You have not just broken laws. You've broken meaning."

The room seethed with rising emotion, but Orion raised one hand.

"They have spoken," he said. "Now it falls to me to decide what justice means, when evil confesses and glories in its deeds."

He turned slowly, his steps echoing through the quiet chamber. For a long moment, Orion stood in stillness at the centre of the Circle of Judgment. Then he lifted his gaze, voice low but resonant.

"I remember Anton's last breath," he said, his words cutting through the silence. "I remember the scorched cities and the screams of children. And I remember what it cost to bring hope back from the edge."

His voice rose, wrapped in starlight and sorrow. "They revelled in apocalypse. I will answer with judgment. Let every world know, Orion's silence is no longer mercy."

Around him, the chamber darkened. Stars shimmered across the ceiling dome, a constellation forming behind him in brilliant arcs, the sigil of the Old Ones.

The weight of memory, of divine purpose, settled around Orion's shoulders like a mantle.

Orion stepped back from the centre of the Circle, the weight of testimony still echoing in the stilled chamber.

"Enough for now," he said, his voice like thunder pressed through velvet. "The truth has begun to surface, but the judgment will not be rushed."

He turned toward the Echo Wardens. "Reinstate full bindings on the prisoners. Let no part of them remain free until the final word is spoken."

The Echo Wardens obeyed instantly. With solemn precision, Star magic flared around their gauntlets as reinforced shackles of pure celestial alloy spiralled around Josnan, Lucandr, and Strixium once more. The containment pillars shimmered as their forms were returned to stasis-like lockdown, conscious, but restrained.

Orion addressed the room once more. "This court is in recess. Prepare yourselves. The next time we gather, it will be to witness my judgment."

The chamber lights dimmed, and the dome overhead flickered into dusk-mode, starlight rippling across the ceiling like a great sea turning to sleep.

And so, the chamber emptied in silence, not with resolution, but with the breath before the end.

# 38. The Quiet Between Judgments

The heavy silence of the chamber gave way to the low hum of Atlantis beyond its crystalline walls. For the first time in what felt like lifetimes, Orion let the silence breathe.

He stepped into the sky-gardens above the tribunal, far from marble pillars and starlit domes. The sun filtered through translucent leaves that shimmered with residual Star magic, and the wind carried the scent of starmoss, saltwater, and smoke.

Pragor walked beside him in lion form, silent and watchful. Occasionally, he nudged Orion's arm with his mane, a quiet gesture that said: You are not alone.

Eymd was the first to find him, perched cross-legged on a floating terrace, her left arm wrapped in a healing wrap, faint scorch marks trailing down to her elbow.

"Not bad for your first intergalactic tribunal," she muttered, tossing him a ration bar with a dry smirk. "You held it together. Mostly."

He caught it and smiled faintly. "Is that your version of comfort?"

She shrugged. "You're not alone. That's mine."

Soon, the others arrived like gravity pulling in constellations.

Verjast offered only a grunt of acknowledgement before sitting heavily on a crystal bench that groaned under his weight. One side of his face was bruised, a gash across his chest still pulsing with residual light.

Snjallt handed Orion a flask of something glowing teal, her fingers trembling slightly, a split lip and bandaged thigh betraying the cost of the last battle.

"Don't ask what's in it," she said, flopping beside him. "Just drink."

Rachel leaned against the glass railing, her emerald eyes scanning the ocean horizon. One sleeve was torn, and blood was crusted along her temple where a wound had only just begun to heal.

"When you speak, the galaxy listens," she said softly. "But that doesn't mean it understands."

Aaron stepped up beside Orion, hands tucked into his jacket pockets, his eyes unwavering. His ribs were tightly bound beneath his uniform, and a bruise darkened one cheek.

"You did the right thing calling a recess," he said. "Gives us time. Gives them time."

Orion looked around at them, the Intenarii. His family. Each scar, each breath, a testament to what they'd endured.

"Tomorrow, the universe changes. Again."

Vilantina stepped forward, her wings folding behind her like veils of woven light.

"Then let it change knowing truth stood its ground."

Orion nodded, the weight in his chest easing ever so slightly.

No strategy. No speech.

Just being.

Then, laughter. And the sound of hurried footsteps slapping against polished stone.

"ORION!"

Jake barrelled through the archway, cheeks flushed, eyes wide with joy. Without hesitation, he flung his arms around Orion in a hug so fierce it nearly knocked him off-balance.

"You kept your promise!" Jake blurted into his chest, his voice thick with emotion. "You said you'd come back. And you did."

Orion dropped to one knee and hugged the boy tightly.

"I did," he whispered. "And I always will."

A gentle rustle followed as Aurorina stepped into view, her presence radiant, calm, and luminous. Her silver-white hair fluttered in the breeze, eyes shining as they settled on her son. Behind her,

Lillithan walked with graceful strength, her expression soft but observant. Lawrence followed with a relaxed gait, hands in his pockets, a crooked half-smile playing at his lips.

"We thought you might need some grounding," Aurorina said gently, brushing a lock of hair from Orion's brow. "You've carried the stars on your back long enough."

Lillithan placed a hand over his chest, her palm warm, anchoring.

"The battle's not over," she murmured, "but you're still here. That matters."

Lawrence stepped forward and ruffled Jake's curls.

"Told you he was too stubborn to die."

Jake beamed, and for a heartbeat, the universe seemed less fractured.

And above them, high in the council tower, the stars continued to turn.

The final judgment awaited.

The following morning arrived veiled in silver mist. The corridors of Atlantis buzzed with restrained energy as delegates, soldiers, and emissaries filed into the Grand Council Chamber. Above it all, the sky pulsed faintly, as if the stars themselves anticipated what was to come.

Orion stood alone in the corridor just beyond the judgment dais. He had donned ceremonial robes interwoven with Star magic threads, each shimmered with symbols of his lineage and the cosmic forces bound to him. His eyes closed briefly, drawing strength from the silence before the storm.

P.I.L.S.S. chimed gently beside him. "The chamber is secure. All required parties are assembled. The Echo Wardens confirm the prisoners remain bound and conscious."

"Thank you," Orion said quietly. "Initiate final protocols."

The doors opened.

As Orion entered, the chamber fell into reverent silence. The Star Council and Earth Council were already seated, their expressions solemn. Behind them, rows of onlookers from across worlds waited, hearts pounding.

In the centre, the three surviving members of the Great Four stood cuffed and bound by luminous Star magic, each flanked by two Echo Wardens.

Orion ascended the dais slowly, each footstep echoing like a tolling bell. When he reached the apex, he looked out over the sea of faces, witnesses to history.

He raised one hand.

"This court is now in session. Let no force of deception take root and let every voice that speaks be heard through the truth of the stars."

The air thickened with cosmic gravity. The final judgment had begun.

Orion looked upon the prisoners, Strixium, Lucandr, and Josnan, and allowed silence to fill the chamber once more. The stillness was not peace, but reckoning.

He stepped forward, his voice low but carrying the weight of starlight.

"You have confessed your crimes, crimes of genocide, deception, desecration, and joy in destruction. You were given the mercy of stasis once before. That mercy bred ruin."

The Star magic threads of his robe glowed brighter.

"I am Intenfli Orion I. As son of Intenfli Auren and Intenfna Aurorina, as Starforged of the Old Ones, and god of the new age, I pass judgment."

The chamber brightened with a dome of radiant light, reality warping with the force of Orion's declaration.

"You will not be imprisoned. You will not be sealed. You will be erased."

Gasps rippled through the gathered crowd. The Great Four did not cry out, but the void behind their eyes flickered.

"Your existence will end," Orion said. "Not as revenge, but as restoration. The damage you wrought, the lives you ended, remain. Your erasure does not undo the grief, nor absolve you of the weight that clings to your legacy. It ends you, but not what you caused."

A circle of golden Star magic flared beneath the prisoners, the ancient symbols pulsing with a force that reached beyond time.

"This is not cruelty. This is consequence."

He raised his hand. "Echo Wardens, step back."

The chamber held its breath.

"Let the stars remember your final silence."

Orion lowered his hand slightly and stepped toward Strixium first.

Strixium met his gaze and... laughed. A deep, guttural, echoing sound that cut through the chamber like a blade of mockery.

"You think we were difficult?" he sneered, his voice curling like smoke. "We were nothing but a pinprick. Our master is the storm behind the stars. Compared to them, you've only glimpsed the first shadow."

Orion didn't flinch. "And yet here you are. Broken. Forgotten."

The ground before Strixium split open with a sudden tremor. From the fissure rose a colossal figure sculpted from dusk-hued stone laced with veins of shimmering Star magic. Its eyes burned with silver fire, and across its chest glowed the sigil of the Final Rite. Death's Warden had come.

In silence, the Warden stepped forward and seized Strixium in its massive hands. Strixium snarled, violet flames erupting around him, but they extinguished the moment they touched the Warden's chains. His body twisted and strained, face contorting from mockery to disbelief as the chains tightened, drawing strength from his defiance.

Chains of starlaced bone and ash coiled up from the floor, pulsing with a rhythm older than time itself, latching around his limbs like ancient oaths.

"There will be nothing for you in death," Orion whispered. "No memory. No echo. Only a void where you once stood."

He raised his hand.

"I unmake you."

The air shattered like glass. The world trembled. Strixium arched once, then unravelled into ash and starlight.

He ceased.

He turned next to Lucandr.

The stitched one tilted his head, a smile curling across too many lips. "Will you at least remember me, Starborn? One last twisted dream?"

"No," Orion said. "You will become less than a whisper, forgotten by time, rejected by memory."

The ground beneath Lucandr warped like heat haze before rupturing. From the shifting stone emerged another Warden, not of death, but of unravelling. Its body shimmered with mirrored fractures, each reflecting a thousand broken realities.

With mechanical precision, it extended clawed hands and clasped Lucandr's shoulders. The mocker of minds tried to shift, to phase, to slither free between dimensions. But every escape twisted back into itself, every manipulation denied.

Bands of radiant Star magic lashed from the Warden's chest, winding like thread pulled through a needle's eye. They stitched through Lucandr's form, undoing his monstrous patchwork, unwriting the abominations he'd woven.

He gasped once. Then his body trembled, convulsed, flickered out in a burst of scattered memory.

He did not scream.

He was unmade.

Then Josnan.

The blind titan raised his chin, his coiled beard writhing weakly. His voice, low and resonant, rumbled through the chamber. "Make it quick, Intenfli. My bones have known ruin since before you breathed."

Orion regarded him calmly. "You wielded destruction without remorse. Now destruction claims you, without malice."

The marble beneath Josnan split with a groan like grinding stone. From the depths rose the third Warden, a monolithic figure of twilight iron and deepwood, its frame scarred by planetary wars. Its presence radiated the slow, certain weight of inevitability.

It walked toward Josnan with the solemnity of a funeral march. The serpents of Josnan's beard hissed and struck, but the Warden moved through them like a tide washing over roots.

Its hand fell on Josnan's shoulder, and vines of ethereal iron erupted upward, coiling through his limbs and spine. The titan let out a sound, not of pain, but resignation, as the coils tightened, draining all motion from his colossal frame.

Orion stepped forward. "You go not to judgment, but to silence. There is no beyond for you. No story left to echo."

He raised his hand.

"I erase you."

Josnan's body shook once. Then, like a mountain collapsing inward, he crumbled, not to dust, but to nothing.

The chamber remained still for a long time. No cheers. No mourning. Only the weight of history reshaped.

Orion lowered his hand, voice quieter now. "Let the stars bear witness: justice has been served."

And across Atlantis, a pulse of golden light echoed skyward.

The chamber remained in heavy silence, as if even the wind dared not speak. Then, slowly, the members of the Star and Earth Councils stood. Some bowed their heads. Others watched Orion with solemn awe, eyes shadowed with the weight of what they had witnessed.

Orion turned from the dais, the luminous threads of judgment fading from his robes, replaced by the simple shimmer of Star magic. The effort had cost him something unseen, but necessary.

He descended the steps slowly, his face unreadable.

Aaron was the first to meet him, placing a hand on his shoulder. "You did what no one else could."

"I did what I had to," Orion replied quietly.

Rachel came next, her expression sober but resolute. "The galaxy will remember this. Even if those three no longer exist, their legacy ends with us."

Eymd crossed her arms, nodding once. "So what happens now, Starborn?"

Orion looked toward the crystal dome above, where the light still shimmered faintly from the echoed erasures. "Now... we begin to heal."

Vilantina approached, wings trailing silver particles in her wake. "And when their master comes?"

Orion met her gaze, fire flickering behind his eyes. "Then we'll be ready."

The Intenarii gathered around him in silent agreement. For now, they had earned their moment of peace.

Behind them, the council chamber slowly emptied, murmurs of disbelief and reverence trailing in every direction. Yet not all had left.

Queen Alexandria stood near the high archway, her armour dulled by ash and time, but her presence resolute. She approached Orion with quiet steps and gave him a nod that spoke volumes. "History will remember this day not for what you destroyed, but for what you preserved."

Orion bowed his head slightly. "Let's hope they remember the cost, too."

From one side, Pro approached with hands behind his back, now wearing the form of a young man but radiating the deep, anchored power of the planet itself. "The earth breathes easier now. She felt every footstep of their march. And she thanks you."

"Tell her it wasn't for her alone," Orion replied, managing the faintest smile. "It was for all of us."

Snjallt limped closer, her arm now in a sling. "So, do we throw a feast or start fortifying for another apocalypse?"

"Both," Verjast rumbled as he sat beside her, unwrapping bandages from one arm. "Preferably in that order."

They laughed, tired laughter, raw, real.

Aurorina emerged from a side hallway, her eyes fixed on her son. She said nothing at first, only wrapped her arms around Orion and held him.

"I watched you give them mercy once," she whispered. "This time, you gave them truth."

Jake peeked from behind her, then ran toward Orion once more. "Are they really gone? Forever?"

Orion crouched and nodded. "Yes, Jake. They won't hurt anyone again."

Jake's eyes glistened with relief, and he gripped Orion's hand tightly.

Above them, the last glow of the judgment dome flickered out.

And in the hearts of those gathered, leaders, warriors, and gods alike, there bloomed something deeper than peace.

Hope.

Orion turned his gaze skyward, just for a moment. His thoughts drifted through the silence, not to the trial just ended, but to the days that would follow. There would be questions. Doubt. Some would fear what he had done. Others would worship it.

He closed his eyes and let the weight of the galaxy rest on his shoulders, not as a burden, but as a promise.

P.I.L.S.S. pulsed quietly beside him. "Orion," it said gently, "long-range sensors indicate planetary resonance anomalies, some species across the quadrant felt the erasure."

"Then let them feel it," Orion whispered. "Let them know the tide has changed."

Pro stood silently at his side, arms crossed. "Judgment closes circles, Orion. But healing? That's the long walk ahead."

Orion nodded. "Then we walk."

Rachel stepped to his other side, a rare flicker of vulnerability in her eyes. "I dreamed of this moment... but I never imagined it would feel this heavy."

Aaron added quietly, "It always does."

Together, they looked out over the city of Atlantis, bathed in the first light of a new era.

And high above Atlantis, the stars continued to turn, no longer watched by the Great Four, but guarded by those who remained.

# Epilogue: Between the Stars and the Endgame

A full planetary cycle passed before the feast was held.

In the heart of Atlantis, every avenue, skybridge, and amphitheatre bloomed with celebration. Star magic lanterns danced in the air, casting golden patterns on the sea-glass domes and bioluminescent terraces. Music thrummed from every spire, old Earth instruments blending with harmonic tones from across the cosmos. The air carried the scent of roasting fruits, sea-salted meat, and pastries that shimmered faintly with cosmic sugar.

The people gathered in tens of thousands. Survivors, soldiers, children, and elders, all beneath the hovering emblems of every world that had stood with Earth.

Orion walked slowly into the plaza at the centre, flanked by Pro in his chosen form and the Intenarii. Children ran alongside them, laughing. Flowers bloomed where Orion stepped, not from power, but gratitude.

He raised a hand and the plaza quieted.

"Let us eat," he said, voice warm and resonant, "not because we forget the cost, but because we remember what it saved."

And for a moment, the city held its breath, a world blinking back tears it didn't yet know it carried.

Later that night, when the crowd had faded to murmurs and the fireworks gave way to distant starlight, Orion slipped away from the plaza to a quiet overlook beyond the crystalline walls of the city.

Aaron found him there, leaning on the edge of a luminous balcony, the ocean far below catching every flicker of light from above.

"You always vanish after the speeches," Aaron said, his voice soft.

Orion smiled faintly. "I'm not made for applause."

They stood side by side, the silence between them easy.

Aaron's hand brushed against his.

"I still remember," Aaron whispered, "that night in the hospital. When you said you could hear me, even when you were lost. I never stopped speaking to you."

Orion turned to him slowly, eyes glinting with starlight and something gentler.

"I never stopped hearing you."

Orion's gaze dropped for a beat. "There were nights I wished you hadn't," he said. "But now... I'm glad you did."

Aaron hesitated for a breath, then leaned in. Their foreheads touched, and then, slowly, their lips met in a kiss both tender and overdue. It wasn't rushed or grand, but quiet, grounding, like the moment itself knew the weight of what had passed and the hope of what might come.

Beneath them, Atlantis glowed like a heartbeat in the dark.

And above, the stars bore witness to something soft, and real, and deeply human amidst the divine.

Far above, Orion's gaze lingered on a single point in the sky, an unremarkable star to anyone else, but to him, it felt different. There was a pull to it. A whisper on the edge of knowing.

"I don't know who you are yet," he murmured under his breath, "but I can feel you watching. And I will be ready."

Even if I have to face it alone, he thought, though he did not say it.

Cheers erupted. The sky above bloomed with light, not weapons, but fireworks of stardust and memory.

But far from the celebration, in the silent black between galaxies, a single star flickered and died.

In its place, something awoke.

A presence vast and old stirred aboard a ship hidden in the cold between galaxies, a vessel formed from obsidian glass and starmetal, drifting silently through the void.

In the command chamber, a shadowed figure stood, her form cloaked in layers of dimensional mist that shimmered like silk beneath starlight. There was a grace in her stillness, a terrible beauty wrapped in unknowable age. Beside her, something that appeared to be a child tilted its head unnaturally, eyes like pinpricks of darklight.

"He did well," she murmured, voice a lilting rasp, as though sung from the bones of forgotten stars. "Far better than I anticipated, especially in such a short span."

The Hollow Kin smiled, too wide, too knowing. "Shall we stop underestimating him, then?"

She nodded once. "Yes. From now on... we play properly."

She had seen gods rise before. And fall harder.

She turned from the starlit window, and the ship began to shift, its engines igniting with a soundless pulse of shadow.

The Great Four had failed.

But the game was far from over.